WATERLOO

FARRAR, STRAUS AND GIROUX

NEW YORK

WATERLOO

Karen Olsson

FARRAR, STRAUS AND GIROUX
19 Union Square West, New York 10003

Distributed in Canada by Douglas & McIntyre Ltd.
Printed in the United States of America
First edition, 2005

Library of Congress Cataloging-in-Publication Data
Olsson, Karen, 1972–
    Waterloo / Karen Olsson.— 1st ed.
        p.   cm.
    ISBN-13: 978-0-374-28626-2 (hardcover : alk. paper)
    ISBN-10: 0-374-28626-4 (hardcover : alk. paper)
    1. Middle aged persons—Fiction.   I. Title.

PS3615.L755W38   2005
813'.6—dc22

                                            2005007065

Designed by Gretchen Achilles

www.fsgbooks.com

1   3   5   7   9   10   8   6   4   2

FOR JOHN

WATERLOO

WATERLOO (POP. 600,000). This provincial capital, known for its friendly, laid-back atmosphere and vibrant local music scene, is nestled between blackland prairie to the southeast and limestone plateau to the north and west. The Alameda River dips below the center of town like a fat man's belt. The city is home to the state's flagship university and its governing assembly.

Surrounded by attractive hills and spring-fed streams, Waterloo is regarded as a pleasant city by locals and visitors alike. Its climate, however, is often unpleasant. In most years a thick, hot haze descends upon the region in mid-April and suffocates the populace until late October. A north-south interstate highway, built fifty years ago and annually responsible for dozens of traffic deaths, divides the city: poor sections to the east, downtown to the west. Farther west are violet hills that used to afford genial vistas of the town, before the smog and subdivisions arrived. "From the hills it is possible to view the city overall, and draw therefrom an impression of sweet curving streets and graceful sweeping lawns and the unequivocally happy sound of children always at play," a writer once observed. "Closer on," he continued, "the feeling is only partly confirmed, though it should seem enough to have even a part." That writer died in 1978.

The majority of Waterloo's residents don't bother themselves with the city's history, such as it is. During the early years of the Republic there was much debate over where to locate the capital, until a commission of the region's gouty elder statesmen chose Waterloo, a frontier encampment, over a more civilized but fever-prone rival on the coast. The encampment became a town, and pioneers arrived, full of grand ideas, but they soon discovered that the thin soils were inhospitable to their more ambitious schemes. They settled. They suppressed their fantasies and consoled themselves with books, music, and ale. Waterloo grew to be a center of learning, a good town for live entertainment, and an incubator of laziness. Rather than visionaries, the city would eventually harbor state legislators and musicians, two populations who, despite their very different styles of dress, were united in their desires not to have to work too hard, to be locally renowned, and to drink beer paid for by somebody else. In this they were generally content, though when the weather shifted, one could occasionally catch a whiff of old buried ambitions.

Only then, only after Waterloo had spent more than a hundred years wallowing in the sun, was it hit by boom times, much as this ran counter to its indigenous spirit. At the turn of the twenty-first century, the city sprung an economy like a leak, like a tear in the cloud cover, and money poured down, into new enterprises created with the toss of a wrist, a couple of keystrokes. High technology sent its conquistadors; builders rushed into action. The air grew thick with sawdust and receipts.

And the poor old musicians, the state employees, the bookstore clerks—they stumbled through the malls and office parks, bewildered, uneasy, cursing under their breath, hoping that some portion of the windfall might find its way into their own ragged pockets, yet forever wishing it had all turned out differently. They couldn't help themselves.

PART ONE

One

His ability to put tasks in sequence was the first thing to go. William Stanley Sabert, the former congressman, ambled into the kitchen, carrying in his good hand, the left one, a glass tumbler. With the weaker hand, the only partially recovered right, he pressed a sheaf of papers to his ribs, but not carefully enough: his attention slipped and then the papers slipped, they fluttered to the floor. Pick them up, he told himself. He could not. Certain capillaries in his brain had gone dry; they dangled like shrunken empty gloves. He couldn't pick up the legal-pad pages he'd covered with notes or the hearing transcripts or—where did that come from?—the Christmas card that slid out from the sprawl. The notion of retrieving all of it loomed and then faded, as showers of tiny particles, boluses, bits and pieces of the midbrain clot that had just exploded inside his head, infiltrated the network of his vessels. He couldn't pick up the pages on the floor because first he would have had to put the drinking glass down. He would have had to lean over. He would have had to reach for the papers and clasp them with his good hand. The sequence of steps had escaped him.

It was his third stroke, though, and he did have an idea of the enemy. He fought back. He'd come into the kitchen to fix something to eat. He intended to do that. No matter that making a sandwich was a more complex task than fetching the papers that had fallen.

He opened the refrigerator and set his drinking glass on the top shelf next to the orange juice. He closed the refrigerator. He took a bag of English muffins from the breadbox, pulled open the oven door, and placed the bag inside the oven. Next, tuna fish—but as he straightened himself Sabert saw only color, throbbing reds and greens. When the room returned, pale and blurry, his eyes were flooded. He touched his sleeve to his face.

Dishes sat in the sink; errant cashews and flakes of cereal lurked under the cabinets; mice lived in the breadbox. And that was just the kitchen. There were also the hairs clouding the bathroom floor, the towels heaped in a corner, the bottle of chardonnay forgotten in the toilet tank. A shelf in the bedroom closet had collapsed, and a hail of campaign buttons and umbrellas and old photographs and the silver serving forks from his first marriage (Delia had taken the spoons) had landed among shoes and old pine inserts. For all his storied acuity, his talent for clarification, for cutting through legislative knots in a few incisive strokes, Will Sabert had always been a force of entropy.

And now these papers spilled across the linoleum. He'd collected them to show the reporter, to help explain the work that had engaged him over the past year. What a relief, a pleasure, to have stumbled upon such a project, one that gave shape to his solitary days. High time he revealed it to someone. A legal method: he had discovered it, having devoted to that end many weeks of research, quite a lot of sorting through precedent and records of international tribunals. A method to end all wars, this was, entailing minimal adjustments to current statutes and treaty agreements. He had condensed the argument in favor of it, that is to say the argument for ending war, to a simple, watertight petition that could be understood by any high school student. It was clear, after all, that the wars of the twentieth century had been unjust, unnecessary, and, without question, inefficient from the point of view of costs. He'd hoped to live long enough to expand his premise into a book, but lately he'd begun to fear otherwise. Hence his plan to go over it all with the reporter. There was some doubt in his mind, though, as to whether the reporter had already come and gone.

The first stroke had been almost twenty years earlier: a tingling on the way to the cafeteria, and by the time he sat down to eat, his hand and arm had gone numb. He pretended to have lost his appetite. By later that afternoon he was back to normal. He went on working just as before.

The next one had followed his retirement. A headache, unlike any headache he'd ever had. Icicles splitting his skull into pieces. A trip to the hospital, a poor prognosis. That time his whole right side crumpled, and proper names hid themselves. He could say the words *son* and *daughter* but the names of his own children wouldn't give themselves up.

Now his mind was beset by a cascade, a closet shelf falling, an avalanche of old possessions. His children, his mother, his first bicycle, his dog. The fountain he and his brother had ridden their bicycles to on the terraced grounds of the state Capitol, a fountain long since bulldozed to make way for office buildings and parking garages. Its water had spouted from pink gargoyles' mouths: there, one terrible hot day when he was ten or eleven, an older boy trying to hawk a few bruised peaches had taken a swing at Will, after Will had called him a capitalist. He dodged the punch. His little brother Robbie had gotten it instead. Smacked in the face. Bloody nose. Scared to fight, Will had grabbed Robbie's arm and run away. This was his last memory.

No one was there to see the former congressman back up against the countertop and slide down the cabinet face. His shirt caught against a drawer pull and tore; his hip fractured; his great old moppy head fell to one side and was still.

Two

The ballroom was packed and anxious. As usual there were no windows. Swags of royal-blue bunting hung above a long dais, and tacked to the bunting was a banner, red with white lettering. HARDAWAY, it read. More words below, something-something VALUES!—but Nick couldn't see the first two words for all the heads and waving arms in front of him. A cheerful crowd of the neat and tidy had filled the hotel's third-largest function room, arms touching, hairdos glistening under the television lights. People scanned the room, signaling one another with raised hands and open mouths.

Nick did not wave, nor did anyone wave to him. Having been swept up by a current pressing toward the coffee urns, he was floundering in an eddy of middle-aged women wearing scarves and stickpins. He bobbled silently in their midst.

He was a reporter, albeit not the most dedicated. He made phone calls, he knocked on doors, he injected himself into other people's lives, into situations, at times unpleasant or terrifically dull situations that most people would take pains to avoid. Then he wrote about them for the *Waterloo Weekly,* an alternative newspaper specializing in music listings and futon advertisements. As Nick himself was an avoider by instinct, the going wasn't always smooth. Or even ambulatory. In work as in life, he delayed, he argued with himself. He waited for some kind of a sign. Once, he'd heard his name announced over an airport public address system, and a woman with a nice-sounding voice had instructed him to proceed immediately to gate number seventeen—this had excited him.

He covered news and politics. He'd never been a bona fide politics junkie (since the type of gossip that gave the junkies their fix, such as who might be angling to enter the next race for state comptroller, numbed his very organs), but chronicling the follies of those in power had for a time imbued him with a sense of purpose—however limited, however faltering. That sense of purpose had faded, though. The disappointments of politics were like the weather: unpredictable as the daily fluctuations were, the same seasonal patterns repeated themselves year after year, so that the only real change lay in the fact that things were slowly getting worse. Global warming, productivity slowdown, a sluggishness spreading among the citizenry, right-wingers in the ascendant. Nick schlepped around to press conferences and wrote about them in a weekly column. He tried to avoid longer assignments. At thirty-two, he had almost relinquished the idea of conducting himself with purpose, indeed was bearish on the very possibility of conducting himself at all, rather than forever feeling as if he were being dragged along behind his own life by means of a rope attached to his pants.

"Can you hear me? Is this okay?" On the dais, a lone gangly figure bent over the microphone, his cheeks pink, his long tie a pendulum, his hands in his pants pockets. He looked out at the row of cameras across the room, and a couple of cameramen raised their thumbs in reply.

Oh, to be a cameraman. The cameramen, really more like camera *guys*, like guys you'd invite over to watch a ball game or help build a carport, were endowed with a kind of silent geekish authority because of their equipment. Big black video cameras on six-foot tripods anchored the camera guys to a particular spot, where they belonged, where they stood with feet planted wide. Everyone else was in motion. Everyone else squeezed and nudged and if necessary resorted to outright pushing, and when they found a spot they still weren't still; they craned their necks and bounced up on their toes. They clapped, at intervals, for no reason at all. The worst were the campaign staffers: sleep-deprived, half-deranged people with stickers on their lapels and cell phones clamped to their ears, ducking this way and that, colliding and then parting again. But even the reporters in the press area were—with the exception of the inertial Sonny Muñiz, political columnist for the *Standard-American*—circling their territory like big dogs in a very small park.

Nick himself avoided designated press areas, media sign-in tables, question-and-answer periods. He'd never been keen on joining that particular club, and as a writer for a barely respectable publication, he wasn't quite the club's cup of tea either. He kept his notebook in his back pocket and removed it only when necessary. He didn't dress like a reporter, not like the middle-aged newspaperman in his baggy flak vest full of pens, or the television correspondent in her stiff suit. Nick wore glasses with black plastic rims and black boots and black jeans, thick dark items to offset his lack of bulk.

Over a loudspeaker music started to play. Electronic horns, electronic drumming: the theme from *Rocky*. Not a tune that lent itself to clapping, but people were clapping anyway, searching for the beat, eager for the show to start.

There it was: a bubble in the collective chest. Nick could feel it. The staffers, the lobbyists, the old-timers, even a few onlookers from hotel management had all gathered, not unwillingly, here in the Lamar Room with its stain-resistant wallpaper and obese chandelier. They seemed happy to be here, on tiptoes although there was nothing to see yet. No one was safe from it, even Nick, hard as he tried to keep his pulse from elevating in situations involving politicians and the *Rocky* theme. And what was *it*? Difficult to say. Something mysterious conjured like life in a test tube by this roomful of human chemicals all sweating and waiting and clapping, excited because the television cameras were here, excited because elected officials were here—jazzed by a second-rate candidate for statewide office, yes, but jazzed anyway! Never mind that the evening news and elected officials were normally subjects of ridicule. It was a bad movie that made you cry in spite of yourself. Nick was a sucker for those sentimental movie moments, and his heart was thumping now. To the theme from *Rocky*.

Nuh-nuh nuhhhh, nuh-nuh nuhhhh.

The candidate was making his way toward the podium, accompanied by a man Nick recognized as a state senator and a woman he thought he recognized but couldn't identify. He'd seen her picture somewhere. In a cranberry-colored suit and shimmery blouse, her plucked eyebrows arching high over her eyes, her teeth flashing, she looked like an official photograph.

Nick scanned the crowd again and accidentally made eye contact with Hardaway's press secretary—a short, stolid woman who spoke in short, stern sentences, a former daily reporter and a fixture of the political scene. Looking at Nick, she pointed to the designated press area: Go. People associated with campaigns, Nick had noticed, liked to give orders. He peeped over at the reporters' area, a disagreeably small, thronged corral, and stayed where he was, pretending not to have noticed the instruction. Out of the corner of his eye he could tell the press secretary was still signaling him to move.

All right. Fine.

But blocking his path was a broad woman in a wrinkled jacket. "Excuse me," he said. The woman didn't react. He touched her jacket and tried again: "Excuse me?"

The woman turned and looked at Nick as if he were slathered in shit, then stepped several millimeters to the left. He wormed his way past her and through the audience and into the reporters' area. For the sake of something to do he took his phone from his pocket and checked its digital window for the time. On it was a picture of a question mark doing some sort of end-zone dance: missed call. Maybe from Liza.

Earlier that morning, Liza had phoned, which was not her habit. He'd been sitting there in his work area, in his socks, staring at his screen saver of busy fish, and had arrived at a decision to stretch. Lifting his arms overhead, he'd caught sight of Trixie Moss marching grimly in his direction, inclined forward and frowning, which could only mean that his last (admittedly quite lame) column had incurred her copy editor's displeasure, or that there had been some new development in her divorce proceedings. Swiftly he brought his arms down and snatched up the phone to pretend he was on a call, but instead of a dial tone he heard Liza's "Hello?"

"Liza?"

"I didn't hear the phone ring."

"It didn't."

"But you answered it?"

"It was an accident."

"An accident."

"A good accident," he added in vain. Her voice sounded flat, and he wondered whether something had happened, and then whether somebody close to her had fallen ill, or perhaps died. Without quite intending to, he thought of Miles, a friend of hers from childhood (though very much full-grown now, brawny and carnivorous) whom she'd started dating after she and Nick had split up. He thought of Miles keeling over, of Miles giving the bucket a good manly kick. He was still working through this idea when Liza asked whether he could meet her for a drink that evening. He'd said yes: seeing her was something he wanted to do just about every evening, and he'd allowed himself, if only fleetingly, to hope that something might come of it. Yet he guessed by her tone of voice that she hadn't asked him for a drink so that they could make out afterward in front of her parked car the way he was imagining, nor was she going to disclose that Miles had unexpectedly perished, and so although he wanted to see her in general, the prospect of this particular rendezvous, its purpose unclear but serious, made him queasy.

Now he flipped open his cell phone and saw that the recent call had come from his uncle. He snapped the phone shut.

The tubby, perspiring Senator Comal, who because of his untelegenic appearance and two divorces would never be tapped to run for statewide office, began his introduction. I want to tell y'all about a great man and a great leader, Comal began. Raised in a small town. Has small-town values. Educated at our state university. Enlisted in the United States Navy. Farmland Insurance. City Council. State Assembly. A wife and two children. Parents still living in the same small town. At last Comal yelled out Hardaway's name and the candidate stepped forward to the microphone, squinting a little and mugging at the row of cameras with their gaping black eyes. The clapping quickened; girlish "whoo!" noises floated up from the crowd; flashes whined and strobed.

As Nick understood it, Mark (Shares Your Values!) Hardaway had been plucked from the obscurity of a City Council in the western part of the state—having impressed the local kingmakers with his cast-iron jawline and treadmill physique, not to mention a congenial malleability when it came to his positions—and thrust into one race for State Assembly, and five years later into another for his current position, commissioner of the Department of Human Needs. Now he was running for governor. Everyone knew this already, but he hadn't yet officially announced his candidacy. To announce you had to have cameras and bunting and a speech.

Hardaway had already started. Nick's entire experience of politics was recapitulated in the progression from theme song to speech: he was excited by the fanfare but turned off by the rhetoric. "I am proud to stand before you today," the man was saying. "I have a record of leadership and the experience to handle the challenges of the future. I have a positive vision." His delivery was mediocre. Mostly he stared down at the podium, reading from a script, but every so often, so as to look into the cameras, he would abruptly jerk his head upward.

"...I come to you today with the experience, the enthusiasm, and the vision to lead our great state into the twenty-first century . . ."

Nick took his notebook out of his pocket but did not uncap his pen.

"...Some want to turn back the clock, raising taxes, undermining accountability, ignoring personal responsibility. I will work hard to defend our state against the forces of mediocrity that would take us backward instead of forward, and I will make no concessions to them . . .

"...I believe the promise of America is yours to inherit if you have the capacity to dream, and are willing to pursue those dreams!"

Nick watched Sonny Muñiz, ahead of him, taking notes. The driest man in the Capitol press corps, a widower, furrowed and whiskered, Muñiz explained the same things week after week to an audience that would never remember what a conference committee was, or how the state had voted in the last presidential election, and yet he never seemed to grow jaded, at least in print, never seemed to tire of the long parade of Hardaways with their visions and dreams, the tomorrow and tomorrow and tomorrow of state elections. He had secured his place in the middle of it all, taking his notes, writing his columns, fixed like a boulder in that river of platitudes and pledges. Nick envied him that.

"A positive vision," he heard Hardaway read again from his notes. "With the blessings provided us by our Creator, we are harvesting the seeds of a better tomorrow! The best is yet to come!"

The thing was, it didn't seem to Nick that the best was yet to come. At one time he'd seen all this sort of political talk as a façade and imagined himself capable of puncturing it, of writing about what really went on, behind all the posturing. But gradually he'd concluded that the people doing the posturing believed in their own postures. There was no simple underlying truth behind or beyond.

"I believe we must curb frivolous lawsuits. We must eliminate government waste. When we lower taxes on our working families, we create opportunities. We are one nation under God! Together we will forge a brighter future for our children!

"The test of leadership is not whether you are the loudest critic or the biggest cynic. The test of leadership is standing for something. As your governor, I will stand for something, and I will not yield!" An obligatory volley of cheering drowned out the next few words.

Behind Hardaway, Ms. Official Photograph smiled absently. She was thin and fastidious-looking, a conservative in appearance and presumably in philosophy as well, and no doubt she spoke in platitudes just like all the rest, but right now she didn't look so sure of herself. Nick felt, if not quite sorry for her, glad at least that he didn't have to sit up there behind Mark Hardaway. A name rose up out of the nowhere of his brain: Beverly Flintic. That was who she was: a state assemblywoman, newly elected to represent Waterloo's northern suburbs.

The doors beckoned. He had a way of taking off early from these things, after convincing himself he'd done all he really needed to do. Next to the exit, the same woman who'd dispatched him to his present location was setting a cardboard box on a table. Transcripts of the speech, Nick guessed. If he picked one up . . . It had become so hot in the room—but there was no leaving. It was too crowded. Sweat trickled down his back while he stood there in the press corral, warm and drowsy, catching himself as he swayed involuntarily forward toward Muñiz. When the speech ended the audience cheered on and on, and Hardaway held up his arm as though he had just stepped off an airplane and might wave, only he wasn't waving. He was holding his arm straight up in a creepy führer way and letting the still photographers take their pictures.

All at once the corral began to move. Hardaway had stepped off the stage, and the reporters migrated toward him. Nick bumbled along, conjoined bodily to the overweight editor of a politics news-letter. As they neared the candidate, the reporters thrust their tape recorders out, encircling Hardaway with a ring of outstretched arms, like a team huddling before the game. At the end of each arm was a small silver or black recorder that would capture the candidate's additional words, his tidings of positivity but not the ruby tear of a shaving cut on his cheek, not the strange, early-eighties television hue of his tan, not the shadow of alarm in his eyes. Nick thought he should ask a question. He wanted to ask a question—he wanted to ask a smart question. Only he didn't have a smart question for gubernatorial candidate Mark Hardaway. What he had was a dumb question, a basic, dumb question that baffled him whenever he went to one of these things. Why would anyone subject themselves to this? To the cameras, the scrutiny, the press conferences, the thousands of handshakes, the permanent smiling—why? Why? Why?

Why?

A silence had fallen around the reporters' circle. Hardaway was looking right at him. Nick hadn't meant to ask his question out loud, but he'd done just that. The word had risen up through his throat and leaped out of his mouth.

The entire circle waited for him to finish the question. Hardaway looked at him, confused.

"Beg pardon?"

"Why . . . are you doing this?"

"Why am I doing what?"

"All of it."

The candidate's face grew somehow longer. He mashed his lips and glanced down. There was a pause. Then he ventured: "Why did I decide to run for governor?" Nick didn't know how else to put it. He nodded. Hardaway repeated some lines he'd delivered earlier about leadership and the rewards of public service.

As soon as he was able, Nick slipped out of the pack, his cheeks still hot, swiped a speech transcript from one of the stacks near the door, and left. He jogged down a half-flight of stairs and examined the transcript.

"My fellow taxpayers," it began.

He folded the speech in half, then in half again, then once more, and dropped it in an ashtray.

He followed an exit sign to a rear door and shoved his right side up against it and tumbled out into an alley. A woman was standing a few feet away. It was Beverly Flintic, no longer looking so official with her jacket off and draped over her arm. She was smoking a cigarette. Alone, half in the shadow of the building, one pump heel planted slightly in front of the other, taking a modest puff and then considering the cigarette between her fingers as if it had been a while since her last one, she might have been a deer or a hare, some furtive animal who, when startled by the opening door, quickly brought her hand down by her side and then stood motionless. Her stance was pigeon-toed. Unstable. She stared at him, caught, while smoke trailed off her thigh. Her lips parted, as though she wanted to smile or speak but could not.

"Did you drop that?"

"Excuse me?"

He pointed at the ground next to her foot, to what looked to him like a book of matches.

"Oh!" she said.

"Here, let me."

"No no no," she said rapidly, dropping to a half-squat before he could reach for the matches. "I got it." She held her left arm high in the air to keep the jacket from touching the ground, and grabbed the matchbook with thumb and finger of the other hand, the same hand that held the cigarette. She was off balance, and for a second or two Nick thought she would tip over sideways. Then she stood back up, awkwardly.

"Sorry," she said. Her hair had fallen out of its place and down over her forehead.

Sorry for what? Nick couldn't think of a response. He tried to return the way he'd come, but the door was locked. After tugging at the handle for a while he took a step back and pointed solemnly at it. "Guess this is locked."

"It looks that way," she said.

He breezed by her, down the alley and into the street.

Three

As soon as she entered the house she knew the old man had died. It wasn't the smell, which had been about him for some time, or the plate he'd left, typically enough, on the sofa, or the uncapped bottle of Macallan on top of the television set. Nor was it the collective scratching of mice behind the walls: she was used to that. A month ago, when she'd come upon a brood of them in the breadbox, nesting in the remains of a loaf of whole wheat, she'd announced that she was going to buy traps. Sabert had stared at her, taken aback, or at least pretending to be, and had protested that mice needed to eat just like any other creature. "And furthermore," he'd said, pronouncing it *futhehmoah* in that no-longer-conscious imitation of a no-longer-living former colleague from the Deep South, "*futhehmoah,* I can't possibly manage to eat that entire loaf of bread all by mahself." She came to suspect that he'd bought that bread specifically *for* the mice.

It was the stillness. Alive, the congressman had been incapable of crossing a room without picking up a newspaper and putting it back down, or knocking over a vase, or drawing his hand over photos and houseplants, touching things as other people are taught not to do when they are children. He had never learned that restriction, or had forgotten it, and would orient himself manually in relation to a room's chairs, tables, books, drapes, ashtrays; his eyes traveled everywhere and his hands followed. No matter if he was crossing his own living room: this was his habit. Dust had never been allowed to accumulate. Inanimate objects seemed always to have just settled into place, like children pretending to be asleep.

But walking into his house that steamy September evening, Andrea might as well have been walking into a summer cottage that had been empty since July. From the foyer she could hear the AC's condenser rumbling out back, that and the scurry of the mice and nothing else. She went straight to his bed, where for some reason she imagined he would have staged his departure, with his usual deliberation and fine manners, after one last bowl of orange sherbet and a final brushing of the teeth. He'd been a creature of habit even after his stroke, so that when she didn't find him there, and saw that the bed was unmade, she thought that maybe she'd been mistaken, that he'd left the house. In a hurry. Run off, was what occurred to her, as she stared at the white sheet and ink-blotched quilt hanging from the mattress, but she remained sufficiently aware of the other possibility to search the rest of the rooms. In the kitchen, a yellow-and-tan galley well suited to an old bachelor who baked his meat gray and ate vegetables from a can, there were papers all over the floor. The oven door was ajar. And there he was, slumped down against a cabinet. His head lolled to one side, and beneath fronds of hair his eyes were open.

Her first thought was that he would never speak again.

No more would he call her a long cool drink of water, or tell her that she was well advised ("My dear, you are *well advised*") to avoid eating poultry raised in the state of Arkansas, or announce that her father had been one hell of a good fellow, or explain that mice, too, required sustenance. After a couple of strokes he'd slurred his words, he'd forgotten names, sometimes he'd failed to complete a thought, but his voice had retained its resonance—even if the vibrato did sometimes turn to shaking—just as his speech had retained its patrician quality, even when the sentences themselves began to detach from one another and crumble into fragments. "The deep difficulty of a reply, in this instance," he might say, apropos of nothing, his dark eyes fixed, but not entirely fixed, on some spot on the floor. "I have always been very lucky, very lucky indeed," he would begin with his right hand in the air. "It is most striking," he'd said the other day, and then again, more softly: "It is most striking." Then just a mumble: *It is most striking.*

"It is most striking," she said to herself now.

She didn't know what to do—what one did, in this situation. Meaning the situation of a dead person. Who was it you were supposed to call first? An ambulance? He was already dead. A funeral home? The family wouldn't have made arrangements. Sabert had been in decline for years, and so it had become easy enough for them to think of this as a permanent condition, as though his actual death had been forestalled by perpetual dying—if they thought about it at all, that is. He'd had the nurse who came every morning, and Andrea, who'd taken to checking on him once or twice a week, after work or on her days off. As far as she could tell, the younger daughters rarely called, while Katharine, the oldest, phoned occasionally and winged into town once every couple of months to fret and chatter in person.

Andrea hadn't given thought to the arrangements either, but that hadn't been her job. Just because she'd knocked on the door one day and found him all alone in that musty house, scribbling illegible notes on loose-leaf paper? And after that had fallen into the habit of stopping by, of sitting with him and talking—or not talking—while the radio purled and popped: Did that obligate her? It no longer mattered. She had to call somebody.

But first she would clean up. Whoever came to take him, that person didn't need to see papers on the floor and mouse pellets. Andrea washed the dishes in the sink and wiped down the counter. Later she would ask herself how she could have done this, sweep the floor with the body right there, but at the time it seemed proper, if also ironic: he had never allowed her to so much as take a plate of his to the sink, as if all his old stands would have been for naught, as if the pillar of equal rights itself might have cracked were a black person to do his dishes. She had tried anyway, and had poked fun at his high-mindedness, and privately had even been suspicious of it. Was there something too abstract about his principles? Had she been, for him, a concept?

And he for her?

The first time she'd come over, he'd answered the door in stained old clothes, untucked and unshaven, his thin face all shadows and stubble, an enormous toe sticking out of one sock. He'd welcomed her inside, as she wondered *Who is taking care of you?*

She'd spent an afternoon on the phone trying to figure out the answer, calling names from a wrinkled phone list taped to the refrigerator and reaching, in succession, an ex-wife, a doctor, a nurse who came twice a week, and a Methodist minister. They all told her not to worry about Sabert. His personal hygiene left something to be desired, it was true, but he was in decent health. He preferred to live alone. He wouldn't let his daughter hire him a housekeeper. He was stubborn.

So she'd begun checking up on him herself, but sometimes it had seemed as if he were the one tending to her, giving advice or quoting verse in his cracked baritone. One evening, he had looked her right in the eye and said, "You must simply ignore the unpleasantness as much as possible. In spite, in spite of . . ." His voice fell off. Then it came back. "Just smile, my dear."

It was hard to know what to do with that.

Then there was his exercise regimen: Sabert would head out of the house in nothing but a pair of skimpy orange running shorts and worn-down sneakers, his shoulders forward, his chest pale and hollow, his hair sprouting wildly from the confines of an ancient headband. He would vigorously pump his elbows as his feet crept along the pavement, two blocks to the post office and then several times around the parking lot, looking for all the world like a man fleeing involuntary confinement. The postal workers knew him, as did the lifeguards at the pool—he swam, too, Mondays and

Wednesdays. He read pulp Westerns and biographies of the Founding Fathers. He filled lemonade glasses and coffee cups with scotch. He watched the afternoon talk shows.

Andrea consulted the phone book and called a funeral home promising "complete services," and went to make his bed. Then she returned to the kitchen. With a dishtowel she dabbed tentatively at Sabert's rigid mouth. She closed his eyes and backed away.

In the hall that led to the bathroom she paused to look at the old photograph that hung on the wall. Taken at a political convention or some such event, it was a black-and-white image of a crowd gathered in front of a big public-looking building. Men in bow ties and straw hats were hoisting signs into the air; other men held up their hats; women waved. Some had umbrellas or newspapers over their heads: it was raining, but not too hard, wet faces smiling. Most of the people nearest the camera were white, but there was a cluster of black men toward the back, and off to one side was a mixed group. One man reminded her of her father, because of the high set of his chest and his unsmiling expression, and the way that he stood slightly apart from the others. Some were in shirtsleeves, but this man wore a heavy suit, and was solemn even as the others were cheering.

Just that week a guy at work had told her she was a serious person. He hadn't meant it critically, only as an observation, a comment, and in fact the comment was accurate. She was careful, like her father. But it wasn't necessarily what she would have chosen to be.

The doorbell rang.

For some reason she'd been expecting a man in uniform, a public official even, someone to give Sabert his due. But it was just two large women, one in long shorts and one in jeans, carrying a blue stretcher and a body bag. "This way," said Andrea. "He's right in here."

Four

The rose-tinted dome of the state Capitol hovered to the north of the downtown skyline like the airborne skirt of a faded party dress. The building's style was "Renaissance Revival"—all cornices and pediments, joined to a stalwart frame that had held up, uncomplaining, under this tedium of having been born and born again. And again: the interior had been retrofitted for modern devices. Spitoons had been replaced by electrical outlets. Miles of computer cable had been routed beneath exact replicas of the original carpets. Delegations of algebra teachers and agents of the optometrists marched past joyless oil portraits of former governors, while schoolkids scratched and prodded at marble effigies of men whose status as heroes had lately come into question.

If the Waterloo air sometimes grew thick with a warm, fond, vague idealism, a dreamy groupthink that rarely funneled itself into definitive action, but instead pooled around selected backyards and nonprofit offices, the Capitol operated to reduce that element. This was where good intentions ran out of gas, or were deflated in midflight by the raised fist of Lady Freedom, an unattractive stone woman who'd been installed on top of the dome during the First World War. Occasionally some draft of principle blew through an open window, but for the most part the interior was shielded from the higher winds, buffered by the ranks of silver-tongued (and some not so silver-tongued) emissaries who circled the building and used up all the oxygen nattering about job creation and dollar amounts.

A slow evening, quiet under the dome. Few footsteps sounded on the terrazzo; few office halogens illuminated the frosted glass of members' doors. The Assembly and its entourage had moved on to cocktail receptions, to restaurants. But the lights still blazed in one basement office, where a recently elected assemblywoman from the nearby Waterloo suburbs had been mounting a valiant but futile effort to grasp the logical underpinning of state water rules—futile, because there had never been any such underpinning. And in the hallway outside stood an emissary, not known for diligence yet somehow reliably informed of comings and goings, of votes and non-votes, of who was screwing whom, and in particular of the fact that he would find Beverly Flintic in her office this evening, a fact that had led him to postpone the day's first vodka sour. Kenneth "Bones" Lasseter waited outside her door, tucking in his shirt, disgorging his nicotine gum, like a veteran performer carrying out his pre-show rituals. A little dance step into the reception area, a compadre smile, the curtain rises . . . for years he'd kept a roof over his head just by winning people over. He had that knack.

He found her alone in her back office, at her desk, a fat bound volume of civil code open in front of her. She was, he saw, one of the grinds, who treated this place like college, trying for their A's in Appropriations and Agriculture and Administrative Affairs. Wasted effort. Of course some background knowledge didn't hurt, but expertise went only so far when you were thigh-deep in a mudbog. And it wasn't worth shit if you lost the next election.

Beverly stood up. From the other side of her desk he proffered his card. She scanned it and at the same time extended her slender hand, as if for him to examine in turn.

"Assemblywoman."

"Just Beverly is fine."

"Just Ken Lasseter. Or you can call me Bones. Pardon the intrusion—"

"I'm sorry, but I'm trying to catch up on a few things," she said, dropping the card on her desk. "If you could come back tomorrow, I'd appreciate it. I'm not really even here." She indicated, as evidence, her pale yellow sweatshirt, something worn in the privacy of her office during times of heavy air-conditioning. Her white shirt collar hung neatly over the neckline. She was decent looking, Bones thought, although it was a shame that so many of these women got rid of their hair, of all but a sprayed-stiff little pot cozy. He'd heard some rumors about Beverly Flintic—but in any given year it seemed that more than half the members had been linked to one or another coarse rumor. She had espied lint on the sweatshirt; she picked it off and—he was struck by this—turned to flick the lint into a trash can, not onto the floor.

"I apologize for barging in and I promise no business. I saw you had your light on, is all. I thought I'd drop in and introduce myself." His breathing was pronounced, and his words had the sound of having been pushed through a long dank tunnel before arriving out in the open.

"Oh. Thanks." She recognized that she'd been brusque. She was often brusque, unintentionally. "Hello."

"So," he said, and sat down on the corner of her desk. "Your first session. Are you getting the hang of things?"

"I don't know. I haven't collapsed yet."

"To you I may look like some old boy just coming out of the woods, but I've been on this beat for longer than I care to think about. If you ever need anything, that's my cell-phone number right there. The damn thing's always on. Call me whenever."

"I appreciate that."

"You want to know what anyone around here is all about, just ask."

"All right." With her right thumb and forefinger she twisted her wedding band in a circle. "How about you. What are you all about?"

"Moi?" He grinned expertly. "Oh, naturally I just want the best for the people of our fair state, and my clients in particular."

"Naturally."

"You scratch where it itches." His phone rang. "See what I mean? Always on," he said. "I am that A-hole in the movie theater." As he fished the phone out of his shirt pocket, a chewing-gum wrapper poked out along with it, then fell to her desk—which she noticed, and he did not.

"My wife," he said. "Excuse me." He strolled out to the reception area. Beverly could still hear him: "You're kidding . . . The bastard . . ." She checked her watch. It was ten after six. She felt it was rude for a stranger to drop by her office at ten after six. She reached for the gum wrapper and threw it away.

When Bones returned he seemed dazed. "A great man has left us," he announced. "A good man, anyway. You ever meet Will Sabert?" She shook her head. "He was in Congress. From here. Big heart, big brain, not much sense . . . That mold got broke a long time ago. And he's gone and died, the old fuck."

"I'm sorry."

"He had it coming."

"I do remember him."

"You wouldn't have voted for him."

"No."

"No," he said contemplatively, as if this were a subject he'd been trying to get to the bottom of for a long time. Then he stood straight and held out his hand. "I barged in, I'm barging out. Forgive me."

"Nice meeting you," said Beverly, though nice wasn't quite the word for it.

After the better part of a year in office, the protocols of the place still eluded her; the longer she was here the more coded everything seemed. There was a surface layer of information, the loose soil and carrot tops they fed to the reporters, and a second layer of wormier stuff you became privy to according to your position, and then beneath that were more strata and gopher holes and decommissioned sewers full of trivia, histories, grudges, petty paybacks she didn't know how deep. Much as she tried to learn, there was never enough time. She wondered what else Ken Lasseter had meant to say before the phone interrupted him. She wondered whether the phone call had really been from his wife, whether this man Will Sabert had really died. She never used to be a suspicious person.

Five

iza was the first woman Nick had been serious about in a
long time. He couldn't bear losing her, if only because it
seemed to condemn him to another long spell of six-week entan-
glements, of capsule biographies traded over beers on the first date,
of trying to insinuate his general outlook on life (or rather, a more
charming and positive version of same) between entrée and dessert
on the second. Of long silences on the third. It was over with Liza,
he had lost her, but in his head he was still in the process of losing.

His story wouldn't interest her; she didn't care about an interview he'd done the day before. Yet he heaved it along.

"The man is in his eighties," he said. "Eighty-three, eighty-four,
something like that."

"Who did you say he was?"

"And drinks like a fish. He used to be in Congress."

"A politician," she said.

"A real old-school old guy. A liberal. He seemed out of it. I'm
not even sure he knew who I was."

"Out of it how?"

"Not totally out of it. But not totally with it either."

"Didn't you tell him who you were?" She looked past his shoulder, though there was nobody behind him. Tables and chairs were
enough to draw her attention away. She'd told him to meet her here,

a downtown bar near her office called B2B, foreign territory, thinly populated with a thinning-haired assortment of older men who sat at the bar and who were all curiously short. Even the bartender, who spoke into a phone headset as he handled the beer pulls, stood well under six feet.

Nick, on the other hand, was tall. He had nothing for Liza but meager anecdotes.

"I did tell him who I was, but I'm not sure it registered," he said. "He wasn't making much sense. He started asking me what I was doing there, and I said I wanted to ask him about his career, and he blew his nose. That was it, he blew his nose. Loudly. It was probably the loudest nose blow I've ever heard."

Nick tried to make a kind of foghorn sound, thinking he might get at least a smile out of it, but she didn't smile. Nothing. Her lower lip had been subdued by her teeth, her hair was pinned back: worrisome signs, in someone normally prone to loose strands and wisecracks. Why had she called? Why was she sitting on her hands?

Five months since the breakup, and they still met every couple of weeks for coffee or drinks, mostly—always, until today—at Nick's suggestion. The first time he'd proposed it, Liza had made him promise he wouldn't try to discuss what had gone wrong in their relationship. "Because I really don't want us to sit there and . . . regurgitate," she'd said.

"Absolutely not. No regurgitation."

"Okay, then."

That time and the next and the time after that, he'd stuck to the rules. He hadn't mentioned their past or the possibility of getting back together. He told himself that they might remain friends, or become friends—since only now that they'd not had sex for five months did it seem they were beginning to get along.

But any further progress was obstructed by the problem, the well-over-two-hundred-pound impediment, of Miles. Liza and Miles had moved to Waterloo at around the same time. Nick's hypothesis was that he'd followed her here. Miles was big but didn't throw his weight around; he was all but apologetic about his size, the same way he was about his business success. He'd gone from desultory studenthood to running a local chain of coffee shops—they sold a kind of muffin with fifteen different ingredients that dominated the "best breakfast treat" category in the *Weekly*'s annual reader survey. Liza had always insisted to Nick that she thought of Miles as a brother, that she wasn't attracted to him, that he was her oldest friend, et cetera, et cetera. After she'd dumped Nick they'd started going out almost immediately.

Nick wanted to think that Liza had called him, at last had called him and not the other way around, because she and Miles were having problems. He wanted to really talk. He wanted to tell her he'd been thinking about her, but couldn't think of how to say it. *I've been thinking about you* didn't sound right, but that was just what it was. He'd been thinking about her, and about a particular pair of yellow tennis shorts she used to wear, sometimes with turquoise flip-flops, and about her long legs stretching between those two items—so that when she showed up at the bar in professional black pants, Nick had felt a ridiculous pang, which her stiff-armed hug did not exactly relieve.

"How's work?" he asked.

The two partners at her law firm were splitting up, she said; they were competing to hire away the rest of the staff. One of them had called her into his office that afternoon to ask whether the other one had offered her a job.

"It's pathetic," Liza said. "Neither of them wants to hire me, but they both want to keep the other one from hiring me. All I want is to get out of there."

"And do what?"

"Go work for a different firm," Liza said as if it should have been obvious. It was obvious. She'd graduated from law school in the spring, and now she was a lawyer. Still, Nick kept expecting her to renounce the law, or at least corporate law, and go on to something else. He was always expecting she might do various things she was never going to do. That she would start liking Vietnamese food, or take an interest in politics: he hadn't believed it when she told him it made no difference to her who the president was. You mean, you think there's no difference between the candidates? he'd asked, and she'd said no, that wasn't it. She just didn't care. It wasn't going to affect her life one way or the other. Nick had tried to argue the point but had soon given up.

"How about you?" she said, sounding as if she might yawn. "How's the paper?"

"Oh, you know. McNally's still a pain, and I don't think he'd be sorry if I quit, but we're coming to a sort of understanding."

"McNally's the new guy?"

"Yeah." McNally had become editor of the *Weekly* right before their breakup. To say that McNally and he were coming to an understanding was misleading, but not entirely false. McNally had killed his last story; Nick had been expecting it. When McNally had threatened to reassign him to the sports section, Nick had pointed out that the *Weekly* didn't have a sports section. "That's correct," McNally replied. Whether that meant Nick would be fired, or that he would be forced to take charge of a new section on sports—about which he knew nothing and toward which he harbored a certain resentment—Nick wasn't altogether sure.

"So what else is going on?" Nick asked.

"Why are you whispering?"

"I guess it just seems quiet in here."

"Looking for a house," she said.

"You're going to buy a house?"

"Our realtor's this actress. She was in *Coal Miner's Daughter.*"

"The movie?" Our realtor?

"No, they did a rock opera of it here a few years ago."

Before going to law school Liza had worked for a theater company, and she still had a hand in the Waterloo theater scene, a scene Nick had always admired for its valiant efforts to keep a fading art afloat while never exactly pandering to popular tastes. He tried to support it by attending shows, some of which he liked more than others. That was how they'd met, at a play.

Liza's phone bleated. "Would you mind if I took this?"

Nick shook his head and asked whether she wanted anything else to drink. With her fingers wedged under her thighs, she'd hardly touched her beer. Nick, on the other hand, was ready for another.

"I'd love an ice water."

Though there weren't more than a dozen people in the bar, it was as if they'd all decided to buy another round at the same time: Nick waited for the bartender, who at long last started toward him but then was interrupted by a phone call. He held up his index finger to Nick. Nick wanted to show this guy his own index finger in return—how's *this* for an index finger—but he just waited. He felt like the only person in the city who was not getting a call.

When at last he turned back to the table with his beer and her water, Liza was watching him.

"You're too nice," she said as he set down the glasses. "You let people tell you what to do."

"I do when I don't mind doing it."

"When was the last time you stood up to someone?" She put an ice cube in her mouth and let her fingers rest on her lips.

Other women described Liza as slutty. Not as "a slut," in reference to actual sexual events, but as "slutty," because of her predilection for boob-flaunting low-cut tank tops and heavy eye makeup (the makeup was ironic, she claimed) and maybe also because of the way she talked to men, like she didn't really give a shit in general but liked you well enough and might even sleep with you were the wind to shift in the right direction. Nick had fallen for that, but not only that. There was, in addition, her vast bank of disorganized knowledge: though she rarely read a book, she retained all sorts of weird facts from newspapers and magazines; she knew every celebrity marriage and recent archaeological discovery and world leader. Nick had tried to convince her to drop out of law school and make millions on the game-show circuit, but Liza said the thought of any of her ex-boyfriends turning on the television and seeing her on *Jeopardy!* made her sick to her stomach. She had a lot of ex-boyfriends. One night at dinner she'd inadvertently revealed that she remembered blow-by-blow the way everything had played out in the former Yugoslavia in the early nineties, and Nick had accused her, only half jokingly, of having had an affair with Richard Holbrooke. The way she'd rolled her eyes, as if she personally knew Richard Holbrooke to be an enormous prick, did not eliminate all doubt from his mind: she was the one woman he'd ever known who really could have slept with Richard Holbrooke. Her father had worked for the State Department; there was a tobacco fortune on her mother's side; she'd grown up in Bolivia and New Orleans; she'd graduated from Yale. Nick, on the other hand, had dropped out of Southwest College his sophomore year.

"Is that why you called me here? To tell me what a pushover I am?" His tone was too sharp. He'd never been able to respond to her banter in the right way.

"When I said I thought maybe we should break up, you never even tried to talk me out of it."

"Maybe I thought it was the right thing to do."

"Maybe it was."

"Maybe it was," Nick said. Christ. Their talent for pushing each other's buttons was uncanny. He'd never fully believed it would succeed, their so-called relationship. She would make plans without consulting him beforehand; he would retaliate by showing up an hour late. Neither of them had had anything to say to the other one's friends. She'd told him he had bad breath—and what could you say to that, no I don't have bad breath? That was exactly what Nick did say. Then they'd argued about it—though from that day forward, over the year they were together, Nick had chewed more gum than he ever had before in his life. Sore jaw, sore heart: what he missed, it seemed, was the misery of her company.

"Miles and I are engaged," she said quietly.

"What?"

She didn't repeat it.

"But you're not—" He stopped himself before finishing the sentence. In love with him was one possibility. Interested in marriage was another. At least, that was what she'd always said.

"You don't know me as well as you think you do," Liza said.

Nick snorted.

"What is that supposed to mean?" she asked.

"I wouldn't say I know you," he said. "At all. But congratulations."

She was silent.

"When did he propose?" Nick pictured Miles lowering himself down on one knee and offering her a satin-lined box that contained, instead of a ring, a large muffin.

"I asked him," she said. "Two weeks ago. We went out to dinner and I asked him."

"How romantic."

"I guess it was a bad idea to tell you this," she said. "I thought you should at least hear it from me and not someone else."

"You want me to thank you?"

"Is there a chance at least that you might be happy for me?"

"No."

"I see. In that case . . ." She stood up abruptly. "Take care."

But wait: it hadn't really been misery. For all their quarreling, she'd been his girlfriend. She'd had his back. When he would complain about some perceived slight, she would take his side—most of the time—and when he'd had a cold she'd brought him obscure homeopathic remedies, and when he'd accused her of ignoring him at parties they went to together, she'd apologized and started paying more attention. In private she had a silly streak, a fondness for Adam Sandler and fart jokes, and such a humane tolerance for her neurotic, bitchy friends that Nick had almost started to like them himself.

When he met her she'd been selling tickets to a play. The theater was in a former warehouse on the south side, with a crude carnival-style ticket booth out in front of the loading dock. Liza had been standing in the booth, her head and chest an animate portrait framed by plywood painted red and yellow. Her insubordinate hair was half pulled back and her eyelids were ringed with a thick stripe of green liner; her T-shirt was black and tight. From the first, it was always *fuck you* and *fuck me* with her, not necessarily in that order. "What'll you have?" she asked.

"One ticket," he said.

"Just one?"

He nodded.

"Your date stand you up?"

He was about to say no—the truth was, he'd wanted to see the play, and none of his friends had been interested in going—but instead he said, "Either that or I got the night wrong."

"Or the play," Liza said. Her "enjoy the show" had a sarcastic ring to it, as if she doubted it were possible. In fact, he did not enjoy it. It was set in the Belgian Congo, and if the review had divulged that some scenes were pantomimed, or that the actors played two different roles by painting one side of their bodies black and the other pink and remaining in profile throughout, Nick had somehow skimmed over that information. Maybe if it had been a better play he wouldn't have spent the entire two hours thinking about the woman in the ticket booth. As it happened, he made up his mind to talk to her after the show, but when he went looking for her, she was nowhere to be found.

A week or two later, he'd gone up to the university campus to do some background research for an article, and had passed Liza on his way to the library: she'd had one hand planted in her hair and the other holding a cell phone to her ear, as if fixing her head in place. "Whatever gets your rocks off, Mom," he heard her saying as he walked by. He followed her to the lobby of the law school building, then on down a set of stairs, and through a door that led to a low-ceilinged hall with a row of dark-blue lockers on either side. There was no one else around. He couldn't very well pretend he had an excuse. She looked right at him.

"Are you following me?" she asked.

He hesitated, then answered: "Yes."

She squinted. "I know you from somewhere."

"You sold me a ticket to a play. A shitty play, I might add."

"So you want your money back, or what is this?"

"Get a coffee with me? It's the least you could do."

"Not the very least," she said, and was about to say no—her head was already shaking, just as Nick had expected it to shake. There was every reason for her to say no, but what she'd said was "You know, I really don't feel like going to class." The reason she'd so much as given him a chance was that his rival for her affections that day had been Taxation with Professor Wedelbaum.

In the beginning she'd told him she wasn't up to dating anyone (a polite way of saying she wasn't interested in dating him, he assumed), but she'd given him her number. In the weeks that followed, they'd talked on the phone; they'd met for lunch. It was at one of their lunches, at a diner near campus where she liked to eat a cheese omelette before class, that he figured out (or thought he did) why she kept stringing him along. They were sitting at a booth near the door, and a couple of dweeby classmates, a man and a woman in student regalia—law school T-shirts, law school backpacks, law school caps, and bar-review-course water jugs—had stopped to say hello to Liza, who that week was teasing her hair to look like Madonna's in the era of *Desperately Seeking Susan*. What struck Nick was how uneasy Liza had seemed—all three of them were oddly formal in the way they'd greeted one another—and it dawned on him that for all her peacockish splendor, and maybe in part because of it, Liza didn't exactly have chums at the law school. She didn't have any normal friends at all, except for her childhood friend Miles. Everybody else she knew was semi-exotic: they owned galleries and made films; they were always leaving to go to Bombay or Ibiza. Around a pair of run-of-the-mill law students Liza had become downright deferential, and, perversely enough, that had given Nick the strength to continue his courtship. He'd detected in Liza a yearning for a normal American life. He was normal, more or less; he had that to offer. He started taking her out to all-you-can-eat buffets. He took her shopping for a car. He persevered until one evening she'd agreed to go to a Jean-Claude Van Damme movie with him. When they kissed, finally, in the wake of a series of violent explosions, it was as if she'd just grown tired of resisting him: she sank into his arms.

In keeping with her moneyed upbringing, she was a great taker of lessons, and afternoons after her law classes were over, while her classmates trudged to the library with a hundred pounds of textbooks harnessed to their backs, Liza would change into pedal pushers and a pink visor from the Luxor casino and head out to the country club to practice her golf swing. Nick had gone along once. It was impossible not to observe that her drives never traveled in the direction of the hole, but she did have a powerful swing, and she liked to root around in the woods for the errant balls. Better than Civil Procedure, she'd said with disdain in her voice, as if there were something unsavory about courtrooms. That was the thing about her becoming a lawyer: she hated to argue and wasn't much good at it. Her usual tactic was to concede, sometimes genuinely and sometimes with a toss of the hair and a "Well, if that's my fault, then I'm sorry." She'd broken up with him all of a sudden, in May, a couple weeks before graduation, as if the prospect of introducing him to her parents had driven her to it. On the day of her graduation ceremony, Nick had snuck onto the golf course with the fifty-dollar bottle of champagne he'd intended to give her in celebration, and managed to polish it off and collect half a dozen stray balls before club security escorted him off the premises.

★   ★   ★

Some hours after Liza delivered the news of her engagement, Nick woke up on the front porch of his house, in the dark, lying on the sofa that had been passed down from tenant to tenant, a sodden Salvation Army reject he'd long been meaning to haul off to the landfill. He didn't feel well. His tongue lay thick in his dry mouth like a leech in the sand. A Big Star song bleated in his head: *Take care, oh, take care* . . . He brought his hands to his face; they smelled of dirt and grass, as if he'd crawled across the front yard. And as he lay there, the desire to move backward in time rather than forward, though hardly new, hit him more brutally than ever before, not just nostalgia but nausea, not just regret but exhaustion.

The sofa sank beneath him. His face burned. He was ashamed of himself. So he had lost her again, he had lost her months ago. His pants were mysteriously torn, and some overachieving bird was already squawking like crazy.

Six

Because of an increase in traffic, Nick seldom drove to work. The *Weekly* office was downtown, where lately all sorts of new businesses had opened, drawing more cars into the central city even as a rash of roadwork had reduced the number of available lanes on many streets. Also, the cars themselves had ballooned in size, leaving Nick's exceedingly compact Daihatsu under constant threat of being smushed by a combat-type vehicle. Plumes of auto smoke billowed along the streets, scaled the sides of bank towers, and wafted over rooftops before diffusing around the brazen peaks of the city's tallest buildings and the construction cranes that lit out across the sky. Most days Nick rode his ten-speed to the office. A milky, sunless glare was typical of Waterloo mornings, and he had taken to wearing dark wraparound sunglasses and a motorcycle helmet with a nuclear hazard decal stuck to the back of it. On a good day this getup made him feel sort of postapocalyptically virile.

Not today, however: his leg still half numb from his night on the sofa, he almost fell over while waiting for a light to change. He pedaled slowly.

The thing about Waterloo was that it fooled people. It was all too easy to overestimate its charms. The trees and lawns were so green and nice-looking that when most people thought of Waterloo, they thought of green, nice things. They thought of playing guitar on a porch, riding a bicycle, watching the progress of clouds across the sky. Swimming holes and cut-off jeans. Beer and margaritas. Not the prodigal quantities of water and noxious chemicals that gave the lawns their color, or the traffic idling on the highways, or the luxury-living communities that had replaced the outlying pastures, or the downtown that had lately turned slick, succumbed to slickness like some kind of wasting disease.

Just across the street, for instance: half-attached to the top floor of a high-rise not worth noticing, a brown brick building with paneless windows and an antisuicide rail around the roof, was a giant red banner, flapping in the breeze like a loose scab. URBAN PIONEERS, it said. LOFTS AVAILABLE. If Nick had been a superhero, he would have leapt to the top of the building and whisked away that offensive banner, replacing it with a new sign, fashioned out of his superhero cape. "DON'T MOVE HERE," it would have said.

As a superhero, Nick would not have subscribed to the whole good-versus-evil routine. If Nick had been a superhero he would have been Pettyman, his mission to fly around the city deploying his superhuman powers in the service of niggling objectives.

The *Weekly* building was a dust-ridden, deteriorating brick box. The owner had died five years ago, and its fate was now in the hands of the children, who could have made a fortune selling the place to a developer had they not been so busy suing one another over the title. Their lawsuits dragged on, though, and the building was left untouched, crumbling amid the city's modern offices and hotels.

Nick had been a writer for the *Weekly* long enough now that if he published a serious feature, his mother, who subscribed from New Jersey, would call to congratulate him and then ask whether this one might be his springboard to a major news organization. No matter that he'd told her a hundred times that major news organizations were all stifling, self-censoring, corporate entities: they both knew he'd never worked for one and so didn't really know what he was talking about.

His cubicle was a dozen or so feet from Bob McNally's office, a location he had lately been trying to avoid. It was dominated by the Pile: a large inanimate object, wedged up against the cubicle's north partition, somewhat larger than his desk. In fact it contained his desk—within a cocoon of newsprint and papers—but as none of the brown Formica was visible, it was first and foremost a Pile. Press releases, interview transcripts, legal documents, drafts of old stories, magazines, loose subscription cards, newspapers, takeout menus, Web pages he'd printed out, receipts, pens, phone messages, junk mail, library books, campaign literature, contact sheets, and income-tax returns all rose toward the ceiling, banked on one side by the file cabinet, itself crammed with manila folders into which he had unsystematically deposited the items he occasionally skimmed off the top. Nick was always careful around the Pile, because its equilibrium was easily disturbed; other people, if they entered his workspace at all, gave it a wide berth.

He lowered his bag to the floor as softly as possible and stepped gingerly toward his chair, hoping McNally wouldn't hear him.

The man seemed to be equipped with partition-penetrating sonar. "Nick," he yelled out from his office, "you got a minute?" He was from Wisconsin originally; the words came out *Ya-gadda-minit?*

Sure. Minutes upon minutes. He reported to the office, singing out "Yell-o," and exhibiting himself in front of McNally's desk. There was not a loose piece of paper in sight. The wooden desktop shone—the lemonish scent of furniture polish hung in the air—and was clear of all but a folded copy of the daily newspaper, a photograph of McNally's young daughter, and a coffee mug with *Why Not?* printed on it. McNally was staring at the painting on the opposite wall: an undistinguished watercolor of a lake, the contemplation of which, he had once explained, helped him relax.

A year earlier, the *Weekly* had been bought out by the Metro Media chain, and all the writers had been put on a quota system: so many long features, so many short features per year, and an annual review meeting to address "performance issues"—they'd actually called it that, performance issues. Bob McNally was the new editor they'd installed, transferred from Minnesota. "McNally, like the atlas," he'd said on his first day, and Nick had been struck by a vision of McNally as Atlas himself, the great mountainous world perched on his hunkering shoulders, its root systems tickling his sweater vest. McNally was a juice-drinker, a midwesterner, finicky about keeping everything clean—clean desks, clean copy!—a man who didn't hide the fact that he kept a toothbrush in his top drawer. He was well versed in Metro strategy, and he'd told all the writers that if they wanted to hold on to their idealistic notions of investigative journalism, fair enough, but in the meantime they'd have to consider their audience. He was talking about service pieces: best restaurants, top doctors. He made Nick write an article about long lines at the Department of Motor Vehicles. "But everyone already knows they have long lines there," Nick had objected.

"Maybe it's time we stopped turning a blind eye and confronted the problem," McNally had said.

He wore bow ties; everything about him was round and soft and scrubbed clean; and as much as Nick might have complained about the man, there was something cute about McNally and his earnest competence that kept Nick from actually disliking him. He hoped the secret lack of dislike was mutual.

"Is this the guy you were writing the story about?" McNally said. He held up the front page, which had a small picture of Will Sabert in the bottom right-hand corner. Nick nodded and reached for the paper. "He's dead, apparently."

"Dead."

"Yep."

"I just talked to him on Monday," Nick said.

Monday afternoon, when he'd arrived—late—at Will Sabert's house in west Waterloo, he'd found the front door wide open. He'd called out, but no one had answered. He'd stepped inside and paced around and called out again. Only then had the old man lurched into the room, wearing a jaunty straw hat, also an ash-stained dress shirt and a pair of dingy white pants buttoned high on the stomach and falling barely to the ankles, leaving his feet exposed: two battered ships rigged into sandals. Beneath the hat his eyes had roved needily over the furniture. At last they'd fixed upon a jelly jar on an end table. Sabert had made his unsteady way over to it, picked it up with a trembling hand, then raised his head and squinted at Nick.

"So you've come to do me the final disgrace," he'd said.

"Looks like you got that interview just in time," McNally said now.

It hadn't been much of an interview: Sabert had fallen asleep a few minutes into it, and Nick had left. He stared at the newspaper. Died yesterday, it said. Not on Monday—Nick was relieved about that, since some part of him feared that what he'd taken for sleeping might have been dying, that he might have witnessed, or even somehow caused, the congressman's death.

"He was the last of his kind," Nick said, reading from the obituary.

"What kind is that?"

"You know. The old liberal kind. The old southern gentleman liberal."

"I thought they said that guy who died a few months ago was the last of the old liberals, Ron, Rob—whatever his name was," McNally said.

"Well, yeah, him too."

"I assume we no longer have our story?"

If there ever had been a story. Before going to his house on Monday Nick had seen Sabert a few times at the Inwood Park pool, sunning himself in a lawn chair. That was how he'd had the idea for the article, such as it was. A retrospective profile, a tribute to the eminent resident; after securing McNally's lukewarm approval Nick had looked Sabert up. His number was in the book. The old man's voice had wavered as he agreed to an interview, in such a way that Nick wasn't entirely sure that he had understood the proposition, or that he would remember the appointment. Possibly he wasn't all there upstairs, but Nick had told McNally three weeks prior that he would do the story, and at the time of that phone call had only just been getting started. Backing out would have meant revealing that for the past three weeks, as for the three weeks before them, while collecting his regular salary, his main achievement at the office had been writing columns based solely on faxes and e-mails he'd been sent. Otherwise his accomplishments lay mostly in the areas of reading magazines and newspapers, sending and receiving e-mails, and downloading software he didn't need and couldn't get to work properly.

An icon, said the obituary. A protector of the little guy and of the environment. Author of two books, said to have been working on another at the time of his death. Nick had been one of the last people to talk to Sabert before he died, then had tried to convert the experience into a funny anecdote to tell Liza, and had failed to amuse her at that—he felt bad about it now. The man might have been drawing his last breath just as Nick had been making fun of him.

"We could do something," he said. "I could go to the funeral."

"All right. An obit. That sounds fine. Now let's talk about what else you're going to do, long-term. What else are you working on?"

An excellent question.

"I'm looking into a few things. A few different things. I'm waiting on a few calls back, you know, to see if they pan out."

Prior to the new regime, one of Nick's specialties had been debunking. With the encouragement of his old boss, a graying, bearish old SDSer named Harold Krueger, Nick had drawn on his general complaints about Waterloo's unchecked growth to generate lengthy indictments of various municipal functions and state entities, which had run in the *Weekly* under the heading "Special Report." Let the boosters talk, was the idea. All their vaunted development projects were turning into nothing but congestion and headache. The fact that a city had good public pools and plenty of moderately priced restaurants was no safeguard against deterioration, no defense in the face of the traffic, the construction, the wanton dumping of tires, the striped wooden roadblocks set down willy-nilly, the straight-ahead lanes switched to turn lanes overnight, the heavy equipment, the lack of sensible planning. The kowtowing to money. The disregard for the public.

But McNally had made it clear he was not a fan of debunking. He wanted no part of Nick's occasional column ("The Scowler"), nor was he interested in Special Reports. He'd never said as much outright, but Nick figured that McNally had aligned himself with all the readers who'd complained that Nick's articles were too pessimistic and "know-it-all," and "demonstrated the writer's callous disregard for the people and institutions of our city." Nick would have liked to tell Martha Bisbee, M.A., author of this last remark, that she was exactly wrong. Criticism was not the same thing as disregard. Nick had lived here all his adult life—was that disregard? He never missed a fireworks display, never failed to admire the Christmas lights, dutifully voted in every election—was that callous? It was precisely because of his deep-down esteem for Waterloo that he wrote as he did, because he kept hoping for the best, hoping that the city would live up to its promises, that those on the side of progressive improvements would prevail over the forces of greed and sloppiness, that wise public officials would beautify the downtown and lift up the disadvantaged, that Waterloo might have its own Roosevelt! After all, bitter people were nothing but a subset of the optimists. It was as a result of persistent optimism that Nick kept being disappointed, over and over again. He was bitter because he'd never stopped hoping.

McNally's eyes were slanted slightly downward at the outer edges, and at times they seemed to creep down even farther. "What sort of things?"

"What sort of things. Well, one of the things is that thing the enviros have been trying to get us to do."

"Which is?"

Nick strained to remember whatever it was that the woman from Nature's Defenders had e-mailed him about. Not nuclear waste. Not air pollution. Had it been the aquifer? Power plants? "That thing about the land trusts and corporate tax breaks," he said, free-associating. "I've got the details on my desk."

McNally frowned, as if he were thinking about Nick's desk, with its precarious stacks and its surface that had rarely seen the light of day, much less furniture polish. "Why don't you bring that up at the next story meeting," he said. Then he cleared his throat. "I don't want to pry into your personal situation, but I'm just curious whether there is something going on that would explain your performance lately."

Nick nodded gravely. "My performance has not been good."

"No, it has not been good." Nick was decidedly behind on his article quota, and though he had every intention of catching up, he hadn't thought of any good ideas for stories lately. He had been, as they say, unmotivated. McNally had not asked him to sit down, and Nick was shifting his weight from one foot to the other.

McNally swiveled to face his computer. "I just read your Rancho Grande piece," he said, jogging the mouse until the text of the article appeared on the screen. In the weeks since Nick had written it and turned it in, he had forgotten the story entirely. The takeover of a popular local restaurant chain by a twenty-seven-year-old multimillionaire had seemed like a good subject to begin with, but the multimillionaire had turned out to be so deadly boring that Nick had walked out of the interview with only three pages of notes, one of which consisted of nothing but the lyrics to "I Wanna Be Sedated." Later on Nick hadn't been able to get a hold of the restaurant chain's general manager or its former owner. Truth be told, he hadn't tried very hard.

"This story," McNally said, gesturing his head toward the computer screen, "is inadequate."

"I know," Nick said.

"Was there some problem I should know about?"

"I had trouble getting anything decent. I can go back and work on it—"

"Don't bother," said McNally. "This story is going in the trash." As if to prove his point, he turned toward the computer again, closed the story file, and dragged its icon over to the trash can at the bottom of the screen.

He swiveled back around to face Nick. "We all have our dry periods. Everyone gets in a slump sometimes. Right now, you appear to be in one."

"Fair enough."

"And so we have to figure out a way to get you out of that slump."

Among friends, Nick would've been the first to admit that he was in a slump, but hearing McNally say it and watching his work be dumped in the trash—well, it was unpleasant. He looked away. McNally's office had a big window with a view of a leafless tree, a tree that Nick could not remember ever having seen with leaves on it. Maybe it was dead. Maybe he should quit.

"I have an idea for you."

Nick braced himself.

"A profile of Beverly Flintic."

"I don't know." Nick said, his foot tapping. "I don't know if I'm the right person for that story." Harold Krueger would have seen fit to skewer her, but that wasn't what McNally had in mind.

"Did you see that piece in the *American* the other day? She's an up-and-comer," McNally said. Ah, thought Nick. The daily had done a story about her, and now McNally was hot to do a better story. Though in theory the two papers were competitors, they competed like a pair of neighbors: if one guy got a riding mower, the other guy had to get a better riding mower. If a story appeared in one paper, the other one would do an "in-depth" story on the same subject.

Even if it was a fluff piece about a suburban conservative. She was in her first term and was expected to run for reelection. As best Nick could tell, she was expected to win—incumbents usually did. They had stuck her up there onstage with Hardaway: an endorsement. Nick saw no reason to grease the wheels with a flattering article in the *Weekly*.

"The thing is," said Nick, trying to think of another way to say it, "I *really* don't think I'm right for that story."

"I think you are."

"What I'm hearing is, you want me to do this," Nick said. McNally nodded. "You're the chief," Nick added. McNally didn't refute it. "And I would be the guy paddling the canoe." He turned toward the door.

"Once you get into it, I think you'll find there's a lot there."

"Paddle or no paddle."

His relations with Bob McNally had started off badly and never quite recovered. After the Metro Media sale, Harold Krueger had quit without notice, and there had followed a month of desperate scrambling as the former managing editor, the sweet, ever-worried, sixty-eight-year-old Susan Farleigh, rose temporarily to the editor position, and everyone else tried to do more than one job. Then Marie, the office manager, had her baby, her maternity-leave replacement joined the Rosicrucians and was never heard from again, and in seemingly calculated acts of vengeance on the part of the office equipment, everything broke down in rapid succession, first the Xerox machine, then the laser printer, then the fax; without Marie no one could find the phone numbers for the repairmen, and finally the phones themselves went down. The last malfunction was at least explicable, for it happened one morning in April during an electrical storm, as rain blew down from the charred sky and the office's sickly fluorescent overheads flickered on and off. The flickering had made everyone loopy. At least that was Nick's excuse: though it had admittedly been his idea to fashion a substitute "phone system" out of office supplies, in his mind that act had been a creative expression of the staff's vital collective spirit, gone somewhat off course as a result of prolonged duress and bad weather.

His original notion had been to go the standard route of string and Dixie cups, but lacking those components, Nick had rounded up some paper-towel tubes and plastic forks and FedEx envelopes, and cut the FedEx envelopes into strips an inch wide, and used packaging tape to join all of it into a twelve-foot long chain with a couple of paper-towel tubes at either end. Nick and Trixie had had a test conversation on the ground ("Come here, Watson, I wish to speak with you," Nick had said), and then they got the idea to hoist the chain over top of a cubicle so they could try out the phone while sitting at different desks. By then the storm had reached its height; all you could see out the windows was the occasional piece of debris blowing by. Nick climbed carefully from his desk chair to the top of the Pile, tugging the new phone system along, and fed a paper-towel tube over the partition. On the other side, Trixie took hold of it. From atop his desk, Nick gained a new perspective on the office. None of the other cubicles were as messy as his.

Then the front door blew open. A pudgy man in a trench coat, with a broken umbrella in one hand and water dripping from the tip of his nose, heaved himself through the entrance. A Big Gulp cup blew in after him. "Gosh," he said, removing his glasses and fruitlessly wiping his face with the dripping sleeves of his coat, then rubbing the glasses against his stomach.

Nick, who was watching all of this, temporarily forgot that he was standing on a desk with a taped-together chain of cardboard and plastic cutlery in his hand. He called, "Can I help you?" The man looked slowly up at Nick, then at the mysterious object extending from his hand, then back at his face.

"Do you work here?" the man asked.

"Yes."

"Bob McNally," the man said weakly.

"Say again?" called Nick, bringing the tube up to his ear.

"McNally," he said, "Like the atlas."

"If you need to make a phone call, I'm afraid the lines are down."
He wiggled the tube as evidence.

"I'm the new editor."

"You are?"

"I spoke to Ms. Farleigh on Monday. She made an announcement?"

"Ah. She's ill," Nick said, guessing now that she wasn't sick at all but pouting over her loss of authority. He stepped backward, to descend from his perch, but in so doing he gave an accidental horizontal shove to a tall stack of court transcripts. He hopped onto his chair and was just returning to ground level when McNally reached the entrance to his cubicle. At the same time, the two feet of transcripts freed themselves from their stacked position and slid splendidly to the floor.

"Sheesh," McNally said.

Nick stood and held out his hand. McNally didn't notice at first, because papers were still sliding toward them. They made an appealing sound, like wind through grass. "Nick Lasseter."

"You work here." Nick couldn't tell if it was a question or a statement; nodding, he shook the wet, chilly hand of his new boss, who was looking not at him but at the papers at their feet. McNally's pant legs, dark with moisture, clung to his shins. He wore a sweater-vest with a pattern of diamonds down the middle. He stood with a slight forward tilt, and his large dewy eyes blinked methodically behind his glasses.

Nick had wanted to apologize but hadn't known how to do it. Instead he showed McNally around the office, somewhat despondently, saving the kitchen area for last. Forty minutes earlier he'd eviscerated the tubes from four paper-towel rolls and the semi-unraveled paper towels were where he'd left them, flowing over the counters and onto the floor in long white ribbons. McNally hadn't remarked on it. He'd just asked to be directed to the men's room, and then excused himself, as Nick crammed all the paper towels in the garbage.

Now, back in his cubicle, Nick felt his body contract; the Flintic assignment literally depressed him. His mail had been left for him on the seat of his chair. Also, the voice-mail light on his phone was blinking. He hesitated before listening to his messages, for fear that they were from readers wanting him to do a story on, say, trash service delays in their neighborhood, or wanting to complain about something he'd written—but when the two messages turned out to be from his friend Roger and from somebody named Christy with North American MasterCard, he was disappointed. No readers were trying to call him. A journalist lives only as long as his last story, a week or two being the most he can hope for, unless he unearths a major scandal or manages to write something funny, and then it's maybe three weeks. By the standard of reader phone contact, Nick had been dead for a while. His mail was only slightly more heartening: along with a couple of press releases and a "special note from Victor Navasky, Editor"—he'd let his subscription to *The Nation* lapse, it was true—there was a letter from his most faithful reader-correspondent: Mike Cummings, Department of Corrections #565629A.

He was about to open Cummings's letter when Trixie appeared at the entrance to his cubicle. "Howdy," she said. "Mr. Bob just asked me to give you this." She held out a Xeroxed newspaper article: the *Standard-American*'s piece on Beverly Flintic. "What's going down?"

"Bob's not too pleased with my performance. I've been under-performing."

"Sorry to hear that," she said.

"Otherwise nothing. I have no life."

"You're not still moping over that lawyer, are you?" Trixie had met Liza twice and hadn't been too impressed; ever since, she'd referred to Liza only as whatshername, the Louisiana chick, or that lawyer.

"I wouldn't say moping. Thinking. Reflecting. She's getting married. Not to me."

"Ah," Trixie said. She paused. "I'll work on finding you some prospects. I've got single friends."

"They're all divorced," Nick said.

"So? It's sexy. They're *divorcées*."

"You know how I feel about French words."

"I say this as your copy editor: You should get over it," Trixie said. Whether she meant his aversion to French words or his fixation on Liza, he didn't know. "Can I borrow a few bucks for lunch?" she asked.

After Trixie had taken all the money in his wallet—a ten-dollar bill with a message scrawled along the edge in purple ink: I'D RATHER PISS ON YOU THAN TAKE YOUR DAMN PISS TEST—Nick checked his e-mail. He had maybe been hoping for some message from Liza, even more than he'd been hoping for reader feedback. But there was nothing from her; there were no messages at all except for the September e-newsletter from Death Penalty Moratorium Now! and a misdirected inquiry about obtaining back issues.

He put the letter on top of the file cabinet and sat to read the article from the *Standard-American*. Its focus was a bill Flintic had introduced to declare part of the east side a "Business Improvement Zone." BIZ was the acronym. Flintic was a conservative whose victory almost two years ago had confirmed the rightward tilt of the city's northern reaches—a land of curving terraces, big houses, and six-lane highways with vast stores out of which hardware, bath towels, and kitchen things were continually being transferred to the houses, until those houses were full, and they had to build new houses. Typical upper-scale suburbs, in other words, with nothing old in them except for the trees. Even some of the older trees had been done away with, replaced by younger trees.

The article was paired with a photograph of Flintic at a meeting, leaning over to say something to the man in the next seat. Hers was not an easy face to read. Attractive but not exactly pretty, she might have been mean or shrewd or stupid or none of those things.

Nick's interest receded as he looked past Beverly Flintic to the setting of the photo, a committee room full of white men sitting in brown chairs. As much as he wrote about politics, politicians unnerved him still. There was that way they always seemed shorter than they were supposed to be. And the way they would look you in the eye and say things that didn't sound like spoken language. The way they would turn regular people into examples of things—of course, that was Nick's job, too, but he liked to think he was better at preserving the individuality of the people he wrote about. Politicians turned them into anecdotes about the human spirit and medical insurance.

The Xerox of the Flintic profile had also captured a piece of an adjacent article about a subject much dearer to local hearts than any committee hearing: the imminent closure of the Sunset, an old rock club on the east side that had lost its lease.

The article reminded him to call Roger, with whom Nick had spent many, many nights at the Sunset. He dialed Roger's number and was greeted by a croak at the other end of the line. "Hello?"

"Roger?"

"Nicky," he said, his voice restored to normal, "how big of you to return my call."

"You home sick?" Nick asked.

"I am home, and I am sick if it's the office calling."

"You work for the state, Roger. Nobody there cares if you're not really sick when you call in sick."

"True enough. But I like to think my standards are higher than that."

"I'm glad to know you're restoring some professionalism up there."

"I do what I can," Roger said. "Can you meet me over at Gloria's? There's something I want to talk to you about."

"Sure, you want to say six?"

"How about now?"

"It's not even noon. I'm at work," Nick said.

"So? Knock off early." Whenever Roger wanted to do something, he wanted to do it immediately, even if that meant convincing other people to drop what they were doing. Especially then, in fact. He liked persuading people to ditch their plans.

"I've got stuff to do."

"Oh really." His dry barb was on target: Nick did not in fact have stuff to do.

"I'll meet you at six," Nick said.

"All right," Roger said moodily.

Nick spent the afternoon trying to read articles online about the State Assembly, but mostly reading other things. At quarter of six he biked down to Gloria's through heavy traffic. Christ, women in cars! It was heartbreak at every intersection. In the time it took a light to turn from red to green, a woman would pull up right in front of him, moisten her lips, sing a few words along with the radio, gather her hair off her neck—and then drive off, never to return.

And today every woman driver was Liza. He kept trying to integrate the idea of her engagement with other new information he'd acquired recently: the rising price of gasoline, the likelihood of rain over the weekend, data about Beverly Flintic. But this concept, the engagement, didn't fit. Had he and she gone out for longer, would he have proposed to her eventually? Nick didn't know, but he did wish he'd met her later on, after he'd figured out a few things.

Gloria's Icehouse was a laid-back beer joint, the type of place where you could, at dinnertime, sit on the porch with a magazine, drink a beer, and eat a hamburger. In the broken shade of the oak trees that rose through cutouts in the deck, a hot afternoon became almost tolerable, and muggy evenings seemed not quite so muggy. Originally a dry-goods store or some such thing, it had run through a series of owners and names and varieties of patron: three years ago it had been called the Thirsty Goose, and gaggles of recent graduates in polo shirts had flocked around its edges, but then a manager from another local bar who'd come into some money had bought the place and hired spiky-haired barmaids to intimidate the fraternity types. Now on a nice night you could sit at one of the picnic tables on the deck and talk and watch passersby. And drivers-by.

Odds were you could find Buzz Mikeska and Roger Herman at Gloria's, drinking at one of the porch picnic tables, their backs to the wall, looking out at, as they put it, "all the other losers," and feeding each other running commentary about whatever or whoever happened to pass before them—ordinary things and people, almost always, and so the sport of it was to come up with something to say about them, though it was Roger who ventured most of the comments, while Buzz agreed or hmmmed. Both were old friends of Nick's. Even when he didn't want to see them, part of him was glad to see them.

"How's it going, Scoop?" Buzz said, sighting Nick over the top of his pint glass.

Nick shook his head. "Truth and justice remain elusive."

"And the American way?"

"What about it," Nick said. "What's up with you guys?"

Both of them grunted and waited for the other to volunteer something. Roger was finishing off an order of jalapeño poppers and licking his fingers. He waved at the waiter. "Oh, *mesero,*" Roger called to him. "Another pitcher, please, and another glass." The waiter saluted and disappeared. A song started to pump softly out of a speaker above the door, and Roger clapped his head in a caricature of dismay. "I cannot understand why Gary doesn't change the fucking jukebox."

The jukebox had been left by the previous owner. U2 was one of the choices.

Only to be with you.

Only to be with you.

"Who would pay to hear this song?" Roger said loudly. "I'm going to at least ask Gary to at least get rid of this CD."

"Gary doesn't want to pander to you," Nick said. "If everything was perfect, you might come here every night."

Roger took a swallow of beer and made a sound like he was coming up for air. "I do come here every night," he said. "Practically. Gary should pander to me before he panders to these . . ." and he looked around as if to locate the person responsible for the offensive selection.

Roughly two-thirds of the picnic tables had people at them, and most of those people seemed harmless enough. An Indian-summer after-work crowd, shirt-and-pants people, college graduates, salaried, polite at least for the first few rounds; nearly every table had someone's phone on it. Later in the evening the mood would shift, as more of the old crowd came in—the old crowd was how Nick thought of the after-dark set, even though it wasn't as if they'd ever been a cohesive unit, nor were they so terribly old. It was just people in their thirties and forties, who'd been in Waterloo for at least ten years or so, a lot of them married now, others divorced; after Gloria's opened, it had somehow become a place where they all tended to go when they wanted to drink too many beers, eat too many nachos, talk too loud, and indulge their collective addiction to reminiscence. Survivors of an extinct club circuit, who had once been sort of hip but weren't at all hip any longer, no hipper than you could be with two kids, driving a station wagon, and complaining about the traffic and house payments. Although Roger and Nick and Buzz had no kids or station wagons, they blended easily enough into that crowd. Most of the regulars didn't have so much in common anymore, if they ever had, but there were still nights when if you tracked who had slept with whom over the years, and applied the transitive property, everyone in the place would've slept with everyone else.

This was not the case during happy hour. A tidy little monogamous scene.

". . . these people," Roger said. The waiter came back with a glass, and Nick helped himself to the pitcher.

"So I think I might get fired. Or quit," Nick announced.

"You've said that before," Roger said.

"Yeah. But usually what I mean is, they ought to fire me. This time I think it could actually happen. McNally chewed me out over something I wrote, and then he gave me this assignment he knows I'll hate, and I think maybe he just wants me to blow it off so he can fire me."

Because Roger worked for the state, unless he started going to work in the nude on a regular basis, he would never be fired. "You're too radical for them?" he asked.

"No, it's McNally, man. I'm not, like, upbeat enough for him. He's so corporate." Nick swallowed a burp. "He has no tolerance for sarcasm or whimsy. Plus I've kind of been fucking up lately."

Roger slapped the table. "But you're not going to let it happen, because you're not a quitter."

"No, I am a quitter."

And Roger knew it. He and Nick had met right after one of Nick's Big Quits: dropping out of college. At the age of twenty he'd moved to Waterloo and not long after that had rented a room in the house where Roger was living, an old firetrap with five bedrooms and, at any given time, at least that many residents. Though a dozen years had passed since then, that house was still there at the base of things with him and Roger, their friendship like an old cactus that neither grew nor shrank.

Buzz got up to use the bathroom. He, too, was familiar with Nick's capacity for quitting. They'd been in a band together for a couple of years, called Real Real Gone. Nick had never cared for the name—it was a reference to an Elvis outtake, but everyone thought they'd named their band after a Van Morrison song. At more than one show someone had requested "Brown-Eyed Girl." He'd quit not long after the drummer had moved to New York: at the time it had seemed to Nick that the band was falling apart, and by then he'd been at the *Weekly* for almost a year—with a job that required overtime and deadline vigils, finding time to practice had become a serious pain in the ass. Though he didn't really regret leaving the band, he did miss hanging out with Buzz and Melissa and Davy

Mullins and Stuart King. Playing music was a good way to spend time with people you didn't have much to say to.

Nick looked at the window, which was tinted, the figures inside shadowy. He made out a woman who reminded him of Liza, standing at the bar. Too often he was reminded of her—he needed to stop doing that, he told himself—but how could he keep from being reminded?

"Yoo-hoo," Roger said.

"Sorry," Nick said.

"There's a reason I called you here."

"What's that?"

"The Sunset is closing down."

"I know. Good."

"Why is that good?" Roger asked.

"It's too small, it smells terrible, and unless you're one of the first twenty people there you can't see the stage. I always hated playing there."

"It's the Sunset! It's historic."

"Historic, right. Historically useless. What is it, ten years old?"

"Sixteen."

"Okay. Call in the National Trust for Historic Preservation," Nick said.

"Club years are like dog years," Roger said. "It's like a hundred twelve in club years."

The same thing happened anytime a place in town closed down, as long as it was a small place with some claim to coolness—a club, a bar, a coffee shop, a bookstore, a record store, a café. People acted as if it were the end of the world and all the fault of Starbucks. They were still eulogizing the greasy burgers at a campus luncheonette that had been shut down years ago by the Health Department. They told recent arrivals to the city that *you should have been here when* . . . When rent was still cheap and the music was better, and you could smoke weed outside the City Council building. With a city councilman.

In the past Nick had chimed in plenty of times, adding his own stale romanticism to the mix, but today he just wasn't in the mood. Not on behalf of the Sunset, at any rate.

"We're not going down without a fight, though," Roger said.

"Who's *we*?"

"The Campaign to Save the Sunset."

"Who?"

"It's me and Buzz and Davy Mullins so far. Right, Buzz?"

Buzz, who was just returning to the table, gave Roger a weak thumbs-up.

"What's the matter?" Roger asked.

"Nothing," Buzz said. He'd never been even a half-decent liar.

Roger pressed him. "What? Did you see your mother inside or something?"

"Just a person we know."

"Who?"

"Did I used to go out with this person?" Nick asked, straining to see if the woman in the window was still there. People were standing in the way. "Is the person Liza?"

Buzz pointed at him: yes.

"Crap," Nick said.

"Crap is right," Roger said.

"What's that supposed to mean?" Nick asked.

"You know what I think. She's a humorless snob."

"No she's not," Nick said, but he was in no mood to mount a vigorous defense.

"Plus, she did you wrong."

"I don't know if I'd put it that way."

"Did she or did she not dump you with no explanation?"

"Could we change the subject?" Nick asked.

"Time for another pitcher," Roger said, though there was plenty of beer left in the one on the table.

"She's engaged."

"Who? Liza? Who's she getting married to?"

"Miles Richmond." Nick peered in the window again.

"He's in there, too," Buzz said.

"That guy? Mr. Entrepreneur? Jesus," Roger said.

She was still at the bar. He could see her silhouette; the guy next to her must have been Miles. Had they seen him? She was reaching for her glass, her arm parting the fall of her hair. Just watching her blurry shadow, Nick could smell her hair. She was wonderful to watch, even from a distance, through tinted glass, her back turned and her fatuous fiancé by her side.

"We're still building our membership," Roger said. "We're also try-ing to get a meeting with the city landmarks people." Then he paused and snapped his fingers to summon Nick's attention. Roger's skin was moon-white and damp. "We're going to need media coverage."

"Don't look at me," Nick said.

"I am looking at you."

"Don't."

Roger made his eyes go big. He was several years older than Nick, pale and red-haired, with a soft face you couldn't easily guess the age of, and bright blue eyes. He had meaty arms, a round, slump-ing back, and a paunch that grew and shrank with the seasons—if not for his straw cowboy hat and sideburns he could have passed for a coach or a middle manager, one of those guys who've been brought up to believe there are rules that a man should play by. But he talked twice as fast as one of those men, and on and on. Probably one rea-son Roger didn't like Liza is that he'd bored her and she'd never bothered to keep that a secret.

The mature thing, thought Nick, would be to go inside and say hello. But was it really the mature thing or did he just want to go in and see her and get depressed? Why not skip that part? Why not skip straight to the getting-drunk part?

"My boss is not going to go for it," Nick said. Then: "I'll see what I can do. But I'm betting on nothing."

"A bad bet, nothing."

"I told you, I'm about to get fired."

"For real?" Roger asked.

"Maybe. I don't know."

Just then Miles and Liza came out the door. To judge by the way her face changed when she spotted Nick, Liza hadn't seen them from inside. They hadn't come out with the intention of stopping by the table, but now they were compelled to stop by the table. Liza and Miles. Miles and Liza. Miles was broader and flusher than he used to be—and in the past, he had already been plenty broad and flush. His mouth dropped open like a puppet's, in mock shock. "Oh my God," he said. And then: "Howdy, howdy," and went around the table, trying to shake everyone's hand. When he got to Roger, Roger held out a limp hand for him to kiss, and Miles kissed it with beery gusto. Liza stood behind him, smiling but after some quick eye contact not really looking at anybody. Her hair was down and frizzing out the way she hated and Nick liked; she was patting at it and drawing it back behind her head and staring at the table.

Her clothes—a white blouse with a tie at the waist and a striped skirt—looked like they could be hanging in a window display, like they had cost a lot of money. That was the problem. She was turning rich. She had always been rich, of course, but for a time she'd wanted to wear the same clothes as anybody else. That had changed: she'd graduated, become a lawyer and bought new clothes, and now she was marrying Miles, who had money.

"Let me buy you guys another pitcher," Miles offered. He was on his way out the door as he said this—couldn't she see that he tried too hard?

"We're good, thanks," Nick said.

"You're about to finish that, aren't you?"

"We're okay," Roger said.

Liza looked at Roger and asked him how things were going.

"They're tearing down my favorite club, and my buddy here's depressed," Roger said, looking at Nick, then turning to Buzz, "and this guy can't find anyone to play music with, and I'm getting fat. Otherwise, I guess things are all right. How's it going with you?"

"It's going," she said.

"Yeah," Roger said. "Have you noticed how no one's ever, like, really good anymore? Like everyone is fine or okay or else they're just, like, 'I'm so depressed'? No one ever says, 'I'm great,' or 'I'm fantastic,' do they?"

Probably he meant this to be entertaining.

"Miles says that," Liza said.

"I do?"

"You do."

She faced Nick like she was about to say something more meaningful than what she did say, which was that she'd gotten a new job.

He couldn't interpret her expression. He wanted to pull her aside and ask her what she meant by it, but that wasn't an option. "Congratulations," he said. He raised his glass up to the level of his nose and then took a drink from it.

Miles stepped back and put his arm around Liza. "Ten grand more than her old job. Hey, we're having a party, a week from Saturday. Instead of a shower and all that. No gifts required. You all should stop by."

Much of last night had vanished from his brain, but Nick was pretty sure Liza had not mentioned any party. Had they just decided to have one? She was biting her lip. Say something, he thought. Then again, what could she say? *No, that's a mistake. Don't come to our party.* She looked nice in those expensive clothes.

Liza glanced around the bar restlessly. Nick's heart skipped and fell, and he looked down at the table. Typical: she showed signs of losing interest, and so he pretended he'd already lost interest.

"And after that we're going to New York for a few days. We just bought the tickets," Miles announced.

"How fun," Roger said.

"All right. See you guys at the party, I hope," Miles said.

"Bye, you guys," Liza said.

"Bye, you guys," Roger said derisively after they had gone. "Hey, have you all heard the new Radiohead?"

Liza had barely talked to Nick, had barely even looked at him. The idiot sector of his brain concluded: Therefore she still had significant feelings for him. She was afraid to look at him, afraid those significant feelings would somehow plop right out onto the table. A logician would not have been impressed with that type of reasoning—shit, Nick wasn't impressed with it either. The best course of action, he understood, would have been to leave town, maybe even the country, until she was safely married and he was safely over it.

"I'd like to just confirm that we are not going to go to that party?" Roger asked.

"Right," Nick said. He looked in the window and noticed the silhouette of that same curly-haired woman, still sitting there at the bar, and laughing now. That woman wasn't Liza and never had been her.

Seven

They sat on opposite sides of the bed, backs to each other, and put on their socks. Beverly faced the windows, framed by heavy drapes they had not bothered to close; through the glass she could see the upper stories of an office building and a blank slab of sky. Hardaway regarded himself in the mirrored door to the closet, meeting his own eyes as he turned his second sock right side out. It was a king-size bed, and so they sat well apart, the top sheet twisted into a cordon marking off their separate sections of mattress. The sterile smell of mass laundering still clung to the bed, while most of the human odors had already been sucked up into the ventilation system. He aimed his feet into limp brown dress socks; she worked her thigh-high nylons up around her calves.

His cell phone rang.

Mark Hardaway walked to the window in his shirt and shorts and socks, and planted himself right in front of Beverly, his back to her. She checked the clock beside the bed. It was ten after one.

He told the phone that he was just finishing lunch and fixing to leave right now.

The backs of his legs were tennis-firm and tan beneath curling dark hair.

He said no, I didn't forget the meeting.

His long blue shirttail hung down to his thighs.

Okay, he said. Just hang tight.

Those very broad shoulders of his, broad like in cartoons of soldiers or airline pilots, went tense, and Beverly rested her gaze on the place where his thick electable hair met his neck. His head was cocked to the left, bracing the phone as he buttoned his shirt. The stubby antenna popped up above his ear.

Okay okay okay, he said.

That she was sleeping with him was remarkable to Beverly. Once, naïvely, she'd thought that the fact of marriage would protect her from something as trivial as this liaison. She had not thought of herself as the type to have affairs. The very word *affair* had seemed made-up, a tacky thing from television or California, like *hot tub* and *limousine* and *singles bar*. And to wind up with Mark Hardaway— who did seem like the type to have an affair, but with a twenty-year-old, one of those college girls who trotted around the Capitol in heeled sandals and tight sleeveless shirts. Not a fellow elected official, not someone married and thirty-nine. The first afternoon she'd found herself lying naked in a room not unlike this one, what she'd really wanted to do was to call one of her college friends. *You'll never guess where I am.* It had seemed funny, the whole thing like an early-morning dream in which someone you've never thought about in any sort of sexual way takes on erotic significance. It hadn't exactly felt as if she were *cheating on* Owen—another odd notion. It didn't seem to have much to do with him.

Mark, pacing now, told the phone that he'd be back as soon as he could, and after ending the call checked the time on the display. "Shoot. You mind if I leave first?" He reached for his pants. They had a rule about staggering their arrivals and departures by fifteen minutes. "I've got a meeting," he said.

"What is it?" Beverly was already dressed and fastening her necklace. Mark had been the one to leave first last time; she ought to have been first today. The hotel was five miles north of the Capitol, a twenty-minute drive. They wouldn't risk anything closer.

"The Association of Adult Educators. I think that's the name. They want grants for job training."

"Sounds pretty important." Sarcasm didn't come naturally to her, and either Hardaway didn't notice her tone or he ignored it.

"There's a federal program. Carson said I didn't need to worry about the nitty-gritty. He's got it all under control."

Beverly pulled a loose thread from a seam of her jacket. "You still haven't told me why you weren't at my press conference."

"Honey, you know I was getting ready for the announcement. We were sweating on it all week. Working out my theme."

"Your theme."

"It was 'Traditional values for a better tomorrow.' But we switched out *traditional* for *strong*. So now it's 'Strong values for a better tomorrow.'"

Hardaway wasn't smart and he knew it: he was smart about not being smart. He rarely did anything he hadn't been advised to do. His position, Commissioner of Human Needs, was an elected one, albeit one that appeared far, far down the ballot. Few had heard of the department and even fewer had any clear sense of what the department did, other than to groom candidates for offices higher than the commissioner's suite on the eighth floor of the Horace F. Dow Building.

"Y'all said you would be there. It was the department's bill."

"We sent somebody."

"You sent some kid," Beverly said.

"You're not mad, are you?"

"I just want to know why you weren't there when you said you would be."

He stared down at the floor. His pants, which he hadn't belted, fell around his knees.

The first time she'd walked into his office, Mark Hardaway had been sitting behind his desk, hunched over a handheld video game, rocking slowly back and forth and punching at the thing with his thumbs as it beeped out an uptempo ditty. His main adviser, Carson Yates, had been the one to greet her. A nebulous man, with soft contours and cumulus hair and cloudy eyes behind glasses that never seemed entirely clear, a man whose various roles were lumped together under the nebulous term of consultant, Yates had encouraged Beverly to run for the Assembly early on, and now he had taken charge of Hardaway's yet-to-be-announced run for governor. He wanted to talk to Beverly about helping with the campaign. "Carson tells me I need you on my team," Hardaway had added after Yates made his pitch. By then he'd put the video game away, but it was still emitting a muffled tune from inside a drawer.

Up until then Beverly's first term had been uneventful. She'd duly tried to learn the rules of the game they were supposedly playing, all the while suspecting that there was another, more important game going on simultaneously, in some proverbial smoke-filled room (though only proverbial, as the entire Capitol complex had been declared a Smoke-Free Zone). Guzzling Diet Cokes, she'd stayed up late into the night to study the finer points of regulations. Yet she'd never had much of a feel for where she stood with the right people. Some of these veterans of the Capitol, the small-town patricians, wore blazers with western seams across the back and shoes that had been resoled at least once and shined regularly; their long jowls had been toughened by strop razors, their tapered hair was slicked back with tonic; they grabbed one another and spoke in unintelligible accents and who knew what they were saying? At first glance there was no telling the power broker from the comic actor. Caucus meetings mystified her. She avoided the cafeteria. She was still trying to determine who the right people were.

Yates was one of them, she knew that much. And from the beginning, Mark had made a good impression on her. He may not have been the sharpest knife in the drawer, but he wasn't presumptuous. That first day in his office, he hadn't presumed a thing. "Would you be willing to help?" he'd asked sincerely, his gentle eyes blinking.

Later she understood, or at least thought she understood, why they'd wanted her on "the team." She was a conservative from the suburbs, but one sliver of her district plunged down into east Waterloo, a flashpoint of Human Needs. She hadn't visited it much during the campaign or afterward. The only reason the narrow peninsula belonged to her at all was that during the most recent bout of redistricting, the R's had managed to knock out an ineffectual liberal by shaving pieces off his district and reattaching them elsewhere. It was said that her piece had been the last one removed, and that it had been purposely drawn in the shape of a middle finger extended outward from the fist-shaped mass of her suburban constituency. That story sounded apocryphal, yet it was a wonder they'd even bothered with such a negligible sliver, home to only a small number of voters—and its contours, to her eyes, did in fact resemble a long, churlish digit. So that it did seem like one last F-you to the bereft liberal, who would have lost even had he been allowed to keep that bit of the east side. With much of its area occupied by half-vacant retail space, railroad tracks, warehouses, and abandoned buildings, the sliver was an urban nowhere—and therefore, Yates would explain to her, the perfect place for the department's pilot project, the first Business Improvement Zone. They wanted her to sponsor a bill on behalf of the department, allowing for privatization of services in disadvantaged areas. Something Hardaway could trumpet during the campaign. She'd submitted it two months ago: bill 1275, the BIZ bill.

"I came to your announcement, didn't I?" she asked. "I stood up there onstage with you?"

"You sure did. What did you think? Did I do okay?" His pants were still only half on. He waddled over to Beverly and kissed her on the forehead, then drew her toward him. "I'm glad you could make it."

Beverly let him kiss her on the mouth.

"I did mess up a couple times," he said.

"You did good."

"I'm sorry about missing your deal the other day."

People she knew, especially men, especially men in politics, had come to use the word *deal* as a synonym for the word *thing*. Everything was a deal. Beverly wanted to tell Mark it was okay without letting him think that it was absolutely okay, but she would have had to spell all of that out for him. Nuance was not his deal. What she said was "It's okay."

He kissed her nose.

"Our bill should go to the committee next week," she said.

"That's great," he said indifferently.

She backed away. "Do you even care?"

"Sorry, hon. Busy morning." At last he pulled up his pants and belted them.

"I'm serious. Are you even concerned about this *deal*? I've spent the last month fending off this, that, and the other thing, and it's like the department has left the building." There'd been an onslaught after she introduced the bill. A man from the Council of Waste Mitigators had insisted on a subsection expressly permitting the construction of recycling facilities in redevelopment zones. The environmental people kept bombarding her office with e-mails, and a cement lobbyist wanted to discuss a proposal to stipulate sidewalk width, and a dour woman in a peasant skirt had worked herself into a froth over the lack of affordable housing for the elderly, as if the bill had been designed to prevent such housing from ever existing.

And then this morning, the lobbyist named Bones had paid her a second visit, again shedding business cards and scraps of paper, foil torn from the top of a pack of cigarettes. He'd been more specific this time. Wanted to let her know that he could help round up support for her BIZ bill if she, in turn, would push a different bill due to come up before the same committee. It had taken him a while to explain. At one point he'd gone off on a bizarre digression about Davy Crockett.

The measure he'd wanted her to back had to do with offering tax breaks in return for improvements on some oil and gas lines that snaked all the way across the state—which, it went without saying, would benefit the one company that owned the oldest, most fallible lines, the pipes that occasionally sprung hazardous leaks in the vicinities of farms or schools. Beverly didn't like the idea, she didn't like the idea of tax breaks generally. She was for lower taxes but also for fairness: the rate was the rate for everybody. She had adopted the popular words "level playing field" as a banner of principle, and had reiterated them in both noun and verb forms (*to level the playing field; a level playing field*) over and over since joining the Assembly—had all but reconceived the state as a large, nicely maintained recreational complex—and so, as she'd said to this man named Bones, she couldn't support his bill. Yet she'd sensed that she was saying it all wrong, that she wasn't supposed to just announce what she believed but to finesse the subject somehow. Before leaving, Bones had wished her luck, in a manner that implied she would need it—had that been a threat? She didn't know. She'd tried to call Yates, but lately she was finding it harder and harder to get him on the phone.

"Well, hold on there, hold your horses," Mark said. "All I'm saying is, maybe it's more trouble than it's worth."

"Look. I'm the one going to all the trouble, and the reason I've been doing it is because you all asked me to. If you're not—"

"No, no, I've gone and stuck my foot in my mouth. It was just something that Carson said."

"What did he say?"

"It was nothing."

"What?"

"You know Carson thinks very highly of you."

"He does?"

"Sure. Now, I got to run." He was knotting his tie. She reached for the remote control and turned on the TV to the local news channel. Hardaway watched the screen for long enough to determine that the newscasters weren't talking about him, then put his hands on her shoulders and leaned in as if to tell her something important.

"They've almost got the first ad spot done," he said.

"Great," she said.

"Only, I'm not in it."

"You're not in your own campaign commercial."

He dropped his arms. "Well, I'm in it, like you see me smiling and walking down the street, but I don't say anything. Carson says he wants to wait until after I do the speech training. We're going to have voice-over. We're still working out what it's going to say. What do you think about this," he said, stiffening and raising his chin. "'Mark Hardaway for Governor. Strong Values for a Better Tomorrow.'"

"I don't know."

"Yeah, it needs work." He reached out and tugged at the fabric of her shirt. Then he said, "I can't wait until it's finished and you can see it." He kissed her and then jogged out of the room as if the hall were a stage he would perform on, as if his exit were actually an entrance.

"I can't wait either," she said as the door closed behind him.

Back when he'd first started calling her, it had always been on the pretext of talking about economic development, or thinning the welfare rolls, or what he called "empowering capital"—a term he'd been taught by Yates. Eventually he'd suggested they have lunch to discuss a report his office had prepared called "Preventing Teenage Coitus: New Approaches." He'd shown up at the restaurant flanked by three assistants, and the five of them had squeezed onto the low benches on either side of the table, Hardaway right next to her, so that it had been inevitable that his legs would graze hers, that she would smell his heavy aftershave, that she would notice, when returning from the restroom, exactly how his white collar rode against his sunburnt neck—and that she would agree to go back to his office to have a look at a draft of the document they had been, in theory, discussing. Even though, under the distracting influence of such an unexpected, absurd attraction, she'd paid scant attention to the subject of abstinence education. Mark himself had seemed to have little idea of what the report contained. In his office, as he'd leaned in to kiss her, she'd held up her hand and stopped him, politely. "Why are you doing this?" she'd asked him. He'd apologized and started to back off. "No, really. Why are you interested in me?" What she'd meant was: Why me, married, a mother, awkward, strident, flabby in the hips, other parts starting to sag? Why not somebody else? Or are there others as well? Why all the elaborate business of lunch and the report and . . . she was still trying to think how to say this when he looked at her with a goofy smile and said, "I just like you," as if it were the most obvious thing. This too-handsome man standing there in his red tie and state-flag cuff links. It could have been a load of bull, but so what.

Then there was the sex, not that it was so extraordinary: it was, by turns, exciting and then just so awkwardly, obviously *wrong*, like the affair itself. The first time, for instance, Mark had taken off his shirt—and to Beverly there were few sights more arousing than a trim man in dress pants and no shirt—but then he'd dropped his pants to reveal white briefs with two stripes around the waistband, one yellow and one blue, identical to the underwear she'd bought for her son the previous weekend. Still, she'd forged on ahead. Mark's lovemaking was boyish, all grins and bouncing, which made her giggle, though it didn't exactly make her feel young. From the beginning, none of this had made her feel young. If anything, she'd felt old, older than him. Maybe if she hadn't felt so old she might have been more careful.

Once she'd tried to cut it off, but he'd refused to go along with it. He had breathed out a long sigh over the phone; he'd said they should meet and talk, have lunch at least, and she'd agreed to it in spite of herself. They'd sat in a bright-orange booth at the soup-and-salad place, plastic bowls in front of them—chicken noodle, broccoli cheese—and he'd tugged at a stubborn package of saltines and said, almost plaintively and as if it had something to do with the package's failure to open, "I think we got something special here."

Special. A more sophisticated man would never have said such a thing. Yet his assurance, however blinkered, was contagious, and maybe it was the very thing that had kept Beverly from giving this up: because while her life as a public figure required her to project a confidence, a doubtlessness, she was far from doubt-free. Mark had sureness to spare, and when they were together she inhaled it. That temporary fearlessness did in fact feel special. For an hour or two or three.

And then there were moments like this one at the hotel, when in the aftermath of hosiery and phone calls, their secret life seemed all too penetrated by the everyday. They would be found out, she thought. If they went on like this they would be found out, and worse, it would be news: file photographs of their faces would be shown on television; their careers would be finished; everyone would know. Jamie would know; his friends at school would know. She would not allow herself to draw the easy conclusion, that the risk itself was part of the attraction—the possible ruin of her life that might lead her, however disastrously, toward another life entirely.

She sat down on the bed. *Special.* In the next room and the next room and the next room, there were green-and-burgundy polyester-fill bedspreads just like the one Beverly was sitting on. There were wall lamps with miniature lampshades and gold plating, and the same twenty-two-inch televisions in composition-board cabinets.

Without Mark in the room she could barely picture his face. She tried to, but what flashed into her mind instead was her husband's face—not as it was now, but as it had been when they first met. When he'd been thin, not to mention employed. Last year he'd been laid off. It was time to go.

Back at the Capitol, Beverly stopped in the restroom before returning to the office. Always there was the fear that the sex had made some mark on her, that she'd left something undone, put her bra on outside of her shirt. She straightened her back and sucked in her stomach and walked briskly to her spare little headquarters.

Her chief of staff, Henry Blanco, materialized in the doorway to the office he shared with another aide.

"A reporter called," he said.

"Where from?"

"The *Waterloo Weekly.*"

"The *Weekly*?"

Henry nodded and said that the reporter had requested an interview. What about, he didn't know. Henry spent the bulk of his verbal energies on his faxes and press releases; out loud he did not elaborate. Every day he arrived at five minutes to eight, hair still damp at the edges, and though he never drank coffee or tea or soda he never seemed sleepy. Beverly's own energy level, on the other hand, had become unpredictable, rising and falling more precipitously than was normal; recently she'd found herself reading the labels of herbal supplements in the grocery store—but the labels were barely intelligible, and really no combination of herbs and plant essences would help her get a handle on the situation.

The solution, her father would have said, was to try harder. Yet she sometimes felt she was losing track of what it was she was trying to do, which made the trying harder itself quite a bit harder. The soda cans piled up in her garbage can; the papers accumulated in her inbox; and in her head, lately, she was always giving interviews. *I believe in what we're doing,* she told an imaginary camera. *It's important that everyone out there be aware that drinking and driving will not be tolerated,* she said into a microphone. *With focus and determination and resolve we can get the job done. We have got to teach children right from wrong. And to cherish freedom,* she said, as her words were recorded and copied down into notebooks.

But sooner or later she ran right into the tough questions, like
What will you do about bad schools? and
What will you do about exploding pipelines? and
What will you do about abandoned babies? and
What will you do about child molesters? and
Who is your role model? and
How is your family doing?
To none of these did she have a very good answer.

Eight

etween Waterloo and its northern suburbs lay a nondescript, marginal region, its six- and eight-lane roads lined with doctor's offices, repair shops, and now and again the odd grassy inlet of land, a remnant of some long-ago orchard, where a lonely pecan tree had survived out of luck. Along one such road, on a small, neat lot, was the Rinemiller-Sherwood Funeral Home, a low brick building with a white portico and brass lamps on either side of the double-door entrance. The building had perhaps been designed to invoke something other than a funeral parlor, but for Nick what its red-brick and white-column architecture invoked was just that sort of business—commerce trying to be discreet about itself, a funeral parlor, or a neighborhood bank branch, or an insurance agency. The modest bureaus of debt and death, offering reassurance by way of solid materials and a few classical touches.

On the morning of Sabert's service the sun was bright and miserable over the funeral home, and the parking lot was clogged with old-person cars, so that even though empty spaces lay in plain sight no one could get to them for all the glinting sedans stopped every twenty feet, fragile ladies in brown hose bracing themselves against the passenger doors. Nick maneuvered his way across, braking, starting, braking, cursing. *Hoof it, meemaw*, he muttered at the sight of a matron who had paused in the middle of the lot to paw through her purse, blocking the way. He watched her pull out something that looked like a bingo marker. He wondered: Am I turning into one of those people who curse the world from behind the wheel? By the time he escaped to a side street he felt stupid for having sworn at a bunch of old ladies on their way to a funeral. He resolved to hold the door for somebody, or to find a seat just so he could give it up to one of the hunchbacked men now making their tortoise-like way inside.

But in the end he did neither thing. Within, it was all too close and too stiff: the antique upholstery, the miniature roses, the elderly crowd in hats and brooches. The foyer was clogged with scents— potpourri, flowers, perfume, air freshener—and underlying all that, a powdery sourness that had not come from a store. All around him old friends gripped one another's hands and sighed and uttered the *so good to see you* that meant *still alive, still alive!*

The whole place and everyone in it hearkened to some past time when everything was smaller. Small sofas, small flowers, small people. Nick recoiled. It was strange for him to be around so many old people. His daily life by and large excluded persons over sixty-five. The only semi-old person he knew in town was his uncle, and although Bones was past sixty he hadn't yet hit the real old-person marks. He wasn't retired, his hands didn't shake, and the only early-bird special he took advantage of was the three-dollar well drink.

Speaking of whom. The first person Nick recognized, the only person he recognized in the funeral foyer, was Bones, leaning against a wall and wiping his forehead. Nick had a fleeting impression of him as a man wounded, holed up in a cave with a broken leg and two bullets left in his pistol.

"Is that you, Nick?" Bones hollered. As Nick came closer he dropped his voice. "You know, it's easier to get the governor to return my calls."

"That's probably because you don't call up the governor to bitch about your bodily functions."

"How would you know?"

He was Nick's father's older brother. The two of them had been raised in Waterloo, but Nick's father had gone east to law school and on to a life of conventional respectability in New Jersey, where he was now a lower court judge, while Bones had stayed put in Waterloo, gaining admission to bars and benches of a lower order. In family pictures going back to boyhood he always looked as if he were about to rush the camera, skinny and forward-propelled, full of himself. Now he had flesh to spare and, as he was fond of telling people, a Viagra prescription.

Bones asked Nick what he was up to, and Nick answered that he was on assignment.

"Some assignment," Bones said.

"Yeah, well. How are you?"

"I'm dead, according to the doctors. Anyone with my blood pressure should be dead. I went over there to the doctor and this lady took my blood pressure, and when the doctor looked at the chart he thought she'd fucked it up, it was so bad. So he went and did it himself, and then *he* told me I was a dead man. Called me up three days later to say that anyone with my cholesterol should be dead, too."

The way he talked, Nick could make out only every third or fourth word. The others stuck in his mouth. He had a fullness about his lips, as if he were hoarding some morsel of gossip, savoring it, letting it roll over his tongue until he was ready to give it up. He spoke in swells, his voice rising and falling. In general he was a swollen person. His belly was round; his face was puffy. He drank a lot even for Waterloo, a drinking town, but he acted the same whether he was sober or lit. There was something sloppy about Bones even though his clothes were neat, something uncombed even though his hair, thick and white and soft-looking, fell in a boyish straight line across his forehead.

"Myra says she'd divorce me, but what's the point if I'm about to die anyway. Says she might as well wait and make some money off the deal. I told her she knows there's no money, and besides, I'm leaving it all to you."

"I'm touched. Is Myra here?"

"She's in there with the stiff. You doing all right?"

"I've been better," Nick said. "I've been worse."

"Women?"

"Both sexes. My boss wants me to write a story on Beverly Flintic."

"I don't see why the hell you would write about her."

"What have you got against her?"

"The question is what have I not got against her. She's just one of those *types*."

"You can't judge a person by type."

"I can. I'm a typist. What do you have on her?"

"It's not really that kind of story. It's a straight profile. Who she is, what she's like, and this development stuff on the east side."

"So are you all doing publicity for the R's?"

Bones was a D to the core, out of psychological necessity. Partisanship served him in place of certain ethical distinctions that he couldn't afford to make in his line of work.

"Don't ask me," Nick said.

"You all have the most retarded ideas about politics I have ever heard of. If it isn't saving the salamander, or something going on in Nicaragua, or endorsing a guy for president who has zero chance of winning, it's the R's. Makes sense, I guess. You give all your votes away and help elect one of theirs as president, you might as well just go on over to the other side." Bones was always ready to debate the views of "the loser left," but Nick had no stomach for it.

Taking a slap at Nick's arm, Bones said he had to go look for somebody or other. Nick was left at sea in a room full of strangers. Near the entrance to the chapel stood a man and two women greeting people as they crossed the threshold. "How *are* you?" said one of the women, over and over. Nick guessed she was family—Sabert's daughter, maybe. Her voice carried across the room. She wore long flowing sleeves, a blue scarf, and a wide-brimmed straw hat, as if in disguise, though her voice was a stage voice that no one could keep from hearing. Several feet away from her was a younger woman in a maroon dress, monitoring her as though waiting to talk to her. The woman in maroon was the youngest-looking adult in the room, and the only black person. She was very pretty, in a solemn, watchful way. Abruptly she turned and caught Nick looking at her, and he flashed her a stupid smile.

He could feel the inanity of it in his mouth and jaw, and regretted it at once. No doubt what he had inadvertently produced was a dopey "Welcome, Negro!" smile. With a pathetic little side note of "Hey, baby." She did not return it. In his embarrassment he looked away, and when he peeked back, he saw Bones.

At first it didn't seem that the two of them could possibly exist in the same frame. Bones was a blotch, a finger over the lens. He was accosting the woman, however; they were interacting. From the woman's expression Nick couldn't tell whether she was horrified or amused or bored.

Was this the person Bones had gone in search of? Nick walked over to them.

"I guessed you were kin to John Carter," Bones was saying. He turned to Nick. "This guy right here's related to me, though as you can see I got all the looks."

"And the personality," Nick said.

"Her daddy worked for Sabert. Smart man." Nick didn't know if Bones meant her father was smart or Sabert was.

The foyer was emptying. The woman excused herself. Nick and Bones followed the others into the chapel, a low-ceilinged room whose walls were smothered in pale-green damask. Already, the pews were nearly full.

Bones headed for a pew, but there weren't enough seats, so Nick hung back. From his position on the wall he had a clear view of the open casket up at the front of the room. He could see a ripple of white satin lining and a piece of Sabert's profile—specifically, the nose: a bluish beak rising out of the coffin. When Nick had gone to visit Sabert the nose had been sizable, and active, but now it appeared even larger, huge really, as if at the last it had achieved its rightful dimensions and was now sneering at all the insignificant noses arrayed before it. Looking at that nose made Nick want to touch his own nose. He shrank against the wall, all the more conscious of Sabert's body and of these people who had come here to encircle it, to consecrate it, to do something that he, the reporter, was not here to do. He was left staring at the nose.

A string quartet sallied forth from some hidden speaker. The usher was closing the doors when the black woman skirted through them and took a spot on the wall not far from Nick. He didn't want to give her another lame Nick-the-friendly-white-boy look, and so he inspected his shoes.

The hard work of conjuring Sabert had been entrusted to men who were not accustomed to imaginative labor, it seemed, men more used to speaking in generalities. They strained as they went along, each in turn standing uncomfortably behind a small wooden podium. The first to speak had a florid block of a head and big hands that held the top of the podium as if preparing to mount it; he was a union leader; he praised Sabert as a champion of the workingman. The next revealed his name, Darrell Robinson, and his profession, state assemblyman (retired), before recalling Sabert's great love of debate and discussion. And so it went, this summoning of a man, no magician when it came to working a room but indisputably a master of the legislative process, of the complex compromise—old-fashioned, sentimental, a good negotiator, an innate pacifist who brushed mosquitoes away rather than slapping them dead. One by one, the speakers did their best not simply to call him up but to raise him as high as they could.

Still, it was possible to read between the lines. He made more concessions than some would have liked—"knew when to fold 'em," said Robinson—he committed himself to too many things, divorced too often, and drank too much. These things could be inferred from what was said and what was not.

Prior to his failed interview Nick had seen Sabert every so often, around town, mostly at the pool: in his beach chair, his trunks and the faded chair fabric and the man's own skin all sharing the same slack quality; or in the water, paddling slowly. Once Nick had walked into the locker room—an open-air changing area, a slab of pavement surrounded by doorless stalls—right as Sabert was pulling off his trunks. It had been just the two of them there. Nick had turned away but had still heard Sabert's breathing, slow and complicated, and the soft rustle of an old man's clothes, his decades-old pants. Nick knew who Sabert was, and part of him felt he should go up and tell him that, simply acknowledge it: *I know who you are, sir.* But the man was feeble, and dripping wet. He'd had a stroke, Nick had heard; they said he was a drunk, the old liberal warhorse, the people's champion, this man with whorls of wet hair plastered to his sunken chest, this naked, wheezing, lumpy old man. And what could Nick have said? He hadn't known precisely what Sabert had done, he knew only that the man had been on the right side of things and had acted accordingly. Sabert needed no résumé; he was a liberal hero, and how exactly do you address a naked old hero? Nick hadn't said anything.

Maybe one reason so many people had come to the funeral was to thank a man they hadn't known how to thank, or even talk to, when he was alive.

Sabert's career would have been a more worthy and interesting one to follow than Mark Hardaway's, Nick was sure. Or Beverly Flintic's. Yes, it was a trap to romanticize the past, but this much—that Sabert was the preferable assignment—seemed beyond argument. Today's politics paled by comparison. Heroes were in short supply. People were having enough trouble just making themselves presentable.

He heard the familiar sound of a throat failing to clear itself. To Nick's surprise Bones was walking toward the podium, though Nick had never heard him mention Sabert's name. Nick had also never seen Bones look nervous. He took quick short steps, head down, until he reached the podium.

"Friends," he began. His eyes darted unhappily over the pews, as if he couldn't see a single friendly face. "There's an old story about Davy Crockett that reminds me of Will Sabert, so bear with me, because I'm going to tell it. It's a politics story, one that Crockett told on himself after he was elected to Congress from the state of Tennessee. Though being a politician, he may have stretched the truth from time to time.

"Goes like this. Crockett was out on the campaign trail, and he came to a fair out in the country where he was supposed to give a speech. So he gets up on his stump, the crowd gathers round, and he starts up with the usual bushwa. Gets about five minutes into it when the people stop him. They won't listen to a subject as dry as the welfare of the nation unless they wet their throats first."

Nick worried that a funeral service was not the place for one of his uncle's monologues. Then again he hadn't been to enough funerals to know what was acceptable and what was not. He stole a look at the woman nearby, as if her expression might tell him what to think. But her profile betrayed nothing.

"As it happened, right there at the fair was a clever Yankee who'd anticipated this communal need and set up a liquor tent. So Crockett says to the crowd, let's all go have a round on me. They cheer and head down to the tent. But when they get there Crockett doesn't have the money.

"But it's Crockett, after all, so he takes his rifle out into the woods and shoots himself a coon out of a tree, and brings the skin back to this Yankee liquor salesman. Then everybody gets their drink of whiskey, and they all go on back to the stump. This is back in the day when your orator types really did stand on tree stumps, now. Crockett gets on up there, but the moment he starts again on the welfare of the nation, the people want another round. All right, he says, let's go down to the tent again, but it's the same deal. No money. And now there's not time to hunt down another critter."

Nick was still uneasy. He himself would've liked to have a drink before witnessing this. Every other speaker had been succinct: this was not succinct. Bones was looking up toward the ceiling and starting to throw his arms around. Just when Crockett thought it was all over, Bones was saying, he discovered that same coonskin out behind the back of the liquor tent, where the busy salesman had tossed it. "Crockett steals that same skin back from the Yankee and brings it to him again, like it's brand-new. It works. Another round for the crowd . . . and the salesman throws the skin back on that box. They go two more rounds like this: Crockett steals the skin, the Yankee takes it, pours whiskey for everyone. And the crowd can see exactly what's going on. They love it. They don't give a fig what he says about the welfare of the nation, they're going to vote for him.

"Here's where this story reminds me of Will Sabert. At the end of the day, the Yankee finally figures it all out, and he's not too happy. But he doesn't go after Crockett. He shakes his hand—and says he's better off for having learned to keep a closer eye on his business. And he did get a coonskin out of it, after all, even if he thought he might get four.

"For a long time, this is how it was between Will Sabert and his adversaries in business, the oil companies, the builders. He passed regulations they didn't like, but at the end of the day they respected one another, because he was a worthy opponent, he kept them on their toes, and he was smart enough to give them a coonskin when he had one to give. Especially if he had an election coming up. He used to say one of the ironies of our democracy was that the closer you were to an election, the less attention you paid to the public. You looked more to the special interests who might buy the seat out from under you. Eventually he didn't pay enough attention to those folks and he lost, but he understood that eighty or ninety percent of what goes on in politics, in the statehouse here or in Washington, D.C., is business, and eighty or ninety percent of that is business versus business.

"He was an idealist but not a starry-eyed one. He could be pragmatic, even if he did see fit to dress himself like Colonel Sanders. He had to make hard decisions. It's easy in hindsight to say some of them were not the right ones. Some of them he lost friends over." Bones stopped and looked down. "I could go on all day, but I guess I won't. I've been thinking a lot this past week about what Will's legacy might be, and it's a lot of things, but . . . in the end it's not really my place to say. Thank you."

Those last lines were strange, Nick thought. But then the whole thing had been strange. He glanced again at the girl to his left, though he was pushing it, he'd looked at her too many times already. She was standing even straighter, if that was possible.

The very audible woman who'd been greeting people earlier moved to the front, still in her straw hat. The sun was now streaming through the windows, and her eyes were shadowed by her hat's wide brim, her chin made to tremble by the dancing, leaf-mottled light. She was Katharine Sabert and she wanted to thank everyone for coming, she said.

"When I was in elementary school, they asked us to name the president of the United States," she said, "and I said it was my father, William Sabert. The teacher told me no, my father was not the president of the United States, but he was a member of Congress and I should be very proud of him. But I insisted that he was in Congress and also the president."

People in the audience laughed politely. Then the woman went on about how her father had meant the world to her, not just when she was a girl but up until the end. Much had been said already about her father's accomplishments, "but all that is not the most important thing," she said. "Not the park land he saved, not the schools he brought more funding to, not the clients he represented as an attorney. My father knew how to live. He knew how to live! He loved to swim and he loved to eat, he loved to talk and he absolutely loved to drink whiskey. He knew how to live. If there's one thing we should remember about him, it's his joy. We are here to celebrate that—to celebrate him—and to remind ourselves of what he would have wanted us to do: Live!"

She fell silent, and stepped back from the podium, disoriented. A suspenseful few seconds followed—would she find her way back to earth? She held on to the pew in front of her as she took her seat.

Nick supposed it was a moving speech, but he was still thinking of Bones's unexpected eulogy, and wondering what if anything he could use for the obituary. He tried to remember what the earlier speakers had said. He hadn't wanted to take out a notepad during the service, and so his plan was to hurry to the men's room as soon as he could and scribble down as much as he could recall. The music started playing again, people rustled in their seats, and a detachment of men surrounded the casket, closed it, and carried it out a side door. Nick turned toward the rear exit. That black girl, though: she was rubbing at her eyes and sniffling.

"Tissue?" said Nick, the word half catching as he remembered he didn't have a tissue. She nodded. Her hazel eyes were lighter than her skin, and flooded. Nick looked at her eyes, and only by looking at them did he at last understand that he was at a funeral, because a man was dead. "Hold on," he said.

He located the largest nearby purse, spoke with its owner, and returned, alas, with a crumpled pink tissue the obliging woman had dug up from the bottom of her bag. He offered it sheepishly. She paused before accepting, but took it. "Thank you."

Was he supposed to leave her then? He didn't move. "I'm Nick."

She nodded, wiping her nose, and said something muffled into the tissue, which might have been her name.

"So your dad knows Sabert?"

"My father used to work for him."

She wiped her nose again. The tissue was about used up, and Nick would have liked to offer her his sleeve instead, his entire jacket—all at once he would have liked to take this stranger into his arms, and yet because there were tears in her eyes he was also uncomfortable and wanted to go to the men's room.

"So, do you live around here?" Oh brother, he thought, but there was no taking it back.

She nodded.

"What do you do?"

"I work for the *Standard-American*."

It was not the proper time to be asking her about her job. "I work for the *Weekly*." That wasn't right, either. "Did you know him, Sabert?"

"Not well, but—I spent some time with him. Did you?"

"No," Nick admitted. "I'm supposed to write about this." Also not right, not right. She was very pretty.

She looked around the room.

Just then Bones inserted himself in the conversation. "Will Sabert was a remarkable man, most of the time. And John Carter—" he said. He turned to the girl, and she met his stare. "You know, it's not that you look that much like him," he told her. "But you carry yourself the same way. Your dad always stood very straight."

"Yes he did," she said, her face a polite mask. "It was nice meeting you both." She walked away.

"What was that?" Nick asked.

"Did I interrupt something?"

As they walked out the chapel doors together in silence, Bones put his arm around Nick. "You know I love you, right?" Up close, it was hard not to look at Bones's nostrils, which were ample and sufficiently upturned to offer a hairy interior view. "Yes," Nick said.

"And I would do anything for you?"

"No, I don't think you would."

"Exactly," Bones said. "But if I can help you out on this Flintic thing . . ."

"You got anything for me?"

"I might."

"You might."

"Let me get back to you on that one."

"I didn't know you knew Sabert."

"Thing is," said Bones, shaking his head, "I knew him but I wouldn't say that I *knew* him. His daughter asked me to speak today. I wasn't expecting it. She asked me, so I did."

"Where did you get that Davy Crockett thing?"

"It was the best I could do."

"I'm not saying—"

"I'd rather not discuss it, Ace. I'll call you about Flintic, all right?"

Nick said goodbye to his uncle and wandered down a series of corridors hung with photographs of Waterloo taken in the early 1900s. The city of the dearly departed. The smell of potpourri was stronger than in the lobby. Nick felt a headache coming on. He could already hear Roger's voice needling him about the pretty girl whose name he'd failed to learn.

The bathroom was covered in tiny ocher tiles that reminded Nick of grade school. He leaned against the sink basin and took his notebook and pen from his pocket, but found he could remember almost nothing of what had been said at the podium. Only the last eulogy stuck in his mind, and only the words *He knew how to live!* Hearing them the first time, he had felt distantly accused, but now they returned as a full-on charge. Not even with that message of carpe diem ringing in his ears had he managed to learn so much as the woman's name.

Nine

The service seemed to Andrea to have been exactly that, a *service*, like dry cleaning, like cutting the grass. With religion all but banished, the rituals had been guided by the precepts of customer care. Professionals had chosen the music, arranged the flowers, and suggested what approximate number of speakers would suit the occasion without drawing out the ceremony so long as to incur a surcharge. Everything had gone smoothly—there was something almost merciless in how smooth. Not that she would have wanted hymns or homilies or women beating their breasts. Not that she knew what she would have wanted. Not that it would have mattered anyway.

It was a five-minute wait at the curb in front of the funeral home before the river of cars dried up and she could cross the road, back to the grocery-store lot where she'd parked. The sun was harsh, the blacktop soft under her heels. She was sweating onto her dress. In the lot she came upon a group of five children eating roasted corn on the cob, the oldest girl pushing a cart full of grocery bags. As they passed each other she realized the one pushing the cart was the mother of the other four.

At times Andrea's mind filled with nonverbal streams, half songs or rhythms that surfaced and ran along in currents before disappearing again down below, not sad or happy but containing the seeds of both in the way that music sometimes did. She hummed to herself as she started the car. The funeral had seemed in some way incomplete, and although she didn't have high hopes for the reception, she drove over to Sabert's house anyhow.

It was a blinding day. The roads stretched out before her like animals lying in the sun, and all the shrubbery, the foliage, the plots of grass outside the banks, flaunted their green. The sidewalks had filled with people, whole families suited up and mobilized, walking, jogging, pushing long-snouted sport strollers and throwing tennis balls to dogs. What type of city was this? Her father had grown up here, but she'd never set foot in Waterloo before she'd come to interview for the job at the paper. It made sense to her that her father would have left: this place wasn't like him. Or like her. In her own neighborhood, near the university campus, people seemed to spend all day exercising or sitting in coffee shops. Sometimes she wondered whether any of them had jobs. Even to call Waterloo a city seemed like a stretch: it was too small and spread out, too good-natured, too easy. People didn't seem to work very hard. They drank a lot.

She worked on the metro desk, and after a year at the *Standard-American* she still didn't understand her editors. At every other paper where she'd worked, she'd been pushed to file four or five articles a week. Here, she was averaging two, and the stories they considered most important hardly seemed like stories to her. A recent assignment had concerned a group of trees. The tree beat. It had started when the city arborist announced that six tall cottonwoods at Rio Vista Park had been infested by cytospores and were "scheduled for removal"; scarcely had the press release left the Parks Department fax machine before the first howls of protest sounded. When the television outlets showed a cross section of an ailing tree, a hollowed, moth-eaten cylinder that resembled a ring of housing insulation, protesters countered that obviously the picture was of some other tree that had already been cut down, not one from the park. And even if the Rio Vista cottonwoods were similarly afflicted, they argued, why hadn't the city explored more options? Why couldn't the trees' innards be somehow reconstructed? Andrea had interviewed several in the save-the-trees camp. They had described, in detail, a process that sounded like dental work, in which a trunk might be restored, ring by ring, with a long, probing implement. *People*, she'd wanted to say, *we're talking about trees here*. Just six trees. And diseased. The branches were already starting to go; a strong wind could easily snap off a large, treacherous limb. And though the state had several years earlier passed a law barring tort claims against municipalities and school districts, if a heavy tree part were to land directly upon the head of a small child—Andrea could understand why the arborist had seemed nervous. No one knew exactly to what extent the law indemnified city employees.

The trees came down. While the removal men worked, the park was cordoned around the perimeter; even the parking lot was declared off-limits to all but police officers and the media. Officials called it a safety measure, but the closing of the lot inflamed the small (but vocal) conspiracy crowd, who believed that there were no cytospores, that the whole disease story had been fabricated, that the city had acted at the behest of nearby loft owners who wanted to watch the annual fireworks display from their balconies. Lies and cover-ups. The same thing had happened in 1969, they said, when the university bulldozed a group of elms to make way for a stadium expansion. Andrea had received a number of long e-mails on the subject. She'd consulted with Richard, her editor, who'd approved of her decision not to include the conspiracists in the piece; she'd later received another e-mail alleging that she was "in cahoots" with the loft owners.

Near where the trees had stood, the city installed six saplings swaddled in orange plastic, like a grove of pylons.

The family hadn't yet come back from the cemetery when Andrea arrived at Sabert's house. She didn't know anyone there. She barely recognized the rooms, emptied of litter, the stacks of papers gone, the furniture dusted, the windows de-streaked, the rugs vacuumed. The flowers had been brought over from the funeral parlor and stationed on the mantel and on tables. Someone had set out fried chicken and fruit pies and beer and wine; serious eating and drinking was already under way. An old white man with a bald, ovoid head who wore a green suit and carried a cane hobbled aggressively toward Andrea, large feet and cane thudding against the floor. "Nice to see you," he shouted once he'd come close. "Though sorry it had to be under these circumstances."

"Andrea Carter. Nice to meet you."

The man had not stopped walking, and thumping. "Mighty fine," he said, moving on past her. After another round of thumps she heard him greet the next person.

There was no sign of Hal, Sabert's cat. A moody, overweight feline, he'd been a stray before Sabert started indulging him with shelter and food, and now his personality was equal parts street child and spoiled brat. Maybe he had gone back to the streets—but how would he survive out there, after so much coddling, after canned salmon and milk and pills from the vet?

She passed through the front rooms and into the hall, where a man was studying the convention photograph that hung outside the bathroom. "Hmm!" he said. Or maybe he was clearing his throat. He turned toward Andrea and seemed startled, not exactly by her, but in general—behind his glasses, his monochromatic eyes were wide open. His thick, dark beard seemed in some way Russian, while his faded short-sleeved shirt and knit tie reminded Andrea of one of her junior high teachers, Mr. Loefler, a gentle shlub who'd taken an extended leave after having been tied to a chair by the students he was supposed to be supervising in after-school detention.

"Andrea Carter," he said.

"Mr. Loefler?"

"Alan."

She wasn't ready for "Alan"; he was Mr. Loefler.

He laughed and said, "Oh, how wonderful to run into you!"

In junior high it had not occurred to her that Mr. Loefler might be gay.

"It's good to see you, too," she said. She wasn't so keen to talk to him, since he made her think of eighth grade, and the chair-tying, but there he was. "You still teaching?"

He said he'd pulled out of the eighth grade business and gone back to school for a Ph.D. in communications, then found a job here. Now he taught a popular class on arguing in the university extension program. He added that he was Will Sabert's biographer—saying it as if a biographer were a kind of medical specialist.

"I didn't know he had a biographer." Sabert had never mentioned it, but then again it wasn't the sort of thing he would mention.

"I'm it, for better or worse. Do you live here in town?"

"I moved here almost a year ago. I got a job with the newspaper."

"The *Standard-American*? Wonderful. Are you writing for them or—"

"Local news." I cover trees, she wanted to say.

"Wonderful."

She felt suddenly protective of the photograph, wanting to defend it against wonderfulness. But when Mr. Loefler turned to look at it, his voice dropped respectfully. "Isn't that some picture?" he said. "That was taken when all the liberals walked out of the state party convention in 1952."

They'd walked out, he explained, to protest the party leaders who wanted to cross over and support Eisenhower. She didn't know what he was talking about. She'd looked at this picture many times but had never tried to learn what all those people were doing out in the rain.

"Did you know the congressman?" asked Mr. Loefler.

"My dad worked for him."

"Your dad? Oh, wow, I've got to talk to him."

Andrea said that he had passed away. Mr. Loefler looked stricken. To forestall his awkward apologies, she said some more about her father, that he had gone to work for Sabert in the sixties as a policy aide. Mostly before I was born, Andrea said.

"I'm sorry to be mercenary, but did he leave behind any records? Papers, files, diaries?"

"He was never one for keeping things. After he died, there really wasn't much." Out the window she could see two small kids, a girl and a boy, who'd escaped the party and were running the run of the liberated through the yard's ancient leaves. The girl kept pulling the bottom of her dress up to her stomach.

"Do you think your mother might have—"

"My mother didn't speak to him."

"What a shame. What a shame. Did he ever talk about it? The old days, how he met Sabert? There must be stories."

"No, not really," said Andrea. At least, she didn't care to dredge up what she knew about her father's past for Mr. Loefler, who was scratching his nose with the back of his hand and waiting, it seemed, for her to say something more. Outside, the girl had pulled her dress over her head and was stumbling around blindly. From the kitchen Andrea heard a shout of "Sorry it had to be under these circumstances!"

"My father wasn't much of a storyteller," she said.

"I see. I'm sorry. It's become my job to pry, I'm afraid. Which is strange. But the more I learn about all this," he said, gesturing around himself as if the living room were his subject, "the more fascinating it is."

"I bet."

He presented Andrea with one of his cards, in case she remembered anything, or in case she wanted to have coffee, to hear about some of his research on Sabert—it was fascinating stuff.

The sight of the girl in the yard had made her own clothes itch. Andrea retreated to the bathroom. There she stepped out of her heels, peeled off her cheap stockings, and, though she would probably throw them out later, wadded them into her handbag. Her knees were ashy, her feet mottled from the press of formal shoes. She sank her toes into the shaggy bath rug, flexed them, and dug them in again. Then she looked up at the mirror and let her forehead relax. For the most part she didn't take after her father, though sometimes he surprised her, jumping out of her own face all of a sudden, hovering in a shop window reflection or a snapshot. There was something of him in the worry lines that appeared between her brows, in the way she parted her lips while concentrating. Sometimes when she cleared her throat she sounded just like him.

When he died, Andrea had been in Spain, on a semester abroad. She hadn't gone back for the funeral. That weekend she'd taken a train to Granada, and at the time of his heart attack she had been, as best she could figure, drinking the local sherry in a tourist restaurant. A Moor with a backpack: the souvenir hawkers hadn't called out to her as they had to the Germans and the Japanese. By the time she returned to her school in Seville, her father had been dead three days; to make it home in time for the funeral seemed almost impossible. Almost. There, surrounded by the orange trees and tiled archways, the Africans selling roasted chestnuts and umbrellas, the narrow streets and iron doors, it hadn't seemed like a fact, his death, for nothing had seemed entirely true—there was something provisional about reading a newspaper in a foreign language, or hearing the odd whine of foreign insects, or, for that matter, smelling the very air with its particular mix of exhaust and citrus and foreign detergents. Her mother's voice, when Andrea reached her at last, sounded remote and grudging, as if Andrea's decision to spend an entire semester in Spain was not just bizarre but, at present, extremely inconvenient. "I have been *trying* to get ahold of you all weekend," she'd said. "Your father has passed on."

Over there, the fact of his death had drifted in and out of her awareness, like a dream she remembered not in the particulars but as a mood, an enduring mood that made everything more difficult: walking, paying for coffee, trying to read. Taking note: on the left, this canvas, and on the right, that minaret. When what she would have liked to do was to hole up in a minaret of her own. She'd always tried to watch carefully but had resolved, from that time forward, on increased vigilance—as if she had let something slide, and had lost a father as a result.

In truth she couldn't say when she'd ever had him. By high school she'd found him unbearable. Older than anyone else's father, and formal to the point of pompous, a *father,* not a dad, and barely that. The fact that he saw her only a few weeks out of the year didn't keep him from moralizing when it came to her clothes (too skimpy) or whatever she happened to be reading (trash). He would ramble on about his work, though Andrea rarely recognized the names he dropped. Once in a while he would throw in some tale of his Noble Youth in the Civil Rights Movement, which as far as Andrea could tell boiled down to not much more than having helped to desegregate the libraries in Waterloo, and then having gone to work for a liberal white congressman.

A month or so ago Andrea had learned that the city was planning to tear down the library in question, and she'd assumed that, as with the trees, there would be protests. She'd assumed that her editor would want an article about it. Wrong on both counts: because the building's rot was not hidden within but visible from the street, in the form of missing shingles and plywood over two of the windows, and because as architecture the library didn't rate, no one seemed to care that it was about to be razed. On its own, the fact that it had once been the black library did not argue against demolition. The new branch to be built a few blocks away would display photos of its predecessor in a permanent lobby exhibit, with accompanying text about segregation. When Andrea proposed the building's destruction as a story, Richard had asked if anyone was opposed; when she answered in the negative, he looked back at her blankly. "So what's the angle?" he asked. And when she said (for the second time) that it was possibly of interest because it had once been the black library, his normally lazy face had seized up in an expression of panic—i.e., *Oh shit, I hope you don't think I'm a racist.* Richard encouraged her to do the story for the Lifestyles section. She knew what that meant: it would run on the weekend with some headline like ONE FOR THE HISTORY BOOKS: EAST SIDE RESIDENTS SHARE MEMORIES OF JIM CROW LIBRARY. But why would that trouble her? What other kind of article would it be? The irony was that she'd pitched the story at all; she hadn't listened when her father had tried to tell her about it, years ago.

She splashed water on her face, and groped for a towel and saw between wet blinks that there was no towel. The door to the big cabinet next to the sink was ajar: she swung it open the rest of the way, and then inhaled sharply. A pair of eyes blinked back at her. A furry bellows of a cat body expanded and contracted, breath by breath. It was Hal, presiding over shaving cream and medicine canisters.

He yowled, and she breathed again. Then she yowled back, softly. They eyed each other. The cat was huge. He propelled his shaggy immensity to the edge of the sink and from there plopped to the floor, mooning her and trailing wisps of hair.

Andrea put her shoes back on and picked Hal up with both hands. She was surprised when the animal submitted, resting on her shoulder like a child as she walked him out of the bathroom.

Surprised again: that smoke-blowing older guy she'd met at the funeral home—was Bones actually his name?—crept out of a bedroom, like he'd been hiding there until he could get away clean. His tie was loose and his glass was drained, and for a second he looked as startled as she was. But he recovered. "I guess fat cats really are back in style," he said.

"He tried to jump me in the bathroom."

"You can't blame a guy for trying."

Har har har. His banter had an edge to it, more teeth than humor. The words were stupider than the man, she felt, and the way he looked at her wasn't quite friendly: drawing his head back as if to inspect her. And here she was with a huge cat on her shoulder.

"So then, Ms. Carter. It was good of you to come. How long you in town for?"

"I live here." For now, she thought to herself. "I moved here to work at the *American*."

"Did you now?"

Hal clawed at the fabric of her dress. She lifted him away from her, wanting to let him down but waiting for him to pull his paw away from her neckline. Bones reached out and pinched the paw, like he'd been removing claws from clothing his whole life, and in the process brushed her collarbone with his dry hand. Hal withdrew and Andrea shivered. She lowered the cat to the floor.

"I knew your dad a little, not well," Bones said.

Enough about him, she thought, picking hairs off of her dress front.

"The congressman just loved him," he continued.

"Are you in politics?"

"Mired in it, I'm afraid. Since I was sixteen years old. Thrown away my whole life on it. But it's been fun. I wouldn't have lasted two weeks in a desk job."

Her first sense of the man shifted—his voice sounded warmer now—and she continued in reporter mode, asking him about his work. He said he was a lobbyist. She asked him how he'd become a lobbyist. His answer was vague. He pointed to the bathroom and then went in and shut the door behind him.

Once again she found herself in front of the photograph of that convention. With barely any forethought, she took it—plucked it off the wall and secured it under her arm. She found Hal out on the porch and, emboldened by the first theft, picked him up again. Having filched both property and pet from the congressman's estate, she marched down to her car.

She'd never had a pet. Before Waterloo, Andrea had worked at a small newspaper in Tennessee, and before that at an even smaller paper in Missouri, and all the while she had assumed that her zigzag across the country would terminate eventually on one of the coasts, where she would write stories on weightier subjects than tree rot, for the benefit of a seven-figure audience. She'd leapt quickly, ably, from paper to paper, and had satisfied herself, but for the occasional spell of rainy-night doubt, that talent and enterprise had had as much to do with her agile climb as the almost pathetic eagerness of the lily-white middle-American news staff to hire anyone with skin pigmentation. There was no reason to think she wouldn't continue to leap—Richard's inane assignments notwithstanding—except that after four and a half years, her legs were starting to tire. The work was good, but she'd had about enough of this hopping from town to town. Once, Los Angeles or New York had meant the light at the end of the tunnel; now they meant having to start over again, to find another apartment and meet a whole new set of people and figure out how to get around.

She might as well look after Hal for now, if he wanted looking after.

Her apartment was south of the river, not far from the newspaper office, a pair of rooms plus a tiny kitchen above a garage where her landlord had entombed his dead Chevelle. The apartment's assets lay mostly in what it didn't have: old carpet, roommates, bugs. As she climbed the steps with her arms full of overweight tabby, as he shed all over her dress and beat his tail against her arm, it occurred to her that this was the first male she'd had up to the apartment. Then she thought of the guy who'd spoken to her at the funeral, Nick, who'd fetched her a wrinkled Kleenex and made a few stabs at conversation: she hadn't been all that nice to him. But he wasn't the first man she'd met in Waterloo who gave off a slight smell of wanting to apologize for his very existence.

Waterloo was the farthest south she'd ever lived, and the heat here, she was discovering, had a life of its own. Or various lives: there were phyla and species of heat, and you developed relationships with them. There was the heat generated by walking around, or the heat of an animal against your chest, the heat of the sun on the back of your neck, the heat of the haze surrounding you, the heat of embarrassment, the heat of recognition. When Andrea was almost to the landing, Hal jumped out of her arms and scampered back down the stairs. Well, then. Easy come, easy go. If he didn't want to stop in for a drink, fine, though she did feel a bit misused for having carried him all the way up the stairs.

Ten

At home after Sabert's funeral, Nick listened to two urgent phone messages from Roger concerning a one-night-only screening of short films about robots—this very evening, not to be missed, incredibly cool, etc.—but he decided to stay in. He went to bed early, and woke up at seven-thirty the next morning. This was several hours earlier than he normally arose on Sundays. Wearing his boxer shorts and nothing else, Nick opened the back door and surveyed his forsaken back lawn. More dirt than lawn really. The morning was quiet, except for one loony-sounding bird. The neighbors were all lying in their beds or bowing over their coffeepots, Nick supposed, and he gave in to the temptation to urinate off the back steps. For some reason this made him wish he had a dog. So that they could piss in the yard together? He wandered back inside and then out to the front porch, where he found his uncle, passed out on the sofa.

Bones had taken off his shirt and used it to cover his head; a canvas briefcase served as a pillow. His big chest rose and fell.

As Nick started to tiptoe back inside, Bones coughed, his shirt billowing above his mouth. He grabbed the shirt and drew it down toward his nipples. "This is an awfully comfortable piece of furniture you have here," he said. "Although it smells like doo-doo. You don't mind if I rest on it?"

"No, I guess not," Nick said. Then: "How long have you been here?"

"I'm not entirely sure," Bones rasped. "It was dark when I got here. Myra said she was tired of me coming home inebriated at two in the morning. She says I'm a vortex of dissipation and waste." Bones started coughing again. "You got any beer?"

"No."

"So I'm a vortex of dissipation and waste. She knew that when she married me."

"I often wonder why."

"Hell, we were both high as kites at the time. Remind me to tell you the whole story when I'm not so depressed." Bones sat up and started putting his shirt on.

Nick walked into the house and Bones followed him. "You're depressed?" Nick asked.

"I told you, I'm falling apart. I've got to take this cholesterol medicine, and hypertension medicine, and erect dick medicine. These politicians keep saying they'll do something about the cost of drugs, but between that and the goddamn cigarette taxes it's no wonder about our family finances."

Nick's father had disapproved of Bones, of the way he'd managed to transform himself into a lazy, crass-talking good old boy even though they'd been raised by diligent Lutherans. But after dropping out of college and moving down to Waterloo, Nick had stayed with Bones and Myra for a month while looking for a place of his own, and during that time a loose boozy bond had grown up between them. At the time, Bones and Myra had seemed like the parents of his dreams. They still smoked pot. Some nights Bones would start cooking supper at eleven o'clock, and continue eating and drinking until two. His weekends were parodies of other people's weekends: yard work meant standing out on the lawn, hose in one hand and drink in the other, "watering." Or he'd "run errands," only instead of going to stores for groceries or hardware he drove around to yard sales that had already ended, to see what he might haul off for free. The inside of his garage looked like a refugee camp for lawn furniture.

Since that time Nick and Bones had kept up with each other, though Nick's job at the *Weekly* had muddled things. Bones had always been discreet about his business dealings, but he became more pointedly so, teasing Nick about the paper's weak grip on reality—*If y'all only knew the half of it*, he'd say, smug but also genuinely irritated that people and institutions insisted on clinging to their flawed idealisms after he had abandoned his own. And Nick felt different about his uncle. At twenty he'd had a kind of admiration for heavy drinkers; now he himself was trying to cut back.

"Can I use your shower?" Bones asked.

Nick didn't want him to. "Go ahead."

Once the water was running, Bones started in on Merle Haggard, though his covers were less than faithful. Every other note of "I'm a Lonesome Fugitive" teetered or cracked or fell apart. The ringing of the phone was melodic by comparison.

"Nick, is your uncle over there?" It was Myra.

"Can't you hear him?" He walked over toward the bathroom door, opened it a crack, and held out the phone. "Did you hear that?"

"If he gets to 'Here Comes the Freedom Train' just shut the water off."

"He said you told him not to come home if he was drunk."

"Then I guess I must have. Sober him up, will you? And don't let him smoke too much. And remind him the Wardlaws are having us over to dinner tonight?"

"Sure, Myra. Okay. Talk to you later."

He walked back out to the porch and sat down on the sofa where Bones had been sleeping. The spot was warm and damp. He moved to the front step.

For all his grievances with the city at large, Nick was inordinately fond of his neighborhood, Bowie Park. There was nothing remarkable about it, just a grid of oak-sheltered streets and one-story wooden-frame houses and Mexican restaurants, but if the neighbor-hoods ever went to war, if Bowie were suddenly attacked by Clark Addition or Rosedale, Nick would have been the first to volunteer for duty. A hundred years ago it had been the red-light district—this before Waterloo had installed much lighting of any color—and now and then Nick imagined what those long-ago nights might have been like, ink-dark except for the red lanterns of vice and the blue moon. A place where people weren't so much poor as broke, or go-ing for it. Where men wore dungarees and suspenders. Loose women and loose pigs strutting across the road. Whiskey flowing in the gutters. Only there hadn't been any gutters.

But that wasn't why Nick loved Bowie Park. Nor was it the legacy of the more recent past, an era known locally as When It Was Cheap. Legend had it that in the early years of WIWC, Mexicans and musi-cians had come with their tacos and their hallucinogens, and the south side of town had become known for a sort of addled good hu-mor, an association that still existed even though meanwhile the rents had tripled, forcing the loafers and the working poor to move out to aesthetically less satisfying tracts farther south. Now it was freelance videographers and interface designers living next door to Mexican grandmothers who'd owned their houses since the fifties. Now it was black Labradors on leashes and people coming for tacos from all over the city in really big cars. Nick had no reason to be-grudge them, for he himself had lived here less than five years. If gentrification was a problem, he was part of the problem. Still, he thought of this area as his own. He couldn't exactly say why. It crept up on him, a feeling of loyalty to the little things, to the sno-cone truck that always sat parked on South Street and to the patch of un-cut grass that was the actual Bowie Park, and to the mariachis who played Rolling Stones covers at Paco's on Friday nights.

He had been renting the house he lived in for going on five years, a one-story, one-bedroom cottage in need of a paint job, among other improvements. The interior was sparely decorated—he didn't own much furniture—and not as clean as it could be. The good part was, he lived alone. He liked living alone. He viewed his decision to live alone as an important step in his life, like his first kiss and getting a driver's license and eating salad. Living alone, he'd become more adult. He was capable of staying in at night and waking up early on a Sunday. When he remembered to pay the bill, he had a newspaper subscription. He thought about getting a pet.

He was not in the habit of receiving visitors, however. From the sound of things, Bones was out of the shower now, humphing and grunting and probably flatulating as well. He came to the door wearing only a towel, Nick's towel, with his lips around a bottle of beer. Nick's beer. It was not yet eight in the morning.

"You are an alcoholic," Nick observed.

"I know it," Bones said. "I've learned to accept the things I cannot change. Guess I'll put some clothes on."

"Please do."

"I don't suppose I could borrow—"

"Whatever you need. Clothes are in the dresser in the bedroom."

"Deodorant, actually."

The thought of Bones swiping his moist, hairy underarms with Nick's deodorant was disagreeable. "Bathroom cabinet," Nick said.

"So what happened with you and that girl yesterday?" Bones called out from the bathroom.

"What girl?"

"The one yesterday. John Carter's daughter. Andrea Carter. You going to call her?"

"It was a funeral. I didn't go there to pick up girls."

"That's a sorry excuse for an excuse."

When he came out of the bathroom Bones had put on half of his clothes: a wife-beater undershirt with a damp spot at the belly and a pair of rumpled khaki shorts. He was holding his balled-up underwear in one hand. His round pink arms bulged out of the undershirt like a pair of peeled vegetables. Nick could smell the perfumed deodorant that Liza had left in the bathroom ages ago.

"I know you probably call yourself a feminist and so forth," Bones said, "but what is the deal with using women's deodorant?"

"Oh, that," Nick said. "It came free with some panty hose that I bought to wear under my pants."

Bones sighed. "It's those private colleges. I tell you, I wouldn't let any son of mine within ten miles of one of those places. Unless he was chasing pussy."

"You don't have a son."

"But if I did. C'mon, get dressed and let me take you to breakfast."

Meals with his uncle were trying, since Bones always finished his food in about ten minutes and then started ogling the waitresses. "I'm not too hungry. This might be the earliest I've ever been up on a Sunday. I should probably go back to bed."

"I'll make you some coffee. You got anything to eat around here?"

"Not much, but you're welcome to whatever's in the fridge."

Nick put a shirt on and joined Bones in the kitchen. Already he'd taken the ketchup out and set it on the counter, along with the pair of underwear, and he was sizing up the contents of jars and to-go boxes. "How's that Beverly Flintic story coming along?"

"I'm meeting with her tomorrow." Nick had been dreading it.

Munching on something, Bones walked out to the living room, where he'd left his briefcase, and returned with a stack of papers and a brochure that he handed to Nick: an eight-page prospectus for something called Waterloo Village. Nick looked it over. Evidently this "village" was a proposed east Waterloo development, a dream of a neighborhood sketched in pastels, with rhubarb-pink walkways and green bubble bushes and pedestrians of many races gadding about, their feet not quite touching the ground. Surrounding the people were sensible three-and-four-story brick buildings, with awnings and even (rare though this was for Waterloo) a sidewalk café. Would it accept food stamps? Nick mused, thinking of the adjacent areas—but of course there was no sign of poverty or strife in the drawings. A clean, harmonious, mixed-use, mixed-race development: it was as though the very builders of the Tower of Babel might have avoided catastrophe had they only hired the right architects, had they chosen walkways and restaurants instead of overweening height.

The planner of this utopia was a company called Heritage. It was this same Heritage that had scripted bill number 1275, said Bones, a bill sponsored by none other than Beverly Flintic. This wasn't the sort of thing Nick cared to become informed about early on a Sunday morning, but Bones went right on talking. "It's a real loco deal," he said. "They basically want a big pass on city regulations over half the east side." Private government, he said. A pilot project in east Waterloo, a pilot project somewhere else, and it was only a matter of time before they took over the whole state.

Nick said he didn't follow.

To build what Bones kept referring to as "Heritage Village," the company wanted to establish an "East Side Development Corporation" with the ability to get around regulations and possibly even levy taxes. "You ought to look and see what kind of money Beverly Flintic has taken from the execs at Heritage," Bones said. He frowned as he removed a drooping shaft of aged celery from the crisper and threw it javelin-style into the sink. It had been overly optimistic of Nick to buy celery, he admitted to himself; he might as well have resolved to run eight miles as to eat celery. He'd always been a peanut butter man, and since adding salad he'd been a peanut butter and salad man, but for him there was no getting over the hump of celery.

"Pickles, now that's what I'm talking about," Bones said, opening the jar and then wedging half his hand into the vinegar before removing one spear. He stressed that few givers to the Flintic campaign had been as generous as the folks from Heritage. And she had responded in kind: by introducing legislation which, if it passed, would authorize the city of Waterloo to all but cede authority over the Temple Heights neighborhood—which in the past had been the target of revitalization plans and three-part series in the *Standard-American*—in order to pursue "economic growth and job creation" by means of "public-private partnerships." In the middle of east Waterloo, an island of suburb. A Heritage colony.

It was the sort of thing that a few years earlier Nick might have denounced as an ominous corporate scheme, more evidence of the coming apocalypse; now it just seemed like a mediocre idea, a mongoloid child of the ideological privatizers, without much chance of success.

"It's one big boondoggle," Bones continued. He rarely said anything he didn't think was worth repeating; he went over the whole scheme again.

"Is that really a boondoggle or just, you know, the usual?" The usual legalized corruption and bad policy, as opposed to extraordinary malfeasance—such were the weak lines that distinguished news from non-news.

Bones passed more papers to Nick. "Take a look at those campaign reports, that'll give you an idea. And consider the fact that the honorable Ms. Flintic, who will tell you in her best Girl Scout voice that she is very opposed to any form of preferential treatment, is supporting this. And then consider the fact that this is obviously designed to benefit interests that gave to her, and gave to Hardaway, and are giving to him big-time now that he's running for governor.

"I've got plenty of documents on this," he added.

"I can see that."

"Trust me, this is your story. You got any crackers or chips or anything?"

Nick indicated the cabinet.

"So what ever happened to that tall drink of water you used to run around with?" Bones asked.

"Magda?" Nick couldn't think when Bones had met anyone he was dating.

"No, I don't think she was Polish," Bones said, although Magda hadn't been Polish. "The leggy gal with the curly hair."

"Liza," Nick said. He didn't recall ever introducing her to Bones. "She's a lawyer now."

"Everyone has their flaws."

"She's also engaged."

"Oh."

After an hour nothing edible remained in the kitchen and Nick had been thoroughly debriefed in advance of his interview with Flintic. Bones retired to the couch for a nap punctuated by garbled statements and, at one point, sustained laughter, while Nick perused the bill draft. Something like hope fluttered in his chest—to his surprise. Trusting Bones was never a simple thing—he always had an agenda, and often more than one—but information, so long as it could be verified, was information. Facts could be checked. Responses could be demanded. Company officials could decline to comment. True, the last time Nick had written about a controversial development, McNally had made him identify its critics not as "community representatives," as Nick had originally written, but as members of the "anti-growth contingent." But if McNally wanted jargon, Nick would write it with jargon. You could water a good story down and it would still be a good story. Whether because of Sabert's funeral or Liza's getting engaged or the fact that he'd gotten up too early, suddenly Nick did not want to quit his job, or be fired. He could write a good Flintic story and climb out of the productivity toilet. Next he would write a piece on the Sunset, to make Roger happy, and then, assured of both friendship and the continuation of his health insurance, he could relax. He could maybe call the woman he'd met yesterday—Bones had said her name was Andrea. There was no very good excuse not to try.

PART TWO

Eleven

Will Sabert, the last of his kind: that was how he was remembered, although had anyone bothered to dig, a few other sentient fossils might have been discovered puttering around retirement facilities, soaking their dentures and pleading toothlessly with the attendants to smuggle in one last cigar. But it was more satisfying to declare them extinct, game over, a certain combination of hallowed but fusty ideals buried in the dirt along with the suspenders and wooden radios. Too many years had come between, too much Cold War blood and high technology, for those old things to fit any longer.

On second thought, maybe they had never fit. In the office of his biographer, the Last Southern Gentleman Liberal had been vivisected and parceled out into file boxes and folders. Which contained the noble ideal?

Not "Childhood/Youth." Not college or law school or that first term in the State Assembly: glimmers of promise, ideals here and there, flirtation, but not resolve. Begin the search after that. Begin, why not, with box 4 (1950–52), folder 7. Begin at the May 1952 state party convention at the Allred Memorial Civic Center. Begin with Will Sabert, age thirty-one, marooned in a metal folding chair, wearing a baggy rumpled shirt buttoned at the wrists and tan suspenders and linen pants, his jaw raised toward the ceiling: asleep.

Out cold. Strands of his dark hair lapping in the weak mechanical breeze. The hall dim and hot. The metal fans droning away.

Will slept, until at last he was jolted awake by the persistent strike of a gavel. It had begun in his dream, first as a giant, slow woodpecker, and then as an axe, swinging away at the tree in which he'd been perched, for he'd dreamed that the convention hall had become an aviary, and he a bird, and upon waking he intuited that he might have been, in his sleep, cawing out loud. Awake, he was only a man with a hangover. At a political convention. A frosty caucus. The grand hall had been, in the space of a nap, reduced to disarray. Three-quarters of the chairs had been emptied, and delegates were standing around the aisles with hats removed, hard-shouldered, sprung for some as yet undetermined action, while a female voice on the public address system pleaded with them to return to their seats. Wan sheens upon men's faces, in this steamy cavern. Banners and flags and county placards abandoned. Near the entrance, a man sat on the floor with his bent knees aimed toward the ceiling and his hands over his nose as though he'd been hit. For God's sake let us sit upon the ground. Whatever had happened, Will guessed this was something other than the lunch recess. For God's sake. The gavel drove Will stumbling out of the hall . . .

. . . and straight into the humid embrace of a human mass that spilled down the steps and onto the lawn. Ahoy, comrades!—all the red-hot loyalists had preceded him. The Stevenson crowd. They had poured from the fractious hall and congregated here in a light rain, holding newspapers tented over their heads. And then he remembered, a grackle cawing in the fog of his brain, recall, recall last night, there had been talk of this, a walkout if the leadership insisted upon bolting the party. If the convention went for Eisenhower, the loyal opposition, the Stevenson crowd, had an exit strategy: to head for the exit. A strategy Will himself had learned the insufficiency of three years earlier when, as a state assemblyman, he'd organized a boycott of an unusually pernicious halt-the-spread-of-communism bill. He'd convinced seven others to sit out the floor vote in the men's room, and had made them all famous: from that day forward they'd been known as the shit-house liberals. Only two of them had been reelected, and Will hadn't been one of the two. At the ripe old age of thirty-one, having been voted into office and back out again, he considered himself a worldly individual. Depravity and torpor would win nine times out of ten, he knew. The game was played, if you played it at all, for the other one-tenth.

A brassy, gloomy, rain-laden light filtered over the assembled good souls, over the thick-armed women of the precincts and the bespectacled speechwriters, over the Negroes clustered by the steps, as well as over a company of men hoisting a life-size papier-mâché donkey into the air and parading it before the press photographers.

A man approached. Will didn't remember his name. Aldo or Frank or Philip or Wallace or Fred or Richard—nothing stuck to him, this tall, reedy-necked operator who had stalked the university campus back when Will was a student, he remembered that much. It had never been clear whether Aldo Frank P.W.F. Richard was himself enrolled in any classes, busy as he'd been trying to establish a workers' vanguard on campus. Trotsky's man in the Student Union. Rumor had it that he'd made an expedition down to Mexico one summer in search of his Russian hero, only to come hurrying back across the border singing *sweet land of liberty*. Without ever disclosing what had disabused him of his revolutionary zeal, he'd signed on to campaign for statewide officeholders. Now he wore a jacket with a Stevenson button on the lapel and a short tie. His broad hand enclosed one of Will's. In a soggy, adenoidal voice he said, "Good to see *yew*," and Will remembered that Aldo had come to visit him in his office once when he was in the Assembly, on a labor matter. How it had been disposed of, Will had forgotten, but if it had gone badly that didn't show on the man's narrow face, stamped as it was with a peculiar mix of mournfulness and straining-to-please. "Last night I wasn't altogether sure you were on board," Aldo said.

Last night. Had they seen each other last night? Will couldn't say they hadn't. He knew that he'd gone to his usual place of solace, the beer garden . . . and he believed that at some point during the evening he had delivered a speech. Possibly more than one speech. Will had a weakness for peroration; even elected office hadn't cured him of it. After a few drinks he was inclined to work up a good ironical baritone, particularly in the presence of Eleanor Hix—a thoroughbred girl he might have liked to engage in a little philandering, were it not for Eleanor's celebrated virginity, and his own moralistic hesitation, and the fact that his eloquence had no other apparent effect on her than to occasion visits to the powder room. She had been at the beer garden last night, and had again disappeared while Will was delivering an address on the ramifications of existentialism for cattle ranching, and vice versa.

"This crowd wants speaking to. Why don't you work something up," Aldo said.

"I don't know what I'd tell them," Will said.

"Tell them about cows. Tell them about boll weevils, it don't matter. You're a known quantity."

"Known for having been deposed."

"These people don't fault you for that. They adore you for it."

"And I adore them," Will said, his smart tone obscuring the truth of the statement.

Minutes later a microphone was produced, and he found himself positioned in front of it, its silver bulb staring at him like some intergalactic eyeball. "My good friends," he began hoarsely. "Why do we stand out here in the rain?" For several measures his tongue failed him. He could not answer his own question. Why was he out here? For God's sake. He stalled: "For what do we stand? For stale conservatism? For reactionary values?" A few listeners were gracious enough to call out, "No!" Will looked down as if to find his place in his notes, but there was only the silver bulb leering back at him. "The time has come for new ideas, new leadership, fresh blood.

Friends, let us not submit to the tyranny of . . . of the insiders!" he said, gesturing at the doors to the hall. "Let us stand outside!"

Flimsy though his introduction might have been, he didn't read any disappointment on the sad, eager face of Aldo Frank Richard, or in the applause from the county delegates. If his pronouncements never quite seemed to match up with the muddy river of sentiment underneath, nobody ever seemed the wiser: it was all in the nature of the perorating beast.

And you could lose yourself in the words. Will was warm now, soaking up his shirt as he gave himself over:

Soldiers deserve our respect and honor. There are many former soldiers here among us today. But our nation's power is not only the power of our army and navy. It is the power of freedom, hope, and tolerance.

Let us not succumb to intolerance cloaked in a soldier's uniform.

Let us not hoard our bounty unto the few in the name of national progress.

Let us not imagine Communist bogeymen hiding under our living-room carpets.

Let us continue to stand outside and speak in our American voices, for that is what it means to be a free people. That is what our soldiers have fought to protect and preserve.

And let us keep on speaking until our abundance is shared among all men, and all men can draw the breath of self-respect!

You should have seen me," he told his wife that evening. "Singing like a loon." It was dusk when Will wobbled into the house. The girls were in their rooms, and Delia was nursing a glass of bourbon, waiting for him to come home so that she could go out. The children had been making something out of construction paper: colored bits were strewn like confetti across the front hall, as if somebody else's arrival had been celebrated while Will was gone.

"You don't say," Delia answered. "I'm shocked. Could this be the same Will Sabert who left the house this morning?"

"You know what they told me. They told me I ought to run for Congress."

"Who's 'they'?"

"People. A man called Aldo. That may not be his real name."

"In case you'd like to know how your children are doing, Katharine skinned her knee today. She was riding her pony around the yard and fell and skinned her knee."

"I didn't know we'd gotten her a pony."

"We didn't. It was her pretend pony. We couldn't afford a real pony."

"So what do you think?" Will asked.

"Of what?"

"Me running for Congress."

"You're not serious. Where would we get the money for that?"

Her new refrain: *Where will we get the money?* It will fall from the heavens, he wanted to tell her, just as it always has. When they'd met she was an art student, serious in her old oxford shirts rolled up at the sleeves, specks of titanium and cobalt on the pale undersides of her forearms, her red hair itself like something out of a painting. When he was first introduced to her he changed his name from Willie to Will on the spot. Now she no longer painted. Now that the girls were five and seven she left them with the housekeeper and never missed a party if she could help it.

"I could always sell arch supporters," he offered.

"Mary Alice Miller married a man from Washington and moved there with him, and last I heard they'd been burgled twice in one month."

"We could get a Doberman. Or an attack pony."

"Mary Alice was always such a bore."

"That's what you always said."

"I didn't."

"You did. You wouldn't necessarily have to stay in Washington full-time," Will said. "Though of course I would want you to."

"Would you?"

He was woozy, still high from the convention but gradually ceding to the sadness that had burrowed into the furniture—the empty kitchen table, the unsteady chairs. He wondered whether it was the same with other houses on the block, and the next block, and the next block, whether they, too, felt like artifacts of past intentions. He stood behind Delia and sifted her hair through his fingers. He asked her did she not want to be a congressman's wife? She didn't answer. "I haven't decided anything," he said.

"Neither have I."

"Where are you off to tonight?"

She said something about somebody's having rented a hotel suite, and that he could come, if he wanted to. It was a lackluster invitation.

After she was gone, he took over her unfinished drink, put on a record, and lay back on the living room chaise. A voice sang, *This is always . . .*

What did ponies cost, then?

Could he really not afford one?

In college Will had ridden a not-quite-white horse around campus. He'd traded an old Ford for her, one summer afternoon when the car broke down west of town at the gates of a ranch. She'd poked her head across the fence and he'd been smitten. On the ride back to town he named her Folly, her propensity for detours having been amply revealed by the time they made it back, via a bumblebee's looping route, to Waterloo proper. At nineteen he'd arrived abruptly at all of his affectations: the linen suits and bow ties and the not-quite-white horse, the cigars, the elaborate turns of phrase, polished during his tenure as recording secretary of the Young Gentlemen's Yacht Club and Brandy Colloquium.

He'd been smitten with politics around the same time. Will had enrolled at the university as a major storm blew in, pitting the New

Dealers on the faculty against the businessmen on the Board of Regents. The regents, titans of insurance, railroads, banks, mills, sulfur, oil and gas, having penetrated deep into the frontiers of industry, had had neither the time nor the discernment to attend to what seemed to be minuscule differences between overtime pay and socialism, between the League of Nations and one-world government, when all of it, as far as they were concerned, represented obstacles to profit, and the thing you did with obstacles was not to spectrographically analyze them but to kick them away. They asked the university's president to fire three members of the Economics Department, and when the president didn't comply, they fired him. Students rose up in protest; they walked out of their classes. Thousands marched through the streets of Waterloo and to the governor's mansion. The resident governor, a pipe-smoking rancher and a no-comment man, had refused to come out of the building.

Will had ridden Folly in the parade, leading the way for a fraternity of pallbearers carrying a wooden coffin and a sign reading DEATH TO ACADEMIC FREEDOM. It was a spirited funeral. Will shouted and sang and had his first real taste of mobilized crowd. The next year the ex-university president had run for governor himself, and though he hadn't had any real chance of winning, students and former students turned out to volunteer by the dozen, Will among them. Aloof and dreamy and mischievous, Will didn't have the right temperament for practical electioneering, but politics had hooked him all the same.

He was still hooked. Tonight he had half a mind to call Eleanor Hix. After polishing off Delia's bourbon it was three-quarters of a mind, and he was on his way to the phone when it rang at him.

"Sabert, you goddamned nitwit."

Not Eleanor at all. "Hello, Al."

"If you think you can get elected because of a bunch of waterlogged fools who'd rather piss into the wind than with it—"

Will and Al Meissner had been college roommates and law school classmates. Al's employers, the Marron brothers, had suckled their construction firm on government contracts until it was the largest in the city, and Al had persuaded them to fund Will's first campaign for State Assembly. But the Marrons, and Al, hadn't been impressed by Will's shit-house escapade. They'd declined to contribute to his re-election effort.

"Who said I was trying to get elected?"

"Why else would you have been out stumping today?"

"I was asked to say a few words."

"What I heard was, you all but announced yourself the candidate of the yellers and screamers."

"That's right. The throat lozenge faction. I've appealed to the Sucrets people for a substantial contribution."

The line crackled, and Meissner exhaled static before continuing. "You stick with that eggheaded bunch and you will see your lunch eaten come election day. That's with or without the support of the lozenge industry."

"I haven't said I'm going to run."

"You haven't said you're not."

"What's it to you?"

"I just want you to do a sensible campaign. I think there are some people who would be willing to let bygones be bygones. If they knew they had a man they could work with."

"You don't say."

"Will, we're old friends. All I'm telling you to do is to think before you jump into anything. Do you really want it? If you do, you've got to run so that you can win. The New Deal spirit is gone from here, and anyone who tells you otherwise is living in the past."

"I don't think Delia'd let me run, anyhow."

"Well, maybe you'd better listen to her."

After he hung up the phone it seemed to Will as if a decision had already been made, but wordlessly, so that he didn't know what decision it was. To run for office, or just to run away: one way or another he was already running.

He didn't call Eleanor Hix that night, but the next day he ran into her, by calculated accident, at Bailey's Cafeteria, a luncheonette downtown where she often ate and he sometimes went in pursuit of her. He'd been in half-assed pursuit of Eleanor Hix for several months now. He would flirt with her and she would humor him for a few minutes and then cut him off. Still, there were those few minutes. Eleanor had a job as a secretary, though more than one man had tried to retire her. She said that she liked working, just as she liked eating alone and reading novels.

The interior of the cafeteria was more alley than avenue, with a counter along the left-hand side, booths along the right, and a narrow aisle down the middle. It took Will a moment to get his bearings in the indoor light. The place was noisy with silver and china and with men just starting to come alive at noon. The counter waitress and the big barnacled fry cook shouted back and forth. But at the frontmost booth was a pocket of silence, a vacuum: it was Sherman Marron, sitting by himself and reading the morning *Standard* as he sliced into a plate of skinned chicken. Marron noticed no one, but everyone saw him, shooting their eyes in his direction as if trying to reconcile his power and his plainness. He had straight white-blond bangs and skin strangely young and smooth for a man who'd gotten his start running road crews out in the Hill Country. His lips looked like they'd just been licked, his mouth a wet rubber hole in the broad foundation of his face. His eyes were heavy-lidded and intransigent. He might have been cutting into a live chicken with the same composure.

Will looked beyond him, down the counter until he saw Eleanor at the far end, her short brown hair tucked behind her ears. She was leaning over a book, one shoulder up higher than the other, steadying her water glass along the crease of the binding to keep the book open. She took a bite of something and let the fork hang in midair while she read on, so intently that Will envied whatever it was she was reading.

Next to her was a burly man, occupying more than his share of the counter; Eleanor had tucked one elbow close to her side to accommodate him. The man stood and limped off toward the washroom, and Will quickly advanced on his seat. "Excuse me, ma'am," he said. Eleanor, still in her book, retucked her elbow—until, after a delay, she registered his voice and looked up at him. "Will. Good grief," she said.

"Good grief to you too. What sort of nonsense are you reading now?"

She'd been introduced to the beer garden crowd a year or so ago, and since then had become something less than a regular, but more than just a once-in-a-while. An affiliate. She was dark-eyed and tantalizingly asymmetrical, her beauty a subject of some debate, nights after she left the beer garden. "English nonsense today, darling," she said.

"Darling," Will said, suddenly famished and eyeing her meat loaf, "mind if I have a bite?"

She handed over her fork. "You just think everything is yours, don't you? That you can have anything you want."

"If I did think that, you would've already proved me wrong."

"Oh, garbage."

"Garbage" was something that Eleanor said, and that Will liked to hear her say. She looked past him toward the front of the restaurant, and then down at her hands. "It makes me sick," she whispered.

"The meat loaf?" Will asked. He'd already taken three bites of it.

"No."

Will surveyed the room for sickening sights. It was the same busy café he'd walked through a moment ago.

"That man up at the front. I don't know what he said to his waitress but she ran away crying."

"The pink-faced old boy at the front? Sherman Marron?"

"Who?"

"That's one of the more powerful men in our fair city. I'm supposed to ask for his support."

Eleanor took back her fork. "It was just a few minutes ago. Didn't you see any of it?"

He hadn't. The large man whose seat Will had taken returned, a half-drunk cup of coffee still waiting there for him. Will asked if he'd stolen the man's place, and the man didn't even nod, only stared at Will.

"I guess I'll be off, then." With his help Eleanor had finished her food, but she was in no hurry to leave. Her few minutes of humoring him were up—so much for that. Back to her book.

But what had he been hoping for? An afternoon in the park?

It was his nature to hope for things he knew he wasn't going to get.

Twelve

I t wasn't a long walk from the *Weekly* office to the Capitol, but in Waterloo there were days when the heat seemed to become a semisolid object, a viscous membrane stretched over the city, and walks of any length were to be avoided. Nick hauled himself up the avenue, as rapidly as he could. All around him were the men and women of the workforce, done with lunch and headed back to offices with their half-finished sodas in hand, shirts staining along their spines. Squadrons of pant legs advanced. Delivery trucks rumbled along. Construction crews resumed their work. The sidewalks of Capitol Avenue were beginning to take on their afternoon character, as fat pigeons scavenged for crumbs and panhandlers decamped for the air-conditioned public library.

Maybe Beverly Flintic wouldn't be at her office. In Nick's experience it was not unusual for politicians to cancel interviews without bothering to inform him. Once, reporting a story on a legislative effort to improve the state highway system, Nick had made four separate appointments with the state senator who'd authored the bill, none of which the senator had kept, until Nick, more and more desperate as the deadline approached, had found himself running, in defiance of his natural predisposition toward a more contemplative gait, *running* up the stairs of the Capitol in pursuit of the senator's chief aide, a gangly wonk in glasses, who when he saw Nick immediately started running himself, galloping away and calling apologies over his shoulder.

But if she was there, he would make her sweat, or at least perspire. He would lull her with softball questions and then spring the Heritage stuff on her and watch her react. Or maybe she wouldn't react at all. She would maintain decorum, and Nick would adopt an extra-friendly speaking style, as invisible daggers flew back and forth across the room. Ladies and gentlemen, the Liberal Avenger is back! See how he halts conservative spin in mid-rotation . . . how he pulls the rug out from under his subject with a single yank . . . how he traps her in a net of her very own words . . . He was actually looking forward to this, though not without qualms—every story made him queasy.

Twenty years earlier, for want of sufficient office space, the state had dug its way into the ground and built a subterranean extension, a network of long halls tunneling off from a central skylit atrium. The atrium's glass-paneled roof was set in the middle of the Capitol lawn like the transparent hump of a great whale whose body was submerged beneath the grass; down below, its stomach seethed with lobbyists and tourists and staff members and college students. The whale's intestines extended into the Capitol proper, where the ungainly animal expelled penal code and water law.

Flintic's office was deep in the subterranean stomach, at the end of one of the obscure corridors where they stuck the first-termers. Nick descended to the bottom floor and then lost his way, as usual, among the identical beige halls lined with identical frosted-glass doors. Many of the people streaming past him looked as alike as the doors. Although some were brown and some were pink, some fat and some thin, some old, some young, they looked to him like clones, maybe because all of them were wearing suits and the same professionally pleased expressions.

At last he came upon the right door. No sooner had he given his name to the secretary than Beverly Flintic strode out of her office with her right hand outstretched, foisting a smile on him like a dish of stale mints. Nick apologized for being late.

"You're almost on time," she said.

He followed her back to her office and then sat, as per her instructions, on a couch while she positioned herself behind the rampart of her desk.

"So," Nick began.

"How much time do you need?"

"Forty-five minutes?"

"How about half an hour."

"Sure. Okay."

"It's two-oh-five right now."

"Right."

"And you said this was going to be a profile. Of me."

"Yes," Nick said.

She put her smile back on, resting her hands flat on the desk.

"Well," Nick said, going blank. "Let's get started then."

"I'm ready."

Always this strange nervousness, and pretending not to be nervous, and general fumbling. "You're Beverly Flintic, and this is your first term in the Assembly."

"Correct."

"Were you always interested in politics?"

"Oh yes. My parents were very active in politics. It's all they talked about, practically. I started working on campaigns when I was in high school."

"Your parents must be proud." Nick cringed at the sound of his interview voice. It was so peppy.

"My mom still clips out the articles every time my name gets in the paper. Then she sends them to me. As if I might not know what I'd done." He could tell Beverly thought this was pretty amusing. Half an hour wasn't much time, but he didn't want to tear into the subject of Heritage with no warm-up. Then again he sucked at warm-up. She was pressing her hands hard on the desk.

"You're a lawyer in civilian life?"

"Yes."

"What kind of law do you do?"

"Litigation, mostly."

The assemblywoman sat perfectly still, her eyes fixed on him. Her cheeks and mouth were rouged; her shirt was deep blue; and spouting out of each ear was a white pearl stud, as though an American flag had been her inspiration while dressing. And maybe it had been. Her dark blond hair swooped out of her head, swirled around her ears, and tapered at the neck. Nick imagined her in a Viking helmet, a silver one with horns. It occurred to him that this woman was probably having more sex than he was.

"You're married?" he asked.

"Yes."

"Kids?"

"I have one son, Jamie. He's eleven."

"Great."

"We thought we'd have more, but . . . I think he's happy as an only child."

"I was an only child."

"There you go."

"You like it so far?" Nick asked.

"Having an only child?"

"The job."

"It's challenging. In a good way. I mean, there's so much to learn. You know, Neil—"

"Nick."

"I beg your pardon?"

"Nothing."

"There is just so much to be done. For example, yesterday in one committee we heard two food-stamp bills, one on a sales tax holiday, one on barbershops, one on alcohol sales . . . So it's never dull."

"Never?" Surely it was dull. It sounded very dull.

She eased up, dropped her hands to her lap, and leaned forward. "Almost never," she confided.

"What does your husband do?"

She straightened again: the moment of revelation had passed. "He's in consulting," she said.

So she wasn't one for small talk either. Nick mentioned the plan for a Business Improvement Zone on the east side, and asked her to talk about the enabling legislation. It was what he'd come to talk about, but as he said the words "enabling legislation" he doubted whether any reader could possibly care about this story.

She perked up, mentioned her visits, plural, to Temple Heights. A vibrant community, she said. She talked about housing, new commercial space. A real boost to the area.

Nick asked her who had written the bill, and she told him it had been a "joint effort" with the Department of Human Needs.

"Because what I understand is that a company called Heritage actually wrote the bill," Nick said.

"Not that I'm aware of."

"The language is identical to bills in six other states."

Beverly opened a desk drawer, pulled out a file folder and laid it open. "I wasn't aware of that. But what's the difference?"

"What's the difference?"

"Yes, what's the difference. I think it's still a good idea, at least an interesting idea, and worth trying. Maybe that's why they're trying it in other states."

"Would you say that the community, the people who live in that area, had as much input into this legislation as Heritage did?"

"I can say they had input. The fact is, Neil, they had as much input with me as the company did, though if what you're saying is true, then it sounds as if the company had additional input prior to the time that I became involved. But let me ask you this: Is that wrong? Heritage is a successful company with a lot of experience in the development area. Their input is input worth having."

He'd put her on the defensive too soon. They still had twenty minutes.

"How would you characterize your philosophy?" he heard himself ask.

"I'm conservative, but I'm a practical person. Getting things done, that matters more to me than ideology. I am here to help."

She paused, then spoke again. "I really am."

"I believe you," Nick said.

"I'll tell you the truth, Neil. I never thought I'd be doing this. Some people came to me and asked would I be willing to run for State Assembly. At first I thought they were out of their minds. Maybe they were. But I took some time to mull it over, and I thought . . . frankly I thought I'd be good at this." She started to talk about the campaign, about the people she'd met from all walks of life, about how she'd heard their stories and told them her story. Nick nodded and sighed inwardly. Political figures didn't have ideas any longer, so much as *stories*. "I grew up in a small town about a hundred miles west of here called Bingham. So I'm a country girl. My dad owned an oilfield supply company and had a small ranch, and my mom was a homemaker. I have one sister, and you could say we had a traditional all-American childhood. We went to church on Sunday, we rode horses, our dad took us fishing, our mom baked us cookies, and we were encouraged by both our parents to pursue our educations and to excel.

"I think there's a way of life that people associate with the small-town atmosphere that should be preserved. There are things about it that can be preserved, even if we're living in cities or suburban communities with different kinds of assets and different kinds of problems. I want to help make it possible for people to still have that small-town kind of compass and to pursue their ambitions and dreams."

Hackneyed stuff, but Nick saw that she did mean it. The intractable myth of the small town. If life was so good there, why didn't everyone go on back now? They could telecommute.

"That may sound hokey to you," she said. Her voice was appealingly sensible. Whatever the merits of her pseudobiography, the telling of it had relaxed her, made her seem a bit more like a person. A person Nick didn't hate or even resent all that much, even if she claimed not to know how her own bills had originated, even if she got his name wrong. In general, as he got older he found that he hated and resented fewer people. This had taken a toll on his reporting. There just weren't that many good villains left in state government. Not Beverly Flintic, anyway. He would have to try to muster up a loathing.

"Getting back to your bill," Nick said. "Have you heard from any of the residents about the fact that this bill says the development authority can force them to sell their houses if it wants to?"

"That's not in there," Beverly said.

She didn't even know it was in there: this was good. He got out a copy of the bill's text and pointed out a lengthy subsection of stipulations, one he wouldn't have read himself had Bones not directed him to it. Pertaining to the right of the development authority to block off streets, access water and electric lines, alter sidewalks, erect and remove fencing, put up signs, upgrade roadways, et cetera, ad nauseam. Buried in the middle of the paragraph that would "grant certain powers and privileges," in the middle of a long list of woolly compound nouns, were the words "eminent domain."

"You're right," she said, puzzled.

He couldn't resist. "Is that consistent with small-town values?"

"I'm not sure what you mean."

"How much money did Heritage contribute to your campaign?"

"Let me ask you something. Is this really going to be a profile of me, or are you here to do a story bashing Heritage and the Temple Project?"

Nick started to give a roundabout answer when the phone on Flintic's desk rang. She seized it. "Beverly Flintic." After a few seconds her tone softened. "What's wrong? . . . Sweetie? Just calm down and tell me what happened."

Her son, he assumed. She looked at Nick and asked silently for tolerance.

He held up his hand: *Of course, of course.*

After hanging up she closed the folder and opened an appointment calendar. "I'm sorry about that," she said, "but our time's about up anyway, isn't it? I'll look into this eminent domain question."

"Okay . . . why don't I call—" said Nick.

"Goodbye," she said, and made a show of studying the calendar as Nick slunk out of the room.

ack at the office, Nick noticed his letter from prisoner Mike Cummings resting unopened on top of the file cabinet. Several years ago Nick had volunteered to take care of all the paper's letters from prisoners. It was the only clerical task he'd ever volunteered for, not that it was so onerous a job: five to ten envelopes per month, all of them containing, along with the letters, a slip of paper that fluttered out upon opening, printed in red ink with the words "GENERAL INMATE CORRESPONDENCE * DEPARTMENT OF CRIMINAL JUSTICE—INSTITUTIONAL DIVISION."

Most of the *Weekly's* incarcerated correspondents described themselves as wrongfully convicted and hoped for media coverage of their cases; a few others wanted to contribute letters to the editor, or full articles—once in a while, a well-written essay on prison life, though more often the material was unpublishable. There was the prolific Joe Farmer, for instance, who every few months submitted another section of the Gospel According to Joe for publication. An elaborate jumble of end-time warnings, Jim Morrison quotes, and semihomoerotic encounters between Joe himself and the son of God, the material was not uninteresting, and Nick would sometimes make a copy, stick it in an unmarked envelope, and send it on to the state Christian Coalition headquarters. He kept the originals in the bottom drawer of his file cabinet. Although he had no qualms about tossing research he'd done for a story three weeks prior, he didn't like to throw prisoner letters away.

So many swore they were innocent. "YOU MUST TAKE INTEREST IN MY CASE REQUIRE EXPOSURE." *I am fixing to be Exonerated and will obtain your interest in a cover story on my present situation with Rector County for the last over 14 years devastation horrific scenario, I had to endure!* Or the more eloquent—*I simply did not do it, Mr. Lasseter.* With their letters came court documents, forensics reports, handwritten motions for discovery. Some were pretty convincing, at least on first skim. Nick's job was to cover news and politics in Waterloo, not to chase potential wrongful convictions across the state, but even so, he knew that his dutiful filing of the letters was in part just a way of averting his eyes.

His favorite inmate, and the only one he wrote back to on a regular basis, was Michael Cummings, who'd been locked up for the last three years in the Santiago Unit, convicted of delivery of a controlled substance (over 500 grams). Cummings had owned an RV rental business, catering to retirees on limited budgets who wintered on the Mexican border, and had transported stashes in false-bottomed toilets. In prison, he still took a professional's interest in smuggling, and he'd originally written the *Weekly* because he thought someone ought to write an article about drug transactions among the corrections officers and some of the inmates. Nick wrote back to say that it would be impossible to do the story on Cummings's word alone, was there any way to back up the charges? Apparently not, because in Cummings's next letter he didn't mention the drugs. Instead he asked Nick to comp him a subscription to the *Weekly*. Subsequent letters demonstrated that he'd read each issue carefully: he would comment on Nick's stories, mentioning a favorite line or quote. Often those lines had also been Nick's favorites. The inmate's opinion began to matter more and more to Nick, and although his theoretical audience was the city of Waterloo, there had been times when Nick had felt he was really writing for one middle-aged convicted drug dealer in the Santiago Correctional Facility.

The letter from Cummings was a short one:

Hey man,

Good news. I went before parole and they were nice enough to let me out of this hole. They don't tell you the exact day but it'll be someday this month. I'm outta here. So thanks for all the newspapers. Sorry you couldn't do that article but if you're ever looking for a story this place is full of stories.

I'm not a hundred percent on what the plan is but for starters I'm going to move in with my sister and help her run her rent storage business and try to stay sober. I'd like to get married, do you know any single ladies who might favor a fat ex-con? Heh heh just kidding. We'll see. Thanks again and good luck in the future, you seem like a good guy.

Sincerely,
Mike C.

Nick was happy for Cummings's sake but sorry to learn that their exchange had run its course. He liked Cummings's letters. And through their correspondence he had, in a small way, been keeping alive Harold Krueger's notion of the *Weekly*'s audience. When Harold had been editor, he'd always had a clear idea of his reader: the Ordinary Man. The Ordinary Man, like Harold, drove an ordinary car, ate ordinary food, and took in-state vacations. It was Ordinary Men (and for Harold, this included Ordinary Women and Ordinary Kids) who were society's lifeblood, its oxygen and hemoglobin both, yet their interests were too often ignored by the rich and the powerful, and by the "corporate media." Whenever Harold had received a letter to the editor he particularly liked from someone he perceived to be an Ordinary Man—as opposed to an advanced-degree-holder, a nut job, or a public relations officer—he would show it to the rest of the staff, as if it justified every bit of work they did. Never mind that most of their readers were not the elementary school teachers and sanitation workers and nurses he most admired, but students, attorneys, professors, and people with no set career who hung out in coffee shops. Harold had always placed the Ordinary Man above them. This was probably one of the reasons Metro Media had hired a new editor. But Nick missed Harold. He'd inspired the entire staff, more than any of them had understood until he'd been pushed out, and McNally had started educating them about the paper's "consumers."

Harold's Ordinary Man hadn't lived in prison, but with Cummings out of the picture, the last trace of that ideal reader vanished for Nick. Yet it was with Harold in mind that he dug out a small workspace next to his computer and began typing up his notes from the Flintic interview. Actually typing out the whole interview, and on the same day—it had been ages since he'd done that.

Thirteen

The advance of the city into the northwestern hills had proceeded in stages. At mid-century, a man awoke from a nap one day with a vision of another city, a smaller and more perfect replica of Waterloo, rotated ninety degrees and attached to one corner of the existing metropolis like a kangaroo pup in a pouch. Instead of a river, a highway would border the new town; instead of the Capitol, a shopping plaza would be erected at its center. This man, a former Marine, scouted out the territory on morning rambles, and with his wife's inheritance began to build ranch houses in cedar-chopper country, laying out Waterloo's first subdivision acre by acre, over a period of more than ten years. Then the pace quickened, and the suburbs spread all around the city, an ever-widening span of lawn and garage.

The Flintics lived out in the very glaze of the suburban doughnut, where the houses, excruciatingly new, were sold with warranties: ten years on the roof, fifteen on the AC, two on the garbage disposal. Beverly had done her homework before they'd bought in the Comanche Creek subdivision. There was the pool and the clubhouse; there were nearby restaurants and highly rated schools; there was the general sense that the march of progress was headed in this direction. When they'd moved in, the back of the house had looked out on a cow pasture, but now from the breakfast nook you could see other houses and bulldozed tracts with plastic orange ribbons tied to stakes.

Granted, no neighborhood was perfect. In recent weeks there'd been reports of a flasher around Comanche Creek, a man who exposed himself to women as they were out walking or loading kids into the car. A flyer had been distributed, with a description of the man: about six feet tall, Caucasian, thinning brown hair, jeans and a polo shirt. It wasn't a useful description.

The commute was roughly forty minutes each way, and Beverly normally didn't mind it. Often it was the only time she had to herself. The only time she quite felt like herself: sitting in traffic was a small price to pay for that. She was immodestly fond of her car, a crimson Taurus with pillowy leather seats and digital controls: the temperature could be adjusted to the half degree. She'd splurged on premium speakers. She would nestle into her seat and turn on the classical station and stick calmly to one lane—no frantic weaving around for Beverly Flintic—and tap two fingers against the steering wheel in time with the symphony.

But it was impossible not to think, and mull, and chew. In the four days since the interview with the *Waterloo Weekly*, Beverly had returned to it often, thinking of other things she should have said, rephrasing what she had said, and above all coming up with questions she would have liked to ask the reporter in turn. Such as: How about you? What have you ever done for your city? Beverly wondered how old he was. He'd dressed like he was in school, and it hadn't been only his jeans that had made her think of a student. He had seemed like a person sitting in judgment of the world rather than taking part, like a student in that respect. A pessimist, a relativist: your typical liberal.

And why hadn't anyone bothered to tell her about that eminent-domain clause? She'd been made to look like a fool.

Not long before she'd introduced the bill, Beverly had received a letter from ACT, the Allied Citizens of Temple Heights, inviting her to a "meeting of community leaders and community members to discuss the future of the Temple Heights neighborhood." Beverly had taken "community leaders" to mean that other elected officials would attend, but when she arrived at a place called Eloy's—a murky barn of a restaurant with randomly situated Formica tables, a long, battle-scarred bar, and an old green parrot in a cage next to the register—she realized it was just her and the allied citizens, a dozen people who were all older and browner than she was, most of them Hispanic, a few black, and not a city councilperson in sight. It didn't seem fair, but at that point she couldn't very well have left.

So she'd stayed. A heavy, winded woman draped in a Minnie Mouse T-shirt spoke first, thanking the assemblywoman so profusely for coming that Beverly sensed she was in fact trying to point out how rare it was for anybody official to show his face in "the Temple," as she kept calling it. "We believe that by coming here in person, our representatives can better understand the needs of our community," she said, watching Beverly as she spoke.

A man sitting next to Beverly chimed in. "At least Eloy hires our kids to clean the floors and wait tables. I don't see no jobs for them in some fancy apartment complex and offices." He was small but fierce-looking, and went on to tell a story about losing two fingers in an industrial accident. He held up the maimed hand: sure enough. Beverly started to sweat. In all likelihood they could tell how uneasy she was. Every so often the filmy-eyed parrot would pipe up: *Buenas noches! Buenas noches!* Beverly took her blazer off, and immediately wanted to put it back on, when she saw how her bare forearms had taken on a greenish cast under the bar lights.

An old woman whose tiny ankles dropped out from pink sweatpants spoke next: "We don't need this kind of stuff. We need a real supermarket over here, and a drugstore. Not to mention a hospital would be nice. There's a lot of places around here to buy tacos, but when it comes to diapers or medicine? Ma'am, we got to go a long way, and a lot don't have cars."

The big woman, whose name was Maria, reminded everyone

that what they were there to discuss was the Temple Project specifically, not everything the neighborhood needed—"or we'll be here all night, no?" She smiled, and Beverly relaxed somewhat. This had been exactly her fear: that she would be kept here all night, as a captive of these people. It was reassuring to hear that they didn't want to stay all night any more than she did.

That evening, Beverly hadn't known too many details about the proposed development itself—she'd dealt only with the legislative end, not actual plans. But she did want to attend to the neighbors' concerns, if she could. Never a sloucher to begin with, Beverly sat especially straight in her chair. I am an assemblywoman, she thought, and these people are people I have been elected to represent. When Maria handed her a petition against the project, with two sheets of signatures, she scrutinized it as best she could, though the room was dark. "So what would it take to make this project more appealing to you?" she asked. "Besides a hospital."

The meeting had been a long one, but by the end of it they'd developed a list of objectives: hiring local workers and paying them at least ten dollars an hour. Reserving at least half of the apartment units for low-income dwellers. Retail space for locally owned businesses. One woman wanted community approval of the building designs; another requested that flowers and trees be planted on the lots. Heritage should improve the local parks. It should appoint representatives to a joint company-community board so as to maintain a continuing dialogue with local residents. "What we really want is a say-so," Maria said. Beverly confessed she didn't know which of their objectives might be under her purview as an assemblywoman, but she said she would take the list and the petition back with her, and they'd all agreed to meet again two weeks later.

Flashes of orange caught Beverly's eye. On the other side of the highway, four prisoners in orange vests were picking up trash from a stretch of asphalt that Channel 7 had once named "Waterloo's Deadliest Onramp." The ramp was very short, and every couple of months an entering vehicle, failing to yield, had plowed into right-lane traffic, until at last the city had shut the ramp down.

When she'd shown Maria Galvan's list to Yates he'd laughed; the bill had to do with privatization of services and building permits and city environmental rules, he told her, not trees and flowers. In the end she managed to include two lines encouraging—whenever possible—local hiring and "wages commensurate with or above the prevailing rate in the surrounding area." Even that had drawn the ire of Heritage's lobbyist, as well as a call from Yates. "The whole concept behind this, which I thought you had grasped, is that by *exempting* a company from some of the usual regulations and processes, that company will be *empowered* to do more." And when she'd gone back to Temple Heights for her second ACT meeting, only Maria and two others showed up at the restaurant.

She'd tried for an honest compromise, and Yates had seen it as betrayal. Was Mark right, had the bill become more trouble than it was worth? The whole process was so arbitrary and fallible: start out with a prince, strike a few clauses here, add a paragraph there, and end up with a frog. And then you have to explain the frog to un-sympathetic reporters in grubby clothes who didn't even bother to hide their sneering. Who made unwarranted assumptions. Don't make so many assumptions! she told the bumper of the car in front of her. On it was a sticker: *Your Mother Chose Life.* What if Beverly was pregnant? She imagined herself sneaking into some abortion clinic, being chased by fanatics with crosses and cameras. The music swelled and so did her heart, for a few beats, with nervous force. She lowered the volume.

Most subdivisions made some sort of statement at the front entrance. Whatever the houses beyond looked like, the turn-off to a community was typically marked by a monolith or pillar or arch. At Comanche Creek it was a large mound of rocks. Beverly drove past the mound, and then along streets named after Pocahontas and Squanto and Sacajawea, until she reached her house on Arrow Lane.

"I'm home?" she called tentatively as she walked in from the garage.

She found Owen and Jamie sprawled out on the living room sofa like beached seals, as if a big wave had tossed them onto the furniture and left them there to dry. Immobile, but for the odd jerk of the remote. Also barefoot: Jamie's dirty toes were hooked on the edge of the coffee table, while Owen had conveyed his shins over the top of it, his big white feet dangling from the far side. Between them, a pizza box was in ruins, with the lid half torn off and nothing in it but the patches of crust that had stuck to the cardboard and an oily residue. Beverly pictured the two of them lowering their heads down to the box and applying their mouths directly to the pie. Her men: hearty eaters, foot exhibitionists, burping in front of the television as it made a public service announcement. A familiar-looking actress was exhorting viewers to volunteer in their communities.

Two soiled socks lay discarded on the carpet. Beverly picked them up and walked over to Owen, a sock in each fist. He held up his hands: don't shoot. "I swear I've never seen those socks before in my life," he said.

Beverly leaned over to kiss him, and dropped the socks in his lap.

"Do you know what happened to the mini-vacuum?" he asked.

"Mom," Jamie said.

"Could it be out at the storage unit?" she asked. The mini-vacuum had been Owen's before they were married, and had belonged to Owen's aunt before that—practically an antique, as vacuums go. Beverly had taken it to Goodwill a few months ago, along with a bag of toys.

"Mom," Jamie said again.

She turned toward him and read the words on his extra-large shirt. "Rage Against the Machine?"

"It's a band."

"Looks more like you're wallowing in front of the machine, if you ask me."

"That's an astute observation." The word *astute* had been on a vocabulary list two weeks ago. They were big on vocabulary at Jamie's new school. Beverly was all for vocabulary, but she didn't understand why he only used these new words sarcastically.

"So, Mom?"

"What are you guys watching?"

"Mom?"

"Yes?"

"It's some kind of melodrama about aliens," Owen said.

"Mom? Can we go to that show next week?"

"What show is that?" she asked, as if she didn't know. Jamie's once-blond bangs, closer to brown now, fell almost over his eyes—he'd developed an aversion to haircuts, also to hair-washing, and had worn the same baseball cap every day since August. He was chubby, with round pale cheeks and a tummy that too often peeked out from below his shirts. He'd stopped playing soccer; he was getting big. She wished he wouldn't eat pizza, but Owen argued that putting Jamie on a diet was a bad idea. He's eleven, kids shouldn't have to worry about dieting when they're eleven, he said. I'm not talking about a diet, Beverly had replied, I'm talking about portion control. To Owen, who'd been putting on weight ever since he'd lost his job, that was the same thing. The room smelled like sausage.

"I only told you about it like a hundred times." Jamie brought his knees under his shirt so that "Against" and "Machine" bulged out in the middle. "Can we?"

"We've already been through that. How was school?"

"The same as yesterday, and the day before."

He didn't like the new school, and for some reason wouldn't use the bathroom there. The other day he'd been caught peeing in the bushes behind the cafeteria. The assistant principal had required him to call Beverly and say what he'd done, a call she'd gotten right in the middle of her interview with the *Weekly*.

"I hate everything about that place," he said.

"Sweetie, if you just give it a chance—"

"I know, I'll start to like it."

"It has an excellent reputation."

Jamie picked up the remote control and started changing the channel from one to the next. "Jonas's mom said he could go if an adult takes him."

Next week Jamie's "favorite band" was playing at a club downtown—"favorite," though he'd seen the band perform only once, at a friend's older brother's bar mitzvah. The members of the band were in high school. The name of the band was Tantrum. They were playing an "all ages show," Jamie had explained—she'd hoped it wasn't true, but a call to the club had confirmed it: the boys could go if they were with someone seventeen or older.

However: they were eleven. Beverly didn't think eleven-year-olds should go to nightclubs, even to see fifteen-year-olds perform.

Beverly was still getting used to eleven. This year Jamie had a sign on his door that said KEEP OUT; he had secrets; he and Jonas plotted covert missions.

"Can I go call Jonas?" Jamie tumbled off the sofa onto his knees, and began locomoting toward the stairs, still on his knees.

"Come here and give me a hug first, handsome," Beverly said.

He reversed direction, knee-walked to where she was standing, next to the sofa, and put his arms around her thighs. She ran her hand through his unwashed hair. He said, into her skirt, "I'm not handsome."

"I think you're handsome."

"That's totally spurious. Dad has something he wants to talk to you about." Jamie stood and bounded up the stairs.

Owen folded his hands over his stomach. Then he said he'd been thinking about "this rock-show thing." Beverly, who could tell that

Jamie had paused at the top of the stairs to listen, and who was hungry besides, said they should talk it over in the kitchen.

A lot of newer houses had kitchens like theirs, twice the size of older kitchens, even though these days people did so much less cooking. Her own kitchen looked to her like a demonstration project or a store of some kind. There were yards of black countertop, in which she could see her warped reflection when she leaned over—though she would have preferred not to see it—and for reasons she didn't understand, the refrigerator locked shut for a minute after you closed it. Also, it made a hissing noise. As did the freezer. The Scandinavian dishwasher had a mind of its own—a Scandinavian mind, somber and unforthcoming.

"I was thinking," Owen began.

"I just don't like the idea of them at a club."

The refrigerator contained diet soda, mustard, and a half serving of potato salad—like a game-show category, "Things That Go with Hot Dogs"—only there were no hot dogs. There were a lot of different kinds of mustard. A constituent had sent a gift pack of specialty mustards, and after checking to make sure that its total value was less than the amount permitted under the ethics laws, Beverly had toted it home.

"Is there anything to eat in here besides mustard?" she asked, posing the question to the refrigerator.

"It might even help him, you know, be cool, make friends."

Beverly turned to look at Owen, who looked away as if to dissociate himself from what he'd just said. "I already told him no," she said.

Last year Owen had been laid off by the software start-up he'd joined the year before: victim of the very same fate he'd predicted for his engineer and project-manager friends who'd signed up for the high-tech revolution earlier on. While all those guys had been racking up stock options and buying second houses, Owen had stayed with NBI, playing it safe, until finally he'd decided he wanted his own piece of the boom. But in short order the windfall had turned into a plain old fall. After the layoff he'd been diligent about looking for work, going to interviews, to job seekers' bag lunches at the church, and even to a seminar on "Portable Careers," with a keynote speaker who'd been a child actor on television. Owen had networked his tail off, but without success. Breakfasts, lunches, coffees: he'd gained weight but not employment. At last for lack of a better offer he'd gone to work for a friend who owned an inventory company: from five in the morning until one in the afternoon, he supervised teams of counters as they tallied up stock at superstores.

There were times she thought the difference between Owen and herself could be explained by the fact that he'd been an only child, fussed over by his mother, and she'd been the oldest of three, left alone much of the time. More recently it seemed that their differences arose out of the philosophy he'd adopted after losing his job: everybody should be less driven, and realize there was more to life than work, and bury their noses in the proverbial flowers. But what weighed on her now was just the differences, whatever the reason for them. Why didn't a single person agree with her? Not even this man—her husband.

"I'll take them," Owen said. "What's the worst that could happen?"

Lobbyists everywhere: she gave in. Okay. Fine. Fine, if you'll take them.

I'll do it, Owen said. No problemo. Then he suggested that in return for his taking the kids to the show, Jonas's mom could have Jamie for an overnight sometime. For a whole weekend, maybe, and Owen and Beverly could spend that time together, and do nothing but lie around in what he called states of undress. He had his arms around her waist, and she turned to face him.

"Like bathrobes?"

"That's one possibility."

"Hmm. I keep having to work on weekends, though."

He opened his mouth as if to say something and then looked down. After a moment he said he just couldn't understand how a mini-vacuum could disappear into thin air.

She turned back around and opened the cheese drawer: more mustard.

"I guess I'm going to have to go out and get something."

She would've liked him to come along, but he didn't offer, and she didn't ask.

And when she was alone she was glad to be alone. The supermarket was two birds in one parking lot, groceries for later as well as something to eat now, and so she drove to the older and smaller of the two close-by stores, the one where she was less likely to have to greet constituents, the one where she could stand in the checkout line and read a magazine without being interrupted by somebody who wanted her to sit on the board of something or other.

Here in the Temple, Maria Galvan had told her, we've got to take two buses to get to a decent grocery store.

Beverly hardly knew what food to buy, since the family eating habits had been thrown off by new jobs and a new school. Two-thirds of her way through the store she looked over the cart and saw that everything in it was a snack. She backtracked for eggs and sausage, one token breakfast. Her dinner was a ham sandwich from the prepared foods case.

At the register, a woman close to her own age with limp blond hair and glistening lips and multiple earrings scanned the goods while Beverly stared at a magazine cover photograph of the first lady. Maybe it was a trick of the fluorescent overheads, but even the first lady looked a little worn out.

Beverly picked up a copy of the magazine. "She looks like she could use a drink."

The cashier saw the magazine and sneered. "Yeah, like a Molotov cocktail."

"Excuse me?"

"I can't stand that woman."

Beverly stuffed the magazine back in the rack. She yanked her credit card out of her wallet, swiped the card, and stared at the register screen as her purchases were being tallied. "You double-rang the carrots," she said sharply.

"What?"

Beverly thrust the credit card at the register screen and rapped against it. "See, the carrots. Right here. They're rung up twice."

"Okay, okay. Sorry."

Was this a good reason to get upset? Because a grocery clerk hated the president's wife? But why did she have to hate her? When Beverly was through paying, she gathered up the bags and hurried out of the store. She was ravenous. Before she was out of the parking lot she'd devoured her sandwich, and eaten by accident a bit of its paper wrapper as well. Calm down, she told herself, gripping the wheel. Count to five. Count to ten. Just keep counting.

On her way back to the house, as she was passing the Comanche Creek rock mound, her phone rang: it was Mark. He sometimes called her while he walked the dog.

"Hey," he said.

"I told you—"

"I know, I shouldn't call you in the evening. I was just—I wanted to talk." He wanted to talk. But what about when she wanted to talk? It was impossible to get him on the phone.

"This has been a stressful day. In fact it's been a stressful week for me, really stressful," she said.

"When I said talk I didn't mean—"

"I'm just so stressed out, I'm worried about that interview . . ."

"The what?" he said. "Strawberry, no!" Strawberry was the name of his dog.

"The interview I told you about. I think I might come off badly."

Beverly pulled up to the house and saw Owen framed by their bedroom window—looking at her? She waved; he didn't wave back.

"What did you say?" she asked.

"I said, which station?"

"It was the *Waterloo Weekly.*"

"Sweetheart, print media? Who cares?"

"Do you know who actually wrote that bill? Twelve seventy-five, the version you all gave me?"

"Lawyers, probably."

"Lawyers for the department or lawyers for Heritage?"

"I don't know. Look. Talk to Carson in the morning; he can tell you. Well, I'm back at the house now. Let's talk soon, okay? We should talk."

Owen had disappeared. She thought: I will go inside and tell him I want us to spend a weekend together. But first there were groceries to be put away. Beverly lugged the bags inside and emptied them, then rinsed off the cups around the sink and put them in the dishwasher. She made some noise with the cabinet doors and the dishes, waiting for Owen to hear and come down and say hello. He didn't. She wandered out to the living room and turned on the television and lost track. Drifted off.

A rustle of branches outside woke her. The Comanche Creek pervert had been described as a flasher, but in Beverly's mind "flasher" and "Peeping Tom" were mingled; when she looked up she half expected to see a naked man pressed to the window like an insect. But all she saw in the glass were the reflections of the lamp and the television screen, two glowing orbs against black.

By the time she dragged her body upstairs, her guys were out cold.

She undressed in the dark. What had Mark meant, they should talk? In bed was Owen, lying on his back with his head turned to one side, cheek on the pillow, half under the blanket, a leg and an arm sticking out. There was a smell around him, of stale breath and sweat, of pizza grease, of sheets that needed washing. Everything needed to be washed, or fixed, or paid off, and here was Owen preoccupied with whether Jamie was cool, and with the idea that she and he might have some sort of a romantic weekend.

She lay down next to him and ran her hand over his chest. Then again, a weekend with Jamie out of the house—maybe, maybe she could even find some way to tell him—but then again—she turned on her bedside lamp.

"Are you awake?"

He rolled violently away from her and pulled the sheet over his head.

Fourteen

On the first Sunday in October, Richard sent Andrea to cover a march on the Capitol in favor of gay adoption. Every term at least one liberal-sponsored bill legitimizing the practice and at least one conservative measure to outlaw it clambered through the Assembly's drafting and proofreading process, like wrestlers making their way onto the mat, and then annihilated each other in committee. In the meantime gay couples went on taking in kids, as foster parents and legal guardians, or as officially single people, and cared for them, for better or for worse—rolled them around in strollers, taught them to ride bikes, and eventually sent them off in sedans while the debate wore on at the Capitol, year after year.

The organizers had scheduled the march to coincide with an annual autumn bacchanal, the Decline and Fall, which drew male revelers from around the state. It was hoped that even after forty-eight hours of plumage, pill-popping, pool-hopping, trysts, spats, apologies, a Roman ball, midnight croquet, and a Polynesian-themed barbecue (where the spirit of a generation of suburban mothers had unexpectedly been resurrected in the meticulous tropical decor), some fraction of them might attend the march. The fraction that did turn out was small but vocal. It rained that day, not hard but steadily, so that the ranks of the marchers were thinner than expected, and more bedraggled, in slickers and ponchos, and a few in garbage bags with holes ripped out for their heads to poke through and cinch handles dangling by their knees. Bedraggled but cheerful, and cheering, they were not dispirited but somehow egged on by the rain as they promenaded through the wet and empty downtown streets. With rare exception, downtown marches were permitted by the city only on Saturdays before 10:00 a.m., or on Sundays during daylight hours. In other words, when nobody else was around. Almost nobody ever witnessed a march directly, other than the marchers themselves and the media.

Like many Waterloo marches, this one had begun by the river and was processing slowly toward the Capitol. Leading the way was Kathleen Alford, one of the organizers, walking backward and talking on a cell phone at the same time, in long cargo shorts and hiking boots and a transparent poncho capacious enough to enclose a bulky activist and her backpack. At her side, her lieutenant, a spry, athletic-looking woman with a bobbing ponytail and the taut poise of someone about to sprint for the goal, scanned a clipboard. Andrea had been on the scene for an hour now, trying to manage note-taking and an umbrella at the same time, which was all but impossible. The umbrella's handle shifted and slid under her elbow. Her notes bled. She switched from a roller-ball to a ballpoint, and then to her spare notebook, which soon became as wet as the first one. At last she gave up on notes and took out her tape recorder, though she preferred a written record. In search of more quotes from the marchers, she started toward a group of men, but then she saw that one of them resembled—and in fact seemed once again to be—Mr. Loefler, and so she landed instead upon a fortyish pair of women with two girls in purple raincoats. It was pretty clear that the older girl ("I'm gonna talk too, I'm gonna talk too, okay?") had the rest of the family under her thumb. "No parents are perfect, but we think we're doing a decent job," one of the women said, as if she couldn't understand what the big deal was. "A *very very very*—" began the talkative girl, who then lost her train of thought, dropped her head, shook it vigorously, and looked back up at Andrea. "Very much," she said, and giggled.

Andrea set no great store in marches and rallies—they had become routine, it seemed to her, the only excitement generated by some flare-up with the police, and even that had become predictable, just another ritual. She heard the sound of two engines revving—cops bringing up the rear maybe. But when she looked behind her she saw instead two cars, a white BMW and a gray BMW, stranded in the middle of the march. Each car had four young guys inside; they had rolled down the windows and were taunting one another while their motors growled, oblivious to all the people marching around them. As if they had just stopped at an intersection to flirt. A whistle blew—now came the cops, thought Andrea—but it was the spry lieutenant, having run through the crowd toward the cars, and produced a whistle, and blown into it; now she made a sweeping gesture with her arms that might have signaled a penalty kick. Kathleen Alford lumbered to catch up, her backpack bouncing, her expression stern and stoic, her figure solid even in juxtaposition with a German automobile. She stood in front of the white car with one hand planted on the hood as if it were her own vehicle and these party boys her wayward sons. "Y'all need to turn off your engines and sit tight," she said. The driver of the gray BMW gave its engine a last defiant rev, which was met by an extended, game-over trill of the whistle.

The rain slowed down the marching and, once most of the crowd had reached the Capitol grounds, sped up the speeches. Andrea stood beside two men with a small Chinese boy; the boy held a sign that said WE'RE A FAMILY, TOO! Andrea didn't doubt it: any family that would actually go to a march together seemed like a family to her, like a coherent unit, in a way that the combination of herself and her parents never had been. Even when they were married, her parents hadn't been big talkers; even when they'd all lived together, the three of them were rarely in the same room; by comparison, a couple of gay guys with an adopted Asian kid might as well have been the Huxtables.

At the end of ninth grade her father had left her mother and gone to live with a former ballet dancer named Melanie Johnson. He'd met her at a health club. It had always repulsed Andrea—the thought of the two of them bare-legged and sweaty, making small talk. Melanie was divorced, and strange, obsessive about her clothes. Through fashion she'd tried to reach out to Andrea, by taking her shopping one Saturday, in tenth grade. Andrea had hated everything she tried on, and so Melanie had bought only a pair of dark brown leather pants for herself. Then a couple weeks later Andrea had taken them from Melanie's closet and smuggled them back to her mother's and worn them to school, though they barely fit (Melanie was tiny) and caused her legs to sweat all day long. Melanie had noticed they were missing and called Andrea's mother.

Andrea had been ordered to take the pants back to Melanie's house. "I would have been happy to buy you a pair of your own," Melanie had said, confused. As for her father, it was as if his jaw had grown too big for his face. Everything seemed to sink down into it.

"She'll pay you back for those," he'd said to Melanie, not looking at Andrea.

Never did he ask her to explain herself. Not that she could have explained. Melanie repeated that there was no reason for any money to change hands now that she had the pants back. But he kept insisting, as if Andrea had ruined them, and asking to know how much they cost until finally Melanie told him—and then he looked as if he might throw up. On top of the fact that his daughter had stolen a pair of his girlfriend's pants, and that as a result his girlfriend and his ex-wife had had a phone conversation, came the fact that it was possible for a person to spend more on pants than his parents had ever earned in a year. He'd started walking in circles around the room. "I've been trying to apply reason to this situation," he announced after a while, "but I give up. I'm going out." He left, and for what seemed like hours, Melanie and Andrea had sat silently watching television from opposite ends of the couch.

When he came back, he sat down to talk to Andrea, finally, though he still didn't ask one question. He lectured. He discoursed abstractly on the theme of responsibility and then somehow got on to what it was like to have grown up in a segregated town. That was when he'd told her about that library. As if to prove to Andrea that there were things more important than material goods; it was as if he'd decided that the reason she'd taken the stupid things, the source of the problem, had been sheer greed. Then again, ten years later she still couldn't say exactly why she had taken them.

A burst of shouting cut in on the memory. Downhill from Andrea, on a side street below the Capitol, a group of a dozen or so marchers were jogging in the same direction, yelling and catcalling. They were followed by the gray BMW. A gay mob? She tried to catch up, but by the time she reached the street it was over; everyone had dispersed. That was a relief, really: she already had plenty to write about, and she was wet from her head to her shoes. The rain was at last subsiding, only a film on her windshield by the time she returned to the parking garage.

She drove due east, toward the old Washington branch library. Her story on the march wasn't due until five, and it wouldn't be a hard one to write. Around the time that she'd proposed an article on the library to Richard, she'd written the address in her daily planner, meaning to go have a look at some point.

As soon as you crossed under the highway the signage changed. The rude facts were not so diligently covered up but were instead, in some cases, emphasized with red and yellow paint; large placards with large lettering said CHECKS CASHED and ENVIOS DE DINERO and INJURED AT WORK? and PREGNANT? ¿EMBARAZADA? ¿NECESSITAS AYUDA? The streets deviated carelessly from the grid system, and Andrea groped along what was by no means the shortest route, past a restaurant with no name visible (only a sign that said LUNCH SPECIAL GOD BLESS AMERICA), past a Latino nightclub, a church, a yard full of cribs for sale, and an AutoZone. A song she liked but didn't know the name of came on the radio, and she sailed right by the library, then checked the address and circled back.

It was a small, dull, neglected building. She'd expected, if not grandeur, some element of charm or hideousness, elegant windows or a tarpaper roof, a hint or a clue. But it was just a plain old building, two stories, indifferently shingled, with a tan brick façade that was obviously a façade, a sheet of pseudo-masonry laid over plywood. This defunct library was narrow and long, like a tombstone turned on its side. Two of the windows were boarded up. On the right side of the entrance a few bushes pawed at the windows; on the left a couple of spindly hackberries rose to roof level. The building looked as if it had been stranded in the middle of the lot, with no relation to its surroundings; it might have dropped from the sky.

She didn't think she would do a story. There was nothing here.

Still, she got out of the car and walked up to the front steps for a closer look. Her father had come here every week when he was a kid, he'd told her. The problem with trying to picture it was, first of all, that she couldn't really imagine her father as a boy at all, and second, that she couldn't really imagine anyone here. Not just the building but the block was deserted. She climbed up to the door and tried to see through the glass panes on either side of it, but they were too dusty and it was too dark inside.

With cautious steps she wandered around to the back of the building. Here the weeds were high and litter-strewn, and a brown metal door had been singed by black graffiti. An old sign said NO TRESPASSING. Was she trespassing already? She stood fixed there, wanting to see the inside, though instantly and unreasonably fearful of what she might find. She tried the handle. To her surprise the door budged—a few inches—scraping the floor. A thud came from inside, and then a rodent-like scurrying, claws against tile: she shrank back and returned to the street.

A man was walking in her direction, carrying a sign. She couldn't read the sign because of the angle, but the first word appeared to be *Save*. Her inclination was to retreat, having had enough of people holding signs for one day, but she didn't move. She stared. He was tall and pale, on the portly side, wearing a straw Stetson even though the sky was still overcast, and he walked without lifting his feet very far off the ground, like a kid. He didn't look like he was from this neighborhood—he was whiter than rice, as they used to say in high school. But it didn't seem as if anyone lived in this neighborhood. He might have been one of the marchers who'd followed her over from the rally, only he didn't look gay, either. He looked like a guy who took a lot of naps: his hair and clothes disheveled, his face undefended and sleepy, long stubbled cheeks and puffiness under the eyes. A homeless hipster, maybe. With a cause. Andrea could see the whole sign now; it said SAVE THE SUNSET. That it was in need of saving came as news to her.

He shuffled toward her and said, "That place's closed." She couldn't tell whether it was a question or a remark.

"Yeah, it is," Andrea said.

"So is the Sunset," he said, and then continued, "The club. The Sunset. Down there." He waved his sign at the strip of storefronts at the other end of the block. Each letter on the sign had been written in marker on a blank restaurant check, she noticed, and then stapled to the cardboard backing. "It closed a few weeks ago."

"This is a protest?"

"Yes. Kind of. You know, it was a last-minute thing that was decided on, last night, by some people, and we all made this sign, and—some other people were supposed to show up, but I believe they forgot. I mean, it's pretty obvious that they're not here right now. So I've just been out here, you know, talking to the people. Yeah. I talked to a couple of winos earlier. Also a few people who were walking home from church. So far I've got one hundred percent support. That is, if you're in favor."

"In favor of what?"

"Reopening the Sunset."

"You said it was a nightclub?"

"I saw the Replacements there."

Andrea nodded, not sure who the Replacements were. "They're tearing this one down, too," she said, pointing at the building. "That library. It used to be the black library."

"Really? Really. Huh . . ." He stared at it for a bit and said, "Kind of a chintzy little place, wasn't it?"

"Mmm-hmm."

"Hey, but—hey. Isn't it, like, illegal or something to tear this down? This place has real significance. Not like the Sunset doesn't have significance, but I mean there's got to be people who care about this library who aren't just pathetic aging rock fans."

"Not too many. A building like this, what are you going to use it for? It's not like they're supposed to save every last water fountain."

"It's a part of history, though. Better that than some whatever the fuck they're putting in, condos, offices. *Lofts*. I mean, they tear down half the city and put down this generic anywhereville shit until I don't even know where I live anymore. My name's Roger, by the way."

"Andrea."

They exchanged information: neighborhoods, jobs. Roger perked up when she said she was a reporter. "So you could write something about this?"

"About what, exactly?"

"About the library, and the Sunset. The whole block."

She hemmed and hawed; she didn't think so. To her relief they were interrupted by a bright blue Chevrolet. The driver sailed toward them and gave the horn a hearty honk, as if they hadn't seen him. He rolled down the window and waved at Roger.

"Man, where've you been? I'm all by myself out here," Roger said.

The driver of the car took a bashful look at Andrea. The thick glasses he wore made him look surprised. "You don't seem like you're all by yourself," he said.

"She's a reporter."

"You got a reporter to come?"

"She was just here."

He waved again. "I'm Buzz." She waved back. Andrea.

"I'm headed over to Gloria's," Buzz said. "I just came by to see if you were really out here."

"I really am."

"You want to go eat?"

"I do," Roger said, then turned to Andrea. "Care to join us?"

"I have to file a story. It's due at five."

"So? It's barely even two. Come with us. We can discuss that other article you're going to write."

The bar they led her to had a nice deck and cheerful waitresses with lots of makeup on, one of whom had kissed both Roger and Buzz before taking their order. Andrea wondered if any of the makeup was permanent. She kept seeing the ads for permanent makeup. She'd heard of women going blind from botched eyelash dye jobs.

She was not a drinker: two sips of beer and it was all she could do to keep herself from talking about eyelash dye jobs. They were at a picnic table, Roger and Buzz sitting across from her; she felt under scrutiny and bashful and, in no time at all, tipsy. She wished she were a better conversationalist, but she was your typical reporter—a shy person who'd learned how to talk to people on the job, by asking questions. The good old who-where-what-why-when, and the odd man out, how. In this situation, who, where, and when were easy, while *what,* as in what she was doing there when she was supposed to be back at the office writing a story, seemed hard even to put into question form. But although Roger and Buzz were not impressive by any of the usual measures, she already admired them, their casual jokes, their junky cars, the fact that they were regulars at a regular sort of bar. They had settled here, they belonged. Her interest was in part anthropological—here were a pair of Trobriand Islanders—but also personal. They seemed intelligent, if eccentric, they were friendly, and they weren't in any obvious way trying to hit on her. She'd wasn't too proud to admit she needed friends. Shit, she needed *acquaintances.* These two seemed like good candidates for acquaintance at least.

"Did you guys grow up here?" Andrea asked.

Buzz raised his hand. It seemed he preferred not to speak if any kind of gesture might suffice.

"He did," Roger said. "I'm from Houston. Came here for school and never left."

"I get the sense that happens a lot here. The never leaving," Andrea said.

"I think there might be some kind of mild narcotic in the water supply. Maybe you could do a story on it. I always thought I'd travel more, I'd still like to, but . . . you see me here in my natural habitat. *Homo glorianus.* Subsisting on a diet of pale ale and nachos deluxe, he is a gentle species, relying on his size and wit to deter aggressors."

"You get many aggressors around here?"

As Buzz shook his head, Roger gave a single nod yes and said, "Here comes one now. It's another member of your ignoble profession. Lock and load, folks. Hey, Nicko, we missed you at the Sunset this morning."

"You guys actually went over there?" said the person behind Andrea. He scooted in next to her and she recognized him, after a moment, as the guy who'd given her the tissue at Sabert's funeral.

Yeah, oh yeah, hey: they acknowledged having met once before.

"Hey, maybe you can help me," Nick said. "I've got to write an obituary of Will Sabert."

"Isn't it kind of late for that?"

"It's overdue, yes."

"I'm not sure if I can help you, but—"

"We're not sure if anyone can help him," Roger said. "Let's drink some beer."

Andrea would not have ordered another for herself, but a pitcher came, and the other three kept adding to her glass.

"Oh oh oh oh," she finally said.

"What's wrong?" Nick asked.

"I have to get back to the office to file a story and I don't think I can even drive."

"What's it on?"

"This rally march protest thing I went to this morning. For gay adoption."

"No problem, no problem," Nick said. "We can write that."

"We can?"

"Yes, we can. Get out your notes, and some blank pages from your notepad, and we'll order up a couple of Cokes and we'll write the story. Then we'll take it to your office and you can type it up."

"I don't know—"

"Oh, come on."

Roger and Buzz decided to circulate around the bar, in search of something more interesting than picnic-table journalism. Cokes were ordered, initial sentences composed.

"Okay," Andrea said.

"You say, 'Get me rewrite.'"

"Uh, get me rewrite. Okay. Here goes. Despite rainy conditions, marchers came out in force Sunday to, to . . . to support a measure that would legalize gay adoption."

"Perfect," Nick said, writing it down.

"A crowd of more than six hundred people, many with children in tow, marched up Capitol Avenue to the Capitol and—"

"Avenue, period," Nick interrupted. "Next sentence."

They continued for another couple of paragraphs before the story swerved off course. "The status quo drew harsh criticism from those who wish to make changes," Nick said.

"'I'm sick of this sorry status quo,' said march participant Van MacDougal of Boystown Heights," Andrea added.

"MacDougal, forty-two, sells prostheses out of his home," Nick said. "Opponents also charge that the status quo has caused health problems in the past."

"These include reported cases of respiratory ailments and rashes—"

"And gonorrhea," Nick said.

"Don't put that one."

"Could I get your phone number?"

The guy was odd. Saying the word *gonorrhea* and then asking for her number. Still, he was cute, in a skinny, receding-hair kind of way—was this desperation talking? She gave him her number.

"Hey, isn't that your march?" Nick asked, pointing to a television hanging over the bar inside, just visible through the doors from where they were sitting. They both went in for a look.

"Oh no," she said, not understanding what she was seeing. On the screen was a dark-haired jogger in red shorts and a white shirt, followed by people in their regular clothes and rain ponchos; the jogger was being pursued by the people in ponchos.

"Gubernatorial candidate Mark Hardaway ran right smack into trouble earlier today," the newscaster said. Andrea couldn't hear everything over the noise of the bar, but she could piece together the story now being related via interviews with bystanders. The Commissioner of Human Needs had gone for a Sunday jog, unaware of the gay adoption march, and had collided with it. Still without a clue, he'd switched into candidate mode, introducing himself and shaking hands, but after a couple minutes it dawned on him that he was gladhanding a bunch of queers, and he'd panicked, wheeled around, and sprinted off toward the river. As was clear from the footage of the commissioner booking down the street. A no-comment if Andrea ever saw one. A BMW veered into view of the camera, and someone tossed what might have been a green lei out the window, in Hardaway's direction.

"Could you see what else is on?" a guy sitting at the bar asked the bartender.

"Shit," Andrea said. She had missed it. She had missed the story, plus the news was on, which meant that it was five o'clock. She barely said goodbye to Nick before rushing out.

Fifteen

Bones missed the 1970s. If some lesser devil had offered to deport him to any decade in all of history, he might have been tempted, briefly, by the Mexican Revolution or the California gold rush, he might have fancied the notion of meeting Cromwell or Alexander the Great, and he might well have seen potential gain in getting to the factual bottom of the whole Jesus situation once and for all, but in the end there was no question as to what he would have chosen, and that was the 1970s in Waterloo. By which he would have meant not the decade proper, but the years 1967–77. Those had been times unlike any other, at least in Waterloo, at least for him. Because of some unlikely confluence of cultural winds, a seed layer of human misfits had sprouted and burst into antic song. They had entered into political battles and river rafting trips equipped with the same good spirits—often contained in bottles they'd brought back from the border—and had aspired to serious things without taking themselves too seriously. They had never subscribed to the school of the good night's sleep. Better to live at night, and swim before dawn: they'd lived by the rejuvenating powers of the moon and diet pills. As I live and crash. *Time passes, time passes,* he said to himself, *we all wore mustaches . . .*

His car was an old diesel-burning Mercedes the indeterminate color of water in a neglected swimming pool, with seats that had been covered in an imitation sheep's fur not at all suited to Waterloo summers. He called her Dolores. Because of the seat covers and the crapped-out air-conditioning, condemned to remain crapped out until such time as he discovered a new supplier for the contraband pollutants she required, Bones did a lot of heavy perspiring in Dolores. As well as a lot of smoking. The imitation sheep's fur had absorbed quantities of sweat and cigarette smoke, and on the infrequent occasions when he had passengers, they quickly took the initiative to crank open all the windows and gasp for air. Between the noise of the engine and the air rushing in the windows, she wasn't a great car for conversation, but she was a hell of a fine one for muttering to yourself and for cussing out all the loony tunes on the road—and there were ever more of them, these people who'd apparently gone down to Mexico for driver's ed and stopped for a lobotomy on the way back. Driver courtesy had been the first thing to go after they passed the open container law. Driver sanity had been the second.

The city was barely recognizable. So many boutiques, and it was getting hard to find a muffler shop anymore. He had a lot more use for mufflers than women's clothing. For that matter it was hard to find a decent party, a real mixed-up all-night party like the ones they used to throw every weekend, the long-hairs and the short-hairs, the hippies and the good old boys all sloshing against one another, and asking who were the people who'd shown up wearing monk robes and Afro wigs. In the old days he'd been loosely associated with a group that had ventured out practically every night, as if they'd been on some long, reckless quest. As if by goading one another to the brink of losing consciousness they'd get a peek at something beyond the absurdity to which they'd applied themselves so fearsomely. He remembered the night they'd driven for hours, chasing a rumor about a cockfight south of town, in hopes, one might suppose, that revelation would pour out of the mouth of a slashed-up rooster. He couldn't recall whether they'd ever found the cockfight in the end. They'd never found the grail, or at least he hadn't.

At some point, the grail had receded too far into the distance, into the past.

And nowadays he would never wind up at the same party as someone like Carson Yates. The man was a homebody, a guy who sat down after supper with a glass of milk and plotted the demise of his opponents in a lined composition book. This was how Bones earned a living these days, by making penny-ante pony trades with the likes of Yates—one of the most powerful men in the city, and he looked like the manager of a TGIFriday's. That was where he'd wanted to meet, a TGIFriday's. Bones wasn't even sure if the place would have a bar, never having breached the threshold of a TGIFriday's before.

But it did, he saw when he arrived, a bar with that sour and wharfish odor of a bar early in the afternoon, sprayed and wiped, the plastic cocktail napkin hoppers plump with cocktail napkins, an arsenal of plastic swords at the ready, the place all cleaned up but not quite rid of the film of last night's spilt liquor. Yates was not in evidence. Bones took a seat near the tray of condiments and helped himself to an olive.

"Lasseter," said a voice behind him. Yates had beat him here after all, and hidden himself behind a booth's high bench. Bones took the bench opposite.

"How are you, sir?" Yates asked.

"Not bad for a rickety old relic. Yourself?"

A waitress wearing a glittery visor asked what she could get them.

"Let's do a root beer," Yates said.

Bones sighed and ordered an iced tea. The waitress asked whether he wanted to get some sort of chocolate dessert along with it. Yates looked at him eagerly. Bones said he didn't want any chocolate dessert. The tea, when she brought it, was overbrewed and too sweet.

"Something the matter?" Yates asked.

"I don't normally drink tea this late in the day."

"If you'd like something else . . ."

Bones shook his head.

"I see you've been helping your nephew with his journalism career," Yates said.

Bones circled his straw in his tea. "That was his deal."

"Really, Ken."

"Really what?"

"I know you're frosted because Flintic won't get on board with your pipeline bill . . ."

"I wouldn't use the word *frosted.*"

". . . but an article in that left-wing newspaper won't make a bit of difference."

"Consider it my opening salvo."

"So you were behind it."

Bones shrugged. "I gave him a few documents. God almighty. All we need is that one fucking vote to get that little pipeline deal out of committee. From there the road's clear. I thought I might have some trouble with the nobler knights of my own party, but not a freshman from your side."

"She's an independent thinker," Yates said. "Heaven knows she's not very suggestible. Walks out of the caucus meeting and then just does whatever she feels like. Frankly, she's on thin ice all around."

"It's a pipeline tax, is all it is. What can I give her?"

Yates shook his head.

"Come on. Everybody'll whore for something."

"She hasn't learned how. Besides, last I heard, the speaker wants to wait until next time on that one."

There was a rumor going around that the speaker's older sister, wife of a higher-up at a company that owned pipelines, was headed for a divorce, and that in her bitterness she'd told her brother not to let the husband's company get so much as a Styrofoam cup out of the session. Though Bones had ignored the talk, he had to concede that the rumor might be true. It wasn't insidious enough to have been wholly fabricated: no sex, no bribes, nothing illegal, only everyday spite.

And here was Carson Yates, Mr. Information, Mr. Allow Me to Congratulate Myself, looking smug for no reason except that he always looked smug, as if just before you'd walked into the room he'd completed all his personal goals for the day. Well, one good rumor deserved another. "You know what this reminds me of?" Bones said. "There was a coal-plant bill back in the eighties, eighty-three maybe, and it was the exact same deal. We went down to the wire on one unexpected holdout. Michael Ruggles was his name. Had a relative who'd been maimed somehow in a coal plant, and he wouldn't give an inch until in the end they caught him balling Alma Bradley. Little Alma. She was barely over five foot but used to be known as the Assembly's goodwill ambassador. So they went to Ruggles and threatened to go to his wife, and he flipped over to the yes column real quick. This does take me back, this pipeline situation. Same deal. Only now it's Beverly Flintic, not Michael Ruggles."

"It's similar, but not really the same. That was when you all had some juice. Now you don't."

"Your point being . . ."

"I haven't heard anything scandalous about Beverly Flintic, and even if there was something, I don't think that kind of mudslinging would hurt us as much as it would hurt you all."

Pissant. Trying to deal with Yates was like playing Parcheesi: a boring series of blockades. Bones wondered why Yates had wanted to meet with him—why even bother if all you were going to do was drink root beer and say no. Maybe it was how he liked to unwind after meeting all his personal goals for the day. But there had to be more to it than that. Bones took a long draw of tea and tried to look wounded. "Did I say I was slinging any mud? I'm a practical person. Live and let live, and all."

Practicality had led Bones to go to work for Al Meissner out of law school, after Will Sabert had turned him down for a permanent job. Meissner had taught him all anybody needed to know about the lobby in those days, and after Meissner died, Bones had opened his own shop. Specializing in friendly persuasion: he had good information and he knew how to talk, but he also knew how to take care of other business—finding girls for the randy and cash for the strapped. VMC had been Meissner's biggest client, and then Bones's biggest. After thirty years of bumming around the halls of the Capitol, he was the dean of their lobbying team, if not the go-to guy. Lately, though, none-too-subtle hints had been dropped that he ought to retire, before they let him go. The old methods had fallen out of favor. More and more it was about which party you belonged to, and if Bones wasn't going to switch outright he at least had to prove himself all over again—and, goddamnit, he was trying, even if it did mean TGIFriday's and iced tea and all this sort of bullshit. Practicality had dragged him here.

Ever since Sabert's funeral he'd been visited by memories, things he hadn't thought about in an age and a half. When he was twenty-five he'd spent a summer working in Sabert's office. At twenty-five he'd been a pretentious, shameless fuck. Once he'd quoted Gunnar Myrdal to a girl he'd been trying to pick up—and it worked! Those were some times, not as beloved to him personally as the succeeding decade, but full of naïve convictions and illicit sex. How differently he'd imagined his life then, thinking he'd go to Washington for good, thinking he'd end up more like his brother, in some respectable sinecure. Though he didn't rue the difference. He could remember his old ambitions intellectually but not on the gut level. They'd passed out of his system. It was a stage you went through, and Bones felt glad to be through it and sorry for his nephew, the shmuck, unable to get to the next thing.

"She might even be looking at a primary challenge," Yates said.

"Flintic? You putting someone against her?"

The way Yates kept shaking his head, it was as if the whole world were made up of one crying shame after another. "Rumor has it Dr. Butze may run."

"Dr. Bob! And his brimstone follies?"

"Of course."

"That show has got to be at the dollar theater by now, he's been putting it on for so long. What's his deal this time—posting the ten commandments on football scoreboards? Quarantining gays? You don't actually want that guy in there. He's a taco short of a combo platter. Several tacos."

Yates didn't answer.

"Oh, I get it," Bones said. "You have him beat up on Flintic for a while and then run some fresh young face right up the middle. Am I right?"

Yates still didn't answer.

"So who's it going to be?"

"You ever meet Ed Vela?"

Bones had not. It might be in VMC's interest to support Vela, Yates insinuated. A meeting might be arranged, if Bones was amenable. Oh, you know me, Bones replied: amenable is my middle name. Kenneth Amenable Lasseter.

He left the restaurant with a stomach full of tea and a date with an upstart conservative. The best he could say was that Yates had paid for the tea.

Sixteen

et another Saturday night. Yet another sunset glazing the newly mown lawns, yet another warm dusk lapping against the hull of the night proper, yet another tumble into dark and drunkenness, yet another swallow of regret just before last call. Yet another slow drive home.

Nick was still telling himself he might not go to Liza's party. His only plan was to meet Roger at the Spider and listen to Buzz and their friend Davy play an early set. When Nick arrived at the club it was not yet dark.

Buzz and Davy had been trying to get a band together ever since Nick had quit Real Real Gone and their drummer, Davy's ex-wife Melissa, had moved to Brooklyn. But they weren't having any luck. Decent drummers were in short supply around the city, never mind bass players. The shortage of suitable musicians saddened Roger more profoundly than it did Buzz and Davy, as if it were his first gray hairs, or his favorite shirt springing a hole. "Where *is* everybody?" he would lament. He bitched about musicians who had stopped playing and were starting up families instead. About friends who were awash in tricycles. A conspiracy of parents ruining his music scene. From time to time he would urge Nick to go back to playing, but having planted an unsteady foot on the shore of his thirties, Nick didn't want to risk it. Going back.

So Buzz and Davy would find some kid and then it would turn out the kid fancied himself the second coming of Keith Moon. Or they would rope in some old friends, practice a couple times, and conclude it just wasn't clicking. In the meantime, they played as a guitar duo, billing themselves as Uncle Albert and opening at clubs where they were friends with the managers.

Davy was one of a group of guys Nick had spent a lot of time with, eight, ten years ago, when they all worked minimum-wage, minimal-effort jobs and didn't have serious girlfriends and would go out night after night to the Sunset, staying through to the last set of whatever band was playing, then pressing on to someone's place to take some drugs and sit around and try to keep the night from ending. Back when Nick had lived with Roger in that run-down house across from the Tamale Hut. Plenty of nights they'd sat in that living room, in chairs salvaged from curbsides, passing around the beers and the guitars, spinning theories and parts of songs, mentioning various women, and breaking out spontaneously into some silly rendition of some silly song—"Don't Bring Me Down," say— fast and loud and exaggerated, with much percussive banging of bottles on the coffee table. Followed by something crooning and out of tune. Followed by a descent into fairly unbearable noise.

Yet Nick had pulled away, eventually. He'd woken up one too many times on a floor or in a pool of something, or both, or been roused by threatening phone calls from his bosses, and as determined as he'd been not to turn into an uptight career creep, he'd started to worry about the way things were trending. He'd moved into his own place, cut back on drinking and eliminated the other drugs, and succeeded in holding on to a job at a record store through such suck-up-to-management tactics as regular attendance. On the side he'd started writing reviews and brief items for the *Weekly*. To his surprise, they'd offered him a job. Which he'd managed to keep, even after the drinking picked back up again. He was closing in on a six-pack a night these days, more on weekends, but he still had his job. For now.

Over time Nick had lost track of Davy, who still had that dirty-blond bowl cut and too-short pants. Tall and shaggy and cheerful, he loped around the stage. Uncle Albert's act was half music and half improvised shtick. Davy would say something like "It used to be a lot easier to get laid in this town,"

and Buzz would say, "Yeah, Davy hasn't gotten laid in a really long time,"

and Davy would say, "Why else would I be up here doing this?"

and Buzz would say, "All you ladies in the house put your hands in the air!"

and then they'd play a few bars of the *Pink Panther* theme. Then one of them would ask, "So are there any drummers in the audience?" It worked better indoors, but tonight they were playing the Spider's back deck. It was a small club with a downward-sloping yard and a deck at the bottom that functioned as a stage, covered by a plywood awning strung with blinking white Christmas lights. At ten o'clock the darkness had barely settled in. A small group of faithful fans stood around, a dozen people loyal to Davy and Buzz, all of them old friends except for That Guy Bruce, a philosophy graduate student who came to all the shows, not quite anybody's friend, and seemingly not quite right in the head, judging by the ardor of his dancing and the excessive way he clapped after songs.

As usual, Nick preferred to stand at the rear, to lean against the wall of the club and survey the scene. When he was younger this had been a conscious affectation, but somewhere along the line it had just become habit.

The backs of women were long in the outskirts of the stage lights, their bare shoulders pale and in motion, while along the fence their animated shadows sipped shadow drinks and nodded to shadow friends. Maybe they were talking about the day's events and where they had eaten dinner and rising house prices, but all of them, if they weren't careful, might start reminiscing about that time all those years ago when Davy had fallen off the stage, or the time Buzz had argued with that cop and gotten arrested. For most of the day it had rained off and on, bursting and subsiding, and it was still cloudy, gusts of heavy air shaking the small leaves of the live oak trees behind the stage. The shifting weather put an edge on things.

Roger had planted himself at a side table and was sitting, to Nick's dismay, with his ex-girlfriend Evie, a cherubic eyelash-batter much younger than Roger, probably in her mid-twenties, though she could have passed for seventeen. A year ago, when they'd started dating, she had hung on Roger's every word, but now she'd taken to flirtatious challenges and insults at every turn. She was drawn, she had once told Nick, to men of intensity. It was obvious that she did not include him in that category. Fair enough, thought Nick, he probably wouldn't include himself in that category either, yet he disliked her; what with her having sized him up as intensity-challenged, and Roger's subjecting himself to her as she came and went, and meanwhile seeing as how Nick felt the sort of unwanted attraction one sometimes felt toward a cute girl with her chest peeking out of her low-necked shirt and her legs packed tightly into denim pedal pushers. Evie wasn't so dumb that she couldn't tell—both that he disliked her and that he tended to notice her tits. Now that she and Roger had broken up, Nick wished they would quit sleeping together.

Nick joined them at the table, and Evie afforded him the curtest of hellos before resuming her story, about a cousin of hers who was always leaning on her to baby-sit. "Just because I'm good with kids," she said. "I took a personality test once and it said I was the nurturing, mothering type. Not that you should go by what one of those tests says, but I think it's true, don't you?"

Roger looked confused, his glasses slipping down his sweaty nose. Nick felt sorry for him. When Roger didn't say anything she prodded at the lime in her drink and dropped her chin. "Don't you want me to mother you?" she asked archly.

"No," Roger said, sounding suddenly confident. He shook his head vigorously. "No, I don't." He turned toward Nick. "So, my old friend. Don't you miss it?"

"Not really."

"Nick used to play bass," Roger said.

"Did you, now," Evie said. She tilted forward and sipped her drink through its straw.

"Evie's not interested in our inglorious past," said Roger. "She hates it when I bring it up."

"Blah blah blah," she said. She was too emphatically cute, in Nick's opinion, with her hair in pigtails and a bandana around her head, a piece of jewelry hung or fastened in every available position, including a rhinestone nose stud that caught the light when she leaned over. "It's like that campaign you're doing to keep that club open. It's just a club. It's closing down. Get over it."

The idea that he might end up taking Evie's side in an argument pressed Nick into preventive action. "So how's that going?" he asked before Roger could start to argue.

"Pretty good. I've got about sixty names so far, though none of those people showed up at my protest. I've talked to all the papers and some of the television stations. I don't suppose you've talked to your boss yet?"

"I'll mention it, I promise."

"I'm not going to bug you about it now, but I will bug you about it later. For right now, I want to return to Evie's previous assertion that something called 'it' needs to be gotten over. In fact, it is precisely because Nick's musical career should *not* be over and done with that I bring it up. How do we get him playing again?"

"Money?" Evie proposed.

"Money, women, and alcohol are indeed the usual enticements, but I think our friend Mr. Lasseter is a peculiar case."

Nick wanted to change the subject. Only when he stopped playing had he realized how much hope he'd invested in it, hope that something would come of it, whatever that meant.

"So tonight's that party at Liza's," Nick said.

"And we're not going?"

"I don't know."

"You want to go, don't you."

"What party? I want to go to a party," Evie said.

"You wouldn't like it," Roger said. "It has to do with things that are over."

"Who's having it?" she persisted.

"An unwitting sadist. It's a masochism party. Nick here will be prostrating himself at the feet of a woman who dumped him."

"I will not be prostrating myself. We're friends now. We've hung out as friends. I'm thinking about stopping by. Just stopping by, you know."

Davy and Buzz finished a song by hopping simultaneously into the air, kicking their feet back and then landing in silly poses, pursing their lips and darting their eyes. Then Davy walked up to the mike and said, "I'd like to thank everyone who got a sitter for tonight." He must have been forty now, thought Nick, but it was hard to believe; under the soft lights of the stage, with his boy's mouth and long bangs, he could have passed for someone in college. "This next song is called 'Ex-Wife Birthday Card.'" Davy started to strum fast, and cocked his head and leaned into the mike to sing. It was a melancholy song, its verses offering advice to the future children of the woman in question. Both Davy and Buzz were really playing now, given permission by the warm red lights and the almost-empty pint glasses set like amber relics on the stage's outer railing. Buzz was watching his own hands, looking down at his guitar and walking back and then forward again. Davy had a voice, a good one. They were both good. Nick was proud of these guys, his friends, in whatever dumb way. He was proud that he used to play with them, and hearing them now as they played some of the old songs, he thought surely it hadn't been so foolish to think they could go further than a local club full of their friends, had it? Not that any of them had talked seriously about that: it had not been too cool to want to be successful. They were just doing it to do it, not to be famous. But if you were good at it, and there was an audience for it, and you loved it, did it have to always come second to all the other things, the silly jobs, the nagging from parents, the daylight world?

Once everything had been loud and timeless and possible; all that he'd needed had been right there; he had been smitten with all of it, even the bad music, even the assholes. That's how he remembered it, at least. He sometimes thought that in the past he'd lived more in the present. The graffiti on the bathroom wall at the Sunset had said *Whosoever playeth onstage shall never die*. But also *You wish!* and *Fuckwad* and *If you can piss this high you should join the fire department*.

L iza's apartment was west of downtown, off Sutherland Road, in an old suburb that was now considered part of the city, where professional types lived in forties- and fifties-vintage houses updated with Saltillo tile and translucent curtains and walls painted the colors of savannas or seashells. A washer-dryer in every bonus room, Asian lettuces in every garden plot. Corner stores with copies of *Marie Claire* and *The New Yorker* in the magazine racks.

They had all squeezed into Nick's car, Evie in the front seat, Roger, Davy, and Buzz in back. "Why are we going to this again?" Roger asked. "Remind me what our goal is here?"

"All we want is a good time," Nick said.

"You realize that odds are you are not going to have a good time at a party thrown by your ex and her fiancé."

"You expect me to take your advice?"

"Obviously not. I am like the blind prophet Teiresias, speaking to one who will not heed me."

"Roger, I want you to know I'm rolling my eyes right now," Evie said.

"You are like a very black pot with an unhealthy fixation on kettles," Nick said.

"What are you trying to say?" Roger asked.

Nick checked the rearview mirror. "So, Buzz. What'd you do today?"

Buzz sat up tall. He could be disarmingly erect. "Took Mrs. Adams to get her hair done, and then we went grocery shopping," he said. Mrs. Adams was his landlady, a widow with wild white hair and bulletproof eyeglasses, about three hundred years old and roughly the height of a bicycle rack. She refused to go into a home or hire help, and she was always asking Buzz for favors, knowing he would oblige. "T-bone steak was on special."

"Jesus Christ. Didn't you have work today?" Roger asked.

"They know about Mrs. Adams. They let me leave early."

"Man, I hate it when you do that."

"Do what?"

"Let that woman take advantage of you!"

"I don't mind it. My rent is cheap. Plus, she takes me out to dinner once a month."

"Sitting in the city's oldest and worst Tex-Mex restaurant eating enchiladas with Mrs. Yoda hardly seems like a reward."

"She's lonely, I guess."

"That's no excuse," Roger said. "Who isn't lonely?"

No one said anything.

"Okay, it should be coming up. It's a brick building with a blue porch light," Nick said.

"I see it, I see it," Evie said.

Nick swerved hard to the curb and parked abruptly, and they all hurried out of the car as if it had filled with fumes.

Her apartment was on the second floor. They climbed the stairs, each step, for Nick, part of a question, the *what will be* that was almost always more appealing than the answer later on, the *what has been*, the hungover effort to review the night's less fortunate moments. At the top of the stairs they pushed open the door and entered the living room, lit by paper-shaded lamps and a streetlight just outside one of the windows. When Nick used to come here, there'd been more furniture: What had happened to all of it? Just two people were in the front room, a couple sitting quietly on the sofa as if waiting for a bus or a train. Lawyers, probably. There were a few more people standing around the dining room, and beyond that, the sounds of voices and clinking bottles coming from the kitchen, a patch of its pearly tile visible through a doorway.

"Greetings," Roger said to the couple on the couch, and the five of them filed through the front room, like freshmen in high school crashing a senior function. It was a smaller party than Nick had expected. He would have liked it to be larger, would have liked to spy on Liza from within the safety of a crowd. Roger and the rest of the interlopers stopped at the refrigerator for beers, but Nick kept on going, on through the kitchen and out onto the deck behind the apartment. The air seemed thinner than it had at the club, and smelled of the damp tree branches stretching out above them. All around him people he'd never seen before were chatting. Nick recognized a face or two, but Liza's people, the handbag designers and film producers, had always been unimpressed by Nick and were surely wondering why he'd come. He, too, was wondering this. Liza herself was standing in the corner, facing away from him, one hand on her hip. And now he might sing praises to her legs, long and slender below her short skirt, or the rise of her back, her capable arms, her . . . But he stopped himself. No praises, no daydreams. No thoughts of . . . of things he shouldn't think of.

"Nick Lasseter. Haven't seen you in a while." Miles held a high-ball glass out in front of him like a lantern. It had been only a week and a half since their run-in at Gloria's.

"Hey, man." When Nick had first met him, Miles had been a music enthusiast and a serial undergraduate, taking a few classes each semester, going out every night; but then he'd bought his first coffee shop, borrowing money his father had wrung out of Baton Rouge real estate. His business gene activated, Miles had shifted course. No more Modern European History or Painting II. He'd opened a second shop, then a third. He was a regular capitalist now—a dissident capitalist, fending off Starbucks, listening to the Mekons as he reviewed his monthly statements. Eating at restaurants where he was friends with the owners. His navy guayabera was starchy crisp; his hair was in a ponytail; one of his small ears was pierced.

"I've been busy, really busy," Miles said, rubbing his free hand down his side. "The stores are doing great." Not waiting for Nick to ask. "What about you? You still writing for the *Weekly*? Fighting the good fight?" His face was conventionally handsome in a ruddy, blue-eyed way that Nick didn't find handsome at all. He touched Nick's negligible bicep with his glass. "Glad you could make it."

Nick, wanting very much to sock him, could hear a voice in his head telling him to chill out: The man was trying to be friendly, was he not? The thing to do at this point was to remove himself from socking distance, but before he could formulate his parting words Liza joined them.

"Nick, glad you could make it," she said, the echo so exact that it all but proved she and Miles had at last gotten involved in a way that included nakedness and borrowing from each other's speech patterns. Then she, too, touched his arm.

"Nick was about to say what he's been working on," Miles said.

Was not. "Oh—a profile of one of our local officials. And trying to find out more about this deal on the east side she's got going."

"A good deal or a bad deal?" Liza asked, drearily polite.

"A bad one, I think. It's not that interesting."

Liza and Miles were waiting for him to say something else. "This is such a great place," Nick said, as if he'd never been there before.

"You know how I got this apartment? My mother found it for me. Isn't that pathetic."

"Is it pathetic?" Nick asked.

"I don't think it's pathetic," Miles said. "Madelyn really has the knack for that sort of thing."

"It's true," Liza said.

"I love being on an upper floor. When I was a kid I wanted a house with at least four stories," Miles said.

"I wanted a house with a tower room," Liza said.

They both turned to Nick, waiting to hear what he had wanted. He didn't know. A swimming pool, with a slide. "Anybody want a beer?" he asked.

"I'm sorry," Liza said, "I should have offered."

Nick felt unreasonably insulted by the apology; it was as if they had met recently, as if he were a mere guest in her apartment. Liza and Miles both raised their bottles to signal they didn't need anything. They were fine.

Davy had camped out in the kitchen, next to the refrigerator. He was standing against the counter and not talking to anyone. Davy was self-sufficient that way. Nick leaned up against the counter next to him.

"You guys should play more often," Nick said, opening up a bottle of some novelty ale. It felt like the first of many. He asked Davy if he had any other music projects going.

"I was playing with the Laminators. But I had to quit. Robert is too psycho."

"Really," Nick said.

"I don't know, man. We were having practice a couple weeks ago and we were doing some bong hits and got kind of fucked up, so then we start playing, and all of a sudden in the middle of the song Robert just starts screaming."

"Screaming?"

"Like, 'Aaaaaaaaaaaah!' On and on like that, and we all thought he was joking, you know, he just went 'Aaaaaaaaaaaah!' so we started laughing, but then he got all mad, like, *This isn't a joke, this is Art!* That's what he said. And I was, like, okay, I've been with too many bands where someone breaks down."

"Yeah."

"He's a great guy, but you know, I can't deal with that shit anymore."

"I know what you mean," Nick said. He detected a hollow of

sadness nearby, and this intuition of a precipice made him apply himself more studiously to his beer. He drained his bottle and helped himself to another, then asked Davy how things were going, outside of music.

"I can't complain," Davy said. Which meant: I won't complain. I will drink and not say much.

Nick was sweating; kitchens at parties were always too hot. "I think I'll check out the living room."

"I'm staying right here. Bon voyage."

More people had come; the room was half packed, and Liza was floating out in the middle of it. She took a step forward or back and the rest of the crowd swayed unconsciously with her. She saw Nick and walked over to him as easily as if she were walking across an empty room. "Hey, sorry about that," she said, with a half gesture toward the deck, "before."

"About what before?"

"I don't know."

"You don't need to apologize," Nick said.

She started to say sorry again, caught herself, and stuck out her tongue. Then she smiled. Her teeth were just this side of too large, long and even. They'd argued about her teeth before; he'd told her they were beautiful teeth, and she wouldn't believe him. But they were. You sound like my dentist, she'd said.

"How are you?"

"I'm all right. How's the law?"

"The law is the law." Liza let out another self-conscious giggle. It was odd; she'd never been a giggler. Nick asked about her new job, and she told him about new colleagues, the new building. It was close to the *Weekly* building; they should have lunch. Here they were, talking. Both of them craning toward each other, mouths too full of the wrong words. He could state for the record that he was still drawn to her in a way he was not drawn to anybody else, and she was standing close enough to him for him to sense some reciprocation, but what did that even matter anymore.

Behind her, Nick saw Miles, framed in the archway between the living and dining room, looking disoriented—but only for an instant before he started toward them. Nick sent a telepathic *get lost* in his direction, but to no avail. Miles walked with feet turned slightly outward, as if he were fat. Nick had made it out of the last encounter without needling him, but he didn't want to push his luck. He mumbled the word *restroom* and left Liza to receive the Good Ship Richmond as it veered into harbor.

Back outside, his people had reassembled by the deck rail, Davy having abandoned his kitchen post, and Roger and Evie and Buzz all slouched together, conspiratorial, faces shining.

"Don't you guys know how to mingle?" Nick asked.

"Is that what you're doing, mingling?"

"Meaning?"

Roger raised his eyebrows, held out his hands, and then sang, "Come back, Liza, come back, girl—" Buzz joined him for *water fall from me eye.* Nearby attorneys turned and looked and turned away.

"Okay, stop."

"My friend, I think what you need here is a strategy," Roger said.

Nick crossed his arms. "Do tell. Strategy for what?"

"I saw you guys talking. You still want her."

"I do not."

"Do too."

"She's getting married." Nick took the beer from Roger's hands and drank from it. "Can we stop talking about this? Do you guys want to leave?"

"I've got no other plans for this evening. Or do you mean you want to leave?"

"I think we should leave. Let's go somewhere else," Nick said.

But no one moved. Nick kept his back to the rest of the party, screening it all out. And then he was drunk, hearing his own voice get louder as his ability to control the volume fell away, attempting to look squarely at the person he was talking to but not exactly able to do that. It was Evie, and he was taking her in peripherally, the information transmitted to his brain as if she were a danger come up from behind. He had an imprecise sense of the bare space between her neck and her shirt, and the sweat around her hairline—and he was finding it convenient to grab hold of the railing next to her, just to be sure of where he was. He was on the deck outside Liza's apartment, talking loudly to Evie. Evie what? Evie the Girl. Evie the Excessive.

"Evie," he said, "what's your last name?"

Her answer, Nick could have sworn, was "yo fanny."

"What?"

"Giovanni."

"Is that Italian?"

"No, Dutch-Lithuanian," she said in a silly deadpan.

"Oh! A shaft of wit from the Evie Giovanni quiver!"

"Ha," she said. "A turd of sarcasm from your ass."

"You don't think I'm very intense, do you?" All of a sudden they were having an argument about rich people. How had it started? Nick had said something innocuous and obvious about how rich people were sometimes tiresome to be around, and Miss Evie Giovanni had taken issue with that. Her nose stud twinkling as she shook her head. So then of course he had to stake out a much stronger position and stick it to her. Rich people, he said, were all either immoral or hypocritical. Not that he necessarily believed this, but it was what he said to her. "All I'm saying is," he said, "if you have more money than you need, you know it, and you're not, like, offering it to needy people, you're keeping it for yourself."

"But there are charities," Evie said, "there's philanthropy."

Nick cut her off. "You're still keeping the rest of it for yourself, even though you know there's someone out there who needs it more than you. And then you feel so good about yourself if you give a homeless guy a dollar. Like, ooh, I gave him a whole dollar."

"Do you dislike other people?" she asked.

Of course not! he wanted to shout. I am Nick Lasseter, lover of men and women! "Why do you ask?"

"Well, you dislike rich people. You dislike me."

"I don't dislike you."

"You act like you do."

"Why would I dislike you? How could any man dislike a woman of your intelligence and charm and your . . . proportions?"

"Oh God." Evie took a drag of her cigarette and spun around to face Roger, who was, of course, talking.

I'm sorry, Nick mouthed at her back, letting his eyes drop to her tightly packaged butt. I've had too much to drink. I'm not myself.

Time grew harder to account for. He was asking Davy about his houseplants; he was talking to a woman he didn't know, again about Davy's plants; he was flirting with this woman until her boyfriend joined the conversation; he was laughing weirdly at things that weren't that funny; and then Roger was saying he'd called a cab for them all, since "driving is obviously not in your repertoire right now."

"But the party's not over yet," Nick complained. There were about a dozen people left. It's one-thirty, said Roger, and it's over enough.

One-thirty. When the hell did we ever quit at one-thirty?

They were in the living room now, and they could see Liza in the dining room, picking up empties and taking them to the kitchen. Roger said, "Let me suggest to you that this would not be a good opportunity for you to make a move."

"I'm not making a move. I just don't want to go yet," Nick said, not meaning to sound as whiny as he thought he probably sounded. "I don't want to have to come back tomorrow for the car. If I wait an hour I'll be all right."

"That is such bullshit."

"I swear," Nick said.

"If you want to stay, fine." Roger pulled his beat-up billfold from his back pocket and, cradling it in his hand, took out a clean twenty.

"If you want to stay, fine, but do not drive home. Take a cab, all right?"

"Thanks, Dad."

So they left, and Nick stayed. Later he would have a hard time figuring out what had happened, as opposed to what he might have dreamed. It seemed he'd ended up sitting on the sofa. He, Miles, and Liza the last ones left. Had the two of them been standing over him? Miles frowning? Liza rubbing her eyes? Maybe he said something like, These paper lamps are really nice. The whole place, really; your mother has such good taste. And then it seemed that Miles, Miles the valiant, Miles the entrepreneur, Miles the fiancé was asking Liza whether he should take Nick home.

Because I could take him home, he said, in the Saab.

I'm not getting in a Saab with that guy, Nick said.

Don't worry about it, Liza said. He can stay here.

And then did Miles kiss her quickly on the lips? Nick lay down on the couch. And then was it five minutes later, an hour, some time passed and then Liza came back and sat down next to his head, which was pirouetting on the inside, though when she sat there her thigh grazed his crown, and that seemed to steady him.

I'm sorry, he said. This isn't how I want to be.

That's good to know, she said.

Maybe you should call me a cab.

She let her hand drop to his head for a moment. Stay here and talk to me, she said.

If I stay here, I'll fall asleep.

That's okay.

Do you remember when you tried to teach me how to play golf?

Yes, she said.

I clocked you in the shins with a club.

I remember that.

It was an accident, he said. He tilted his chin so that the top of his head was in closer contact with her leg.

I know.

Do you remember when we drove out to Dos Rios and I forgot to stop for gas and we ran out and had to sleep in the car?

Yes, Liza said. Remember that guy we got a lift from the next day?

A man in need of an orthodontist.

A man in need of a shower.

A man in need, Nick said.

Anyway, he continued, I remember those things.

Do you remember, she said, that we never wanted to go to the same places?

Your friends didn't want me at their parties.

You didn't want to be there, she said. Do you remember when my grandmother died?

Nick did not. He was ready to swear that she had never told him about this grandmother, but instead he closed his eyes. Later on he wouldn't feel entirely sure that this conversation had taken place. When he woke up Liza had gone, and there was a cotton blanket covering him, a blanket he remembered from when they were together. He was hot, and he pulled the blanket off, then gathered it up in his arms and squeezed it to his chest.

His back hurt. He didn't want to wake up the next morning on Liza's couch. What time was it?

He didn't know until he got back to his car, and the clock on the dashboard said 4:30. Nick drove home. It was still dark, the stoplights were blinking red, but the night was over.

PART THREE

Seventeen

By the summer of 1954, John Carter had completed three years as a high school teacher. September to May he taught school, and summers he did what he could. Picked up work where he found it. Even during the school year he was something of an odd-jobs man, teaching geometry and government because Riverside High didn't have instructors in those subjects. Teaching was all right, considering the options, though at odds with his personality. He was shy. Worse: children scared him. The younger the child, the more unnerved he was.

Here came two of them now: Hawkins and Dalton. Ninth grade, going on tenth. They raced around a corner and almost raced right into Carter, until he yelped: "Hey!" George Dalton and Theodore Hawkins skidded to a stop, panting and apologizing. They were both of them skinny, pulsating boys with long necks and knobby knees. Sons of janitors, they'd already realized that misbehavior was their one and only birthright outside of the broom closet. The important thing, Carter reminded himself, was not to be intimidated, or at least not to let it show if you were intimidated. "Where're you two in such a rush to get to?"

"Roller rink," George Dalton said. "It's colored day."

The year before, a roller-skating rink had opened on the north side, off limits to non-whites except on Tuesdays. To Carter the whole arrangement was an insult, but the Tuesday-evening skate had become very popular in the community, and a few months earlier he'd been prevailed upon to give it a try. This had been the activity portion of his one and only date of the past year, a setup inflicted upon him by a couple of bored church women. He'd fallen three times, winding up with bruises all up and down his left leg and a new nickname among the students, Mr. Bumpty Bump. After that he'd denounced colored day more strongly than before and had advised the students not to waste their two bits on the white man's bread and circus.

Bread and what? Nobody had listened. Both Hawkins and Dalton carried a pair of makeshift skates: short planks of plywood with what looked like furniture casters attached. Carter took one from George Dalton and inspected it. The casters were bolted into the wood, which was splintering and flecked with white paint, as if it had been crowbarred off of a shack.

"Are these supposed to be skates?"

"Yes, sir," said George Dalton.

"How are you going to wear them?"

"We got rope to tie them on with."

Theodore Hawkins was now holding a skate against either shoulder and bending his knees and then straightening them again. Excess momentum: common enough among boys, though Carter hadn't had it at that age. Every joule of surplus energy had been directed inward. At night he'd ground his teeth as he slept—still did, as far as he knew. Dr. Gibbons had been the one to point this out, when Carter was in high school: one day out of the blue Gibbons had walked over to him, right in the street, grabbed hold of his jaw and told him to open up. "Ahhh," Carter had said, reflexively. Gibbons had made a squinting face, the mole beside his nose vaulting toward his eye. "I'm not checking your tonsils, I'm looking at your teeth," he'd said. "Practically worn smooth."

Carter handed the skate back to Dalton. "Don't they have ones that you can rent?"

"They got a new rule. We ain't allowed to rent no more," Hawkins said.

"We *aren't* allowed to rent them anymore," Carter said—but standing still had become unbearable to the boys, who ran off before he finished the sentence.

Carter resumed his walk to the library. He'd never planned on teaching, much less these summers of running around town fixing old ladies' toilets and shelving books and mowing the baseball field. He ought to have been an engineer. As a student he'd been drawn to the subjects of engineering and physics—what little he knew of physics, which was very little, because the only physics books at Riverside High were ten-year-old physical science texts written for pharmacy students, which emphasized the description of atoms and molecules and were riddled with errors so basic that Carter often spotted them himself. Each mistake needled him, reminding him yet again that these cast-off old books, which had evidently never been proofread, were all that they had.

His junior year, he'd been studying one day at the Washington Library when he came across another mistake—two numbers added incorrectly in a sample problem—and slammed the book shut and threw it on the ground, with a thump that resounded in the otherwise silent room. Mrs. Vane, the librarian, had raised her head, and he'd hung his own in response. "John Carter," she said, and when he looked up again she was summoning him with a reproving finger.

"I'm sorry," he whispered, hangdog in front of her desk, "I got frustrated."

"And is that the fault of the book?" she said.

"Yes, ma'am. It's a bad book. We ought to have ones that are at least accurate."

"You want a different book, there's other ways to get it besides you throwing things on the floor."

But throwing his old book on the floor had, in a sense, produced a new one. He hadn't known he could request books from the other libraries—but, as Mrs. Vane had explained that afternoon, although the other branches were off limits to coloreds, he could still order any book in the system, to be delivered to the Washington branch. Carter didn't know the names of other physics books, but he'd invented titles and written them down. *Physics. Engineering. Introduction to Physics. Introduction to Engineering.* "Anything like that," he'd told her.

What arrived, one week later, was *Introduction to the Principles of Civil and Structural Engineering,* by Professors Connor, Tuttingham, and Spunk. It was twice as thick as the physical science book, full of tiny type and line drawings and trigonometric equations. Carter had been so taken with it, and taken with himself for possessing it, that he'd toted the book everywhere he went. The print was embossed into the thick glossy pages; the principles of engineering could be perceived through the hands. He was enchanted to learn that everything oscillated: walls, rooftops, the earth itself. Nothing was as stationary as he'd believed. Then one afternoon he was sitting in the park, beginning a new chapter, when he heard someone approach the bench from behind and read out, "Levers and gears . . ." Without turning around, Carter knew the deep voice belonged to Dr. Gibbons.

"What is that you're reading?"

But before he could answer, Dr. Gibbons bent down and reached one of his long arms over Carter's shoulder, slipping his hand under the book's cover and folding it most of the way shut, so that he could see the title. "Principle number one," he said. "No colored students admitted to that School of Engineering up there." He gestured toward the university tower to the north.

Some called him the Bronze Mayor of Waterloo. With his giraffe's legs and lolloping gait, he might have been a particularly suave marionette, one who often wore a three-piece black suit, impressively tailored to cover the length of his limbs, and a camel-colored hat with a black band. He'd invited Carter to walk with him, and they'd walked. Dr. Gibbons had greeted everyone they passed by name, and along the way he'd elucidated his views on Socrates (a browbeater); Keynesian economics (good); the rumor that all property on the east side was owned by Jewish bloodsuckers (erroneous); Paul Robeson and the Communists (the man should have stuck to singing); and good nutrition (the keys to longevity were packed inside bananas, walnuts, and sardines). He was a rambler, but by the end of the hour he'd persuaded Carter to assist him, Dr. Gibbons, with some of his projects: the children's shoe drive, the Christmas party, the visits to City Council.

Middle of summer and the city was warped by heat. Windows melted, floors buckled. Awnings sagged over storefronts. The complaints of car horns bored through the haze. And here on the east side, on blocks of rotting boards and high weeds, the rooftops sank, the porches crumbled, the doors drifted open like jaws struck dumb. But the dumb blocks were outnumbered by the decent ones, as Carter reminded himself whenever he hit a dilapidated stretch. By and large it was a decent community. East Waterloo was practically its own small town, a poor but friendly one, with some people straight off the farm and some who owned businesses and some whose parents had been slaves and quite a few who rode the bus every day to the white side of the city for work. Most would have said it was a nice place to live. Plenty of trees, several parks, and a growing number of paved streets—Dr. Gibbons reminded City Council regularly of the road improvements it had pledged would be made on the east side.

From time to time Carter still lent Dr. Gibbons a hand with his projects. He went along to meetings of the Negro Citizens Council and occasionally on one of his ambassadorial missions to talk with city leaders, but the doctor, who was actually a dentist, no longer enjoyed the near-universal popularity he'd once had. That Dr. Gibbons been givin' and givin', people said, telling us who to vote for, and what do we get for it? One day at the roller rink?

A falling-down library?

The library was inadequate, outside and in. The building was small and flimsy, the collection minimal. Two bodies were buried beneath it, figuratively speaking: the first that of Dr. Horace Mc-Cray, who had bequeathed ten shelves of books and five hundred dollars toward the creation of a Negro Library; the second, that of a sixteen-year-old colored boy whose body was found one morning outside the gate to the municipal dump—provoking a gesture of reconciliation from a nervous city government, in the form of a library. The same structure had once housed the white library, but by the time of the boy's death the city had been awarded a Carnegie grant to build a new central branch, and the old building had been trucked across town as a gift to the city's colored.

Carter walked inside and smelled the familiar must. The oscillation of his own feelings toward the city were somehow rooted here, in this sorry excuse for a library, which had fed some of his earliest hopes as well as his adolescent recognition of how thoroughly the deck was stacked against him.

"Good afternoon, Mrs. Vane."

She still greeted Carter the way she always had. "John Carter. What trouble you going to stir up now?"

It had always been a joke—dropping a book on the floor had been the extent of his high-school-era rebellion—until a few months ago, when it had become something more than a joke. But all that had since quieted down.

"I came by to remind you I won't be here today."

"You're here to say you're not here?"

"I've got to do the chairs for the concert over at Ridgeway Park."

"That's all right, I got no use for you anyhow. What I need is someone to buy me some new window coverings." So as not to dwell on all the deficiencies of the Washington branch, Mrs. Vane focused on one: the tattered window shades, which caused her no end of shame, as if she had personally taken to them with a scissors and then regretted it later.

"No use for me?" Carter asked.

"I thought I heard that concert was canceled. Or postponed or something," Mrs. Vane said. "Because they got some kind of an election or I don't know what going on over there."

Carter said he didn't know how they could be holding an election at a park in the middle of July. "All right, all right, not an election," Mrs. Vane said. "Something like that, though."

"You're just trying to trick me into staying here and helping you."

"Everything's put away."

There was never very much for him to do. The library's entire store of books fit into a single room. Odor rather than light penetrated: there was a smell of the street, of exhaust and humidity. The high ceiling didn't lend the room airiness so much as it allowed smells to accumulate. There were two long tables with fans set on top like centerpieces, and spread out across one of them were copies of the *Standard* from Monday, Wednesday, and Friday mornings—on the days the library was open, Mrs. Vane bought a copy on her way to work, and occasionally she brought the Tuesday or Thursday evening *American*. If normally the job of the librarian was to impose order on a plentitude of materials, at the Washington branch it was another thing, trying to expand the slim holdings into an abundance, fanning out the papers, or standing books on end in front of the gaps in the shelves.

"Uh-uh. I told you, I don't want you around here. Make my life harder. After all your foolishness I'll be surprised if I ever get my shades."

It did seem foolish now. Had it been more than vanity? His grand protest. His test of the system. Last March he'd handed her a sheet of bond paper with a typewritten list of book titles and explained that he wanted all of the named books from the Central Library. She'd tugged at the collar of her dress and objected that there were two whole encyclopedia sets on the list.

We don't have those here, he'd told her.

"What you up to?"

"Research."

She'd acted suspicious but had called anyway, asking the Central branch for two full encyclopedia sets, the papers of Franklin Roosevelt, and any novels written by, as she pronounced it, Honoree Day Ball Sack.

No, ma'am, she told the Central branch librarian, I'm afraid we don't have our own encyclopedia over here. Yes, the borrower specifically said he wants to see both of them. Yes, ma'am. Yes. It's a research project, a very large one, as I understand it. All right. I can see how that would take some time. I'll tell him. Next Wednesday.

By the time the books arrived, Carter already had another list prepared: *The Dictionary of American Biography.* The Harvard Classics. Bound volumes of *Life* magazine. He'd come with the new request to present to Mrs. Vane, and had found her hidden behind a four-foot wall of books stacked up on her desk, fat piles of reference volumes and thinner towers of novels and histories.

"What are you going to do with these ones, then?" she'd asked, a baffled, disembodied voice from behind the encyclopedias.

"You can call the Central branch and have them come pick those up," Carter said. "I got what I needed."

It hadn't taken long for word of the book transfers to spread among the city's librarians, many of whom might well have agreed that it was redundant to maintain a separate branch for coloreds—but in no who's who of the city's powerful interest groups would anyone have included the reference professionals. The George Washington branch may have existed because of an unwritten rule, but it was a rule nonetheless, not to be altered by the library staff. Carter could request all the books in the world; to actually see anything done about the situation he would have to go to the City Council. Which he did. Before five council members, four men and a woman, he'd made his case, over the wails of a child in the general public area. As he argued in favor of equal access, he could read the outcome on the five white faces. He'd sat down and watched while a proposal to desegregate the library system failed, two votes to three.

T he city's designers had elected to arrange its streets around not one main square but four smaller ones, a square of squares marking off the core of the business district, with the Capitol to the north and the river to the south. Three of the squares were flat and crossed by stone paths, but the fourth one, Ridgeway Square Park, was a tilted bowl of St. Augustine grass, with a large white gazebo on its eastern slope, and pecan trees and civic buildings around the perimeter. On the north side stood the granite New Deal courthouse, all vertical lines and tall, ambitious windows; on the south was the twenty-year-old Carnegie Library, an Italianate villa with painted grotesques beneath its sandstone vaults; and so the legacies of Franklin Roosevelt and the Steel Trust were confined to opposite sides of the square, like frozen boxers who would never get their chance at another round. It had long been a favored location for public speeches and concerts; and although most Negro events were confined to the east side of town, every year the City Council granted permission for the Delphic Choir to present its Jubilee Concert in Ridgeway Park.

As Carter approached he saw what Mrs. Vane had meant by an election. A man on the gazebo steps was giving a speech. Carter had seen his picture in the papers: a candidate for Congress, Will Sabert. The chairs would have to wait, and so Carter waited, off to one side, listening. High-sounding words wound out of Sabert's mouth, while Carter thought of Hawkins and Dalton and their so-called skates.

Carter knew enough about the campaign to know that it had been a bland one so far, as both Sabert and his primary opponent sought to imitate the popular retiring incumbent, a genial bon vivant who had not sponsored a single bill in more than twenty years of service, and who every time he was asked about a position had waved his hand reassuringly and said the same thing—"I'm all right on that issue"—before taking the next question. Each of the current candidates had taken mincing steps toward the middle. Though it was known that Sabert had a liberal record and had been encouraged to run by the left wing of the party, he'd grown cautious after having lost his bid for reelection to the State Assembly. He was hedging.

The afternoon had turned muggy, the sky a low ceiling of oyster-shell muddled with oyster-meat clouds. Sabert, a pale man in a tan suit, had a grave face but spoke animatedly. The cut of his suit was old-fashioned but his wide stance was youthful: a young man in spite of himself.

"I am for putting an end to petty feuding at all levels of government," he was saying. "I am for working together to solve our common problems, so that our beloved land might take its proper place as one of the richest areas in the world.

"I think people are interested in good government," he continued, and then paused as if he didn't remember what came next. "Will Sabert has a positive, practical, forward-looking program for the betterment of our state and our nation . . ."

When he was through he took questions. An out-of-breath young man in the rear of the group introduced himself as Robert Mahoney. Reporter for the *Independent*. He was wearing a white shirt with short sleeves and thick black glasses. He articulated his words as if giving a sort of speech himself.

He began by mentioning an antilabor measure passed the year before. "You have said you would not have supported it had you been in office when it was proposed," he enunciated. "You have said you do not favor the restrictions on labor strikes currently in place. Would you vote for a repeal of the law?"

Standing beside the gazebo was a man holding a folded umbrella like a nightstick, swinging it back and forth. His eyebrows were thick and set low, and his mouth was pursed around an unlit cigar.

"There's no such bill before the Congress," Sabert said.

"But if there was one, would you vote for it?"

"I'd have to see some specific legislation before I could comment on that," he said.

Each time Sabert answered, it was as if the man with the unlit cigar had been spared some insult he'd been expecting.

"What about integration of our public schools?"

Sabert took a couple of slow breaths. Carter watched a grackle drop to the lawn and start pecking at the ground.

"No prejudice is so dangerous as the prejudice against men because of the color of their skin," Sabert began. "When we in the South speak against a particular civil rights proposal, we are not speaking against the Negro race. I am opposed to federal control of our schools. I think that it is something that should be carried out gradually and carefully by the state and its school districts. I am for state control of the schools." This seemed to please the man with the cigar. "And now if you don't mind, I'd like to shake hands with the folks who came out to say hello," he said.

He moved toward the small group of bystanders, as if performing for the reporters, barking: "Hello there! I'm your next congressman, Will Sabert. How yew?"

Carter walked over and stood quietly among the well-wishers. Next thing he knew Sabert was seizing his hand and learning his name. Up close he seemed bonier, more fragile, his eyes melancholy.

"John Carter. I hope I can count on your support," Sabert said.

"Likewise, sir," Carter answered.

Then came a boy, gangly and wet-haired and couldn't have been much more than sixteen years old, tripping down the gazebo steps with a handful of Will Sabert buttons, which he began to distribute among the people like they were money. "Button, ma'am? Button? Show your support for our next congressman, that's right. Don't lose that. Button?"

"Bones!" Sabert called. "Gimme one of those."

The kid was quick to oblige. Grinning, he held out both palms, a button in each. "Take your pick." He watched Sabert expectantly. The candidate grabbed both and handed one of them to Carter, just as a photographer for the *Waterloo Standard* swooped in for a candid. Sabert smiled; Carter did not.

Seconds later, the man with the cigar beat a path to the photographer and took the camera out of his hands, then examined the back of it, as if deciding whether to open it or to smash it with his umbrella. His thumb was on the release. The photographer was pleading with him. Promising him something. At last the man gave the camera back, and Carter felt sure that no photograph of the candidate standing with a colored man would appear in the morning paper.

But he'd had another impression, beforehand: that Sabert hadn't felt comfortable saying what he'd said. The suit didn't fit properly. Although Carter had just listened to him advocate for states' rights, what he concluded was that this might be someone who could help.

Three days after his Ridgeway Park speech Will Sabert was in his office, on the phone, doing his best to defuse, or at least deflect, Al Meissner's wrath. Al had been appointed—had effectively appointed himself—Will's campaign manager and took it upon himself to berate Will at least two or three times per day. He was still upset that Will had stood for a picture, for a newspaper photograph no less, with a colored man. The way Al talked about it, you would have thought they'd both posed in their birthday suits.

"Al, you heard me talk to those reporters. How much clearer could I have been? I came down solid on the side of you and the Marron brothers and all the other cretins, didn't I?"

"Yes, but no one is sure which side you're really on," Meissner said.

"What does that even matter? What does it matter what I think, so long as I do what they want me to do? So long as I say what they want me to say? So long as I bend over when they tell me to—"

"All right, Will, all I'm saying is, the Marrons need someone they can be sure of, not someone who's going to go befriending niggers on us."

"I've got an idea. How about it. As soon as we're done talking I'll go see my good friend Sheriff Stanley Klansman down in Coonass County, the two of us'll strip down to our loincloths, and then we'll drive all around my future district with a megaphone, and every time we see a man, woman, or child of the Negroid complexion, I'll get right on that loudspeaker and say, 'Hi there! This is William Stanley Sabert, and I want you to know that I AIN'T YOUR FRIEND!'"

Meissner didn't say a word for a long time, so long that Will thought he might have put the phone down and walked off. Then, finally, he told Will in a low voice that it would be a good idea for him to call on Sherman Marron. "Promise him a . . . a naval air station, or a power plant or something. Otherwise, it's been nice working with you."

As soon as Meissner hung up, the bubble of Will's semi-righteousness, not resilient to begin with, collapsed. He didn't know whether he could win without the Marron brothers' money. Probably he could not. One wrong photograph, or a few wrong remarks, and it would be back to lawyering.

Will rested his head on his desk. He didn't mind lawyering. In a courtroom, with just one client's interests to promote, he could argue with confidence. The needs of a man facing five years in the penitentiary were usually clear-cut, the proper balance between the oilman's interests and the farmer's almost never so, and during the campaign Will had wondered more than once why he was ready to give up the straightforward demands of the former for the morass of the latter. He was not a natural campaigner, though he did have a good memory for names, which was useful. His real talent and inclination was for the law itself, that extensive apparatus, with its technicalities and subsections, its pretense of infallibility, like an immense unfinished railroad network whose tracks had to constantly be shifted, bit by bit. And then every so often the engines them-selves had to be replaced. The mechanics of legislation had con-sumed him in the Assembly, though that work hadn't drawn a tenth of the headlines of his restroom rebellion, and they would consume him again if he made it to Congress. That was one reason, maybe the reason, he'd decided to run: he knew he was good at something not very many people were good at, for the simple reason that he saw an intriguing puzzle in something that put most people to sleep. The law was fallible, authored by humans who couldn't have anticipated every nuance of their society's future; and it was the necessary fine-tuning that Will delighted in, the track-shifting, the slow work of picking up one cross tie and then the next.

When he opened his eyes, he was no longer alone. Robert Ma-honey, notebook in hand, pen behind the ear, sat in the chair across from Will's desk, wearing the same shirt and tie he'd been wearing the last time Will had seen him, at the park.

"Where did you come from?" Will asked.

"I was hoping you'd allow me to follow up on my questions the other day," Mahoney said.

"Would you excuse me a moment?"

Will walked out to his secretary's desk. "Can you tell me," he whispered, "how Mr. Mahoney managed to sneak into my office?"

She raised her head, startled. "Someone's in there? I—"

"That's all right. I just don't particularly want him to stay. If any-one else comes to see me, send them straight in. And if no one comes in twenty minutes, and I'm still in there with Mahoney, tell me I have a phone call or something."

There was a stubborn quality to the thickness of Mahoney's legs and arms, and to the way his small feet in mulish black work shoes dug into the carpet. After five minutes Will had yet to figure out whether this was an interview or not, since Mahoney was doing all the talking, about the loyalist-liberal program and the rising tide of labor and the possibilities for a liberal statewide campaign.

"Oh no," Will interrupted. "That'd be suicide."

Mahoney started to answer but Will shook his head. "Insurance, drought relief, tax reduction. Bread and butter and a little bit of jam. I've got to stay moderate for the election."

"You'll lose your liberal support. Aren't you worried about that? If you keep shilling for the segregationists?"

"Let me tell you something. I'm tired of people telling me what I'm for. Damnit, I'm a moderate. Not a segregationist, or an integrationist, or a disintegrationist or a congregationalist! All in good time, is what I say, that's what I've been saying. It's got to move at the proper pace or we'll have riots. We've got to take a moderate approach, and in the meantime put more money into Negro education. We've got to do something about poverty in this state."

"And where's that money going to come from?"

"General revenue."

"And which southern representatives do you think will vote for putting a dime of general revenue into Negro schools?"

Sabert kept on wishing he could shoo the man out of the room. "I'm explaining my positions," he said. "Whether they become law or not is another question."

"But as long as it's a long shot, why not take the high ground? Why not *lead*?"

"The high ground seems like a fine place, but it's awfully far off. Certainly it's a long way off from Capitol Hill. If you want to lead the people, you've got to start close to where they're standing. Can't lead them from miles away." Will was parroting someone else, he didn't remember who. Meissner, maybe.

"So you remain opposed to desegregation."

"Once again, and then I won't say it another time: I am opposed to immediate desegregation forced upon us by the federal government. I am for a middle course of action. Look what happened in that cotton town up on Highway 20, where they tried to do it all at once. Utter mayhem. We don't need that here!" His voice was too loud, and now there was another figure in the doorway. John Carter.

"Pardon me," he said. "The secretary told me to come on back."

All three men were quiet. And quiet. And then Will asked Carter to come in and have a seat.

"I don't mind standing."

"Mr. Mahoney was on his way out."

Mahoney understood that he'd been dismissed; his round face fell into a pout. With a sigh of self-pity he drew himself out of the chair, raised his hand in a farewell salute, and departed—which left Carter and Sabert in a state of uneasy solidarity, having rid themselves of the third man but not sure how to begin.

"What can I do for you?" Will asked.

"I came to talk to you about what you said the other day."

"What did I say?"

"That you wanted my support."

"That I do," Will said warily, and then picked up where he'd left off with Mahoney. "Let me say that—well, what I was trying to say just now, to that reporter, if that's what he is, is that I am a proponent of moderation."

"All right."

"That is to say—" What was he saying? And why was he saying it now? He was suddenly desperate to explain himself. "I have put my trust in the viability of compromise and gradualism despite all the evidence that it is unworkable, that splitting the difference leaves you with exactly zero, and that I might as well claim to be the man in the moon. Moderation is a losing proposition. I've got to choose. Big bidness or the eggheads—and all of my so-called friends want another Stevenson!" He flung his arm in the direction of the door, unable to stop. "All I've got to do is shave off a bunch of this hair and say I'm the new Adlai—even though they know perfectly well that even the mighty Adlai himself isn't too popular here outside their little whiskey-drinking club. Still they want another lamb to sacrifice at the temple of their high holy idealism. And maybe I'd be better off . . . Would I? Is that what I should do?"

Will had a clump of his hair in his fist, as if he were thinking of cutting some of it off right then and there.

Carter had watched this performance impassively. "I don't know," he said. "I'm not for Stevenson or any of them so much as I'm for . . . for what I would call the principle of the lever."

"I don't follow."

Carter had never really tried to put this to anyone. His theory of how things should work. "Not the schools, not yet. They're a tinderbox. Folks go crazy whenever it's their kids involved in a thing. You put colored children in the white schools right away, it's going to be hard on those kids."

"Precisely."

"The problem is changing people's minds. It's not going to happen overnight."

"Exactly what I've been trying to tell—"

"Only that's no excuse for sitting on your hands. You got to use that lever. There are several possibilities. Number one is the library system. Why not open up these libraries to everyone, white and colored."

"The libraries. That's that proposition that failed at City Council, isn't it?"

"It almost passed." Carter was still on his feet. He started describing to Will his tactics at the library, forgetting himself as he talked, or at least forgetting that his audience was a candidate for U.S. Congress, not a classroom of fifteen-year-olds. He spoke of fulcrums and wedges, a dynamics of social adjustment he'd worked out privately and, until now, kept to himself.

Points of pliability, that's what he would eventually call them. The notches and soft patches in the social order, the skin stretched thin, the gaps into which a lever might be wedged: to him society was not a fixed thing but rather a kind of vibrating machine, stable in some places, loose-jointed elsewhere. There were components that might be adjusted or reshaped or, once in a while, replaced outright.

"You do all that and then what?" Will asked. "At best, you've got something that only helps the few people who use the library. Might as well integrate the golf course."

"Why not the golf course? It's gradual, moderate change, just like you said."

Will shifted back in his chair and sighed. "I come out in favor of something like that and my opponent'll be thrilled. Just thrilled. Sure proof that I'm another ultra-intellectual parlor pink doing the bidding of the NAACP."

"I'm not affiliated with the NAACP."

"Doesn't matter."

"Some might view it favorably."

"Are you saying you think this would help me win?"

"No, I'm saying it's the right thing to do."

"Do what, exactly?"

"Make a statement. And if you win—"

"I'm running for Congress. In Washington. I'm not even sure what I *could* do—"

"Funding. Find more money for the libraries here, and they might well favor letting us in. If you make it clear they don't get one without the other."

"Plain old pork—"

"Who goes to libraries? Lot of well-mannered people, middle-class people, students. Enlightened folks. A lot of them embarrassed about our southern way of life. And a lot of them are quiet people. Readers. They like to stay home with their books, not make a big fuss because there's a couple of dark-skinned patrons in the building."

"I'll see what I can do."

"You'll see."

"I'd like to be able to promise."

"But you can't," Carter said. This might have been going too far, but part of the reason for it was Sabert's expression: as if there was more he wanted to say but didn't, as if he were weighted down by all that he wanted to say but couldn't. Carter wanted to nudge it out of him.

Will lit a cigarette. "What will you do if I don't help you?"

"I've been bringing this issue to the attention of some people, and I hope to have it before the City Council again before too long."

"Some people such as . . . ?"

"Such as various people." All right, he was bluffing, and Sabert knew it. But he was also in the right, and Sabert knew that. The young candidate leaned forward and put his elbows on his desk. "I can't do it now. But I'm glad you came to see me and I hope you will support me, and if I do win I will help you, only I can't make any kind of promise in public."

"What about in private?"

"I've said what I can say."

Eighteen

Nick called Andrea, and they endured about five minutes of stilted conversation. Jingles might have been whistled between statement and response. She said she was "fine." Nick was "pretty good." He'd been "meaning to call sooner." She'd been "busy too." Her voice low but not too low: something in it made him picture her smiling, but smiling out of pity.

It had been two and half weeks since they'd met, or re-met, at Gloria's. During that time Nick had been occupied with the Beverly Flintic article, though not literally working on it—stalling on it, rather, using work as an excuse for not doing other things but not working. He tossed his mail on the kitchen table, fished shorts out of the laundry basket to wear a second time. He went to get his teeth cleaned: a grandmother in rubber gloves savaged him with floss. At the office he read old magazines and created small sculptures out of tape and pen caps. He melded three unrelated rumors to make a column. He tried to knock out the Sabert obituary, which was by now seriously overdue, but got bogged down in the details of natural-gas legislation Sabert had passed in the early seventies.

At last he made the necessary calls to the Department of Human Needs and to a few of Flintic's colleagues and to Maria Galvan, east side über-activist, whose subsidized apartment he visited on an overcast afternoon two days before his deadline. She'd promised to round up several members of the Associated Citizens of Temple Heights, but when he arrived it was just her, in a tiny apartment with file boxes stacked high against cinderblock walls painted a ghastly yellow. There were lists of contact numbers and e-mail addresses typed out and inserted into binders, and carefully preserved newspaper clippings that she unfolded and handed to him like family heirlooms. The hermetic activist: Maria Galvan wasn't Nick's first. Hungry for justice, heavy with loss—loss of friends, of siblings and spouses who'd tired of the endless battles—they reeled off thirty-minute answers to simple questions and made Nick feel bad. No matter how sympathetic he was to Maria Galvan, he was pretty sure he would disappoint her in the end, by failing to see the situation as starkly, as urgently as she did.

The night after the missed deadline, Nick wrote the article. It was a long, slow night of red wine and salty snacks, of feeling oppressed by insect noises, of the usual crises of confidence, but he was able to borrow enough conviction from Maria Galvan, his uncle, and the vintners of Chile to make up for what he lacked in himself, and sometime between three and four in the morning he wrote the last paragraph and crawled to bed.

And after handing in the story he called Andrea Carter.

"Would you want to get dinner some night?" he asked after a few minutes of tortured back-and-forth.

"Okay. That would be fine."

He had a sinking feeling about the prospect of a date—he still thought about Liza all the time—but he'd asked, and Andrea had said yes, and he went ahead and scheduled a haircut.

A few years earlier he'd made the switch from barbershop to hair salon, a decision that had led to one winter of unfortunate blond highlights, to fancy shampoos, and to ritual pre-date visits to his haircut person (he would not call her his stylist), Shauna of the Products. She was a zaftig Michigander with a rabbity overbite and, on this occasion, a sort of Cubist hairdo that, like her prior coiffures, indicated too much downtime at the salon. Nick's relationship with Shauna in a sense paralleled his relationship with his mother—she thought he should be one way, he thought another— and he avoided thinking about whether he visited Shauna before first dates because he wanted to look good (when invariably she cut according to her own opinion, took off too much hair, and sent him away looking like a balding six-year-old) or whether there was some creepy Freudian prerogative at work.

Shauna, who kept up with the horoscopes, told Nick that it wouldn't be a great month for him romantically. "On the other hand, it's a good time to take a closer look at your finances," she said.

"What you just said is true of every month of my life," Nick said, viewing his new haircut in the mirror. "I look like a dork."

"You look like an adult, instead of that shaggy grad-student thing you had going on when you walked in here."

"I don't feel like an adult."

"That's your problem."

He was never satisfied with Shauna's haircuts but felt obliged to tip generously, as if that might make the date go better. He wondered whether he would get away with kissing Andrea. The vibe he got from her didn't invite kissing. Hers was a lonely vibe, one of the more dangerous vibes around. Nick would have to tread carefully. Whether or not he was able to work up a romantic interest, at a minimum he wanted to show her a good time. Whenever he met a newcomer to Waterloo, even one who'd already been in town for a year, he wanted the person to like the city, to see in it what he saw. Of course if the newcomer had been a hairy old man he might feel less invested in this than he did in the case of a pretty woman close to his own age, but when it came to Andrea, Nick wanted to jump on the welcome wagon. He wanted to take her out and show her around and let her see what Waterloo had to offer.

What *did* it have to offer? That was the problem; there wasn't much to see. The places and things Nick cared about were superficially unexceptional; either you liked them or you didn't. They were bars and streets and train tracks. They were dogs traipsing around the neighborhood, people picnicking in the backs of trucks, prickly pear cactus, yard art, purple neon, tortillas. You couldn't very well show a woman a tortilla and expect her to be impressed.

"You got your hair cut," Andrea said when she opened the door of her apartment. She had him wait while she put on a pair of dangly earrings, which he could see her doing through the open bedroom door—it for some reason pleased him to watch this— and when she came out she said, "It looks good. Your haircut." He would have liked to watch her put on earrings for a while longer, but didn't feel he could suggest anything like that. Her face didn't match his recollection of it: her neck was longer, maybe? Her nostrils more flared? Or maybe it was nothing in particular, only the discord between imagined and actual. Above one brow were two small darker patches of skin, like tears that had fallen in the wrong direction.

At the car, he opened the door for her and then hurriedly threw newspapers and a pair of sneakers from the passenger seat into the back. "Where are we going?" she asked.

"Uh-huh. That's correct."

She smiled. "We're going out to eat, right?"

They hadn't made a plan ahead of time. Nick asked her what she wanted to eat, worrying that her answer would belong to some cuisine not readily available in Waterloo, food from a more cosmopolitan city. He wished he'd remembered to take the smelly sneakers out of the car before leaving the house. She said she wasn't picky when it came to food. He took her to a restaurant serving "new American cuisine" that he'd been to once before.

"I noticed they did some editing to our story on the march,"

Nick said. He'd checked the paper the next day: there had been a big photo, paired with a short article by Andrea that did not resemble what they'd composed at Gloria's, even before they'd veered off into nonsense.

"Let's just say they weren't too thrilled."

"Did you get shit for it?"

"I got some, yeah."

"Sorry."

"Not your fault."

"I bet that doesn't happen to you very much. I bet you never get in trouble, do you?"

"I was always pretty well behaved," she admitted. "Shy. I didn't want to draw attention to myself. I don't think I've ever turned in something late before."

"Never?"

"Not unless there was some reason, like some late-breaking thing I had to put in at the last minute. I'd rather just do it on time."

"You've never turned something in late."

"Not really."

"We should celebrate, then. Your first time."

"What about you? What happened to that obituary you were going to write?"

"I had to finish this other piece on Beverly Flintic."

"I saw that," said Andrea.

Not *I liked that* or *It was good* but just: I saw that. In fact Nick had few illusions that his article had been much good. He'd managed to split the difference between the sort of toothless profile McNally might have wanted at the outset and something more substantial by focusing on one lousy bill. He'd laid out its flaws, with the help of Maria Galvan, asked Flintic about it, and quoted them both, thereby bringing the issue to the public's attention. If there was such a thing as public attention. Now that the story was written and published, though, he suspected his approach had been wrongheaded. What was one bill? It didn't seem to be going anywhere; maybe it had never been a serious bill at all. At the Capitol there were shadow bills and shell bills, chassis without engines, sham proposals the sole purpose of which was to distract attention away from the genuine ones. The reason Nick had taken Flintic's measure seriously was that she'd seemed to take it seriously—and so had Bones. A mistake, maybe.

At the restaurant, which had once been considered one of the better ones in Waterloo, before there were many nice restaurants, the waitress disappeared for the better part of an hour. This was Nick's first-ever date with a black woman. He tried not to think about the fact of its being his first date with a black woman, and so of course kept thinking about it. Meanwhile the conversation suffered, until they wandered onto the subject of their dads. That is to say, Nick started talking about his dad, *my dad the judge*. Nick had called him just last week. He'd called both his parents, as he tended to do when he was avoiding writing an article. The guilt of not completing an assignment merged in his bloodstream with the guilt of not having called them, so that he tried to shuck off one guilt by taking care of the other. His father always had some comic but also loaded story about the most outstanding loser (his word) to have appeared recently in his courtroom—and no matter how radically different from his own life was that of the Armenian pimp, or the hearing-impaired speed dealer, or the eighty-year-old tax cheat, Nick interpreted these stories as warnings. His dad had never fully recovered from Nick's dropping out of school and moving to the very backwater he'd escaped himself. For all the good-natured banter, Michael Lasseter feared his son was a hopeless case, Nick could tell. And though Nick sometimes wanted to scream—but, but, but! *I've got a job, I've got friends, I'm not in trouble, I've got a life*, et cetera—he couldn't, because he feared the same thing. He had courted failure and not even accomplished that. Lacking the guts to really hit bottom, he trailed slowly along through the murk like a squid or a shrimp.

Tongue loosened by wine, he managed to explain much of this

to Andrea before it sank in that he was, on a first date, telling her that he had failed at failing. "I don't know how I got off on this whole thing," he said finally. "What about your dad? I bet he's proud of you."

"He died when I was in college."

"Oh, I'm sorry," Nick said, feeling like an idiot.

"Before that he didn't know what to do with me," Andrea said. "Especially when I was in high school. A teenage girl. I don't think he'd ever really known one before, not well. He told a lot of stories on himself, and I used to hate it. One thing about losing him when I was nineteen: now I wish I knew those stories and I don't remember them very well. I didn't listen."

"No one listens when they're in high school," Nick said. If ever, he thought. "And it's hard to remember unless you write them down or tell them to somebody."

"I didn't do that."

"Maybe it's not too late."

She didn't respond.

The food came at last; it was lukewarm; the bar they went to afterward was too noisy. They still couldn't really get the talk rolling, but each long pause only spurred another attempt: they were sufficiently attracted, and sufficiently lonely, that instead of ending the date early with a polite peck and a halfhearted pledge to do it again, they drank too much, and then drank some more, and fumbled up the stairs to Andrea's apartment and ended up in Andrea's bed, naked and miserable.

"Sorry," Nick said.

"It's okay."

"I guess I had a little too much to drink."

"It's okay. Just relax."

"I am relaxed," he said moodily, flicking the condom onto the floor.

Maybe some old-fashioned sexual scruples would have saved

him from a regrettable situation, but that thought always came too late. Maybe his dick had scruples. Maybe that was the problem. "I guess I'd better go," he said after a while.

He expected some token invitation to stay, but none was extended. He didn't know whether they would so much as talk again, but he did kiss her goodbye, and she responded in kind. It felt like their first decent exchange since leaving the restaurant.

The Sabert obituary was now four weeks overdue. Though another editor would have let it slide, McNally did not. It had become a matter of principle, though what principle Nick wasn't sure. Trouble was, the longer the delay, the higher the bar. A weeks-late obituary had to justify itself, it had to be more than just a quick sketch. Nick felt obligated to illuminate the man's character through succinct but winning anecdotes, to render historical context with something beyond the usual fuzzy catchphrases (the "turbulent sixties," the "shadow of Vietnam")—but that meant additional research. Like a gerontological private investigator, he'd tracked down both the man's ex-wives; neither had understood why he was calling. Nick wasn't sure he understood it himself.

"I'm writing an obituary," he told Mrs. Delia Sabert Humphries, when he reached her at the Zanzibar Senior Community.

"Did he die again?" she asked, after a long pause.

If he could only write it—and there was absolutely no reason for not writing it, just sitting down and writing it.

Except: he had obituarist's block.

Instead of sitting down and writing, he contacted Professor Alan Loefler, a man Andrea had told Nick about, and though he, too, seemed confused as to why anyone would still be working on an obituary, he invited Nick to his office to have a look through what he called, in a languid voice, his voluminous files.

Then late one morning, Nick received a summons, the standard one—"You got a minute?"—but without its normal bounce and hopeful quality. As if McNally had a cold or a problem. He stepped into his boss's office and saw what the problem was: Beverly Flintic was sitting on McNally's couch. Because the couch was low and her legs were long, her knees stuck up in front of her and her narrow shins were poised underneath them like tools waiting to be used.

Nick hadn't planned on seeing her again. After he wrote about anything, he usually wished for that thing to disappear from his life, and usually that was what happened. He moved on; the people he wrote about moved on. Never had one of them appeared a week later in his boss's office looking pissed and holding a copy of the story in two taut hands. Nick could see that parts of the text had been underlined and circled; comments had been scrawled in the margins. Beverly Flintic had come to confront him. Before she said one word he was flooded with remorse.

"Hello," he said finally. This greeting was too short; he wanted to add a "Welcome" or a "How are you?" but the customary lubricants were not going to fly, he could tell. He had an urge to introduce himself. To pretend they'd never met before.

Her voice was not so much angry as it was airless. She skipped hello. "I came to talk with you about this article which . . . you wrote," Beverly said.

Maybe she had come to get him fired. That couldn't be too hard; whatever points Nick had racked up with McNally would be wiped out if she discredited the article. There would be no reason not to fire him. Nick realized that he did not want to be fired.

"Really, I'm curious," she said. "Were you planning this to be a hit job from the beginning? I don't understand why you even came to interview me. I gave you information, important facts that you didn't put in the article, and then you write this story that makes it sound like I'm scheming to take over half the city. You're attributing things to me that I'm not responsible for . . . and it is just a bunch of slop!" She emphasized her last words by hitting the newspaper with the back of her hand.

McNally exhaled pointedly. "Assemblywoman Flintic, we appreciate you coming down here and letting us know your concerns. I think it would help if you were a bit more specific?"

"I wasn't planning on coming over here, if you want to know the truth. I was going to have my office send a letter, but then I read this thing over again this morning, and—it's just dishonest. He went out of his way to try to make me look stupid."

"Maybe some specific parts of the article."

"There are all these so-called critics that he doesn't even identify. Who are these people?"

"If a source requests anonymity, we generally try to honor that request," McNally said.

"So if everyone wants to be anonymous, they're just anonymous? Don't I get to at least respond to them? Wouldn't it be fair to mention that I met with Maria Galvan twice, and tried to bring her into the process? Look, this bill came out of Human Needs and you hardly even mention the department. Instead it's my plan for a corporate takeover of east Waterloo. Let me ask you this. Have you spent any real time over there? Even if there was a plan to entirely privatize a neighborhood, and that's a big oversimplification of what they actually want to do, even if it was that, wouldn't that be better than nothing at all?

"I also looked into the part about eminent domain," she continued, "because I had overlooked it, and I'm seeing if I can get an amendment on that. I can't just snap my fingers and make it happen, okay, but I'm doing what I can, and you never followed up on it. And then there's the fact that your uncle the lobbyist has it in for me because I won't give him his pipeline subsidy."

Nick hadn't known that Bones was lobbying her. He should have guessed, though. Bones was a lobbyist. The woman was right: he'd been careless; also naïve.

"Before Nick came in, you mentioned there were some factual errors?" McNally said. It was surprising, to say the least, the way the man was going to bat for him.

"For example," she said, scanning the marked-up copy of the

article, "he wrote that I needed six votes to get that bill out of committee, when in fact I only needed five."

"I see. Nick?"

"That's true," Nick said. "I got it wrong."

"We'll run a correction," McNally said. "Were there any other factual errors?"

"The whole thing's an error, in my opinion. But I can see I'm just wasting my time here." She stared at Nick. He did his best to withstand it. A tendril of her hair had fallen out of her helmet, and it hung forlornly, like a lamp pull, in front of her ear. Her lipstick was bitten off. Her face was wilting.

"I'm sorry you thought the piece was one-sided," he said. "I tried to be fair." He said it but wasn't so sure.

She stood and marched out of the room, letting the copy of his article fall on the ground next to the trash can.

Once she was gone, Nick fully expected the ass-chewing to commence. McNally was frowning. All Nick could hope for was a quick trial, a mild sentence (anything other than immediate termination seemed merciful enough), and a long, wet lunch after it was over.

"Geez," McNally said. Then he sighed; it was his second or third sigh since Nick had entered the office. "Well, Nick—" he began.

"Well." McNally balled his hands together and rested his head against them. "Well."

"I'm sorry about that—"

"That woman was totally out of line," McNally said.

"She was upset—"

"Thinks she can just march in here and bitch and whine. Because she's so important. Jesus, what is it with women these days?"

It wasn't clear to Nick what McNally was talking about. "I'm not sure."

"You know what my wife said to me this morning?"

"What?"

"I couldn't tell you. I couldn't even give you the general idea."

"Really."

"She's been studying Portuguese. She bought these tapes to listen to in the car." He looked up. "Why Portuguese?"

Nick shook his head.

"So how's that obituary coming along?" McNally asked.

"It's coming," Nick said.

Afterward Nick felt uneasy. The fact that McNally hadn't yelled at him was somehow disappointing, even worrisome. Unsettled, he resolved to tackle his desk. He skimmed a bunch of papers off the top of the Pile and started putting them in files or in the recycle bin. After ten or so minutes of this the phone rang.

"Save the Sunset party, two weeks from Friday," Roger said when Nick picked up.

"Okay."

"Have you started your article yet?"

"Not in so many words."

"Have you talked to your boss about it?"

Nick didn't answer.

"What the hell is wrong with you?"

Nick still didn't answer.

"Is there something you're not telling me, because there's something I'm not getting here, and that's why you can't do me this one favor. Frankly, it doesn't seem that hard. You work at a newspaper. This is a story you could easily do."

"I know."

"Do you have something personal against doing it?"

"No, I've been meaning to—"

"Meaning to is nice, but this thing is in two weeks, which means the story ought to go in the paper next week or the week after, right? I'm calling to see if there's any chance you might get off your ass between now and then?"

"Quit yelling at me."

"I will not quit yelling at you. I'm calling to yell at you. You need to be yelled at."

"Yeah, but—"

"But what?"

"I'll see what I can do."

"You've said that before," Roger said and hung up.

Nineteen

As the law required, the Hardaway campaign had pitched its headquarters well away from his state office, in a rented suite downtown. Not a long walk from the Capitol, but Beverly took her car. Her phone had been quiet the past few days: Mark hadn't called. He'd said they should talk, but he never had called. She'd waited; then yesterday she'd left a message for him. Today she'd tried Yates, who'd been short with her. "Could you come down to headquarters," he'd said—not asked.

"You mean now?"

"It's as good a time as any."

The Taurus had balked twice before starting.

When she arrived at headquarters everyone was already shouting, or at least talking at top volume. Her office, her car, the elevator, all had been silent, and she flinched at the noise, as if everyone were shouting at her. The barren rooms were hectic with people, the riot of their voices competing with ringing phones, a radio, and a television turned to a cable news station. One old woman, a volunteer having second thoughts maybe, had clamped her hands over her ears and was looking around the place in wonderment. Telephone cords crisscrossed the carpet, some at ground level and some a few inches off it, like trip wires. Every flat surface was encumbered with file boxes and pizza boxes and soda cans. There weren't many lamps, and so the office was bright by the windows and desks, dim elsewhere. Maps and Hardaway signs had been taped to the walls, next to dry-erase boards colored with faded words, traces of abandoned slogans that had been wiped away with paper towels. A clock on the wall was set five minutes ahead.

Then she saw Mark, and she bit her lip to keep from smiling. He was stationed in front of a music stand. On the other side of the stand were a man and woman in matching ball caps.

He looked up. "Beverly!" he called out. She smiled in spite of herself. "Hey, you should meet my mom," he said, pointing at the woman with her hands over her ears. The woman smiled weakly, and Beverly nodded at her. I can't meet your *mom*, she thought. Honestly.

He studied a sheet of paper on the music stand. Across the room, Carson Yates sat at a desk, talking on the phone. Beverly shifted her weight and knotted her hands together, wishing Yates might at least wave her inside.

Yates's authority was palpable, though it had no obvious source. Not his voice: his doughy cheeks enclosed his mouth like a pair of parentheses, and everything he said had the flavor of an aside. But for his thinning hair, which had a loose relationship to his head, ground cover rather than grass, Yates looked like a schoolboy on the verge of puberty, forever smirking about something he hadn't known the day before. He made no effort to counter his boyishness. He wore round-rimmed glasses and short-sleeved oxford shirts, and drank root beer by the liter.

It was Yates who'd persuaded her to run for the Assembly, three and a half years ago. At the time, she'd been on the school board—at the time, that was the extent of her political ambition—and working as a litigator with Lyman, Ross. Then one inconspicuous day she'd taken a call from Carson Yates. He was a political consultant, he said. He wanted to talk to her. Could he take her to lunch?

A bizarre invitation, but she'd accepted it. At a strip-mall Thai restaurant he'd produced charts that showed (he said) that someone like her had a strong shot at the State Assembly. Someone like me? He told her she had name recognition and "the right factors." She thought he was joking. He told her about the new district, the open field. Eight months later she'd filed as a candidate. Her campaign manager, her direct-mail guys, her polling firm had all been recommended by Yates, but after that lunch she'd rarely seen him in person. Sometimes he sent her e-mails, and occasionally he called to question her vote—on bills she'd believed unimportant if not silly, like the one that would have barred HIV-positive adults from becoming foster parents. There was already a shortage of foster parents. Beverly had voted against it, though the conservative caucus had endorsed the bill.

The woman in the ball cap shut off the radio, muted the television, and returned to her spot. The shouting abated. Mrs. Hardaway removed her hands from over her ears. Mark cleared his throat, and started to read slowly from the papers in front of him.

"One hundred years later, the life of the Negro is still sadly crippled by the manacles of segregation and the chains of discrimination," he read aloud.

"One hundred years later, the Negro lives . . ." he continued, until the same woman—fortyish, with protruding hips and tiny feet and tough skin—said "Stop!" She jabbed a pencil into the air and barked, "What do you do after you finish a sentence?"

"I pause," Mark said.

"You pause for how long?"

"Two potato."

"That's right, let me hear you count it out loud."

"One potato, two potato." The woman kept time with her pencil, lunging forward to beat it against the music stand.

"You should be counting that after every period," she said. "Okay, let's keep practicing."

"Just a minute." Mark arranged the papers, threw back his shoulders, and gazed piercingly out into his imaginary audience.

"Good, good," the woman purred.

There was another clock on the shelves behind him, not synchronized to the clock on the wall. On the shelf it was two minutes earlier than on the wall. Mark started to speak again. "I say to you today, my friends, that in spite of the difficulties and frustrations of the moment, I still have a dream. One potato, two potato—*shoot*! Sorry."

"That's all right, you can count it out loud for now if you want. Keep going."

"It is a dream deeply rooted in the American dream. One potato, two potato. I have a dream that one day this nation will rise up and live out the true meaning of its creed . . ."

A phone rang. Hardaway kept going.

"Let freedom ring from the heightening Alleghenies of Pennsylvania! One potato, two potato, three po—uh." He winced.

"Two is enough. Two potato."

Beverly backed up against the wall. The man she'd been sleeping with—there could be no denying it—was a numbskull, and yet she already missed him.

Yates hung up and folded his arms over his chest. He didn't greet her as she approached, just started talking. "He may not sound perfect right now, but these people know what they're doing. Don't you, Roxanne?"

The speech coach hushed him. They went from potato to protein: she gave Mark a can of beef stew and instructed him to read the ingredients off the label as if he were giving a speech to a group of donors in a large city. Seasoned cooked beef, artificial grill flavor—short phrases were his forte, and he was really getting into it now, his jaw sweeping forward with each meaty particular.

Yates pounced to his feet and signaled to Beverly to follow him to the window. In the direct light, his head seemed not so much round as amorphous, a blob against the blue sky behind him. Beverly, who was taller than he was, knocked her knees to better hear whatever it was he hadn't yet said.

"The week after next is the Daughters of the Star of Freedom banquet. He's going to be there giving a speech."

"What day? Should I be there?"

Yates shook his head. "Not this one."

"Okay." She wouldn't have cared one way or the other, but she was bothered by the way Yates was shaking his head.

"It'll just be him and possibly Lynette," he said.

Beverly looked over at Mark. Surely he wouldn't have told Yates.

"We have to shore things up. Make it look like they're a strong couple." It was as if, having caught on to exactly what Beverly was worried about, he was trying to assure her he didn't know anything.

Maybe he didn't. "Whatever you need me to do," she said.

Maybe he did. "Or refrain from doing." His watery eyes fixed on hers. "Stay out of the papers."

"You mean that *Weekly* thing? The sooner forgotten, the better."

"I'm sure it has been forgotten, by most people."

"What do you mean?"

"Next time, if you're going to introduce a bill, maybe you should read it first."

Just then Hardaway came bounding over, looking for a moment as if he might kiss Beverly—he stood close enough, with his hands behind his back, chest out, *beaming* for chrissakes. So happy! Maybe it was just his happiness that Beverly had fallen for. "Hi," he said, happily. "How was I doing?"

"Great," Beverly said. "Carson was just explaining why I shouldn't come to your event next week."

"I'm sorry, darlin'," Hardaway stuttered. "You'll come to the next one, won't you?"

One of the young minions broke in. "Commissioner, you have a phone call." Hardaway stepped backward and said, "We'll talk soon, okay?"

He didn't wait for her response. What did soon mean? She was ashamed, unexpectedly and all at once. Every last shred of misgiving she'd been trying not to feel—all the doubts surrounding not just the sneaking around to hotels but her very foray into politics, this whole stilted performance—now coursed through her.

Yates took her limp arm, and she let him lead her toward the door, as if she'd made a scene and were now being escorted out of the building. And on to the seamstress who would sew a big scarlet A to her rayon blouse.

"I can still amend the bill. I could take out eminent domain," she said.

"You know, if you're not on somebody's side, you end up on nobody's side." Yates's tone was almost paternal. He led her to the elevators and then stopped, still grasping her arm. Go ahead, she thought, start twisting. "If necessary we'll find another person who can do this bill for us," Yates said. "Bargeron's been a strong supporter."

Louis Bargeron was the CEO of Heritage. The one time they'd met, he'd been dismissive. A few adjustments might mollify the concerns of local residents, she'd begun, but Bargeron had cut her off, insisting it was too late for that. "If you were in business, you'd understand there's constraints you have to recognize in order to see a real profit," he'd said. She'd pointed out that the reason he was in her office, the reason his project required a bill at all, was so that it could receive exemptions designed to help him make a profit.

"Too-*chay*," he'd said. "That's my point. There hasn't been much profit in the history of the east side, has there?" He was a tall man, sunburnt, with an evangelical sweep of snow-white hair and an open collar. "This project is going to help those people over there, whether they realize it or not."

Then he asked, "You fly on planes much?"

"Some."

"I do some of my best customer research on the airplane. Could I afford to sit in first class? You bet. Hell, I could buy my own plane if I wanted. But I fly coach every time. I get great responses from people who I just happen to end up sitting next to, and you know, they are just average ordinary people who are giving me their honest opinion. So, it's great. I say this because you're in politics, you're in a situation where you're interacting with the public, am I right? You want to know what they are thinking, get on an airplane. That's where they are." He pointed straight toward the ceiling. "They are flying on airplanes."

Beverly looked up at the ceiling and then back at Bargeron. "Okay," she said. "And?"

"And I know what people want. They believe in individualism. They want private, business-oriented solutions to problems such as the decay of our cities. At heart, I'm a philanthropist. But I'm also a businessman. This project is going to be good for the east side, and it's good business."

"I'd like to see it work," Beverly said. "Why don't you have a meeting with some of the residents, and see if you can't get the kinks ironed out."

"We're past that stage. It's already been focus-grouped."

"In that case, I'm not sure what more I can do."

"In that case," Bargeron spat, suddenly agitated, "I'm not sure I can be of help next election." Then he'd thrust his sizable self up from his chair and hightailed out of the room, as if about to burst into sobs.

Now Yates was making that same point, with even less subtlety. "In case it hasn't occurred to you," he said, "support from a man like Bargeron is probably more important than the support of a few disgruntled welfare freeloaders in your district." When she didn't respond, he added, "In fact, it is definitely more important." He didn't twist, but he did squeeze, his chunky fingers pressing just above her elbow. "I suggest you do some thinking about this."

The elevator arrived. "Do some thinking?"

"Frankly, we were hoping you would be more of a team player. There've been other bills."

"What do you mean 'other bills'?"

"There was the pipeline thing, and abortion waiting periods, and the ban on foster parents with AIDS"—three bills on which she'd voted contrary to the conservative caucus's recommended position. Three negligible bills. "What I told Bargeron was that sometimes an investment just doesn't pan out."

She wanted to ask him what he meant by that, but she was on the elevator and the doors were closing, and anyhow, she knew what he meant.

Every part of the process had been too hard. From day one. The initial leg of her campaign had been conducted from her house, where she'd had a second phone line installed for the purpose of begging— hello my name is, this is, I'd like to introduce myself, my name is, and the reason I'm calling today, I'd like to talk to you about, my name is Beverly, Beverly Flintic, my name is, I'd like to talk to you, I need your help, I'm asking for your help, Beverly, I'm a fiscal conservative, *my name is Beverly and I am a fiscal conservative,* can you pledge one thousand today, could you help me out, for Beverly Flintic, hello, hello, and how are things over at M—— Industries, hello, good, nice to talk to you, my name is Beverly FLINTIC, *so pay up, buster,* that's F-L-I-N-T-I-C. Her ear warm and tingly, her elbow on the kitchen table, her head propped up by a telephone handset, her back straight, then curved, then bent and stiffening. Having discontinued her own income in order to ask other people for their money. Having neglected her own family to talk about strengthening families. Having—what had she done, anyway? A hundred events, a thousand meetings, and what had she done?

"Sweetheart?"

She almost didn't recognize Owen's voice on the phone, stretching itself over a word he seldom used. "What's the matter?"

"Well. There's good news and bad news."

He paused. Both varieties of news were slow to emerge. The good news: a company called Vigilient had offered him contract work. Short-term, but maybe it would lead to more . . . but who knows . . . but the thing is . . . sweetheart . . .

"The thing is what?"

"I have to start tonight." Something about a system crash, a reinstall, a Monday deadline, working around the clock until then. "I know I promised to take Jamie and Jonas . . ."

"Oh no." No no no.

"It's only a few hours."

"I'll tell them the show is canceled."

"You drive them down, you stand there for a while, you leave. What's the worst that could happen?"

Jamie had outfitted himself for Tantrum in a long black T-shirt with an un-smiley face on it, baggy shorts, and high-top sneakers with the untied laces tucked inside the uppers. A looped metal chain dangled from his pocket. His hair was divided into sticky spikes, and it smelled of eggs. *What's the worst that could happen?* Forget *worst*, Beverly thought. Let's talk about the fact that our son has put tomorrow morning's breakfast in his hair.

In her purse: a box of earplugs, a travel pack of Kleenex, a bottle of Motrin, a pack of spearmint gum—but equipment couldn't save her. She missed the days when it could, the hyphen-strewn days of Handi-Wipes and Capri-Suns and Band-Aids.

And the Taurus was small comfort now. Jamie and Jonas spent the ride downtown discussing a couple of girls named Jessicaca and Barfera. Beverly tuned out for a while, then heard Jamie say, "That's because she has maggots flying out of her butt."

"*James Flintic.* Keep it up and I'm turning this car around."

"Keep what up?"

"And we will go straight home."

"We'd have to drop Jonas off first."

"I mean it."

They parked in an unattended lot. At the pay box Beverly realized she didn't have any small bills and cursed under her breath. Jamie and Jonas snickered. "You didn't hear that," she said, wedging a twenty into the slot.

"Yes we did."

"What are you both going to do once we get there?"

"Stay close to where you are," Jamie said. "But—"

"Correct."

"What if you have to go to the bathroom?" He giggled, and Jonas cupped his hand over his mouth.

The club was on a street she'd driven on during the day but never at night. The sidewalks were full of young people and there was a smell in the air like gasoline and old lemons. Beverly was not a night person, much less a nightclub person. You couldn't have paid her to wear one of these skimpy getups all the girls out here were wearing—how old were they? A lot of them seemed very young—and drunk, though it wasn't yet nine o'clock, on a Tuesday night. They were shouting and hooting, bumping purposely into one another. Even the young men wore clothes that were too small. The girls were wearing too-small clothes that looked new and the guys were wearing too-small clothes that looked like they'd come from a church rummage sale.

What she did not see on this street were junior high kids or their moms.

This was Owen's fault. She settled her hand down on Jamie's gunky head; he jerked it away. She would've liked to have the boys on leashes. For that matter she would have liked to walk the two of them directly back to the car. Sorry, boys. Change of plans. A black man with an odd gait limped toward them carrying a long piece of metal. Beverly steered the boys toward the outer edge of the sidewalk, before she saw that the thing the man was carrying was a microphone pole.

They entered the club, and she held her breath. A man at the door stamped some sort of inky hemorrhage on the back of her hand. A minute later, a girl spilled beer on Beverly's new white canvas sneakers. Another drunk girl: "Sorry!" she called as she sauntered away. On the walls were paintings of ghoulish figures, and though the actual people in the room were not so gaunt and goth-looking, the lights tinted their skin purple and put socket shadows under their eyes that were very unflattering. They all looked older than sixth graders.

The room was gauzy with cigarette smoke. Beverly had smoked in college and law school and then had cut back—but picked it up again whenever she'd had to make a court appearance. Now she only snuck out for a cigarette every once in a while, and never in front of Jamie. Now all this smoke hurt her eyes. The boys wriggled toward the stage. She tried to follow but was uncomfortable in the dense pack toward the front. People jostled around her as if she weren't a person. She was dizzy. Her toes squished in her wet socks. Her new sneakers, soaked.

Times she had cried in public: in high school, after rear-ending a priest in a Ford Falcon—she'd been driving her father's car, a Thunderbird—and after her team lost the district championship in volleyball. At a party in college she hadn't wanted to go to—her first and last experience with tequila. The evening Owen proposed to her, after a baseball game. The day Chet Baker died and they played "My Funny Valentine" on the radio while she waited to find out whether she was pregnant. She'd cried in spite of, or maybe even because of, the fact that Chet Baker hadn't been such a nice person, apparently.

She held it in. Just because she was in a place she didn't want to be and her sneakers were wet, that was no reason to cry. The band had taken the stage, three boys and a girl, fiddling with their instruments. Beverly swallowed a couple of times and watched the girl watch her fingers on a guitar. She remembered Carson Yates saying *If you're not on somebody's side, you end up on nobody's side*—and tears came defiantly to her eyes. She exhaled and rubbed them off and looked to make sure she could see the boys. The one thing she could see was Jamie's hair. She was on nobody's side. And this was her punishment.

The band started playing, terribly. There was nothing like a melody, only guitar noise and shouting. Even with earplugs it was awful. She wanted to call Owen, hold up the phone so that he could hear it. She half expected Jamie and Jonas to come running back to her, out of the crowd, ready to go, for who could like this so-called music? But they weren't going anywhere. Jamie's hair bobbed in and out of view.

As Jamie had foreseen, she had to use the restroom. She struggled in the direction of the boys, to tell them, and then gave up— they weren't going anywhere. She fled to the bathroom, colliding with yet another drunk girl on the way in.

"Watch *out*," the girl said.

She walked head down into a stall where she sat for a long time, blowing her nose, collecting herself. When she came back out she checked again for Jamie's hair, and then made her way to the bar to get water for herself and the boys. The bartenders didn't notice her. Bottles of beer were dispensed to either side, while she held out a ten-dollar bill and craned her head around and back, an eye on the boys. When at last she was able to relay her order of three waters, the bartender, a chesty young woman with an earring in her nose, said it was three dollars apiece, and then she said something Beverly couldn't make out, pointing to an orange jug down at the other end of the bar. There was glitter in her cleavage. Beverly, confused, handed over her ten dollars and then pushed her way to the jug and poured three cups of water. What a rip-off. Was the bartender calling after her? Or calling her a name perhaps? Beverly spilled half the water as she squeezed back to where she thought the boys were.

They weren't there. Don't panic, she told herself. They are not gone. They are here in this club. She shoved her way around the room, more aggressively this time, crushing a cup in her hand. She turned onto a ramp that led outside—could they be outside? She didn't see them among the pockets of kids standing around the yard.

"There you are." It was the bartender, holding three bottles of water.

"Oh," Beverly said, only now understanding that this was the kind of water she'd bought.

"You paid for this and then walked off," the bartender began, but then stopped. "Are you all right?"

"I'm here with my son and his friend. Two boys. Have you seen two boys?" The yard was full of teenage boys. "Younger boys."

"God, my mom never would have taken me to something like this." Beverly was about to explain that she herself never would have done it, when the girl added, "That is so cool of you. Isn't this band the worst?"

"I was hoping I might understand the music, but"—and here Beverly's voice caught—"I don't get it at all."

"Oh, hey," the girl said, sympathetically. At this Beverly started to weep. "Hey."

"And now I don't even know where they are."

"I'm sure they didn't leave. I'll help you find them. Remember, you are getting big mom points for this."

That was the whole problem, Beverly thought. Points. Why should she be trying to get points? What happened to rules? "This isn't for kids his age."

"What do they look like?"

Two small, chubby figures, one of them with pointy hair, appeared at the top of the ramp.

"Mom?" Jamie said. He was directly underneath a floodlight attached to the side of the building, and there was a glow around him. He held his arms rigid against his sides. "Where did you *go*?"

For a moment she thought he would run down the ramp and throw himself on her. She would have welcomed it. "I'm right here," she said, taking out a Kleenex and blowing her nose.

"How can we stay by you if you go somewhere else?"

"I was looking for you two."

"We were looking for you."

"Hey, I don't think your mom's feeling so hot," the bartender said.

"Who are you?"

"I'm Evie," she said. She was still holding the bottles of water, and now she offered two of them to the boys. "I think these are for you." She wasn't much taller than Jamie. He looked at her in the way he'd once looked at the costumed characters at Disneyland. "So, do you guys like the band?" Jamie and Jonas nodded silently. "Were they awesome? Now that you got to see them, I think it's time to take your mom home."

"She's not my mom," Jonas said.

"Okay," Jamie said, looking down at his bottle of water and then back at Evie.

Twenty

In Professor Alan Loefler's office, Nick was unaccountably nervous. Loefler might as well have been his junior high school principal, dispensing with the usual preliminaries before removing the paddle from its hook on the wall and getting down to business. As he described the contents of his voluminous files, Nick heard the particulars of an indictment. His right foot raced like a heart. His underarms went swampy. He stared at a photograph of Loefler in a French's-yellow raincoat with his arm around another man. Gay men sometimes made him self-conscious, but this was different—it wasn't Loefler. Not the way he bit his lip between sentences, which because of his full mustache and beard made it look as if the bottom of his face were one continuous muff. Not Loefler's shirt, its fabric poxed with tiny polka dots. Not the overreaching ivy on the windowsill or the stack of progressive-rock CDs next to a small round boom box.

It was as if he'd at last been arrested. As opposed to merely gone off track: there was no track in sight. He had taken a few tentative steps toward the semblance of a track, by completing a feature story and taking out a woman who wasn't Liza. But he'd done very poorly at both. The published article had been met with silence—no one had called to compliment or e-mailed a comment until Beverly Flintic herself had come barreling into the office. And after that

Nick had reluctantly read back through the piece, with growing disgust at his lame attempts at wit—the bad jokes shamed him even more than the sloppy reporting. He'd set it aside before he reached the end.

And he was trying not to think about Andrea, about that whole forlorn evening, though the memory of it dogged him. How she'd opened her legs as he crawled clumsily over her, looking down for a moment at himself and perceiving the dark shape of her thigh turned outward, resigned. The uneasiness of her smile. Pushing against her and failing, sorry, wait, ah, there, no, sorry . . . failing, failing. But along with the humiliation there was the memory of her body—he wanted another chance. Ha. As if she would be interested in that.

He had always been slow. From junior high on, everything he did, he'd begun at a measured pace and then decelerated as time wore on. "You started out the season strong, Lasseter," Coach Veal, the junior varsity soccer coach, had told him once, hovering right behind him. "But lately, I've noticed you're always the last one to practice." There were times when Nick still felt that hand on his shoulder, that deep voice resounding in his ear.

He thought of how he'd waited months after his sixteenth birthday to get a driver's license, how he'd worn that really awful tie to school sometimes (a skinny, solid black tie), how year after year he'd kept on going to summer camp, reupping for Counselor in Training and Junior Counselor summers even after most of his camp friends had moved on to jobs or summer school or chasing girls at the beach. How he hadn't even gone out with a girl until senior year of high school, and that after she asked him.

"When I started this project, I wasn't so sure about it," Loefler was saying, "but since then I've really become engrossed." He emphasized the word *engrossed*. "There's tons and tons of great stuff; I don't know where to begin. Do you have any particular time period you're focusing on?"

"I'm not so sure what I'm focusing on."

"Oh. Well, I can relate."

One look at Loefler, who was short and bearded, balding on top, spreading elsewhere, and spattered with polka dots, was enough to confirm that he spoke the truth, that he was no stranger to disorientation. "I guess all I really need is a few things I can quote from," Nick said.

The professor gave him a quizzical once-over and then started to pull pages from folders. In the general silence, the rustle of fingers on old paper made Nick's feet and hands itch. A few sheets from this one, a few from that one: soon there was a binder's worth on the desk. A pink Mardi Gras necklace hung from one of the drawer pulls. "I'll be right back," Loefler said. Alone in the room, Nick stared out the window, trying to figure out when was the last time he'd been engrossed. He wished he could ask this man how it had happened. He thought of Andrea again, and reddened. Loefler returned holding a stack of Xeroxes and handed them to Nick. "Why don't you start with these," he said, "and then call me if you have questions or something in particular you want to go into depth on. Would that be all right? Do feel free to call me."

A nice person; Nick was surrounded by nice people. It was upsetting. He thanked the professor and left, and read the first page in the elevator, part of an interview Sabert had done in 1959 with a weekly paper that had long since folded, the *Independent*. Asked to offer his observations about the workings of Congress, Sabert had said, "It is an institution that attracts good men and some less good, all of us burdened with a noble ideal. We do struggle with it. We manage as best we know how. Sometimes we fail, but the struggle has merit nonetheless."

You just couldn't *talk* like that anymore. You didn't have noble ideals. You had a Daihatsu. You had a Fender Stratocaster that hadn't been tuned in two years and an Emerson TV-VCR unit and a Sony stereo. You had trouble sleeping. You had aches: head, back, internal organs. You had night sweats, and now, it seemed, day sweats as well.

On his sweaty way back to the office he drove by Liza's apartment, a detour of several miles. In the middle of the afternoon Liza would not be home. Several hours yet before she left work, and then there might be some sort of attorneyish fraternizing, a lawyer happy hour or a lawyer spinning class, after which she would stop by the upmarket market and pick a few things out of the prepared-foods case and then, at eight or nine, arrive back at the apartment, where she and Miles would eat already-grilled salmon and already-roasted vegetables and watch television together.

Later that night he thought to call Andrea but dialed Liza's number instead. She answered after five rings, her voice sleepy and irritated, and he hung up.

id you call the house last night and then hang up?" It was Liza. Nick was at work, or so they called the place even on those somnolent mornings—the week's issue had been put to bed the night before—when nobody was turning in much of a performance. While cleaning out a closet at home, Trixie had found an old Nerf Velcro dart set and had brought it to work to make sure her soon-to-be ex wouldn't get it, and now members of the editorial and art departments were marveling over it as if it were a priceless artifact. Someone had brought in pastries, and there were trails of crumbs and sugar winding across the floor. Even the fish on Nick's screen saver seemed less busy than usual.

The phone's ring had startled him. Liza sounded cranky.

"I dialed your number by mistake," Nick said. "Sorry."

"Did you drive to my place yesterday afternoon and then sit there in your car?"

"Why would I do that?"

"Miles was home. He said he saw you lurking."

"Miles is wrong. I wasn't lurking."

"I think we need to talk," Liza said wearily.

"If you think I'm stalking you, I'm not."

"I don't think you're stalking me. I'd just like to talk to you."

"Talk away."

"In person."

"You have another big announcement for me? Are you pregnant or something?"

Silence.

"*Are* you?"

"No. Jesus. Will you be home tonight?"

"I might be, I don't know," Nick said.

"I might stop by."

"All right."

She might stop by. The day contained all too many hours. He worked on cleaning his desk for a while, read an online report about an emerging human rights situation in Africa, and then gave the Nerf darts a try. On his first effort, the dart overshot the target and hit the stomach of a pudgy lady who'd stopped in the office to ask for directions.

Midday, he dawdled at the sandwich shop. When Trixie caught him returning to the office, she peered over top of his cubicle. "Long lunch," she said.

"We're all going to die someday, Trix. I intend to enjoy my lunches while I still can."

He spent the afternoon in that same spirit of resolute joie de vivre, and went home exactly at five, so as not to miss Liza. He waited inside, with the newspaper, hoping it would be less obvious he'd been waiting than if he sat on the porch. When he heard footsteps he sprang up.

Only it wasn't Liza, it was Andrea. She was standing on the porch, back to the door, looking around as if she'd misplaced something. He opened the door. "Hi," he said, and in one continuous motion she spun around and stuck out her hand. He took it, and they moved their clasped hands back and forth in a semi–soul brother way, which was embarrassing.

"Is this your watch? I found it this morning under the bed." She hiccupped on "bed." She said she'd called and got no answer, "but I thought I'd swing by and drop this off . . ."

Figuring he wouldn't be there. "How did you know where I live?"

"Phone book. I'm sorry to just show up like this, I didn't think—"

"No, no, I'm glad you're here." It was the truth. "Do you want to come in?"

"How long have you lived here?" Andrea asked as Nick held the door for her. The sight of his own living room appalled him. The inside wasn't nice. It needed painting. It needed furniture. He looked at his old James Brown poster, ripped and curling at the edges, and wondered how it was that he still Scotch-taped things to the walls. The thought of his mildewed bathroom made him hope that Andrea wasn't one of those women who had to go to the bathroom all the time. How had he not seen all this squalor before? But then again he had seen it before, whenever a woman came over for the first time.

"Five years," Nick confessed. "I'd like to fix it up some." A half-truth: he wished for it to be fixed up.

"You own this house?"

"Rent."

"Still, five years, that's impressive."

"It is? Are you impressed?"

"I've never lived in a house for that long," she said. "Or a city, since I was a kid."

Nick offered her a beer, and she said ice water would be great. He thought the better of having her stick around for a beverage of any kind, only it was too late.

"Or we could go somewhere else?" he asked.

"This is fine."

They sat on the front-porch sofa. He stared at her feet. She was wearing that kind of rope-soled shoe, Liza had taught him the name: espadrille. These were tan and tied at the ankle, in generous bows that were Andrea's only adornment; otherwise she wore a plain white shirt and short black pants and no jewelry. The bows seemed ornate by contrast; they made Nick want to see her bare feet. He supposed by now it had become obvious that he was staring at them.

"How's work?" he asked.

"They're talking about having me do more politics. They need another person now that the campaigns are gearing up."

"Sorry to hear it."

"Why?"

"It's such a pain in the ass to cover those people. All that ego, and not much happens that's interesting, not that you can print, anyway."

Andrea seemed to consider this and then reject it. "Doesn't seem so bad to me."

"It's torture."

She smirked. "Why is it torture?"

"It just is."

She started to take a sip of her water, but the ice had stuck to-gether and fell in a clump toward her lips, while water streamed down her chin and onto her shirt. She looked over at Nick and wiped her smiling mouth with her hand. "Uh-oh," she said. Nick was trying not to look at her wet shirt, but he peeked in spite of himself.

Then came the question he'd been dreading. "Can I use your bathroom?" she asked.

"Do you have to?"

"What?"

"Never mind," he said. "It's the second door on your right." Nick cast a limp arm toward the inside of the house. "It's, um . . . just try not to inhale while you're in there."

She went in, and seconds later a car pulled up to the curb, a sil-ver Jetta. Liza's car. Indeed she was the driver, and now the parker, bringing the car to rest antiparallel to the direction of traffic, so that the driver's door opened onto the curb. It was as if a movie star had taught her to exit vehicles, the way she swung her legs out, paused, and then stood. Even in flip-flops she walked as if on red carpet.

But she seemed in no mood for smiling or waving. She barely looked at Nick. Fatigue or maybe sadness had deformed the regions around her eyes, and although she almost never went out in public without having taken care with her appearance, at present her hair was all tangled, and she was wearing an old ratty black T-shirt that Nick recognized as once having belonged to him. He'd thought he'd lost it. "Hey," said Nick.

"Hi," she said, so quietly that Nick thought maybe she'd been fired from her job: those weren't work clothes she was wearing. "I tried calling first, but you didn't answer."

"I haven't been home long."

"I'm glad you're here."

"What's up?"

Liza sat down on the end of the couch where Andrea had been sitting. "I might not get married," she said.

Andrea came back out the door. Now she, too, was wearing one of his shirts. "There," she said, "I didn't breathe but one time." Only then did she notice Liza. "Whoops. Sorry."

Liza stood up quickly. "No, I'm sorry. I didn't—"

"It's okay," Nick said, not sure whom he was addressing. Himself, most likely. *It's okay, it's okay.* He ran through the introductions and tried to figure out what to do next. He didn't have any idea. Andrea dug into her pocket for her car keys. Nick didn't want her to go before he'd somehow clarified the situation—a difficult goal given his own unclear state. He planted himself at the edge of the porch stairs, blocking her path to the street. Not a subtle gesture: she took a step toward the couch and perched on its arm. The shirt she'd borrowed was a checked button-down, baggy even on Nick, a smock on Andrea, and with the sleeves rolled up she looked ready for Sunday afternoon, for lounging around or painting a room. At the thought that she had gone into his closet to borrow the shirt, Nick was both pleased and unnerved, but mostly pleased. He liked the shirt on her. He wished it were that Sunday afternoon.

Liza sat back down and crossed her legs. Nick shot a quick

glance in her direction, nothing she could catch and hold. Potential subjects of conversation were not exactly leaping to mind.

"How do you guys know each other?" Liza asked Andrea.

"We met recently," Andrea said, warily. "What about you two?"

"We used to go out. And are you guys—"

Nick interrupted. "Liza."

"What?"

He paused. "Can I get you anything to drink?"

"No."

". . . should get going," Andrea was saying.

"No," Nick said. "You just got here."

"Still—"

"I didn't realize you were going to have company," Liza said.

"I'm just going to duck in and get my shirt." Andrea disappeared through the door.

Liza looked at Nick. He ignored her and went inside the house. "You don't have to leave," he called after Andrea. "Hey." She was in the bathroom with the door shut. "If you want, you can keep that shirt for now. I'll get it from you later."

She emerged in her own shirt, still semitranslucent, and handed him the other one. "That's okay," she said. "But thanks."

"I'm sorry."

"No, I'm sorry for barging over here."

"You didn't barge over," he said, following her back out.

"I did."

"Some other time?"

"I'll call you," she said, walking down the stairs and waving goodbye.

Liza had positioned her legs on the edge of the couch, and she had her hands on her shins. He was annoyed with her—for what exactly?

"Did I interrupt your date?" she asked.

He was about to say no, it wasn't a date. Instead he took a seat on the other end of the couch.

"We're thinking about calling it off," Liza said.

It sounded as if she were trying to convince herself of it. "You both are?" No answer. "Or just you're thinking that? Does Miles know?"

"I don't know what I'm doing."

"This is not really my department, but I think I read somewhere that doubts and jitters are common before people get married."

"I think it might be a mistake."

"Can I ask you something? Why are you telling me this?"

"I don't know," she said miserably.

"I can't give you marriage advice. I'm still in love with you."

"You are?"

Her question threw him. He sensed for the first time that he might be able to wound Liza, and he was tempted to, and it was frightening. She drew her legs closer to her chest, as if she sensed it as well, and yet managed to scooch closer to him at the same time. She touched his knee. "So can I have some water or do I have to drink from your new girlfriend's glass?" Andrea's glass was sweating onto the porch floor.

"She's not my new girlfriend," Nick said. He got up and walked into the house, and Liza followed. In the kitchen, which was dark and hot and stank of burrito, he gave her water to drink, and she gulped it down. Then she said, "I miss you."

What the fuck. He remembered his early days of courting her, waiting and waiting for the green light, always following her lead—he was doing the same thing now. "I miss you too," he said.

He would not let himself be seduced. If anyone was going to make a move here, it would be him. He marched across the kitchen and stood directly in front of her. "I miss you," he said. He kissed the top of her forehead, and she leaned toward him. When he kissed her mouth she kissed him back. This went on for a couple of minutes, long enough to establish bodily contact, long enough to imagine it continuing for a couple of days, a couple of weeks, a beach season of kissing before she went off and married someone more responsible. Then she pulled her head away. "This isn't what I want to be doing," she said.

"Go figure."

"You're allowed to be angry at me," she said.

Oh am I now. He speculated that if he pushed her back against the sink and kissed her again, angrily, if he forced it a little, she'd give in to it.

"I am angry."

"I—"

"I hope you and Miles figure things out."

"I'm sorry," she whispered.

They hugged and he smelled her hair and then she was gone.

Nick sat on the porch for a while, pouring sweat like a wrestler, but he couldn't sweat enough. He couldn't sweat her out. He was pissed and sweaty and he wanted to take the afternoon back and redo it. But the afternoon was only the tip of the revisionist iceberg. His whole life could stand a little editing. He could see it all marked up in red pen, unnecessary adjectives and gratuitous complaints crossed out, possible improvements scrawled in the margins—in his mother's handwriting—with recommendations for how to dress better attached as an appendix.

If drinking wasn't the answer, then maybe it was the question. He finished off the few bottles in the refrigerator and went to Gloria's.

He sat at the bar inside, where it was cooler, where you sat if you were alone at this hour of four-tops and six-tops and ten people crammed around a picnic table. The bartender was a woman who'd rebuffed him ten years ago, then pursued him later on, when he was no longer interested. Now they were friendly, but tonight she was too busy to talk to him. She slid him free drinks between the ones he ordered.

Then Roger was there next to him, grabbing him close to the neck, too tightly.

"Where did you come from?" Nick asked.

Roger made some joke, said something like "From your mother's house," but Nick wasn't sure he'd heard correctly, and when he tried to say that his mother lived halfway across the country, it came out as "My mother doesn't have a house." Roger's face went blank, and he took the drinks and walked away.

"Where are you going?" Nick called out after him, too late. He stared across the bar at a warped pale shape that seemed to be his reflection in the brass strip below the beer pulls. A pot of coffee was souring on a hot plate. Other people were talking loudly, but he couldn't make out individual words, except for repeated cries of "No!" from one guy who was listening to another guy tell some story. The songs playing in the background were all about dreaming or love or love gone south. "No . . . no . . . no! . . . No *way!*" Something in the "No way" reminded him of high school, of how they used to talk. He did not miss high school, but thinking back to adolescence was like being yelled at by some man not right in the head, feeling guilty and not quite knowing why. He hadn't understood *anything*, least of all the way the people he knew would all vanish. They were gone, the eighteen-year-olds, they'd turned into adults. This was to be expected, but something about it moved him in a way that the disappearance of age twenty-two or twenty-seven did not. Those eighteen-year-olds were the people he'd tripped blindly out of childhood with—and now he was starting to forget how it had happened, which movies they'd watched, even some of the names were starting to go. One more drink and he would go home and search online for Kenny Wunderlich. He would track down Matt Luria. He would call up Melinda Cox—he definitely had some questions for her.

Roger walked by again. Nick reached out and stopped him.

"Hey, hey. Listen. I'm sorry I dropped the ball on the Sunset story. I'll do something next week. I promise."

"I'm not mad." Roger looked away. Then: "I'm sitting outside with Evie, if you want to join us."

"She doesn't like me very much."

"No. But come sit with us anyway."

"That's all right."

"Come on, man."

"Okay."

Nick sat with them and didn't say anything, while Evie told a bartending story, about a mom with two kids who'd come into the club the other night, for some sort of battle of the high school bands. The kids were so cute, she said. And the mom? Roger asked. Miserable, Evie said.

Nick drank steadily, and an hour or two later when it came time to get up he couldn't stand very well. He could hear Roger murmuring, *Come on, all right*, a refrain blending into the hum of the night, as he came over to Nick and caught him around the back with his heavy arm. Then, bracing his other hand against Nick's elbow—*Come on, come on*—he walked him toward the parking lot, all but lifting him off the ground as Nick's head lolled back and he saw out of all the corners of his eyes the sky up there moving around. Come on, Roger said, I got you.

Twenty-one

At work one morning Andrea found her desktop sprinkled with hundreds of eraser shavings, as if someone had sat there late into the night, erasing away, and then had left all the shavings behind rather than sweep them into a trash can. In fact this was the only explanation she could think of for why there would be tiny pink filaments all over her desk. It was odd, since she rarely saw anyone at the office using a pencil to begin with, much less erasing, and by the number of shavings it looked as if someone had written a letter or drawn a sketch, or had started to take a standardized test but then had thought better of it.

It wasn't so odd that this nocturnal erasing fool would have chosen Andrea's desk, however. She always cleaned it off before she left work, unlike most of her colleagues, and she didn't have much permanent clutter: no family pictures or postcards or ceramic frogs. She had only the going-away presents from her prior coworkers, generic gifts: a metal box for her business cards, a fountain pen that she kept, along with her ordinary pens, in an oversize coffee mug. Today, she saw, the mug also contained a pencil, its eraser rounded from use. She picked it out: a plain yellow pencil.

Though smoking had been banned in the building, the newsroom was still lousy with smokers, old-timers who slunk out on the half hour. In its pages the *Standard-American* advocated smoking cessation, regular exercise, and diets low in this or that, but such measures were not popular among the senior editors. Richard Hornfisher, captain of the ship of Metro and State, was one of the smokers, dry and gruff and often grumpy. Toward Andrea he'd been grumpy ever since she'd missed what he called the "Hardaway and the gays" story. Afterward he'd stuck her with another round of small-time assignments—an infestation of spiders at the city's hospice was one. Another was a proposal for a new shopping mall.

Behind her, Richard and Sonny Muñiz were discussing something that had happened at the Capitol.

". . . that deal just blew up in their faces," Muñiz was saying. "They didn't know—"

"No warning at all. Screwed, blued, and tattooed, and all before lunchtime. Flintic just kind of went apeshit."

"Apeshit? Really?"

"Not literally apeshit."

"But apeshit."

"You want to be a player up there, you've got to work with your team. Especially these days. You can't just be running around the outfield by yourself."

These men had a way of conferring about politics that sometimes left Andrea feeling excluded. They used their own language of sports analogies and sexual allusions and pronouncements about the way things work in the so-called real world—a world of endless baseball and fucking. Maybe she was just being oversensitive, maybe that was all there was to it, but then again, the only political stories she was assigned were the ones about minorities or abortion.

Well, it was up to Andrea: she could sit there and feel alienated, or she could turn her chair around and join the conversation. "What are you guys talking about?" she asked.

Sonny addressed her paternalistically, as he addressed everyone. He dealt in the basics. *You see, before a bill can get to the floor to be voted on, it has to be voted out of committee.* After a long rehearsal of preliminaries he explained that Beverly Flintic, the state assemblywoman, had blocked a bill from passing out of committee, out of spite, or so he said. The bill she'd blocked had been nearly identical to one she'd introduced and failed to get through herself.

Sonny and Richard traded guesses about whether this would hurt Beverly Flintic's "long-term prospects."

"You think she's out of there?" Richard asked.

"Might be. Might be. She might be. I asked Carson Yates about it. He thinks she might have really blown it."

"Ah, but *who* did she blow, that's the million-dollar question."

"The question is, do we really want to go there . . ." Sonny began.

"Well . . ."

". . . or do we in fact not want to go there?"

"No, no, no, you're right," Richard said.

"I mean, the last thing I heard was that Hardaway's wife had talked to a divorce attorney, and he got scared."

"Do you really think he and Flintic . . ."

"It's not like she's—"

"You're right—"

"Such a *babe*."

Andrea circled around to face her desk again. She felt sorry for Beverly Flintic, though she knew almost nothing about the woman, except for the things Nick Lasseter had written in what had struck her as an overly strident article, and now this: that she wasn't such a babe.

It had been a week since she'd stopped by Nick's house to return the watch. She'd thought he might call afterward, to apologize, even though he didn't really owe her an apology, just because his ex had shown up. But an apology was an excuse for calling.

She was bothered on all fronts. It bothered her that he hadn't called; it bothered her to hear gossip about Beverly Flintic; and most of all it bothered her that someone had been sitting at her desk and erasing wantonly. Inside one of the drawers was a photograph that she didn't want anyone to find: the one from Sabert's house, inside a brown bag. She'd brought it to work with her in the week after the funeral, out of some nonsensical fear—that it might be stolen from her in turn, maybe, by daytime burglars who were also photography buffs.

The phone rang, and when she heard a male voice on the other end of the line she thought of Nick again, though it wasn't him. It was Roger, the guy she'd met outside the old library. He asked about her story on the Sunset, as if this had been something they'd agreed she would do. She said, almost whispering, that she wasn't on the best terms with her boss at the moment.

"There seems to be a lot of antagonism in the workplace these days," Roger said.

"I'll see what I can do," she said.

"That's what everyone tells me."

"I'm sorry. That's all I can tell you."

"Yeah, yeah. Listen—"

"Yeah?"

"Um, never mind."

"What?"

"No, no. Forget it. Let me know if your boss gives you the green light, okay?"

"Okay."

"Okay. There's something I wanted to ask," Roger said. "I should probably just keep my mouth shut here, but to be honest discretion has never really been one of my strengths. You know a few weeks ago, when we were all at Gloria's? You and my buddy Nick were getting along pretty good, right?"

"Sure."

"I know this is none of my business, but I thought maybe . . . the thing is, he's really had his head up his ass for, like, forever, because of this woman who . . . I won't go into it, but you know, when I saw you guys together, that was the first time I'd seen him look happy in a long time."

"We went out the week before last."

"Oh. Oh, you did. Huh."

"We did."

"He didn't mention it. Any plans to go out again?"

"Um . . ."

"Right. None of my business. Sorry. Look, I don't know where you guys left things, but if you're at all willing to give him a second chance, he's worth a second chance. He needs a second chance. Hey, do you like swimming?"

Roger said that he and a group of his friends usually went swimming on Thursday nights. You should come, he said.

Sounds like fun, she said. Not sure what the rest of my week will be like, but maybe. Thanks for the invite.

She didn't think she would go. The big pool in the middle of town was a popular spot, and one Sabert had loved, but Andrea didn't want to be wearing a bathing suit when she met new people. It might have been ridiculous of her to jump into bed with a guy she barely knew, on the one hand, and to bow out of an invitation because it involved bathing suits, on the other, but that was how she felt.

Still, she was pricked by the same kind of envy she'd had at the bar, envy of these people and their rituals. Maybe Roger was right, she should give Nick another chance, though she didn't know what kind of chance it would be, or whether he would have any interest in a chance.

She opened her desk drawer a crack and put her hand on the bag that contained the photograph. For her fifteenth birthday, her father had given her a photograph, a picture of himself and a man who at the time she'd never met: Will Sabert, his former boss. It was the two of them standing outside, somewhere in Washington, her father in a dark cabled sweater and blocky glasses frames, Representative Will Sabert wearing a light-colored jacket and skewed bow tie. Black and white, dark and light: she remembered the image well, though it had been several years since she'd last seen it. When she'd opened the gift she'd frowned. Her birthday and he'd given her a picture of himself! She'd looked up at him in time to see that he'd been watching her hopefully, but it was already too late, he'd already seen that she wasn't impressed with his gift. He'd told her coolly that if she didn't like the frame, he would pay for a different one.

Andrea had lost that picture. She had no idea what might have happened to it: for a while she'd had it, but in one of her moves from city to city it had been misplaced. That lost photo was one reason she'd gone to visit Will Sabert in the first place. As if another copy might turn up in his possession.

But stealing another photograph had been foolish: she resolved to send this one, anonymously, to Alan Loefler.

"Carter."

"Hornfisher."

"I got one for you."

What now, she wondered. A budget increase for the fire department? A new menu item at Taco Time? Richard handed her a press release. ". . . Daughters of the Star of Freedom Thirtieth Anniversary Banquet . . ." was the first thing she read. Her face went hot. This was possibly the crummiest thing yet.

"These next few weeks are make it or break it for your man Hardaway. After that jogging thing, he's got to nail every event."

She looked back at the press release and read the top line in full. "Gubernatorial Candidate Mark Hardaway to Speak at Daughters of the Star of Freedom Thirtieth Anniversary Banquet."

"What are the Daughters of the Star of Freedom?" she asked.

You'll see, he said, and then laughed wickedly, imitating Vincent Price.

PART FOUR

Twenty-two

It was on a weekend district visit in 1965 that Congressman Will Sabert offered John Carter a job.

The previous Christmas, Al Meissner had bought himself a plane. Real estate deals and then oil deals had made him rich. He'd also grown fat—his fat all centralized, like a pregnancy—and had acquired first a ranch and now this: a snub-nosed old bomber retrofitted with all the modern conveniences. A toilet in the tail-gunner's compartment, a full bar above the bomb door, three armchairs equipped with safety belts and bolted to the floor—Will now occupied one of them, Al another. A deaf and shrunken old man who Al said was his cousin Hugo sat patiently in the third chair, staring straight ahead, while a couple of Vicor-Marron junior executives huddled on the floor with their arms around their legs. One of Al's Mexican ranch hands mixed drinks from the payload area. Will and the junior executives had pleaded with Al not to attempt flight with this many passengers, half of them not belted in, and at last Al had consented, instructing the pilot instead to taxi down the gravel drive toward the highway. Which was what they were doing now, riding in a giant silver hammerhead past Al's various ponds and outbuildings. Always scheming at improvements, Al had retained a foursome of handsome Mexican boys whose job it was to forever be digging ponds and erecting outbuildings and God only knew what else; probably they kept some suffering Sonoran village alive on the whims of their employer.

"You think you could find something for him?" Will asked.

Meissner was leaning across Will's lap so that he could see out the window. "See, that over there is the fence I was telling you about. Jorge's been working on it. *Que linda*, eh, Jorge?" It was a ten-foot-high deer fence extending halfway down the middle of a pasture; Will couldn't see what was so *linda* about it. The man at the bar smiled and *sí-señor*'d and went back to pouring. "A job for Lasseter? Probably. I guess. Hasn't he been working for you? Why don't you hire him?"

"I just don't have a permanent position."

"What's wrong with him?"

"Nothing's wrong with him. You've met him."

"Yeah, he seems all right. Even if he does idolize you."

"He knows better than that," Will said.

"So why don't you have something for him? You're probably going to turn around and hire some Negro, aren't you? I've got the sixth sense. I can tell that's what you're going to do."

"Why a deer fence, Al?"

"Whatever you pay your nigger, I'll pay the kid double. Tell him that." Meissner took a swig of his drink and yelled to the pilot to take a right at the highway. "You folks want to get up early tomorrow and go alligator hunting?"

He was only a year older than Will but had readily, even gratefully, assumed the mantle of middle age, living out this oversaturated *patrón* fantasy of his on a couple hundred acres of infertile ground: wading naked into one of his ponds every morning to float on his back with his belly bulging out of the water, then devouring his breakfast in nothing but a towel. Dressing and driving into town for a bit of business, returning in the evenings for cigars on the porch. Two election cycles had come and gone since Meissner had told Will he couldn't be directly associated with his campaigns any longer. During his first term alone Will had refused to sign the

states' rights Southern Manifesto; he'd sponsored a parklands con-
servation law; and when two members of the State Assembly had
staged a thirty-six-hour filibuster of a segregation bill, he'd given a
public statement of support to all the papers. The kicker was a new
tax on the oil companies—there would be no more money from the
Marrons after that. Meissner still chipped in a little something on
his own—"out of friendship," he said—and Will came to visit when
he was in town. Al had offered to put him up this time (in separating Delia had taken the house, Will the apartment in Washington),
but he'd declined in favor of a hotel in town.

"We can't take this thing on the highway. Tell him to turn around,"
Will said.

"Still scared of airplanes, aren't you." But he obliged, and they
turned back for the hangar. From there they headed up to the main
house for lunch.

It was ten minutes before they realized Cousin Hugo was still
on the plane.

ater that afternoon Will went to pick up Bones, now in his
last year of law school. In Waterloo the winters were more
damp than cold: they seeped through the skin. The day was already
in decline, though it wasn't yet five. No one really out on the streets,
no signs of trouble: he'd read in that morning's *Standard* of a demonstration up on the campus drag, two groups going at one another in
front of a bar that wouldn't serve blacks. Along with the article
they'd run a photograph of a shaggy-haired student whose upper
arms were drawn in toward his chest even as he held out a small paper American flag, forearm extending out from his tucked-in elbow.
An ROTC type was screaming at him. They both looked petrified.

The last time Will had spoken to his eldest daughter on the phone,
she'd told him he was hopelessly behind: she meant politically.
She'd spoken of a multiracial army made up of poor people and students that would wrest the country out of the claws of the military-

industrialists—and one day, if he were fortunate, Will would join them. Katharine was seventeen now. It was true there was a divide between Will and the street demonstrators, the militants. Of course he was for them and against the administration's fool war, but their tactics, their boisterousness, their crowds, and their dope provoked an instinctual response from Will: he didn't want his daughter getting involved with those people.

They had their ways and he had his. Rarely did his legislative work make the news, but through that work—the drafting of the laws as well as the persuasion, the parliamentary maneuver, the vote-trading, and the last-resort sheer pettifoggery—Sabert the populist came into his own, ratcheting up the pipeline tax and regulating chemical plants and stumping for education and declaiming, when necessary, in a pair of old tennis shoes. Although as a congressman he outranked Washington's legions of mid-level bureaucrats, and received more invitations, there were days when he felt he had slipped, and slipped happily, into the anonymous ranks of the deputies and analysts employed by the federal government, the civil servants who puttered along the city's avenues in old cars and subsisted on sandwiches and yogurt.

Bones had spent two summers working for him, time the boy had mostly devoted to chasing women from Capitol Hill to Bethesda and back again, taking weekends at the shore and during the week nosing out complimentary food and liquor like a regular free-truffle-hunting pig, all the while trading on his closeness to the congressman—*Aw, I don't just work for him, he's like a second daddy to me.* Though Will knew he was in no position to throw stones, though he had likewise prized drink and girls over all else when he was Bones's age, though he admitted to himself that he might well have served as a kind of model of dissolution to young Bones, he didn't want to hire the boy permanently.

Had the staff budget been infinite, Will thought, then maybe—but maybe not. Bones was not a good influence on the other young people in the office, the interns . . . maybe he reminded Will too much of his own younger self, who'd waffled and orated and compromised and asked a girl to marry him only to let her down for the next eighteen years.

Bones lived with three of his old fraternity brothers in what amounted to an oversize lean-to a few blocks from the law school campus. The street they lived on was all student houses, every inhabitant still trying adulthood on for size and periodically vomiting over the porch railing, as if in direct reaction to the prospect of leaving the university and entering a profession.

A dog was barking, and someone was strumming at a guitar, and someone else was playing a jazz record, and from a short ways down the street came a grating eruption of laughter from a group of kids sitting on a porch. It was like hearing a bunch of foreigners laughing and not knowing why. Will Sabert, the over-forty intruder, sat in his chilly roadster waiting for Bones to come out of the house. The leaves were off the trees. Will honked the horn again.

Out came Bones with a smirk on his lips and hollows under his eyes, his hair wet, his tie dangling nooselike around his neck. The look of the practiced rake. Bones's act charmed people, all the more for the way he wore his hokum on his sleeve: his country twang was something he'd picked up as an undergraduate, along with a reckless leer, and Will had a feeling that each had been tried out first in the privacy of his dorm room, before a mirror. The last time Will had seen Bones, in the fall, he'd been dressed in a Hawaiian shirt and a straw homburg and was canvasing for donations of ladies' undergarments to something called the North Abyssinian Mutual Aid Association.

"That dog's been barking all *day*," Bones said as he folded his lanky body—now just starting to gather reinforcements around the belt line—into the seat, his wide knees against the dash. "Howdy, Pops."

"For God's sake, don't call me that," Will said.

"All right. If it's for God's sake."

"So how are you?"

"Had a meeting with an assistant dean today. My academic probation officer. Seems they don't want me around anymore. They're threatening to graduate me even if I flunk my exams. Looks like I'm going to have to find myself a job after all."

"You seeing anyone?" Will wished to forestall the subject of jobs.

"About work?"

"Any girls."

"Oh. A few. Nothing serious. Listen, Pops—"

But just then they rounded a corner, and Will hit the brakes. He'd turned onto the campus strip, where normally the restaurants and bookstores and student group offices were full of young people. Today it was empty, and blocked off to traffic by a pair of sawhorses directly ahead.

"Guess they closed it off because of all the ruckus," Bones said.

"You mean that trouble about the bar?"

"It's been going on near every night. Your bohemian do-gooders want old Raymond to start serving the bibulous sector of the Negro population, which he is not ever going to do, not unless the National Guard comes and makes him. Then all these fraternity hooligans come on out here to protest the protesters. Beautiful, isn't it?"

"I hadn't heard until I saw it in the paper."

"What kills me is, if the protesters weren't so goddamn self-righteous about it all, and didn't draw so much attention to themselves, most of those would-be Marines who go out there to yell at them wouldn't give a damn. But every time they open their mouths it's"—Bones shifted into falsetto—"'*I shed hot tears for our imperiled democracy!*' And then one of them starts singing a song about how peace and love are better than war and hate. Like that's a new concept."

"I suppose their hearts are in the right place."

"I suppose they love seeing their pictures in the newspapers. Celebrity nigger-lovers."

"Someone's got to be out front." They stared at the empty street. A young woman in a skirt and a cardigan dashed out of a store and ran across, clutching a bag to her chest.

"Wish it didn't have to be these Students for Dim-witted Speechifying. I've had about enough of them. And then there's that pompous nigger friend of yours, what's his name, the teacher? That whole gang has just about shut down the City Council a few times."

A year earlier John Carter, now the vice principal of Riverside High, had written to Will to request support for an embattled city-wide desegregation ordinance, and Will had called members of the City Council, asking them to vote for it. The local NAACP chapter had sent dozens of people to testify; the folksinger Joan Baez had made an appearance. The ordinance had not passed.

The conversation, like the car, had come to a halt. There was nothing to do but turn around. Just then a pair of horses passed, one on either side of the car, each bearing policemen with sidearms and helmets.

"Here comes half of the apocalypse," Bones said. Will shifted into reverse, hoping to avoid it.

They found the beer garden subdued, a few people administering to themselves in the small inside bar. Whether it was the burrowing instinct of winter, or the meager scene before them now, or the knowledge that he would have to let Bones down sooner or later, Sabert wished there were somewhere else to go. Somewhere well lit and wholesome, somebody's home. If only he knew of a place.

"So how's life up there in Washington?" Bones asked, his leg bobbling.

"Same old."

"I tell you I can't wait to get out of this town."

"I may end up back here if Vicor-Marron and the governor get their wishes granted."

"You got nothing to worry about," Bones said.

If only that were true. VMC was now the largest construction firm in the Southwest, erecting bridges and dams and a naval air station—Sabert had secured the contract, his first term. They'd more or less struck a deal during that campaign. Will had got the Marron brothers what they wanted, and in exchange Sherman Marron had tolerated what he would have called Will's pinko leanings. But it was an alliance bound not to last, as Congressman Sabert migrated leftward, and came around in favor of civil rights, and Marron the baron merged his firm with Vicor Industries, and then died—the wealthiest corpse in Waterloo. Now VMC was churning out airfield equipment to send to Southeast Asia, and scheming with the governor to see Sabert defeated.

"I cannot wait to get out of here," Bones repeated.

"This town's not so bad. I miss it. The land of eternal youth. You move away, you get old."

"You stay here, you get damn sick of the place. You know I want to come work for you."

Will was silent. He gulped at his beer and then choked, coughing like he'd dived into the drink and filled his lungs up with it.

Bones stared at the table. "I been with you since I was sixteen years old."

"I know it."

"Passing out buttons your first campaign."

"I haven't forgotten."

"You haven't."

"I haven't," Will said, and looked up as if to see who had just walked in—but no one had come in or gone out. The door was shut.

"That sounds like a no."

"Right now . . ." Will began, still weighing excuses and suggestions and *maybe in a couple of years.*

"So. You fixing to hire someone else?"

"That's not what this is about."

Bones looked away and stood up. "Thanks a lot, Pops."

"Lasseter," Will said as Bones neared the door, but Bones kept on going and Will let him. He couldn't help picturing the high school kid who'd volunteered on his very first campaign, and wishing that the kid had gone out for the baseball team instead. He'll be better off working for Meissner, better off with the good old boys. Will told himself that, but still felt as if he'd failed to steer him right.

That weekend Will saw decay everywhere—or if not decay, signs of cracking. It had something to do with the way the city was spreading carelessly out into the hills, and something to do with troop deployments, and something to do with the number of hoboes standing on the street corners. On Saturday he was on his way over to the east side when he came to a train crossing just as the lights started flashing and the barrier lowered. He waited there, watching yellow and red boxcars go sorrowfully by, their couplings straining against one another, their cargo a mystery.

He had arranged to meet with John Carter to discuss the current needs of the east side. As it turned out, Carter had other things on his mind. They sat on the steps of the empty high school—he'd said to meet there, and Will had perceived, when he'd seen Carter walk out of the building in his shirt and tie, that he worked every Saturday, and that he would go after their meeting to work some more, or to watch the basketball team practice. Carter wanted to talk about the ordinance that hadn't passed a year earlier. "We're at an impasse," he said.

"But now there's a federal law—"

"A federal law, and an impasse here in town. At the end of the day we still don't have any resources," Carter said. "We got the Central Library to open up to us, but now this one over here is falling apart. They're talking about closing it down. We've got more slum-looking streets than ever. And this brand-new segregation highway."

"Would you ever consider coming to work for me?" Will asked.

The question caught both of them off guard. It hadn't occurred to Will before Meissner had accused him of thinking about it, and even then he hadn't seriously thought it through. "You could help me work on these problems from the federal angle."

Carter said he would think it over, and let him know on Monday. They shook hands nervously, and Will thought of Bones, who would believe he'd been right all along.

elia had thought it best that he stay in a hotel, and he had agreed to it. When you were a congressman they put you high, high up: he was on the top floor, in a room overlooking the river. Staying in a hotel in the city of his birth. Some nights he speculated as to what might have happened, had he not lost his second race for State Assembly, had he remained an assemblyman all these years, had he been able to keep his family together and raise his children. A pillar of the community and all that sort of thing.

Twice, he'd persuaded Eleanor Hix to fly up to Washington to see him. He'd bought her the tickets. Both times, they'd driven out to a Virginia resort hotel and spent the weekend hiking and reading to each other. Then two years ago she'd married an economist named Louis Blumenthal.

He called his wife to see whether she'd eaten supper yet. She said that she had. All right. He said he still hoped to come over tomorrow to see her and the girls, unless she'd made other plans. She paused before answering, as if she had in fact made other plans, but then said they were expecting him. See you then, she said. See you then.

Darkness had set in during the time it took Will to get to his room from the lobby, but not absolute darkness: out the window, he could see the blurring shapes of the city and the section of interstate highway they'd just finished—an asphalt spine separating downtown from the east side—and a misshapen crescent slice of the Capitol dome. Will thought of a former state senator, dead now, who'd been not only voted out of office but exiled from his own hometown after helping a power company bankrupt a group of farmers there: he'd lived in a Waterloo hotel and died a very rich man.

Twenty-three

wo weeks went by and Mark didn't call. Ever since she'd re-fused to vote for the department's substitute bill, she hadn't heard from him, or his campaign, or the department. Beverly would stare at herself in the mirror, trying to see what Mark had ever liked about her. But even if the answer was nothing in particular, and his attentions had been just a device to keep her on the so-called team, she wanted an explanation at the very least.

Then one evening after everyone else had left the office, he appeared. Just popped in as if for a drink of water, panting and per-spiring and wearing a sports outfit. His shorts were flimsy, the scalloped nylon parting to reveal, almost indecently, his pale thighs. On top he wore a T-shirt from his own campaign. Unable to bring herself to look steadily at his face, pink and parboiled in its own juices, she scrutinized a thigh—veined, vulnerable—and asked him why he had come. He seemed wounded by the question. "I came to see you," he said, as if this should have been self-evident, and welcome.

He had come to say goodbye. After a run, or perhaps in the mid-dle of one. Having perhaps practiced his wording as he jogged down the river trail, counting two potatoes after each sentence. He walked to the chair and sat down, his sweaty legs squelching against the leather, and started talking.

Beverly heard only bits of what he said, short phrases that hardly seemed linked one to the next. He was under a lot of stress, he began. *Me and Lynette both. The interviews, the media buys, the fundraising. You continue to learn your whole life. I've cut out fried foods. Not sleeping too well. Recently Lynette had a look at the cell-phone bill and put two and two together. But we're eating right, whole grains, organic. Willpower. Counseling once a week. Grass is greener. Carson thinks at this point it'd be better to just let the BIZ bill go, too much baggage, maybe next year. Maybe you'll be more inclined to go with the program. Of course I didn't tell him about us, but he is a smart man, you know the way he is, and I've got to stay the course, he says. That means keep my dick out of the news. But after the election, things quiet down a little, who knows.*

The funny thing was that as he rambled on he seemed to shrink. Actually diminish in size. This stump of a man had wound up in her chair, a dwarf in jogging shoes—but jawing away in a loud, grating voice. It was just how everything kept turning out to be, noisy and minuscule and pathetic. To think that she'd once thought joining the State Assembly was a large gesture, when it had turned out to be this, a grits-for-brains politician perspiring all over her office furniture.

". . . still really care about you, and I always will . . ."

Beverly cleared her throat.

"Okay," she said. "Please."

"Please what?"

"Please end your remarks."

At last he shut up.

Attraction falls away; horror fills the void—still, she felt a correction was in order. "I was doing my job," she said.

"Did I say you weren't?"

"You said I wouldn't 'go with the program.'"

"I didn't."

"You did."

He dropped his head and raised his eyebrows as if to signal

someone else in the room that this much was to be expected from women. They heard things.

"You're full of it," she said.

"Actually I think I'm a pretty honest guy," Mark said.

He probably did believe it. Whereas she was beginning to buckle under the weight of all the little falsehoods that were involved in, that just seemed to be required by, an ordinary life. She would have liked to point out to him the ways in which he was a dishonest person—starting with his misrepresentations about the economic development bill and maybe moving on to the fact that they'd been having an extramarital *affair*—but what was the use.

"Look. All I was trying to say is, just because we can't see each other right now . . ."

She stared at him.

". . . doesn't mean we don't have a future."

Standing behind her desk, she pressed the tips of her fingers against its edge, pushing them back behind her hands until they hurt. "Well. Thanks. Thanks for dropping by."

There would be no sweaty goodbye hug. He would leave the building and then, she guessed, he would go on with his run.

After he left, she saw that on top of the stack in her incoming mail tray was a white five-by-seven envelope, one she hadn't seen before. Could Mark have brought it with him? But she would have noticed if he'd been carrying an envelope—also, the envelope bore no trace of sweaty fingerprints. It wasn't addressed to her, or to anyone; it was just sitting there in the inbox, with a return address rubber-stamped in spotty blue ink: "Operation Jeremiah," it said, over a Waterloo post office box number.

Inside there was no letter, only a brochure on thick glossy stock. Upside down, it looked like an invitation to an art opening, but when she turned it right side up, Beverly saw that the cover photograph was of a black man and a white man, bare-chested and kissing. The text below the photograph read: "According to State

Assemblywoman Beverly Flintic *these people* are fit to take care of the state's neediest children!"

"Oh my God," she said out loud. Inside, more text asserted that she was the ally of the radical homosexual agenda (a claim which, as far as she could tell, rested on two votes). A Dr. Robert Butze had, after much prayer and consultation with family members and community leaders, decided to run against her in the primary, and an outfit called Operation Jeremiah was urging support for his campaign.

She closed the brochure and stared at the picture on the cover. The two men, both handsome and lean and unblemished, must have been models who'd posed for the shot, but there was something in their embrace that seemed genuinely tender. They weren't literally kissing, she saw, but about to kiss, or else they had just kissed a moment earlier: their faces were slightly apart, and their eyes were open.

Beverly let the brochure fall out of her hand. Then she picked it up again, holding one corner between thumb and index finger, and dropped it in the garbage.

She dialed home but hung up before the first ring. She rifled through her purse, which still contained earplugs—maybe the thing to do would be to wear them all the time—and a dozen crumpled receipts, and her address book. Jonas's mother's name was Natalia. She was from some other country originally, somewhere in Eastern Europe. Was it considered rude in Eastern Europe to ask a woman you didn't know well to look after your son?

Well, probably they did that all the time over there. Natalia told her that of course, of course, Jonas would love for Jamie to spend the night. Jonas had been so happy to go to the rock-and-roll show. Thank you so much for taking them. You are a brave woman, she said.

Then Beverly called home again, suddenly nervous as she waited through the rings. Owen answered. What's up? he asked. Oh, I think I'm losing my mind up here, she told him. Tell me some news from the regular world.

"Out here in the regular world," Owen said, "we're making supper. Why don't you come home and have some?"

A trick question: she could go there and eat, but was it home and was it supper? She wanted to crawl in on scratched-up knees and confess the truth about everything and be taken back, and not return here to this office and the way she had acted in it. There was nothing left to do but go and make her attempt.

On Arrow Lane, Beverly paused at the sight of the front door— it had always looked garish and plastic to her, painted the dismaying green of an exit sign on the interstate—and she remembered how it had once before seemed not tacky but comforting, on a night when she and Owen and Jamie returned from an anxious and rash-ridden trip to the coast, that last time when they'd admitted to themselves that none of them liked the beach very much anymore. For once she walked straight up to that door instead of going in through the garage, as though it were some kind of an occasion.

She could hear voices in the kitchen, over Jamie's music, and when she paused to listen the music didn't sound so bad. She was getting used to it. The television was on, muted, in the living room, and she went to shut it off, then stuck her head in the kitchen. Owen and Jamie were standing intently before the stove, calling out names of ingredients in silly accents. There were stray spines of rosemary on the floor beneath their feet, flour on their arms. They turned around at the same time to greet her, and, exhausted, her legs about to give way, she smiled at them from across the room.

Twenty-four

Fall Activity Day on campus, and the club reps were out in droves. They'd set up tables around a mini-plaza below the administration building, draped the tables with painted sheets, stacked them high with literature and freebies, and taken up positions. Now they voiced happy cries and gave things away. Flyers danced in the breeze. Squirrels made off with complimentary ballpoints.

Down at the bottom of the plaza, wedged in against an iron fence and next to a garbage can, was the Save the Sunset table. Just on the other side of the fence was the street, with only a thin strip of sidewalk intervening, so that at the table it was hard to hear anything whenever a city bus or the campus shuttle lumbered past. Nick didn't care so much about making himself heard, though. He was manning the table as a favor to Roger. Whether a petition in favor of Save the Sunset would have any traction on campus was not his concern—or rather, when he'd started telling Roger that no undergraduate would give a rat's ass about a rock club that had peaked in the eighties, Roger had suggested he arrive by nine-thirty at the latest. In the morning, he added.

With Nick at the table was a guy who'd introduced himself as Ernie Cabrito. He had big spongy pores, a double chin, and eerily blue eyes that hinted of criminal tendencies. Roger had referred to him as a genius, but so far all he'd done was to sit there and read the paper while Nick took care of student outreach. Like Roger, Ernie worked in the state proofreading office, but unlike Roger he had the day off. For sustenance he'd brought along a 64-ounce Coke in a pink plastic tankard and a can of potato sticks. Also a book called *The Idiot's Guide to Anarchism*. Nick suspected that Ernie Cabrito was not his real name.

It had been Roger's idea to make people curious with oblique advertising: a lone piece of posterboard reading "Save the Sunset: Ask Me How" was taped to the listing table. There were no pamphlets or free refrigerator magnets. Nick and Ernie did not wear matching shirts. Nick guessed that the other clubs and organizations here on the plaza had all registered for Activity Day with some Office of Activities. He and Ernie, on the other hand, weren't students, much less a legitimate student club, and would probably be kicked off the plaza sooner or later, though that would hardly render them much less effective than they were currently. So far Nick had spoken to a few kids from the South Asian Association and to a pair of sorority girls, who'd inquired about the Sunset, it seemed, so as to place it into one of two categories: things to dominate, or things to ignore. They'd quickly chosen the latter but had shruggingly agreed to sign the petition, while the South Asians, doubtful that they were getting the full story, had refused.

"So how do you know Roger?" Ernie asked, once he'd tired of the newspaper. It had been five minutes since anyone had stopped at the table.

"We lived together about ten years ago. I don't even remember how we actually met. Might have been at the Sunset."

"Do you go there a lot?"

"Used to. How about you?"

"Not one time," Ernie said. "I've never even driven by the place."

"So—"

"I'm just here as a favor to Roger."

"Yep, me, too." Nick's recollections of the other night were foggy, but he knew it was Roger who'd taken him home and who must have helped him up the steps, into the house, and into bed, where he'd woken up the next morning still wearing his pants, with a glass of water next to the bed he didn't remember getting for himself.

"Being able to count on another person. It's something you don't see as much anymore," said Ernie.

"Mm-hm," Nick said. It wasn't so far from what he himself had been thinking, but proclaimed by somebody else, it sounded dumb, like something a bitter old person would say.

"So what's your game?"

"You mean my job? I work for the *Weekly*."

"Reporter?"

Nick nodded. The other day McNally had asked him how he would feel about switching over to an editing position. "I'd want to think about it," Nick had said. And he had been thinking about it. Thinking maybe it wouldn't be such a bad thing.

"Ah, well, in that case," Ernie said, "let me provide you with my card."

In Nick's experience, proofreaders for the state did not carry business cards—but it wasn't a card for proofreading. The bit of paperboard Ernie coaxed from his wallet with his fat thumb was dark green and said "Derring-Do Productions," in black techno-font lettering that was hard to make out against the green. There was an e-mail address but no phone number.

"We stage direct actions," Ernie said. "Remember when the power went out a couple of months ago?"

"Yeah."

"That was us."

Nick found this hard to believe. "What was the point?"

"That was not an action per se but a training exercise which, to be honest, went somewhat awry. We've got a couple things planned for the near future. If you'll let me have one of your cards I'll give you a heads-up when we're about to move."

What the hell, thought Nick. When McNally made him deputy editor for music listings, he'd have to get new cards anyway.

"Potato sticks?"

"No thank you."

Ernie tilted his head, lifted the can, and shook some into his mouth. Beneath his thin cotton polo shirt, the weird topography of his torso began to quiver, and this worried Nick before he figured out that Ernie was laughing, more or less, laughing with his body if not his voice.

"What?" Nick asked.

But to laugh, even silently, in the course of munching on potato sticks had its consequences: Ernie was now coughing strenuously, red-faced and wet-eyed and bent over in his chair. Students walked in wide arcs to avoid the table. Finally Ernie took a long sip from his giant Coke and then gasped for air.

"Save the Sunset," he said. "Jesus."

A week later Ernie called Nick at work to advise him of "something about to go down" at a business hotel in north Waterloo. He gave few specifics. "Tomorrow morning," he said. "You don't want to miss this."

The hotel was located out in the land of a thousand off-ramps, behind an outdoor shopping area, The Galleria at Spiny Bottom, where the stores sold watches, leather goods, jewelry, crystal, golf bags, chocolate truffles, and cruisewear, as if someone had pillaged a duty-free area, drunk up the liquor, and assembled the rest here. All of it had gone up within the past few years, including the hotel: a fortress of tinted glass behind zones of parking garage and box hedge. Black doormen, scrupulously eager in white uniforms with maroon piping, stepped theatrically around a stage of maroon carpet, tossing car keys back and forth, yessirring brightly, palming fives and tens. Inside the lobby, a desperate profusion of flowers did not quite mask a faint funky plumbing smell. POOL CLOSED UNTIL FURTHER NOTICE said a discreet printed sign near the elevators. Beyond the lobby was an atrium with a fountain (shut off), a restaurant, shade plants, and the entryway to Ballroom B, where, as Nick had been informed by Ernie Cabrito, the annual banquet of the Daughters of the Star of Freedom would be convocated at eleven-fifteen.

The Daughters of the Star of Freedom was a state heritage organization with a complicated hierarchy that meddled in community endeavors and occasionally issued a denouncement of something in the news. Middle-aged women milled in and out of the ballroom. They had arranged themselves according to status and age, with the long-haired real-estate-agent types in one cluster, the dumpy artists in another, the fake-tanned country clubbers and the bossy grandmothers all in their separate groups. Not exactly Nick's scene. After poking into the ballroom he poked back out again. He hadn't seen Ernie anywhere. Why he or anyone else would bother to mess with the Daughters, Nick couldn't fathom.

As he picked up a banquet program off a table in the atrium, a female voice said, "May I help you?" It belonged to a blond woman of indeterminate age.

"Is this the Daughters of the Star of Freedom banquet?" Nick asked.

"Yes, it is."

"I'm with the media," he said.

Sometimes that was enough. The woman took him by the wrist and deposited him in one of the ballroom's back corners, where a table had been cordoned off from the rest. MEDIA, said a sign planted between the salt and pepper shakers. The table was empty except for one person: Andrea.

"Fancy meeting you here," he said. "Did you get a tip, too?"

"Pardon?"

"What are you doing here?"

"I was assigned to cover this."

"Oh. Okay. Sorry. Hi." Nick took a seat on the other side of the table from her.

"You're going to have to crane your head to see the stage if you sit on that side."

"I can always turn my chair around," he said.

"True . . . but then what about your lunch?" At each setting was a white plate with a cylinder of green mousse set on top of lettuce and flanked by two thin triangles of watermelon.

"Looks delicious." He stood—crouched—and half circled the table, for some reason ducking as if he were in a crowded theater, and then, shy at the last minute, sat down one seat away, leaving an empty chair between them. Then he summoned his courage and scooted over to the seat next to her.

He scrutinized his mousse, poking at it with his knife and then with his finger. Andrea wrote something in her notebook. Nick took out his notebook and opened it to a page with a string of onion half stuck to the paper. He flicked it off.

He was curious as to why the *Standard-American* would be covering this event. He wanted to ask her, but by the time he'd decided how to phrase it, a woman was standing before the microphone and clearing her throat. With a kind of practiced feistiness she recited her welcome, then said an opening prayer, during which the majority of the Daughters bowed their heads, while two very pale women sitting over toward the side of the room raised their arms in the air and squeezed their eyes shut, Pentecostal style.

"A-*men*!" the emcee concluded, "and on with the program. So many of our members are blessed with special talents. We are excited to have two of them here to perform for us today, please welcome the Gracettes!"

A pair of zippy homemakers in bright purple blouses hurtled themselves onto the stage and in the direction of a small electric piano behind the podium. Without saying a word, they launched into an anthem called, according to the program, "Daughters, O Daughters, Let the Star of Freedom Shine upon You." Much use was made of the "crystal strings" setting on the electric piano. By the fifth verse many of the real estate agents had begun inspecting their manicures in earnest. Nick looked around at the walls and floor and ceiling, and then at Andrea. She was staring—gawking—at the stage. She turned to Nick, widened her eyes in mock alarm, and they both smiled, quickly, before returning to their notebooks.

At last, the song concluded with an unexpected operatic flourish. The emcee returned to announce this year's recipient of the Outstanding Young Woman Scholarship, high school senior Faye Sleziak, who in accepting the award was revealed to be with child. Disturbed Daughters applied themselves to their mousses; the dinging of forks against china rattled across the room.

The emcee upped the cheer quotient in her voice. "Well, now it's time for the main event. We're so thrilled to have a speaker of this caliber with us today." Nick referred to his program and read the speaker's name at the same time that it was announced: Commissioner of Human Needs Mark Hardaway. Now he understood why Andrea was here. Covering the campaign, in all its wrinkles.

The lights dimmed. Above the stage was a projection screen, on which a series of pictures now appeared—of daffodils, smiling children, a baseball stadium, and people huddled around a computer pointing excitedly at the monitor. The candidate walked across the stage to the podium, mugging at nobody, and set his notes down in front of him.

Since his announcement, Hardaway had added to his repertoire a steely-eyed stare out into the distance. He stared, inhaled, and said, "Freedom."

Then: "Freedom . . ."

"Freedom."

Scattered applause.

"We hear that word a lot, but what does it really *mean*?"

Nick sniffed the approach of a dictionary definition.

"The Webster's dictionary defines freedom as *the quality or state of being free*: as, a: the absence of necessity, coercion, or constraint in choice or action . . ." Hardaway soldiered on through the multiple meanings. Here was an age-old routine: this banquet room, these women, this speech. It was reassuring in a way, to think of the endless sequence of conventions and luncheons rotating through rented spaces, and the ambient faith that something might be gained by so much stilted association, but also just strange, the things people filled their lives with. These women would probably think that Nick's life, his nights watching music, were just as strange. And he would agree with them.

"You and I may have our own definitions of freedom," Hardaway continued. He followed each sentence with a very long pause. "Maybe for us, it's the freedom of childhood . . . Who doesn't remember that feeling of rolling down a grassy hillside, or running down a beach?"

People from the ghetto, Nick thought. Bedouins.

"That's one kind of freedom." Deep breath. "Other kinds of freedom, we've been hearing about since the sixties, with the 'Me' generation. Those 'if it feels right, do it' kinds of freedoms that maybe some of us in this room"—he looked around meaningfully—"don't think we need quite so much of. But when we talk about the Daughters of the Star of Freedom—"

At that moment, the audio system faltered. Hardaway's lips were still moving, but the speakers broadcast only bits and pieces: *inalienab . . . as Thomas Jeff . . . values.*

Then came a loud snap, and the audio returned in full. Hardaway smiled. "That's better," he said. "As many of you know, I'm running for governor." He said he wanted to keep spirits high by keeping taxes low. Pause. He wanted to encourage growth in the private sector. Pause, applause. Today he was announcing a new initiative he planned to implement as governor: special incentives for companies to locate in underserved neighborhoods. No community, he said, need be left behind!

Then the sound system buzzed and sputtered and went silent, but for a low hum. A new picture appeared on the screen behind him—poor-looking Hispanic kids in a schoolyard, with a caption below that said that fewer than half of them had health insurance. Hardaway, busy hitting the microphone, did not notice. Over the pirated speaker system a recorded voice said, "For the kingdom of Heaven belongs to such as these." It might have been Ernie's voice, but there was a lot of distortion and Nick couldn't tell.

Hardaway's mouth drooped. He kept hitting at the microphone with his open palm. Then he stared at his palm. He began to shout, his raw voice not amplified by microphone, "That is not me. That is not me!" Unlikely though it was that anyone would think that the voice *was* Hardaway, he said it again. "That isn't me! Damnit, will somebody turn that off?"

He looked left and right, and something caught his eye: the screen behind him. He spun around and saw the picture of the brown children, and drew back. "What the hell is that?" he shrieked.

The candidate was freaking out. He half crouched, as if about to jump up and down. Then he did jump up and down, three times. Finding himself, on each landing, in the same spot he'd been before liftoff, Hardaway looked increasingly morose. After the jumping he stomped back and forth for a while. "Turn it off!" he kept shouting even after the voice had faded. Nick had a theory that very few people could run for office, produce that many grins and that much happy talk, shake that many hands, put forth all that unremitting hopefulness without eventually nursing deep bilious anger within themselves. To every action an equal and opposite reaction: on the flip side of all that smiling there had to be rage. He wanted to find Ernie Cabrito and shake his big hand. Hardaway moaned. Just then his microphone came back on again—the moan was magnified—and realizing this, he quit moaning and shut his eyes and said:

"Let us pray."

Up went the arms of the Pentecostals, while other Daughters walked out of the room. Nick was delighted. He loved a good meltdown. He was always happy, for example, to arrive at a McDonald's and find fifteen-year-olds behind the registers and french fries all over the floor. Andrea had risen from her chair and was watching the stage with no expression whatsoever. "You were right. It is going to be torture."

"This isn't what I meant," Nick said. "*This* is great."

"How am I supposed to write about this?"

If he'd known, he would have told her. And if he could have thought of something amusing to say, he would have said something amusing, but suddenly his well was dry, and he stood with his hands in his pockets, worrying that she would go away.

Once, disaster for a man like Mark Hardaway would have been delicious fodder for "The Scowler," but there was no more "Scowler." He took Ernie Cabrito's card out of his wallet. "You should e-mail that guy. I think he had a part in this." Their fingers brushed as he gave her the card. Lowering his voice, he said, "I notice you didn't eat your mousse."

"Neither did you."

"Want to get some lunch?"

"I'd like to, but I've got to work the room," she said. Andrea trudged away from the table. She turned back toward him. "Unless you can wait for me?"

Nick loitered outside, watching the doormen. He'd swiped the centerpiece from the table, white flowers in a plastic pot inside a straw pot, and when Andrea came out he offered them to her.

"You shouldn't have," she said, balancing the pot in the crook of her elbow.

"You get anything?"

"Mark Hardaway believes that the responsible party or parties should be located and held accountable. He invites anyone with information to contact his campaign headquarters."

"So—you hungry?"

She said that she was, but there was someplace else she wanted to go first, if he didn't mind.

He didn't. He tailed her through a part of town he didn't know well. The streets ran at odd angles, the numbered streets jutting every which way off the main commercial avenue, a colorfully jumbled thoroughfare with gas stations painted yellow and pink, pickup trucks everywhere, and balloon animals and Popsicles for sale in empty lots. Deep-green tree branches formed an overhead canopy, like the tent cloth above some permanent, ramshackle fair. Nick didn't know where they were headed, but followed her south into increasingly familiar territory and finally onto the street where the Sunset languished. Andrea stopped down the street from the club, in front of a bland, vacant-looking building on a section of street that seemed confused as to its purpose: the building stood next to an empty stretch of grass and across the street from a cheap apartment complex.

They got out of their cars, and Andrea said she wanted to try to get inside the building.

"Inside that building? Why?"

It had been a library, she said, as if that explained anything. "I was scared to go in by myself."

"What were you scared of?"

"Being alone in there."

They walked around the back to a wooden door with a broken latch and a NO TRESPASSING sign and kicked it open. The sign had not served as much of a deterrent. Beer bottles whole and broken had been piled in one corner; white down and bird droppings covered the floor. Unfurnished except for some built-in shelves that had seen better days, its windows covered up, the large main room was a trashed storage locker. Restoration did not seem called for so much as razing and replacement.

"This was the black library," Nick said, only now guessing.

Andrea nodded. Nick wasn't sure how he was supposed to feel. Whatever it had been once, it was now a junky old building that reeked of urine and birdshit. He couldn't really imagine it otherwise. He was just waiting there. He felt as though he was supposed to make the proper gesture, or say the right thing. She had turned her back to him, her shoulder blades visible in outline—even those seemed calm and elegant and interesting—and gazing at her back, he recognized his own idiocy. This wasn't about him or anything he might say. He heard a flutter of wings from up under the eaves.

When they were back outside, she took a piece of paper from her purse and held it up, but didn't give it over, and he stood slightly behind her to read it. Their shoulders touched, the front of his to the back of hers; he could hardly concentrate. It was a copy of an old newspaper article. USE OF LIBRARY ASKED BY NEGRO, said the headline. Below that, in tiny print, were two paragraphs of text:

> *John Carter, a teacher at Riverside High School, appeared before City Council yesterday to request that the main library be opened to Negroes. There is a branch library for colored residents on East 11th Street. "The east side branch is quite inadequate," Mr. Carter said. He added that he had discovered no law or ordinance requiring separate libraries for whites and Negroes.*
>
> *"The council has taken the position that where equal facilities exist, they will be used separately," said Mayor Timothy Mulhouse. However, the mayor said, the council would investigate Carter's allegation of unequal facilities and issue a statement in September.*

"That professor I told you about, Alan Loefler?"

"I went to see him," Nick said.

"He found this and sent it to me. John Carter is my dad." Her father had convinced Will Sabert to help put pressure on the city, she said, and eventually the main branch was opened to everyone.

The building might not have moved him, but he warmed to the story, partial and speculative though it was. Grown-up men doing their best to shift the balance, in their small town with its small ways. Nick stayed right where he was until Andrea stepped forward, away from him.

"Quite inadequate," Andrea said. "I can hear him saying that." Something in her face twisted up and then relaxed. "All right, let's go eat."

"Hey, you know Roger—the guy you met? He's trying to do this thing, Save the Sunset, to try and rescue that club over there." Nick pointed toward the Sunset.

"Yeah, I met him out here, actually."

"Oh. Right. Anyway, he's doing this benefit show for it on Saturday. If you had any interest . . ."

"I might."

He guessed she didn't know whether she wanted to risk going out with him another time, but she hadn't written him off. It was shaping up to be a decent day. At the sub shop where they had lunch he was downright goofy, asking Andrea whether she wanted to see some tricks he knew how to do with mustard. Not really, she said.

Twenty-five

Bones waited in a bar for Ed Vela, the would-be candidate, a young guy with what they called genuine potential. The bar was a dark basement haunt of lobby types and other inscrutables who traded off-color jokes and made deals here and there and vacated any time a reporter stepped onto the premises. A good old girl named Nelda who co-owned the place poured drinks in the afternoons, and she would holler at any known reporter who entered to kindly scram before she went out of business. Right now there didn't seem to be any members of the press on hand. Happy hour had ended, and only a few men remained, the ones unwilling or unable to go home.

Bones was sunk in thoughts of Sabert's last campaign. The late seventies, and Sabert's primary opponent, Floyd Hollins, had called him a man from another era, which was close enough to the truth. On the campaign trail Sabert meandered as if across a wasteland, through half-ghosted towns abandoned by the Saturday shoppers, bereft of the strollers and domino players who'd once flocked to political speeches but had since retired to the suburbs—and in the suburbs Will Sabert was lost. At sea. Picture a man in a white suit surveying the perimeter of a shopping-mall department store as if it were some unscalable fortress, and then pushing his way in through the double doors, and staggering across a bailiwick of makeup and scarves, sick on perfume and all stopped up with dumb words, use-less latinates, idle phrases about the betterment of society that no tired, smiling woman in a smock handing out samples of beauty cream could have wanted to hear. The betterment of skin was her concern. And in the evenings, if she watched television, she would have seen the ads put on by Hollins blaming that soft spendthrift atheistic left wing of the party for violent crime, busing, high gas prices, marijuana, unemployment, general immorality, and litter— the last not stated but implied by the ad's monochromatic montage of run-down, trash-strewn city streets.

We're living in the jet age, Hollins said, and my opponent is rid-ing in a buggy. It was Bones who'd fed him that line. He'd done work for the Hollins camp. At first it had just been a matter of agreeing to hand over his Rolodex, fat with the phone numbers of potential donors, but then Bones had met the candidate and liked him, had started making appeals himself and offering Hollins bits of advice, had even gone so far as to write a speech one surly, hung-over morning when all his old grudges had crawled out into the cavities between skin and clothes. He'd watched Hollins go from underdog to dark horse to stalking horse to favorite to congress-man—and a few years later, after he'd switched parties and remar-ried, on to the Senate. He was a senator still, though he and Bones no longer consorted. Word was that Bones Lasseter was an old drunk; Bones himself knew that. Nobody was too interested in his advice anymore.

Except Ed Vela: that was the pretense, that Bones might offer the kid some tips. But really Yates wanted VMC's backing, or maybe something else. There was no knowing for sure. Yates had motives four layers deep, and might rope people into the fold not because he wanted their help but as a form of damage control. To keep them from helping out the other guy. So be it: Bones couldn't see any harm in a meeting and besides, Yates's shitlist was a club he didn't want to join. To actually help an R in the primary was not some-thing he was used to, but there was a first time for everything.

Sabert must have heard about how Bones had assisted the Hollins campaign, but they'd never spoken about it. They'd never spoken at all after that last race, never again. It wasn't what Bones had intended. He'd always thought he and Sabert would wind up together, or wind down together maybe, old-fart style, sitting out on the porch, shooting the shit. Only they'd both been too stubborn. It was a consolation, their shared mule-headedness, a small insufficient consolation, but in a way it felt almost like love. The first time he ever saw Will Sabert, Bones was in high school and the not-yet-representative was standing barefoot on the hood of a Chevrolet parked in a gravel lot west of the Capitol, his tie loose, sweat streaming down his haunted white face, reciting Roosevelt's second inaugural just for the hell of it . . . *the test of our progress is not whether we add more to the abundance of those who have much* . . . no one listening but for a few pals of his leaning against the car, and then Bones, who had been on his way home from his dishwashing job and had stopped there, a big foolish moon in the sky and a warm breeze blowing and that was it. God, that was it.

Once, a few years ago, Bones had tried to see Sabert again. After the stroke. He drove over to the hospital and parked in the lot and sat there in the car, preparing to go in. Then a sedan had parked a few spaces over from him, and the driver, a good-looking girl, Mexican, got out, took a cane from out of the backseat, walked around to the passenger door, and helped a bent old woman to stand. After a minute Bones recognized her: Sabert's old flame Eleanor Hix. Wearing a striped dress and high-top sneakers; her cane shook. By the way the girl was reacting, Bones guessed that Eleanor was making wisecracks at her own expense. He sat there another minute, watching the pair's careful progress toward the entrance, then drove away. He'd been stubborn but that wasn't the only thing: he was sixty-two years old and didn't want to be. Didn't have the balls to throw himself in the river—the Alameda was too shallow, anyhow—but he did not want to be old.

And then again he didn't quite want to be young, not now. At least if you were born before 1950 there was a chance you'd started out with your illusions intact. When you were disillusioned by junior high, where did you go from there? Toward extreme religion or marathon running or just that sort of ongoing fatalism disguised as fresh outrage. Or apathy. Or muddling along, donating fifty dollars to whatever noble cause showed up in the mailbox.

The door swung open and Bones knew right away this was his man—he was maybe twenty-six, twenty-seven tops. Not terribly tall but broad across the chest, handsome and grinning like he'd just gotten laid for the first time in his life. Just looking at him, Bones figured he would win, it almost didn't matter who he was up against. Genuine potential indeed. A real bright-eyed small-town church-going baseball-team yes-ma'am suited-up best-all-around boy, ready to stride out in front of the klieg lights and promise tomorrow would be a better day. And then the show would start all over again.

Vela was alone. They shook hands. This kid was a prodigy, Bones could tell already. A prodigy of eye contact and righteous intonation, of that tricky mix of manners and Elvis that sucked up votes like a vacuum. Plus he was Hispanic.

"I may look to you like some old boy just coming out of the woods, but I've been hanging around the Capitol since before you were born," Bones said. "If you want to know who's who, you can ask me. Don't be shy."

"Oh, I'm not shy," Vela said. "That's one thing I'm not."

"I've been through some battles."

"I bet you have."

"My first session, we had one of the scariest things I've ever seen: a horde of angry Minute Women on the warpath. They wanted to ban Henry Miller from the entire state. Neither his books nor the man himself was to be allowed across the border, or it was a Class B misdemeanor."

"You were an assemblyman?" Vela asked.

"I was a lobbyist," Bones said. Vela seemed relieved to hear it. "That was my first session in the lobby, up there with a bunch of fire-breathing homemakers."

"Sounds pretty wild."

"Probably seems like ancient history to you, now doesn't it."

"I've always enjoyed history. It was my minor in college."

"Good man," Bones said.

"I think we can all learn from history," he added, making a triangle with his thumbs and index fingers.

"I'd like to think we could."

"An example of that is, I think we've learned that it's wrong to judge a person by the color of their skin. That's why I don't believe in racial quotas in hiring or admissions. Those are just another form of prejudice."

Bones felt something squeeze in his chest. That night so long ago in the parking lot, Will Sabert standing on the hood—*it is whether we provide enough to those who have too little.* There was nothing he could tell this twenty-six-year-old future governor except farewell and fare forward. And: you can count on VMC. Though he wasn't in a position to make promises, Bones was confident that VMC would want to help out with the campaign: a little something now, more if he won the primary. *I don't know if you know much about pipelines? First thing you got to understand is, they cost a lot to maintain.* Vela listened politely. Bones went on telling him about the history of the depletion allowance and the potential for more pipeline-related jobs and growth and enterprise and so on and so forth, as the vise tightened around his heart.

Twenty-six

She learned of the upcoming demolition in the pages of the *Standard-American*: CONSTRUCTION SET TO BEGIN ON WATER-LOO VILLAGE PROJECT. The beginning of construction, Andrea knew, was destruction. The library's time had come, and on her lunch break one day she went over to see it fall. If it hadn't already fallen. On her way over she imagined something dramatic and impressive: a wrecking ball careening through the air, windows shattering, the crumbling perimeter swallowed by clouds of dust. But when she arrived at the site she saw it wasn't anything like that. A marigold-colored backhoe with a long double-jointed arm and a big claw-looking thing at the end had caught the tip of one gable in its clutch and was gently twisting a section of roof away from the sagging walls, as though opening a jar. Much of the roof was already gone—most of what remained was naked frame—and the ground was covered in shingles and boards. At the opposite end of the building from the twisting gable, a worker sat on a rafter sipping a Gatorade. The library had never seemed too substantial to begin with, but it had stood for the better part of a century, and now here it was revealed to be just boards and shingles propped on a flimsy skeleton, something that could be ripped apart without any trouble, flattened in a day.

When her dad had first told her about this place, practically everything about the story had seemed to Andrea like bragging on himself. That he'd gone to this library constantly as a kid (i.e., how smart he'd been); that he'd gradually realized the collection of books was woefully inadequate (how perceptive); that he'd gone to the city and demanded equal access to the other branches (brave and noble), won over Congressman Will Sabert (savvy), seen the library integrated (capable), and later gone to work for the congressman (successful). Only that wasn't the end of the story—the end was returning to Waterloo for a banquet honoring Sabert after twenty years away, not having so much as come back for a visit since his mother's death eight years earlier, and discovering that the town he'd grown up in had for all intents and purposes disappeared. The library he'd roamed through as a boy had been closed by the city for lack of funds, and everything else on the east side had been the same way, the high school he'd once taught at, the streets and sidewalks, all neglected.

That was when Andrea decided she'd had more than enough of that story, after hearing him go on about himself and then turn right around and get misty for the 1950s—*community* was the word he kept saying. At fourteen she hadn't seen his loneliness.

A gargantuan white pickup truck cruised down the street and stopped right in front of her. A beefy man in a suit and a hard hat dropped out. Then he said something to her she didn't understand.

"Hello," she said.

"I said, what do you think?" he yelled, nodding at the demolition, and then, before she could answer, stuck out his hand, which was saddled with what looked like an NFL championship ring. "Lou Bargeron. I like to find out what people like you are thinking."

People like me? He waited expectantly. "Pretty impressive," she said.

"Don't b.s. me now. What were you really thinking when I drove up here?"

"Really I was thinking about my dad."

"I see," he said, nodding for her to go on.

"He used to go to this library when he was a kid," she said slowly.

"How about that. I'd be willing to bet my dad never set foot in a library his whole life."

"Never?"

"Used to beat the crap out of me. Said it was for my own good," Bargeron said. "Nice talking to you now." He climbed heavily back up into the truck.

"Mighty fine," Andrea said as the truck pulled away.

Down the street, she noticed, bulldozers were advancing on the Sunset.

Twenty-seven

Summer weather persisted through October; only at the end of the month did it relax its grip on the nights first and then the days, as bare shoulders dwindled in number and football players breathed easier under their pads and plastic epaulets. Birds moved on. The sno-cone truck stayed put—the midday sun still made a decent showing—but the afternoons brought storms, and water flowed along creek beds that had been dry for months. The water altered the landscape, transporting items that had long lain stranded in gravel to new locations, and to Nick it seemed that even objects well above the floodplain were somehow affected. In his neighborhood he stumbled across odd compositions marooned in the grass: four Natural Light empties arranged around a lone high-top sneaker; a box containing dead flowers and a deflated Mylar balloon in the shape of a heart; a timeline of ancient Greek history drawn on posterboard; a nearly full party platter of raw vegetables with dip. What might have been judged to be plain trash looked, to Nick, like precursors—to new sneakers, new loves, the Roman Empire, the main course.

He met Liza for a drink, and she told him about her trip to New York with Miles, which had been full of quarreling, neither of them able to stop turning the crank. They hadn't broken off the engagement but hadn't set a wedding date, either. They were engaged to be married eventually, at some point. Whether it was the cool late-afternoon light or the genuine uncertainty in her face, Liza looked especially beautiful, and Nick brooded, not because she and Miles were still engaged but because he could see that she had grown older. He remembered whispering with her at the movies, and knew that it would never happen again.

Myra called to tell Nick that Bones had gone into the hospital. "He thought he was having a heart attack, but it was unstable angina. Which means he's clogged up but not blocked. They're keeping him for two days to watch him and do tests." She paused, and Nick couldn't tell whether she was composing herself or had simply run out of things to say. "I guess they're just so charmed by his presence they don't want to let him go."

"I'll go by this afternoon," Nick said. He hadn't talked to his uncle since the publication of the Beverly Flintic article.

"If you do go, he'll work on you to bring him some liquor. He says he can't eat that hospital food without anything to wash it down with."

"Should I take him something?"

"Heavens, no. The one thing I'm not worried about is him starving to death."

Sure enough, when Nick phoned the hospital to tell Bones he planned on coming by, Bones asked him to pick up "some of the good stuff" on the way there.

"You mean weed?" he asked.

"Course not. Just get me something potable. Maker's would do nicely."

"I'm not going to do that. You still want me to come?"

"You might as well," Bones sighed, waiting until Nick had shown up in person to deliver his full rant against the "fanatics" who would deny him a drink in his time of need. "It's my heart that's under suspicion here, not my liver," Bones said, "but they're insisting that I ab-

6666

stain. Whatever happened to those doctors who put liquor in brown bottles and sold it as medicine?"

"Charlatans, I think they were called."

"Still, they were onto something. Right now I'd take a vial of vanilla extract over all the TV in China." He nodded impatiently toward the television. Bones was in a shared room, his area separated from another patient's bed by a pale-blue dividing curtain. On a high shelf fixed to the wall was a small television tuned to a soap opera—a scene was taking place in a hospital room just like the one they were in. Bones elbowed himself up to sitting upright and pointed at the screen. "Gal's pregnant by one guy but she's telling another one it's his so that he'll leave his barren wife for her," he said. "I swear it's the exact same story as when I came in for my appendix in 1982."

"There's more channels now. You don't have to watch the soaps."

"Who says I don't want to watch them? I relish tawdry melodrama. You know, I heard your friend Beverly Flintic and Mark Hardaway were an item?"

"Really," Nick said, half watching the woman on the screen. "That's not something I want to think about." The woman wore a low-cut blouse, and her long straight hair fell artfully down her front, framing her chest. Tears plowed a path through her tan makeup.

"It might not be true."

"I hope not."

"You hear anything from her since that article?"

"She offered some feedback."

"She did?" Bones snorted. "Well, that economic bill of hers is dead for now. And she killed that other one. They'll probably try again next year. Man. I went in there thinking I could get a few changes made—that was how it used to work. These days, seems like it's all or nothing." He looked erratically around the room as if to locate a fly whose buzz was bothering him. "And I can't even drink. Problem is, there aren't enough drunks left in politics. There's no more spirit of *conviviality*. Nowadays everyone's screeching at each other all the time."

Bones took a drink of water and then went on. "Negotiation is a dying art. All I wanted at the beginning was a few modifications. Level the playing field, so to speak. Give companies other than Heritage a shot at some of those contracts. And I was hoping Ms. Flintic would see fit to get behind another bill I had an interest in."

"You fed me all that stuff on her to help your client."

"Nah, my client didn't get anything out of it. I guess I just sorta wanted to give her some grief for having been so insensitive to my needs. You were already doing a story on her. Besides, I thought it would help you. It wasn't bad information. You didn't seem to mind being on the receiving end of it. Might have been a stretch to paint her so hard right, especially since now the party honchos have got their knickers in a twist because they don't think she's hard-line enough. They're going to drop her just because she doesn't goose-step out of the caucus meetings the way they want her to. It's foolish. Used to be, everyone goes away with something. That way you keep them coming back. This hardass bullshit keeps up, I'll have to join up with you all and try saving the whales." Bones drew a breath and held it, letting his cheeks puff up, then practically spit the air back out. "Myra says I ought to retire. That's probably what I'll do. Start on my new life of fake food and fake beer and exercise. Maybe I'll take up Ping Pong." Bones coughed for a long time. "Don't ever get old, my boy."

"I keep trying not to."

His uncle was a calculating person. Nick had known that and had let Bones spin him anyway, out of laziness and wanting to find something bad and strike at it in print. But it was hard to stay angry at somebody in a hospital bed.

"So what's the next big story?"

"Dunno." He didn't know whether there would be any more big stories. In lieu of a Sabert obituary, he'd turned in an article memorializing the 1800 block of East Eleventh Street, a mid-length piece in which he'd roped together (however clumsily) the histories of the Sunset and the Washington branch library—or as much as he'd been able to find out about them, which wasn't all that much.

T hat evening, he found Roger at Gloria's, head sunk almost to table level, his nose practically resting on his pint glass. The Sunset had been demolished, he said. "It took them, like, a day. One *day*."

"One day. Man."

Roger lifted his head slightly. "You know I ought to go over there. I lost a set of keys there about nine years ago, maybe they'd turn up in the rubble."

"I lost a girl there. Maybe she's in the rubble, too."

"You did? Who?"

"She wasn't exactly a girl*friend*."

"Nevertheless," Roger said.

"Her status notwithstanding—"

"She might be over there."

They convinced themselves they would head over to the site and sort through the construction debris in search of lost keys and lost women—after the next drink—and then after the next one— until it was too dark, and Nick was too sleepy.

"Here, before I forget, let me give you one of these," Roger said, handing him a piece of blue paper.

SAVE THE SUNSET was printed in large block lettering at the top of the page. Below that was a small picture of the club, so blurred by the bad reproduction that it might have been any building. "ONE OF WATERLOO'S MOST BELOVED VENUES. Refried 80s Hoot Nite/Benefit @ Gloria's Icehouse 11/1."

"Saturday night. You're coming, aren't you?" Roger asked.

Nick was confused.

"I thought about calling it off, but then I thought, what the hell—"

The first time he'd gone to the Sunset, Nick had been nineteen, and absolutely everybody in the place had intimidated him. He'd thought he was going to get kicked out at any moment, just for not being cool enough—and with the limp Rod Stewart mop he'd attempted to cultivate at the time, he'd not been at all cool. What he missed was that intimidation, the belief that all the people in that club were badass, fascinating, frightening people that he wanted to dress like and talk like and be like. When did he ever walk into a room and feel that way now?

"All proceeds to benefit Save the Sunset activities," said the flyer. Four different bands were listed.

"The Delilahs are playing? Do they still live here?" Nick asked.

"Yes they do, and yes they are. And look who else is playing."

"Real Real Gone," Nick read. "I didn't know that."

"Just a few songs. You're getting together with Davy and Buzz to practice tomorrow. It's high time you guys had a reunion."

"No one told me about this. I don't believe in reunions."

"I don't believe that you don't believe in reunions," Roger said.

Over the next twenty-four hours, in a burst of respectable behavior, Nick had a conversation with his father, e-mailed McNally to suggest they have lunch, went to a band practice no one had bothered to tell him about, and afterward told Buzz he was sorry about the dumb way he'd acted during the demise of Real Real Gone five years ago. He also called Andrea.

"You still up for that benefit I told you about?" he asked her.

"I think they already tore the club down."

"They did, but the party's still happening."

"I don't get it."

"It's not really gettable. Just come. Can I pick you up?"

"Why don't we meet there? Around ten?"

"I'll try to be on time. I should warn you that in general I am often late."

"I should warn you that I think that's rude."

"It is. But it's not like I'm only late when I'm meeting people. I'm late for movies, I'm late for airplanes. I'm just in denial about what time it is." Even as Nick said this it sounded retarded, and he wondered what it was about Andrea that made him want to own up to all his failings and annoying personal traits. What would he confess to next? Looking at pictures of naked women on the Internet? Spoiling the end of a movie for friends who hadn't seen it? He had been known to do these things. "I'll try to be on time, though."

"In that case," Andrea said, "I'll try to make it."

The night of the Save the Sunset benefit was cool but not too cold, a good night to stand outside under a purplish sky and listen to your old friends play covers of old songs. Nick cheered them on, his heart softly stung. It was a sting he'd stopped trying to suppress. No matter what he did, the wistfulness returned, and the best he could do was to ride it out. If nostalgia was an illness, maybe it was one of those that never fully left the body.

He didn't know what Andrea would think of these bands, or how to explain all of this to her. Was it possible to explain?

Roger approached him, beaming, holding a pair of beers high in his hands like trophies. "Isn't this great?" he said. "Here, take one of these."

"Didn't you get it for someone?"

"Yeah, Evie, but," he said, scanning the field of heads, "I'm not sure where she went." The deck was at capacity, full of faces Nick hadn't seen in ages, a bunch of which he could no longer match names to.

Once Nick had taken the beer, Roger hiked up his pants with his free hand and then took a swat at Nick. "I'm glad you're still here, man. I'm glad we're both still here. We're old-timers now, you know?"

"I know."

"I don't see you enough. We should hang out."

"We do hang out. We hang out a lot. You're toasted, my friend."

Roger threw his arms around Nick and told him that he loved him. "Okay, okay," Nick said, speaking the words into his collarbone. "Me, too. Mmmhrrrum."

After freeing himself from Roger's bear hug, Nick spotted Andrea climbing the stairs from the sidewalk to the deck. She wore a pink blouse and was smiling: both things made him happy. He wedged his way into the crowd and met her in the middle of it. Because they could barely hear each other, he took her hand and led her up to the balcony, which was less congested, and then looked around impatiently for a waitress, as if he were responsible for the service at Gloria's. He worried Andrea didn't care for the place. But after a few minutes she said to him, "I like it here." Though he wasn't sure whether she meant the bar or the city, it didn't matter. They looked down over the railing, watching the tide of people go in and out of the bar.

"So how long you think you'll stick around?" Nick asked.

She looked out at the street. "I don't know—I just got here."

"I meant stick around Waterloo."

"I have no plans to leave, for now."

"A lot of people say that and then never leave."

Across the road was another bar with a white awning and a fenced-in patio. By any objective standard, it was just as good a bar as Gloria's was, but Nick and his friends almost never went there.

"Are you one of those people?" she asked.

"I may never leave," he said.

"There are worse fates."

"There are worse fates."

Then it was time for Nick to go play. Real Real Gone's performance didn't rise to the not very high standards the band had never quite gotten around to setting, but no one minded. His monitor kept failing, and so he couldn't really hear himself. He felt stranded in a sea of noise, and he hadn't played in forever and his fingers hurt, but he was also okay. Somehow he remembered what to do, more or less, and he looked out at all those familiar, aging faces and knew they would forgive him his mistakes, at least for three songs. He could have stayed up there for much longer.

When the set was over he found Andrea again. "That was fun," she told him, and he was glad she didn't pretend it was a great performance.

She left soon after—she was an early riser, she said. Nick didn't take it personally. He himself departed not long after midnight. The night as it wore on had grown clearer and sharper, and it seemed to offer to lend some of its clarity to anyone who took advantage. Though he'd driven to Gloria's and parked in the lot, Nick stashed his guitar and amp in the trunk and set out on foot toward the river.

His ears were still ringing from the show, and from somewhere deeper inside his head he heard notes being plucked, a slow, twangy melody falling down the scale. The sounds of humans thinned as he left the bar district and approached the river, which, when he came to it, was almost invisible, a strip of darkness fastened down by long hooks of lamplight and the nail-head reflections of a few stars. Waiting out the night along the banks were the black, misshapen trees and city trash cans, rising lifelessly from the indefinite grays of the grass—but then a raccoon rustled and took shape, barreled toward a tree and disappeared again. Nick followed the trail to the place where it ran beneath the Capitol Avenue bridge, the lights above forcing lurid half colors out of the pillars and the shrubs. A winding set of concrete steps led from the trail to the bridge, and Nick climbed them, a little deaf, a little out of breath. The downtown hotels loomed above him, hiding sleepers, insomniacs, couples screwing, empty beds. At the top of the steps was the avenue, with sidewalks and planters in one direction, the bridge in the other. Cars shushed past, and a man snored on a bench.

Nick looked both ways. He wished he could see more than what was actually visible. Not just a section of downtown, or a piece of river, or a stretch of road, but the entire city was what he was after: he thought if he could see it all, for just a moment, he might understand something about it. If only he could take the city up in his arms and hold it perfectly still, just long enough to know what it meant to call a place your home.

ACKNOWLEDGMENTS

I am very grateful to my parents and siblings for their love and support: Thank you, Olssons. Thanks also to Esther Holm. Thanks to Amy Williams for her enthusiasm and to Lorin Stein for his help and patience. Thanks to the Warren Wilson M.F.A. program, especially Robert Boswell, Tracy Daugherty, Debra Spark, Adria Bernardi, Judy Doenges, and Pete Turchi. Thanks to dogged readers John Ratliff, Paul Stekler, Jay Ponteri, Meghan O'Rourke, and Rosemary Hutzler. Thanks to Steve Collier for the song title. And thanks to all the good people of Austin, Texas.

Langworthy Public Library
24 Spring Street   P.O. Box 478
Hope Valley, RI 02832

NEW 10/05

BRODART, CO.   Cat. No. 23-233-003   Printed in U.S.A.